MEN AGAINST DEATH

Moving with the lethal suspense of a discharged torpedo, this is a tense tale of American Navy men on the destroyers assigned during World War II to eliminate the ferocious wolf packs of German submarines from the treacherous waters of the North Atlantic.

The mission of the crew of the U.S.S. *Dee* was to hunt—and to kill. The slashing ocean gales, the fog and the lurking presence of the U-boats made the search a fierce struggle for survival and victory in which the unseen quarry often became the hunter—and the destroyer.

Charged with unbearable anxiety of desperate battle, this is a novel of men thrown together by the chances of war—of the calm, level-headed members of the crew performing their dangerous sea duties on ship as ably as they did their peacetime jobs on land, of others who broke under the strain.

The portraits of these men, of the heroes and the cowards, their friendships and their antagonisms, their earthy talk of wives, sweethearts, and girls in port or back home, make this one of the most exciting and vivid novels of World War II.

Written by a man who spent two years as gunnery officer on a destroyer in World War II, this powerful novel of grim battle on the high seas presents a striking picture of how men act when they must destroy—or be destroyed.

"An extraordinary performance."
—Saturday Review

The Enemy

by

Wirt Williams

WILDSIDE PRESS

This is a work of fiction, and is not intended as an historical or factual account
of any single naval operation. The characters are fictional characters, and are not
intended to represent or to resemble
actual persons, living or dead. Any such
resemblance is accidental.

To

The U.S.S. *Decatur* (DD 341)

United States Navy, Retired

*"Pursue these Sons of Darkness, drive them out
From all Heaven's bounds into the utter Deep . . ."*

BOOK VI, PARADISE LOST

Part One

1

THE UNITED STATES SHIP *Dee* had four smokestacks. You could look at the four stacks, one behind the other, pointing straight up out of the blue and gray length of her as she lay alongside the black finger of Pier L-5 that jutted into the running brown water of the Elizabeth River half a mile below the Norfolk Navy Yard, and you would know nearly all there was to know about the U.S.S. *Dee*.

You would know from the stacks, throwing slanting twilight shadows across the pier to the water on the other side, that she was a destroyer and carried one hundred and fifty men and twelve officers. You would know, still from the stacks, that she was more than twenty years old, obsolete, badly armed, and good for only the Atlantic war against submarines. You might guess, from where she waited, that she had just finished overhaul in the Navy Yard. But you would know at the same time, and this more than all else from the four stacks, that in spite of all that this Navy Yard and all that the other yards and all that her own men could do, she was crumbling slowly to scrap.

If you walked down the pier, paused close to the *Dee*, and looked at the fresh paint on her hull, the dark blue that started at the water stopping in a straight line halfway up the side and giving way to a haze-gray that swept the side and the upper works and the four stacks, you would know something else. You would be very sure she was ready to go back to sea.

"Any sign of the captain?" Lieutenant Graham, the executive officer, standing on the quarter-deck near the gangway that linked the *Dee* to the pier, wanted to know. He could not go ashore until the captain returned to the ship.

"No, sir," I said.

Graham looked down the pier and scowled. He was worried. This was the *Dee's* last night in port, and he wanted, with painful transparency, to spend it with his wife. He was all ready to leave, in a freshly pressed blue uniform with a starched white cover on his cap, the gold band above the visor matching the two gold stripes and one star on each sleeve of the coat.

Graham grunted. Then he walked, still scowling, in front of the gangway along the deck, turned, and walked into the passageway that led to the ship's office.

The sailor on the gangway watch had kept his back carefully turned to Graham as he stood at the desk mounted on Number Four stack and wrote in the open green ledger that was the gangway log with a yellow, red-rubber-tipped pencil. Now he put the pencil in the middle of the ledger, closed it, and turned to me. He said: "The exec looks kind of impatient."

"He's in a hurry, all right," I said.

"Guess he can't wait to hit the old lady that last time."

The sailor grinned. So did I. His name was Horner and he wore a .45 pistol in a brown leather holster on a canvas belt that fitted tightly around his blue jumper under the round white sailor's hat. I wore a .45, too, strapped around the gray work uniform coat. I was officer of the deck.

"Wish I had something here." He eased forward in two short steps. "Not in Norfolk, though. Never anything in Norfolk. You got to have a wife here like the exec to have anything in this port."

"Can't you guys make out here?" I was not thinking about Horner, nor the exec, nor who could make out where, but was looking at the shadows falling from the stacks and the stump-shaped air vents and the other uncountable projections rising out of the ship's deck, the shadows deepening on the deck in the always darker twilight, and was wondering what the captain would bring back with him when he came.

"Not here." Horner walked to the head of the gangway, looked down the pier, and came back. The rubber heels of his fresh-shined black shoes squeaked on the deck. "They're keeping the old man late."

"They sure are keeping him late."

"I don't like them keeping him so late. It looks like they're cooking up something. You know what I mean? I don't like it." Then he asked the question I knew he had been waiting to ask. "You know where we're going, Mr. Taylor?"

"No." That was true. I did not know. "I don't have the word. Nobody has it, except the captain. He's supposed to bring all the dope back tonight."

"I wish we was heading south down to Cuba tomorrow and then running back to New York. This thing don't look good. Everything's too covered up. Nobody knows what's going to happen."

"When did anybody ever know what's going to happen in this Navy? Quit bellyaching and turn on some lights."

Horner was Old Navy. You could talk to him. He grinned.

"Aye, aye, sir."

He reached up and snapped the switch on the single electric bulb shaded in a green metal cover that was rigged on Number Four stack above the gangway desk, and the bulb ignited into yellow light that fell over the quarterdeck. Then he started forward through the passageway by the galley to turn on the aircraft recognition lights on the foremast. I looked at the mast, where the yardarm made a cross, sixty feet above the waterline, and saw the twin red lights, one on each end of the arm, go on. Above them was the steel rectangle of the radar cage that marked the top of the ship. It was still not dark, but would be soon. On the pier, the shadows of the four stacks, breaking sharply at the edge on the other side, were blurring in the dying light.

I walked across the gangway to the pier. The gangway was a two-foot-wide strip of wood with steel railings on both sides, that came to your waist. The railing was cold against my hand as I stood on the pier, looking down it through the twilight to the white concrete road strip that passed by the tin-roofed red shed for the dock police at the end of the pier. Nobody was on the pier or in the shed, and no station wagon showed on the road. The Navy Yard had sent the captain a station wagon to take him to the conference, and it would also bring him back. I turned and walked over the gangway to the ship.

Horner was back at the gangway.

"See him coming?"

"No," I said.

I walked to the desk and opened the deck log, not the green ledger but the official log in the long black cover, to start the entry for this watch. I turned the pages to the one that had "16 November, 1943" written in pencil in the blank at the top. I wrote, toward the bottom of the lined page, "16-20. Moored as before," and put the pencil down. That was all there was to write, now.

It was November 16, 1943, and Thanksgiving was coming in less than two weeks. We would probably spend it at sea. That would keep the *Dee's* record intact. She had spent, although I had been with her on only the last of each, every Thanksgiving and every Christmas and every New Year's Eve at sea for the past three years. The job coming up, whatever it was, was almost sure to make it four.

Thanksgiving was coming. In Russia, they were fighting hard in the Caucasus. In Italy, the English and American armies were bogged down on a line south of Rome. At a place called Bougainville, somewhere in the Solomon Islands, the Navy had just landed troops in what could be the start of the Pacific push. All over the Atlantic Ocean, German submarines were sinking more ships than could be lost. And in Norfolk, Virginia, the U.S.S. *Dee* was tied portside to Pier L-5 in the Elizabeth River and was ready to go to sea on a job that nobody knew about. Except the captain, and he was not, so far, telling.

I looked again at the "16 November, 1943," at the top of the page and closed the log.

"Wish my relief would come," said Horner. "I could eat the wrong end of a skunk right now."

"I know what you mean."

I looked at my wrist watch. It said five-thirty. Dinner for the officers was at six, and supper in the crew's quarters at five-fifteen. I would have gone below before now if we were not expecting the captain. The officer of the deck had to be there to greet him.

"The skipper back?" somebody asked from beside me. It was Anson, the chief engineering officer. I had not seen him approach. He had come out of one of the engine room hatches.

"Not yet."

"Any word on when we fuel?" He was wearing a sailor's blue dungarees and only a grimy, once khaki, cap with a gold band tarnished to green to show that he was an officer. The dungarees were streaked with grease and smelled of it.

"Nothing so far."

"I wish I could make some plans." He wrinkled his face. "Well. Let me know. I'll be in the wardroom." He walked away through the galley passageway.

I moved, without direction, in front of the gangway. I kept smelling chili con carne. For nearly two hours, the smell had been coming out of the galley, only a few feet from the quarterdeck. The mess cooks had already carried the food below to the living compartments, and only the ship's cooks were in the galley now. These were the cooking cooks, not the mess cooks. The mess cooks were menials who carried food, set tables, and cleaned dishes; the real cooks were personages. They might have some chili left. I walked from the quarterdeck through the passageway into the galley.

Whitey, the chief cook, was standing by a silver-bright steel boiler beside the doorless doorway. He wore a food-streaked white apron over food-streaked white T-shirt and pants. He had no hat and his straw hair flopped wild along his forehead. He was short, thin, and had a pink face set in a perpetual look of persecution. He was filling a partitioned aluminum tray with food for himself. In the separated sections of the tray were a peach, green lettuce, white bread and yellow butter, and rice. He was scooping the dark, red-brown chili from the boiler with a long-handled ladle. The ladle glinted as the light hit it. Smoke spiraled from the chili in the open boiler. He was pouring chili on the rice on the tray. He looked up when I came in.

"It smells good," I said.

He smiled. He liked it when anybody liked his food.

"You ought to try some, Mr. Taylor." He knew what I wanted. "Let me fix you a plate."

"No thanks, Whitey, no time. I'll sample your chili, though."

"Fine." He took a heavy white plate from the shelf above the boiler and began to ladle chili on it. "Plenty of it."

"Just a taste, Whitey."

He gave me more than that, and a big tin spoon. I dug the spoon into the chili and ate in fast mouthfuls. It was good. It was undoubtedly better than the dinner the officers would have in the wardroom.

Whitey watched me. Then he asked it: "Any word on where we're going, Mr. Taylor?"

"No word, Whitey." I said it with chili in my mouth.

He sighed and shook his head. "They're sure keeping it locked up this time."

Horner put his head through the door.

"Mr. Taylor. The captain." ·

I set the plate, that still had a corner of chili on it, on the shelf, and stepped, in a hurry, to the quarter-deck.

"Tell the exec," I said to Horner.

The captain was already halfway down the pier, walking fast on his long legs. You always knew him by his walk, even three hundred yards away. He got bigger coming down the pier, tall in the heavy, brass-buttoned bridge coat, the gold flowering on the visor of his cap telling that he was a commander in the United States Navy. He had a brown leather briefcase in his left hand.

He closed the distance to the ship and turned at the gangway to come aboard. At the foot of the gangway, he stopped, and looked, carefully, along the ship, from the bow to the stern, then walked aboard, his feet clacking sharply on the wood of the gangway and his right hand sweeping to his cap in perfunctory salute to the stern, where the flag had been until sunset, half an hour ago.

"Attention on deck." I barked it like a drill command and saluted militarily. "Good evening, captain."

"Evening, Pete." He returned the salute with an easy lift of his arm.

What he said meant he was in a fair humor, not good and not bad. If he had been in a good one, he would have made a joke; if bad, he would have said nothing. Now he was neither angry nor pleased, but seemed, more than anything else, preoccupied.

He stopped and turned to me.

"Get all the officers in the wardroom."

"Aye, aye, sir."

He walked across the deck to the passageway that led to his cabin.

I was the eleventh and last officer, except the captain, in the wardroom. The others, all in gray uniforms but Graham, were sitting in chairs pulled back from the mess table that ran length-wise through the middle of the room.

Arbry, the gunnery officer, sitting facing the door, raised his eyebrows in a question when I entered. I shrugged my shoulders.

The wardroom was only a little longer than the table. The table was covered with a piece of billiard-table green felt. At each end of it, built into the bulkheads, were brown leather sofas. We called them "transoms." Between table end and transom was just space for one chair. Other chairs lined the sides of the table. In the left rear corner of the room was a two-part door to the pantry. The top part was open. Outside the door, on top of a gray locker that held the silver, was an electric hot plate. On the hot plate were two glass coffee bowls. One was half full, the other empty.

The wardroom cut across the whole ship, a little forward of its middle and widest point, and the room's length was the width of the ship where it was. In this room the *Dee's* twelve officers ate, worked and spent their free waking moments at sea. It was thirty feet long and half as wide.

I sat down on the transom opposite the captain's end of the table. I unfastened the steel catch of my pistol belt and felt the heaviness of the gun slip off. I left it where it rested on the dark brown leather cover of the seat, the black, cross-grained butt sticking out of the tan, new leather-smelling holster that had "U.S." stamped in a circle in the middle of it.

"Tell the captain we're ready," Graham said to Ensign Chase, sitting near the door.

I looked at Graham. Sitting straight in the straight-backed chair, on the right of the empty one at the head of the table that was the captain's, he had both feet on the deck and his hands in his lap, and was trying to set his face into a blank that did not show his chagrin at remaining on board so late. It still showed.

The door opened and the captain came in. He did not have the briefcase. The chairs all scraped on the deck as we stood. The captain walked around the table to his empty chair and sat; then we did.

"Here it is." His glance, circling the table, brought everybody into what he was saying. "We get underway sometime tomorrow afternoon. We fuel and take on stores tonight and we load ammunition in the morning. All departments report ready to get underway at twelve hundred." He hardened his voice. "That means twelve hundred. That's all."

Nobody said anything, nor, for seconds, moved, but sat motionless thinking about what the captain had not told us, about what was in the briefcase: where we were going and what we were going to do. The captain pointedly pushed his chair back, rose, and walked to the magazine rack three steps away. The chairs scraped again, the others got up and walked out of the wardroom to the staterooms behind the curtain. I kept my seat on the transom, picked up a picture magazine someone had left there, and, half looking, turned the pages.

The captain was standing at the rack, deciding on a magazine, when Graham, at his elbow, said, "We've got all the navigation charts you listed on board, captain."

The captain nodded, not taking his eyes off the magazines.

"Guess I better call my wife and tell her I won't be home tonight." The exec tried, unsuccessfully, to make it casual.

The captain turned and looked at him. "What the hell, what the hell. For Christ's sake, the O.O.D. and the chief engineer can handle it tonight. Go on home."

"Aye, aye, sir." Graham wanted to take it nonchalantly, but he beamed. He picked up his cap and walked slowly, not wanting to hurry, to the door.

The door closed behind him and the captain looked at me and laughed. Then, to two white-coated, brown-faced mess attendants, now standing in the corner by the pantry with an air of martyrdom because dinner was already forty-eight minutes late, he called:

"Let's get set up and have some dinner."

2

JAMES BUCHAN, Commander, United States Navy, and captain of the *Dee*, looked perceptibly out of place and time without cutlasses in his belt. This was said first when Buchan was a lieutenant, junior grade, by a certain captain's wife, who had what could have been considered, by the most charitable exercise of the imagination, a maternal interest in him. It had been repeated many times since.

Looking at him sitting at the head of the wardroom table, his officers ranging down both sides from him in sequence of rank, I thought of what the lady had said. Under the long, brown-red hair that was freshly combed and waving slightly was a fair skin burned by the wind to a pink receding smoothly from his high cheekbones; against this deep color, his teeth showed white and even when he laughed. He had an effect, knew it, and used it. In any port in the world the *Dee* touched, he always found a woman. He had been graduated from the Naval Academy ten years before, had been in destroyers ever since, and did not have much time left on the *Dee*. This trip might be his last. They were moving the old destroyer men fast, from the disintegrating four-stackers to the new, twice-as-big destroyers that were sliding, with assembly-line regularity, out of the shipyards.

Now he and the medical officer, two chairs on his left, were quarreling again.

"You don't need to know when we'll be back, Doc." He was irritated and showed it. The doctor could annoy him. "If you needed to know, you'd be told. You don't need to know."

"I just asked," said the doctor.

He glowered at the bowl of clear yellow consommé in front of him. His lower lip stuck out, and he spooned the soup viciously, as though it were the soup which had offended him. His face seemed built around that lower lip; above it was a short, wide nose, two pink-rimmed blue eyes, and a wide forehead running into thin brown hair cropped close to the skull. He was short, and, after more than a year on the *Dee,* a little fat.

The doctor occupied, like all the Navy's medical officers, a peculiar place in the deistic society of the ship which had the captain as a god-head. He was under the captain's command, subject to his orders, and yet in certain well-defined areas he was completely beyond the captain's control. Where medical and sanitary matters were concerned, he was the ultimate authority and could dictate even to the captain. One letter from the doctor condemning health practices on the ship could be disastrous to the commanding officer.

Buchan did not like this hold the doctor had on him, he did not like the doctor, and he did not hesitate to show it. Baiting the doctor was, in fact, one of his solid pleasures.

He leaned forward on the table and laughed, maliciously.

"You ought to find a little more to do, Doc, and take your mind off your troubles. The rest of us have plenty to do, we never worry about where we're going or when we'll be back."

He looked down the table at the rest of the officers and laughed again. So did we. The doctor did have almost nothing to do on the *Dee,* and the rest of us, as much out of envy as anything else, made his idleness a standard butt for wardroom jokes.

Still, we wanted as badly as he to know the answer. And the captain knew we wanted to know. But he was deliberately playing the conversation as though this meal were like any other, as though we were able to push from our minds the only thing that was in them, what it was that was beginning in the morning and where it would take us. It seemed to me that he enjoyed it, that he was teasing us, though I could not be sure. Whatever, we did what he wanted. We picked up the cues. We looked at the doctor and laughed.

"You will grant that it's an interesting question?" The doctor did not look up from his soup as he said it.

He kept his eyes on the consommé as the others stared, laughing, at him. I looked at them, one by one, and thought that this was the first dinner since the *Dee* had come to Norfolk, nearly four weeks ago, that so many had been on board. They were all here but Graham.

Sitting on the captain's right, in Graham's place, was Arbry, the gunnery officer; then Rockwell, the first lieutenant; and Carter, an ensign of all jobs. The left side started with Anson, then moved to the doctor, myself, Ewell, the torpedo officer, and an ensign who had just come on board a week before, named Farnsworth. At the end of the table, facing the captain, was Chase, the senior ensign. That seat belonged to the mess treasurer; Chase was it, as well as my assistant communications officer. Except for the ensigns, the rest of us were lieutenants, junior grade.

Now we all turned on the doctor. He reddened and tried to make a joke.

"I don't know what I'm doing on this bucket, anyway. Nobody contracts anything interesting. Nothing ever happens to anybody but athlete's foot and clap. You don't need a doctor, you need a chancre mechanic. Just somebody to grease the affected parts."

"That's a good job for you, Doc."

"Perhaps."

The doctor froze what he meant for a grin on his face. The captain apparently decided he had had enough, and, still underlining the unanswered question by ignoring it, picked another target.

"Flattop," he called to Chase at the far end of the table. "How do you like sleeping by yourself again?" This was still part of the design, of the pretense that nobody was thinking what everybody else was thinking.

"My feet get cold, captain." Chase knew what was expected of him. "They stay cold all night long."

There was no good reason why we called him Flattop. Some girl in Key West, whom he had subsequently bedded, gave him the name at a time when the villain of the same designation was figuring in the comic strip, "Dick Tracy." It stuck.

"That's what you get for pampering yourself back in New York. You're spoiled." Then Buchan pricked with the needle. "You're going to be without a foot warmer for a long time. You better get used to those cold feet."

"Poor Flattop," said Anson. "All alone on the great big ocean with nobody to sleep with."

"No more of those morning constitutionals for the Flattop." The captain had finished his soup and placed the spoon beside it on the plate. "Remember how he used to come back early from those New York strolls?"

"They really trained him down." Arbry looked at him speculatively. "He lost fifteen pounds in New York."

"He's gained it back since we came to Norfolk."

"He'll lose it when he starts standing sea watches again."

Flattop colored but he did not really mind. He unquestionably enjoyed it. He looked like a cherubic tomcat, with a round unlined face and crew-cut blond hair standing straight up above it. His gray twill coat was tight around his chest; he had gained almost thirty pounds in his year on the *Dee.*

"Why don't you travel with your talent, Flattop? Why don't you bring it to sea?"

"I think the Flattop is a better operator than the rest of you." The captain looked down the table, his eyes crinkled, laughing. "I think you ought to request lessons."

"I believe he does it with his nose," said Arbry. "He just doesn't waste any time in the wrong places."

"When are you going out with a girl under thirty-five, Flattop? Young girls are nice, too."

Flattop was twenty-two years old.

"Each to his own taste," he said. He was trying hard to produce one blow that would annihilate the opposition, but could not make it. Looking at the blushing Flattop, I was all at once aware that I had forgotten, for a moment, The Question, that for a while the talk had been, actually, what we pretended it was at the start.

"Oh." Arbry was suddenly excited. Peters, the mess attendant, had thrust the silver meat-service platter by Ewell. A dummy twenty-millimeter machine-gun shell, mounted on a red lead pedestal, stood by his plate to show it was his turn to be served first. "Look at them. Look at those steaks."

Ewell stiffly forked one of the steaks, dark brown and charred against the silver of the platter, the brown gravy swirling gently around them as the mess boy's hand shook slightly with the weight, and dropped it to his plate. Arbry stared at the platter, fascinated. In the order of serving, he, sitting almost across the table from Ewell, would be nearly the last. He looked at the steaks on the platter as another might at a woman. He loved food; he was almost consecrated to it, with the reverence of the dedicated. He often gave the wardroom cooks recipes for dishes beyond their capacity, and then pridefully supervised the preparation himself. He was, strangely, a thin boy, and never gained weight.

"You and the Flattop," said Buchan. "Always thinking about something to eat."

Arbry was not daunted. "Wait till you try the sauce. I made it myself."

Another mess boy was passing the sauce, in a small silver cream pitcher, around the table directly behind the steaks. When the pitcher came to me, I poured the sauce over the meat; the sauce making a dark red pool on top of the steak and dripping over the sides to spread on the plate. It had a smooth mustardy tang. It was good.

Arbry stopped talking when he started to eat, and a half-smile stayed on his face. I watched him. I liked to watch him eat.

"Good steaks, Mr. Mess Treasurer." He nodded to Flattop.

"Know what we ought to call the mess?" said the captain. "The Flattop's Steak House."

"Sure." Flattop swallowed what he was chewing. "Bring in a few cash customers. Cut down the mess bill."

"Enjoy the steaks while you can get 'em." The captain grinned, with, I was sure now, faint, teasing malice.

"By the way"—he leaned back in his chair—"we're getting a new officer tomorrow."

Johnny Ewell and I looked at each other, and Johnny looked back to the captain.

"An ee-ficient watch stander, I trust?" he said.

"I wouldn't know." The captain looked at him and laughed, shortly. "I wouldn't count too much on it."

"I'll bet he's a hell of a watch stander." Johnny's mouth curled upward as he stared, with the slightest shade of humorous insolence, at the captain. "I'll bet he can stand one in five magnificently."

Whether or not this, or any, officer was a qualified deck watch officer was of supreme importance. The more watch officers, the less watches.

"One in five!" the captain laughed, derisively. "Jesus. You trying to retire?"

"I'm willing."

The captain laughed again. "This guy's name is Crandall. He's a full lieutenant and Deslant's sending him. That's why we didn't get the orders on him in advance."

"Any destroyer experience?" asked Anson.

"They didn't say," the captain answered, abruptly and ending the discussion. He never liked to speak seriously of personalities, particularly when they touched, professionally, his own.

The mess boys were clearing the plates and passing dessert, applie pie with cheese on top. When Peters started to set the pie in front of him, the captain shook his head. He never ate dessert. It might have gone to fat and reduced his operating efficiency. He took coffee instead, and, no longer smiling, lighted a cigarette and smoked gazing expressionlessly at the table in front of him, thinking about something, perhaps what was starting the next day. He said nothing. He never talked business at the table. After the other officers had finished their pie and coffee and were smoking, he spoke abruptly to me.

"The fuel barge comes alongside at twenty hundred. The stores trucks are due on the dock about the same time. Better get your working parties ready." He looked at Anson. "You all ready to fuel, chief?"

"All ready." Anson crushed his cigarette deliberately in the ash tray by his plate.

I excused myself from the table and went topside.

3

I WALKED to the rail opposite the gangway and looked in the slip between the piers, along the dark water that shimmered with splintered reflections of light, for the oil lighter. I did not see it. Then I moved back to the gangway.

Horner was looking down the pier. "Somebody heading this way," he said.

"Where?" I saw nothing.

Horner pointed, and then I saw him. Walking out of the darkness of the middle of the pier into the strip of dim light close to the *Dee*. A middle-sized figure in the belted black raincoat and the gold-corded officer's cap.

He walked very gracefully, but not rapidly, swinging his arms, that ended at the hands in gray gloves, in careful, conscious precision. As he walked closer, he had nothing, absolutely nothing, to set him off from fifty thousand other officers in the United States Navy. And yet. And yet, as he came even with the ships, glancing back and forth at the lights that shone through the open ports and hatches, he gave me a vague uneasiness. I did not know why. Or perhaps I did know why. By the time he reached the gangway, turned to put his foot on it, and glanced quickly to either side and then at me, I completely disliked him.

He walked slowly up the gangway and stepped from it to the deck. He saw me, and then the holstered .45.

He snapped to attention and brought his hand, in the soft gray glove, to the visor of his cap in a stiff salute.

"Sir," he pronounced, with great formality, "I report aboard for duty."

Overwhelmed, I nodded. With the same stiffness of motion, he thrust his left hand across his chest and inside his coat, then drew it back with a folded sheaf of papers and handed them to me.

I unfolded the papers. They were orders, and the name on them was W. G. Crandall. He was, and I knew now that I had known it when I saw him take the first step down the pier, the new officer.

"Fine." I extended my hand. "Taylor. Glad to have you aboard. We didn't expect you until tomorrow."

He jerked off his glove quickly and took my hand. His grip was firm enough but the flesh of his hand was oddly soft and yielding. He smiled, with his mouth, and inclined his head to acknowledge the introduction. Then I understood that he had seen and measured the single silver bar on my collar and wished to preserve the proper gulf between himself and an officer one grade his junior.

"Lieutenant Crandall," he said.

"Yes." I worked hard to be pleasant. "Damned glad to see you, too. We sure need another officer."

He favored me with the smile and hint of a bow again, and now I looked at his face. There was not a line in it. It was even and regular, starting under the cap brim with a broad white forehead and well-spaced brown eyes and making a smooth oval contour to end in a well-made chin. It ought to

have been a pleasant face, and for the second time in five minutes, I utterly failed of understanding. I did not understand
why I found the face offensive. "My gear is in the shed there."
He nodded toward the base of the pier.

"I'll send somebody to pick it up," I told him. "I don't know
where the exec means to bunk you so we can't move you into a
stateroom just yet." I saw him recoil at the word "bunk." "He'll
work out something."

He said nothing."

"Perhaps you'd like to go to the wardroom. They're having
coffee now."

I started away, and then stopped. He was not following. A
tiny crease showed between his eyes.

"Shouldn't I"—he paused—"call on the captain first?"

I looked at him, and saw he meant it. "You'll find him in the
wardroom."

He nodded stiffly.

Shall we go below?" I said.

He did not ask if he were qualified for sea watches.

4

THE OIL LIGHTER turned wide from the river to pass the end
of the pier and crawl into the slip toward the *Dee.* As it made
the turn, I saw only the lights: red on the left, green on the
right, and two white ones, one above the other, in the middle.
Then, as it crept closer, the rest gathered into a black shadow
framed by the triangle of the lights.

The *Dee,* herself, waiting, was yellow with light. From her
bridge, three signal lamps lanced spreading cones that angled
off her decks, the water on one side of her, and the pier on the
other, and fired them together into a mass of incandescence.

The oiler took sharper lines as it closed, went past, and
turned to head back toward the *Dee's* clear side to tie up. Slipping inside the sphere of light, it revealed six seamen on the
forecastle, one with a thin white heaving line coiled like a lariat
in his hands, and heavy brown manila mooring lines laid out
on the deck.

"Stand by!" yelled the man with the heaving line.

When the oiler was twenty feet away, he threw the line with
a side-arm, discus motion to the linehandlers on the *Dee.* They
pulled the light line aboard and then the heavy manila hawser
attached to its other end. They dropped the end loop of the
big one over a round cleat rising from the *Dee's* deck. The line

creaked as the oiler, still inching ahead, pulled it taut; then the line went slack as the craft eased back and settled close to the *Dee*.

It put another line to the *Dee* from its aft, and the two lay together, bow to stern.

"Moored *soixante-neuf* style. They used to call it Chinese gangway on the Asiatic station, but it's *soixante-neuf* to me." Horner said it looking across the deck to the other ship. "Want me to log it like that?"

"Sure. Just like that. And let's put out the smoking lamp."

Horner grimaced, then took his cigarette out of the corner of his mouth and threw it with an overhand wrist snap into the foot of space between the *Dee* and the pier. Then he went into the ship's office passageway, where the microphone for the loudspeaker system hung. A moment later, from the speakers scattered over the topside, came the mechanical bleat:

"Now hear this. Smoking lamp is out throughout the ship. Smoking lamp is out throughout the ship."

Smoking was now officially prohibited. Horner came out of the passageway and stood by me on the *Dee's* starboard side, where the oil ship was tied.

On the oiler, half a dozen men in dungarees, thick blue Navy winter jackets, and dirty white hats, were handing the fist-thick, brass-tipped black hose to as many engineers waiting on the *Dee*. The *Dee's* men did not wear hats. They worked the end of the hose under the bottom lifeline.

Anson and Chief Hawley stood beside them. Hawley was Oil King, the petty officer in charge of fuel and water.

"Hurry it up," he gruffed at the hose tenders.

Two of them picked up the end of the hose, and, both arms under it, hauled it down the main deck.

"Come on, you wop bastard," said the man in front, whose name was Mariotti. "Carry the fogging thing. Carry it like you live."

"Shut your yap," said the other. His name was Almerico. "If I was a wop like you I'd shut my yap and keep it shut."

They dropped the hose by another hose, stretched on the deck forty feet aft of the gangway. This was the *Dee's*. One end of it led through an opening in the deck to the oil tanks below.

Almerico and Moriotti screwed the brass couplings on the end of each hose together. Then they took rags from a pile made ready near the *Dee's* hose and placed them under the couplings to absorb leaking oil.

"You do that good, wop," said Mariotti. "Bet you used to bring towels around in a whore house."

"Sure. I brought 'em around. And you picked 'em up."

"Yeah?"

"Yeah."

"Well, you can blow it. You can blow it straight out."

Mariotti did not wait for an answer but stood and shouted to Anson, "All set."

Anson nodded. "We're all ready," he called to an officer on the oiler's deck. "Let it go."

The officer waved acknowledgement. He said something to the two men beside him, who had their hands on the valve wheels rising out of the deck. They turned the wheels.

Now the oil was passing through the trunk-like hoses, into the *Dee's* tanks.

Anson turned to me. "We ought to be through in about an hour. Maybe a little longer."

Now he and his engineers had nothing to do until the tanks were full. Mariotti and Almerico sat on the deck where the hoses joined and abused each other with great filth and amiability. Anson moved around.

Chief Hawley, a long, cadaverous man with a long face and a short, scraggly brown mustache, stopped by the gangway where I was standing, my weight on my left leg and my right hand resting on the .45.

"Guess we'll need all we can hold this time." He pulled a dirty red bandanna from his back pocket and wiped his hands as he said it.

"We'll need all of that."

"Any idea how many times we'll have to fuel at sea?"

"Plenty."

"I kind of thought this one was going to be a long one."

"It'll be a long one, all right."

He shoved his chief's cap to the back of his head. The heel of his hand left a black grease mark on his forehead. "Well. You catch some long ones sometimes."

He joined Almerico and Mariotti at the after manifold, and stood, hands on hips, looking down at the black hose bent through the hole. Out of the opening came the strong, sweet turnip-like smell of oil.

Jake Warwick, the chief boatswain's mate, walked to the gangway and saluted me. From anybody else, this would have been a surprise. Salutes from chief petty officers to lieutenants, junior grade, were unusual on the *Dee*. But Jake was an unusual chief petty officer. He was, complete to himself, the embodiment of the old, four-stacker Navy, that shuttled from Manila to Panama and from Halifax to Gibraltar, as casually as a liberty-bound sailor sauntered out of the Sand Street gate in the Brooklyn Navy Yard; he was that Navy, melted down and poured into a pot-bellied, khaki-suited, unchanging figurine that was impervious to time, decay, and human fallibility. He was, like the captain, a prop on which the whole weight of the *Dee* rested; he was, like the captain and God, never wrong. Jake moved with quick, eighteen-year-old steps behind a forty-eight-year-old belly that he pushed in front of him like a wheelbarrow.

"Any sign of the stores yet, sir?" he asked. His blue jacket was unzipped, and the big belly, tight against a khaki shirt, poked between the unfastened sides of the jacket.

"No sign, Jake. They were due at twenty hundred. You know these civilian outfits. If they get here only an hour late, we'll be lucky."

"Those civilians." Jake made it an epithet. The *Dee* got her food supplies in Norfolk from commercial concerns that had Navy contracts.

"Hell," I said. "If the Navy Yard sent the stuff, it'd be three hours late."

"Yeah. The civilians and the shore-based Navy. The men behind the men behind. What is it that makes a good man on board ship turn into six kinds of a son-of-a-bitch when he gets shore-based?"

"They get to be bureaucrats, Jake. You get 'em at sea and they're sailors. Bring 'em ashore and right away they turn into bureaucrats, the officers and the men both. They can't move without making six carbon copies."

"The men worse than the officers." Jake breathed heavily. "I never seen a worse bureaucrat than a chief storekeeper in a shore supply office with a piece of line you got to have before you get underway in just an hour. Honest to Christ, I wonder sometimes how the Navy stays afloat. Sometimes I wonder why it don't sink from the carbon copies."

"It sure makes you wonder."

"I got my men all ready, soon as the trucks get here." That ended the stores with him, until they arrived. "How about some joe, Mr. Taylor?"

"You talked me into it."

Jake went into the galley and came back with a thick white mug in each hand. The top of the mugs stuck two inches above the knotty knuckles that had been broken in boxing twenty years before and had healed in lumps. Steam rose from the mugs. The smell of fresh coffee came out of them. The coffee in both mugs was black. Jake and I were alone among the officers and chiefs in drinking it straight black. It was the basis of a friendship. He handed me one mug. The china was hot against my hand. The coffee almost burned my tongue.

"What do you think about this job, Mr. Taylor?" He asked it casually, but in a voice dropped almost to a whisper.

"Just another job. We'll go out and fog around for awhile and come back. Why?"

"I just wanted to know what you thought about it," Jake said carefully.

"What do you think about it?"

"I don't think nothing about it. Just another job. Like you say."

"What do you think about it, Jake?"

Jake did not answer. The belly rose and fell twice with his breathing. Then he said:

"I tell you, Mr. Taylor. I been in the Navy almost thirty years. I been on some funny deals. But I never seen one that shaped up like this."

"How do you mean?"

"This is the first time I ever got underway and didn't have some idea where I was going. I don't know nothing. Not where we're going nor what we're going to do nor who we're going to do it with. You know anything? Anything you can pass on?"

"Not a thing, Jake. I don't know anything."

"I'd just as soon we was running down to Cuba and back to New York."

"We aren't going to Cuba this time, for sure."

"I don't like the feel of it. You can tell when one feels good. This don't feel good. It don't feel worth a damn."

"Hell, Jake. That's bull."

Jake grinned. Lines made a map in his face when he grinned. Then he stopped grinning and erased them.

"They never had nothing like this in the old Navy."

I crossed the gangway to the pier, and looked down it. A pair of auto headlights moved down the road and stopped near the pier. Another pair followed and stopped behind the first. I went back aboard.

"Looks like our stores are here," I told Jake.

He leaned over the lifelines to look. "Yeah. I better get the working parties."

He moved like a pot-bellied ballet dancer through the passageway by the galley. He was heading for the forward crew's quarters. In two minutes, men were coming out of the passageway on both sides of the galley deckhouse, in dungarees, blue jackets, and some in white hats. They milled in the space between the deckhouse and the gangway. They elbowed, punched, and insulted each other.

They were, I thought, the best that was left, a big part of all that was left, of the toughest and the best corps of seagoing mercenaries this country or any other ever had: the four-stacker Navy, which was itself nearly gone, and due soon to be all gone when the *Dee* and the handful of sister ships still working the North Atlantic could not work any longer and made the last mooring in a contractor's scrap yard. But now the *Dee* was working and the sailors were still four-stacker sailors. I listened to them.

"It's always something. One fogging thing after another."

"Ah, blow it. What the fog are you bitching for? You think you'd be shacked in Norfolk if you was on the beach? Who the fog you think you kidding?"

"Let's get started and secure this fogging detail. Where's Jake?"

Jake's stomach, a last handful of seamen in front of it, shoved through the passageway as I stepped into the galley to tell Whitey his stores had come. Whitey took off his apron, put on his blue jacket over the greasy white pants, set his chief's cap on his head, and his face carrying its permanently harassed exasperation, walked over the gangway and down the pier to supervise the loading.

Jake remained on the ship. The men followed Whitey down the pier. They came back single file, the flour bags showing white on their blue-covered shoulders in the yellow light.

They came aboard and made an unbroken loop between the gangway and the after deckhouse at the end of the ship. There, they passed it to Whitey's cooks, who lowered it bag by bag into the galley hold.

The line moved slowly. The stores were going to take a long time loading, much longer than the fueling. That ought to be over soon.

Anson was loitering near the opening to the fuel tanks. Mariotti and Almerico were still sitting beside it. Mariotti now wore a telephone headset, with hearing pieces over both ears.

The smell of the oil came up from the opening. The stores line kept moving. Half an hour passed.

Then I saw Mariotti raise his head, listening to something coming over the phones. He said something to Anson. Anson nodded, and walked to the lifelines by the oiler.

"Shut her off," he called. "We're about full."

The officer on the oiler's decks nodded. The two sailors beside him turned the handwheels.

"Shut off," the officer called back.

"Thank you." Anson went back to the fueling manifold. I joined him there. "Don't uncouple until she drains," he directed Mariotti and Almerico.

They waited for more than two minutes. Then Almerico turned the brass ring of the female hose to unscrew the two. The male hose from the oiler, the phallus in the coupling, slipped out of the socket of the other and trickled black oil on the blue deck. The turnip smell was strong.

Anson cried to the oiler, "Take her in."

The men in the stores line stood clear of the hose. It slithered in a dribbling retreat across the deck as the men aboard the oiler hauled on it until the brass nozzle dropped over the side. The hose left a streak of black along the blue deck.

Anson returned to the gangway. "You can log sixty-nine thousand gallons," he said to me.

The engineers on the *Dee* cast off the oiler's mooring lines. She sounded one long blast on her whistle, her red, green, and white lights went on, and she moved slowly out of the slip toward the stream.

I watched her move away, her sharp black lines blurring into a shadow and then merging with the darkness to show only the red-green-white triangle of her running lights as she backed into the river, turned, stopped, moved ahead and vanished behind the two white lights of a ship at anchor.

I walked through the ship's office passageway and over the narrow space of the well deck to the door of the captain's cabin. The door was only a few feet from the steel ladder angling down from the bridge. The captain could run from the cabin to the bridge in less than ten seconds when he had to. The door opened toward the outside and was hooked back at the top. A gray asbestos battle curtain hung over the doorway.

I knocked on the steel bulkhead.

"Come in."

I swung the curtain to one side, and leaned inside. The captain was sitting in a brown easy chair in the middle of the room, reading *Look*. He had on a white shirt, black tie, dress blue pants, and no coat. A faint scent of shaving lotion was in the room. He looked up at me.

"Completed fueling, Cap'n. Took on sixty-nine thousand gallons."

"Very well." He slapped the magazine on the arm of the chair, as though this information was a signal he had been waiting for, and stood up. "How about the stores?"

"Loading now, sir."

He inclined his head slightly. I stepped back from the

doorway, let the curtain fall across it, turned, and went back
to the gangway.

Men in the working party were still filing over the gangway
and down the port side toward the after deckhouse. They had
been at it for more than an hour.

"Want to break them for a few minutes?" I asked Jake.

"Sure. They can use one, I guess." Jake dropped his hands
from his hips and, from the lifelines, bellowed to the men in
the line on the pier. "Take a ten-minute break. Pass the word
down."

The men with boxes already on their shoulders brought
them aboard and dumped them on the deck. Those at the
two trucks at the foot of the pier crowded along the planking
to the *Dee,* jostled over the gangway, and made for the galley.
Coffee was boiling in the steel urn there. Its smell hung over
the whole ship. Whitey filled white mugs at the urn's tap and
passed them, steaming, through the galley door to hands
stretched toward him. The men took the coffee and spread over
the main deck, clustering in knots of threes and fours wherever they could sit. About half a dozen lounged against the
long steel cylinders of the port torpedo tubes, a few feet from
the gangway and legally just off the limits of the quarter-deck.
The theoretically sacrosanct quarter-deck was forbidden ter-
ritory for loitering.

"How are we doing?" I asked Jake. His back was to the
gangway as he faced me.

"Not bad," he admitted, as though the fact pained him. "We
ought to be secured by maybe midnight." He suddenly straightened and cried, "Attention on deck."

I turned. Jake had seen the captain coming out of the
shadows of the office passageway. I made a quick salute and
took Buchan's in return as he reached the quarter-deck.

He had on the three-quarter-length bridge coat, with brass
buttons. It was a real coat. It made the wearer very military
indeed; for Buchan, it did more than that. He wore his new
commander's cap with the gold on the visor, gray gloves, and a
white silk muffler draped inside the collar of the coat.

He stopped in front of the gangway.

"I'll be back a little after midnight," he said. He had
waited to leave until we had finished taking fuel oil. Something could have happened during the fueling. Now it was
over and he was on his way. He handed me a piece of paper.
"If anything comes up, call me at this number."

"Aye, aye, sir."

The seamen at the torpedo tube watched him walk, the
north wind whipping the end of the coat around his long legs,

down the pier toward the road, his tall figure in the coat outlined in the ship's light until he passed beyond it.

"The old man is a good-looking bastard," one said. "He
gets his share."

"Share, hell. He's the biggest dog on the ship."

Buchan, lost in the darkness, suddenly showed again in the
cone of light at the foot of the pier made by the lamp hanging
from the roof of the police shed. He walked through the gate,
turned left, away from the stores trucks, and slipped into
darkness again. A moment later, about fifty yards along his
way, a pair of headlights flashed on, a motor sounded, and a
car that had been waiting there, unseen, moved down the road
strip, only two white lights with a red one behind them in
the dark to us on the ship.

"Goddamn," the first seaman laughed and smacked his fist
against the open palm of his other hand. "Goddamn. He had
him a piece waiting there, all the time. All the time he had her
right there."

"Oh, he's a dog, boy, he's a real dog."

This was pure admiration. If a companion had had a woman
waiting in a car, they would have been eaten with jealousy;
the fact that the captain had one was not only proper but
admirable.

"You ought to get yourself a deal like that, Mr. Taylor."
The first sailor moved a step toward me. His name was
Kosciuzko. It became, inevitably, Ski. All Poles in the Navy
are, automatically, Ski. Since there were two on the *Dee* and
since he was by forty pounds the smallest, he was Little Ski.
The other, with him in the group by the tubes now, was Big
Ski. "You ought to have yourself something that can't wait,
just like that."

"I'm for it." I edged closer.

"You ought to been gobs, Mr. Taylor, you and the old
man. You're too bigga dogs to like being officers. You could
really go after it if you was gobs." Little Ski grinned. He was
flattering me and he knew I liked it. He was slight, satanically
handsome, and had pushed his white hat back to expose the
peak of brown hair starting at his forehead.

"You can go after it too much. You ought to know that. By
the way, how is your health these days?"

They all laughed, loudly.

"It's all right again, Mr. T. The doc says I'm fine now, all
set again."

"One more dose and you know what's going to happen."

"Aw, Mr. T." Ski made it a mock whine. "She said she
was a nice girl so I didn't use anything."

"Nice girl. Some nice girl. One of them niggers in the ball park down at Aruba." This was Big Ski. He was also a Pole, but was a hundred-and-eighty-degree counter to the little one. Blond hair tumbled about his forehead, over a smooth, ninteen-year-old face. Under the open blue jacket was only a white crew-necked underwear shirt. The big round muscles of his chest pushed tight against it. His thighs strained against the faded blue dungaree pants as he propped his buttocks against the torpedo tube.

"You ought to of seen that, Mr. Taylor. Man, right down in the infield. All you could see was them black knees in the air and something round and white in between. Man, just white and shining in the moonlight. And Ski was right in there, man, he was right in there."

"Something got right into him, too."

"You got to expect them accidents," said Little Ski.

"You tell your wife about that accident?"

"No, Christ. What I want to tell my wife for?"

I had seen pictures of Little Ski's wife. She was blond, plump, twenty, and beautiful. They said she adored Ski.

"What happened to the wife you were going to get, Big? I thought you were going to get yourself a wife. Wasn't that what you got that seventy-two for last week, to get married?"

"Yessir," Big Ski frowned, remembering. "But I tell you, I didn't get married. I decided not to get married."

"How come?"

"I tell you. I brought my girl down here from Brooklyn and we got her a hotel room, her and her girl friend. She brought the girl friend for the wedding. That night I got in bed with my girl, and my girl, she stank. She stank awful. She stank so bad I put her out and got her girl friend in. Her girl friend didn't stink, she was all right."

"You mean you didn't marry her just because she stank a little? You're mighty damn particular."

"I guess I am. But I tell you, she stank so I couldn't stand it. I think I'll marry the girl friend. She don't stink hardly at all."

They laughed again.

"When you think I'll get a chance to marry the girl friend, Mr. Taylor?" Big Ski asked it innocently. "We be back any time soon so I can marry her?"

"Wait and see."

"Give us the word, Mr. Taylor. Where we going? Where we going and what we going to do? We want to know the score," Little Ski wheedled. "Things sure look funny. This whole thing shapes up funny. Give us the word."

"Ask me tomorrow."

I walked away from them, across the gangway to the pier, and along the pier beside the *Dee* to check her lines. When you looked at the *Dee* you did not realize she was longer than a football field; walking up and down the 300-odd-foot length of her, you were completely conscious of it. Her lines were fine. There were six, three forward and three aft. All of them, doubled for strength, dipped easily between the ship and the black wooden dolphins rising like columns through the dirty brown planks of the pier. The lines were made fast to the dolphins. None were tight. I went back aboard. Jake was standing by the gangway.

"I better start 'em." He put the white coffee mug on the gangway desk, cupped his hands, and shouted through them, "Come on, you farmers. Take those cups back to the galley and get it moving."

The men, sitting on the deck between the two deckhouses, stirred painfully. They began to rise, slowly. Jake yelled, "Come on, get it moving."

They moved faster, threaded into the galley to return the cups, went down to the pier, and started the walking line again, carrying the boxes of canned goods.

Little Ski, breathing hard under the box on his shoulder, stopped on the quarterdeck on his way to the hold.

"Let's go over the hill, Mr. Taylor. You and me. We'll go over the hill and go after that stuff and let this old bitch go out and get herself sunk to hell and we won't care a fog. What you say?"

"Next week, Ski. Next week we'll do it."

"Okay. Next week." He jerked his shoulder up to get a fresh grip on the box and walked aft.

The boxes of canned goods were all aboard and the galley hold closed and locked in less than an hour. Then Whitey opened the doors of the ship's refrigerator for the meat. Only the meat was left.

The refrigerator was between the galley deckhouse and the gangway. The box was big inside. After looking at it there on the deck, only a little higher than a man, you were always a little shocked at the bigness of it inside. It carried enough meat to feed 150 men for almost two weeks. Whitey stood by the open doors with black iron tongs in his right hand to pack the meat in the box.

The slabs of meat were harder to carry than the boxes of canned goods or the bags of flour; it was a job for a man to balance a side of beef on his shoulder. Coming down the pier under the meat, the seamen were stiff-moving and bent; aboard, they dropped the slabs one on top of the other, in two piles beside the refrigerator.

Big Ski stepped over the gangway, dropped his piece to one pile, and said loudly: "Sure wish I knew when I could get married."

He caught my eye, grinned, and crossed back to the pier.

The meat was dark red with uneven white edges of fat. Blue inspection stamps were on the white fat. Whitey and a cook lifted the chunks by the ends and stacked them in piles inside the box, except for the biggest, which they hung on hooks from the back wall. The meat came aboard faster than they could pick it up and pack it. The two piles got higher.

Whitey called in two more cooks to pack. The four worked fast, two bending at the knees to pick up the piece on top of the pile, then straightening and swinging their arms together to toss it into the box. Then the other two, Whitey and his first helper, shoved and tugged it into place.

But the piles were still there, as high as a man's hip, when all the meat was aboard, the trucks gone, and the working parties sent below. Whitey and the cooks were still packing.

In spite of the north wind cutting across the deck, sweat showed on Whitey's forehead. He wiped it with his blue-jacketed forearm and stopped to rest.

"That looks like a lot of meat," I said.

"It goes fast, though. That'll be gone in two weeks. Where we going to get the next batch?"

"We'll get it somewhere."

"We better." He jerked his head to the side in what he meant as a gesture of apprehension.

Thirty minutes later, the last piece went into the refrigerator. At the gangway desk, in the dirty green gangway log, I wrote at the top of the page for the next day, "Mr. Taylor—0600." I looked at my watch. It was twelve-sixteen.

"Remind your relief to call me," I told the man on the gangway watch, no longer Horner. Horner had been relieved. He nodded. "I'm turning in."

"Good night."

"Good night."

5

THE SKY was still gray with twilight when I came on the quarter-deck again. Inside the jacket, I shivered from the early morning cold. The .45 felt heavy on my hip. Across the brown water on the next pier, two hundred yards to the right, was a cargo ship with a black hull and one red stack with gray smoke twisting out of it. The smoke curved up until the north wind caught it and blew it toward the *Dee*, the smoke thinning in the wind. The wind stung my cheeks. From the galley came the smell of coffee boiling and bacon frying. I went into the galley.

The galley was hot. Bacon was popping in grease in big square tin pans on the black oil range. The two cooks inside the galley were in T-shirts. The heat from the range felt good.

"How about some joe, Lanny?" I asked Landry, the one nearest the urn.

"Yes, sir!" He was cheerful. "We have got us some joe this morning. This joe will make your hair curly and your teeth white and something else big. This is extra-strong joe."

He took a mug from the shelf and began to fill it from the urn spout as he talked. Steam rose from the black stream.

"You like it straight, don't you, Mr. Taylor?" He handed me the mug. I let it cool a little, then tasted it.

"I see what you mean," I said. "What kind of lye did you put in this?"

"That's good for you."

"Good for my funeral."

He looked up from the bacon pans and smiled. With a long fork he turned pieces of the bacon over. He said, "Where are we going, Mr. Taylor?"

"I don't know."

He smiled again. He did not believe me.

I finished the coffee, got the mug filled again, and took it with me outside. After the heat of the galley the open deck was colder than before. My watch said six-twenty-eight. The sky over the shoreline at the foot of the pier was beginning to color with orange and pink. I moved and drank from the cup to keep warm. The coffee felt scalding all the way down.

"How's it going, Barich?" I asked the man with the gangway watch, standing by the desk on the stack. "Reveille go all right?"

"Yes, sir. Everybody's up." Reveille was at six.

"Good."

He had been on watch since four o'clock, and would go off at eight. The gangway watch was a round-the-clock watch, with each man on it standing the regulation four hours. The officer of the deck had twenty-four-hour duty, from noon to noon. On the *Dee*, he was at the gangway during daylight and when otherwise needed. Big ships kept officers on four-hour watches around the clock, like the enlisted men on the *Dee*.

"There's an ammunition barge due at oh eight hundred," I told Barich. "I doubt if it gets here before. Call me if it shows up."

"Aye, aye, sir."

I left the quarter-deck, walked over the topside to inspect the ship, and went below to the wardroom for breakfast.

Two tugs chugged the ammunition barge, itself a red boxcar on floats without power of propulsion, along the *Dee's* outboard side just after the crew had dispersed from their eight-o'clock muster. The barge made fast to the *Dee*, the two tugs, both on the other side of the barge, took in their own lines, and puffed away, one behind the other, short-bodied, squat, and ugly, their propellers just below the surface churning white bubbles in the brown water as they steamed out of the slip between the two piers and back into the river.

Arbry, as gunnery officer in charge of the ammunition loading, was standing on the deck beside me, his thin cheeks pink from the wind, as the barge was moored.

"Jesus." His mouth twisted as he looked at it. "We've got to unload that thing by noon." He turned to me. "Well, let's have at it. How about piping all hands?"

"Will do."

Baker, the swallow-tailed red flag that, to the Navy, means both the second letter of the alphabet and danger, jerked up, fluttering in the wind, to the *Dee's* port yardarm. Loudspeakers growled: "Now hear this. The smoking lamp is out throughout the ship. All hands lay topside to handle ammunition."

Loading and unloading ammunition is what is called "an all-hands evolution." That means everybody has to do it, except the cooks and men on watch. Before a ship goes into a navy yard, she disgorges all her explosives. When she has completed repairs and is moored, safely for the yard and other ships in it, somewhere outside, the barge offers up the ammunition again and the unloading process of days, weeks, or months before is reversed.

This loading job normally consumed for the *Dee's* crew a leisurely day—or a furious half of one. Today, the ammunition had to be struck below in the magazines and apportioned in the ready boxes topside by noon, less than four hours away.

The *Dee* had already taken her torpedo war heads aboard, the day she left the yard. The depot sent them by truck. It was impractical to take them on board from a barge because of their weight. Everything else had to be handled today.

Two seamen who had jumped aboard the barge now opened

the door to the red shelter by sliding it back. Inside, almost filling the entire warehouse-like structure, was the ammunition, a narrow strip of space cutting through the olive-colored twenty-millimeter magazines that were in the middle of the mass.

"I'll take a look." Arbry bent, slipped to the narrow ledge outside the lifelines, and leaped to the barge's deck a foot below.

"We'll start with the twenty stuff," he called to MacClendon, the chief gunner's mate. "Set up the ammunition gangway and get the line going."

Two of the gunner's mates placed across the foot of space between the *Dee* and the barge a broad piece of planking made with two-by-fours, and lashed it in place.

MacClendon pointed to it and shouted, "You guys make a line here."

He was tall, big-boned, blond, and, for a chief, young—still under thirty. His khaki cap cover and trousers were still brown; they were not old enough to have been bleached to the off-white shade. He had made chief two months before.

As he directed, the seventy-odd men near the ammunition gangway flattened into a line from the barge to the ship. They passed the magazines along the line to the machine guns. After the magazines, moving straight down the line, came the long, brass-bodied, sharp-nosed three-inch fifty-caliber cartridges that were loose and not crated.

"Keep those noses up now, Goddamn it," shouted MacClendon. One clumsy recruit straight from boot camp could blow half a dozen men to pieces by dropping a cartridge on the point of that nose.

Nobody did. When these cartridges were in the ready service boxes at the six three-inch guns, the men, no longer rooted in the line but walking from the barge to the *Dee*, carried the remaining, crated ammunition aboard.

The three-inch stuff was in long, rectangular wooden boxes; the twenty-millimeter, in square, short ones. The men stacked the boxes in front of the after deckhouse, where they made a pile by the open hatch in the deck. The hatch opened to the handling room of the magazine, thirty feet below.

Rigged on the sides of this square opening in the deck was a small crane. On the end of it, directly over the hatch, a pulley was fastened. Through the pulley ran a piece of line one inch in circumference. Attached to the end of the line, dangling over the open hatch, was a rope bridle, to hold the ammunition boxes as they were lowered into the magazine.

Watching the boxes pile up, Arby said to me, in an undertone, "Any dope?"

"No dope at all."

"Not even on when we get underway?"

"Only what the skipper said yesterday. Sometime this afternoon."

He shrugged his shoulders and walked closer to the hatch. "Let's get it below," he said to MacClendon.

"Aye, aye, sir." MacClendon turned toward the moving line of men. "I want twenty of you guys here." With an arm motion, he chopped off the segment of the line closest to the open hatch. "Flattery, you and Shanty put the boxes in the sling. Villarubia, you take these two guys and work the magazine."

Villarubia, a squat Italian with black hair, eyes, and beard stubble, said, "Come on, you guys," and the three walked into the after deckhouse to go below to the magazine.

A moment later, Villarubia yelled up: "Okay. Let 'em go." His voice was hollow in the eight-by-eight, steel-walled closeness of the handling room, straight down from and thirty feet below the hatch on deck.

"Start it, Flattery," said MacClendon.

Flattery pulled a box from the pile, and the other gunner's mate, Hogan, slipped the sling around it.

"All set," said Flattery, straightening and stepping back. He was a slender boy with wide shoulders and brown curls, protruding, undoubtedly by his own arrangement, from under his white hat.

Fifteen men, the nearest about twenty feet from the hatch, were standing, ready, with their hands on the Manila line. They walked forward to ease the box down into the handling room.

While the line tenders were lowering the ammunition, the rest of the crew was still carrying the boxes from the barge to both magazines. At the after magazine, the pile of the long three-inch boxes grew wider and higher, as the twenty-millimeter stack, shrinking with each box that descended into the magazine, dwindled.

"How many more of them twenty boxes?" called the hollow voice from below.

"Eight more." Flattery winked at me. The pile had almost two dozen. "Eight more."

On the twelfth box, Villarubia yelled, "How about them eight more you said?"

"That's right, Ruby." Flattery winked again. "Eight more."

A box banged on the magazine plates.

"Watch it, Goddamn it, watch it," snarled the chief. "You got live ammunition there. Watch it."

They finished the twenty-boxes and started on the three-inch. Forty-five minutes cut that pile in half. My watch said ten twelve.

"How many more?"

"Eight more." Flattery leaned over the open hatch to answer Villarubia, standing in the middle of the cubicle below, looking straight up. "Eight more, Ruby."

"Ah, blow it." Villarubia made an obscene gesture with his middle finger upward at Flattery.

Arbry came to the hatch.

"We can get at the depth charges now," he said. "Let's get them aboard."

The charges started coming. Over the gangway, one at a time, with one man pushing each, they rolled.

The charges were flat-ended gray cylinders that looked like and were the size of garbage cans. On the base was a numbered dial where the desired depth of explosion was set. A charge weighed three hundred pounds; they were only half as big as the charges the new destroyers carried.

In the North Atlantic war, the charges were our primary, real weapon. All the other things, the machine guns, the main battery, even the torpedoes, were only adjuncts. You could not shoot guns at a submarine three hundred feet under water, and you could not fire torpedoes at her, either. We did what we had to do with depth charges. They were what counted.

When we fired them, charges rolled from two stern racks thrusting over the end of the *Dee* to break the water softly, while others arced in the air from the K-guns on both sides of the ship, the squat, forked K-guns roaring with the blast of the cartridge that kicked them upward, and the charges whirling in the air to splash one hundred yards away in a heavy white spout rupturing the surface of the sea.

Then they tumbled downward through the water to the depth that a torpedoman had set on the dial with a fast turn of the hand wrench. When they hit the depth, three hundred pounds of TNT went off, and through the water hundreds of feet down ripped the big percussion wave that smashed anything it hit at fifty yards and battered its target at many times that distance.

The thing was to explode the charges, close, very close, to the submarine.

There was a special magazine for the depth charges. The charges belonged to the torpedo department, and four torpedomen lowered them into the magazine. John Ewell, the torpedo officer, stood by the hatch, his big body dwarfing almost to caricature the slender, short Arbry beside him. I joined them.

"Those are heavy bastards," Ewell said, looking at the gray can on the end of the line inching down through the hatch. Still looking at it, he said to me, "I had something fine night before last. A beast, strictly a beast, you understand, but it was sure fine. Why is it you always line up these fine beasts just be-' fore you get underway? When you come back somebody else is in and you're out and you have to find yourself something all over again. If you could just line 'em up as soon as you got in."

Three men on the line were cautiously lowering the charge.

"For Christ's sake, don't be afraid of it. Give me the damn thing." Ewell grabbed the line in his hands and spread his legs wide apart. "I got it." The three let go the line and moved away. Leaning back on the line, his arms tensed in the blue jacket and his big legs pushing hard at the deck, he worked toward the hatch in short forward steps. The strain went out of the line as the charge reached the deck below.

Ewell handed the line back to the three sailors.

"Don't stop," said one. "We got nearly a hundred charges to go. We'll hold your coat for you. You don't want to stop now."

"I just remembered urgent business elsewhere."

They grinned. They liked him. His strength always impressed them.

The depth charges still covered part of the main deck after the last three-inch box had been sent to the magazine. The sun, cutting through light clouds, was almost at its zenith when the charges were no longer there.

Arbry, looking at the bare deck by the hatches, exhaled hard through pursed lips, in relief, and shook his head. He looked at his wrist watch.

"Eleven-fifty-one. Christ Almighty. I hope we never have to do that again. Four hours to load all the ammunition. Let's report ready to the exec."

Graham was sitting at his desk in the office, frowning at some official letters before him.

"Gunnery department ready to get underway," Arbry told him.

"Communications department ready," I said.

Graham nodded, still frowning, and looked back to his letters. We stepped over the high curving bottom of the doorway, closed the door, and walked across the well deck toward the big hatch to the wardroom one deck below.

Loudspeaker blared: "All hands to dinner. All hands to dinner."

"That'll be their last meal in port for a long time," said Arbry.

We stepped down the ladder to the wardroom.

6

THE MESS BOYS in the white coats served coffee to the officers at the wardroom table after lunch. The captain sipped from his cup, clinked it back into the saucer, and said without intonation, "Under way at fourteen thirty." Then he lighted a cigarette.

The smoke curved thinly away from the white stem between his fingers and diffused over the table, the smell of the smoke mixing with that of the coffee and the clatter of dishes and silver in the pantry sounding clear and loud through the silence of the wardroom.

Anson said, "Better tell the boys to light off the boilers." He raised his cup to his mouth, finished his coffee, put the cup down, rose, muttered "Excuse me," and walked out of the room. The door shut behind him. The silence set in again.

I looked at Crandall. He was sitting very straight in his chair, and was gazing, with an air of great intelligence, at the captain.

Buchan ended it. "You told all of it goodbye, Flattop?"

"Sadly. With great sadness and unspeakable regret."

"That won't hurt you." The captain's eyes crinkled as he looked down the table at Flattop. "Do you good to learn you can live without it."

"You can?"

"You'll find out." The captain laughed, deep in his throat, still looking at Flattop.

We laughed, too. When we left the table we still did not know where we were going, or why.

At two o'clock, I was in the radio shack checking incoming messages when it came.

The loudspeaker on the bulkhead outside brought it through the open door of the shack: "Now hear this. Set the special sea detail. Set the special sea detail."

"Here we go," said the radioman at the far end of a long table against the wall opposite the door. Three of them, all with earphones, were sitting at the table in front of typewriters.

"Here we go."

I left the radio shack and started for the ladder to the bridge, less than ten feet away.

The loudspeaker command had called all hands to their positions for the business of getting underway. My station was on the bridge; as communications officer, I had charge of the ship's communications there. The bridge was the brain that controlled the ship. There she was steered, navigated, her speed set, her battle targets picked, and there she communicated with her friends. Every nerve impulse that resulted in action by some segment of the *Dee's* three hundred by thirty-foot physiology began on her bridge.

I walked up the ladder from the well deck to the bridge.

Ewell, always officer of the deck for the special sea detail, was already there, in gray pants, a gray-covered cap, and the blue jacket stopping at his waist. Around his neck, by a leather strap, hung a pair of black binoculars.

He smiled when he saw me.

"Goodbye, Norfolk," he said.

"Goodbye is right."

"We'll get the word now."

"We'll have to."

He turned to the telephone talker beside him. The talker had earphones clamped to his head by a metal strip across the top of it, and a mouthpiece suspended, by a canvas neck strap, two inches from his mouth. He received reports from the stations spread over the ship, and, in turn, relayed orders to them.

"The engine room reported ready?" Ewell asked.

"Not yet, sir."

I started to check the bridge to see that my men and equipment were ready. I pressed the button to turn on the power for the short-range radio that had a French-style telephone mounted on a box against the rear bulkhead of the wheelhouse. A button-size light on the box turned red to show the radio was working. Also inside the wheelhouse was the helmsman, standing in front of the spoked mahogany wheel. Standing at the wheel, he could look straight ahead through a glass-covered porthole along the path of the ship. A gyro compass repeater hung directly above the wheel from the overhead.

The wheelhouse was the core of the bridge. The two open wings, where the officers and the signalmen did their business, unprotected from the weather, flanked it on each side. Behind it in the same four-walled steel cube, were the sound shack and the chartroom, separated from each other by a thin board partition. At the rear of this cube was a strip of space connect-

ing the two wings. On the back side of the space was the flag
bag, where the ship's signal flags were kept.

I went through the door of the wheelhouse to the port wing
to see if my signalmen were there. They were: one for each
of the two signal lights, two for the halyards by the flag bag,
and one for the radio telephone.

"Officer of the deck." The captain was on the port wing. His
face was freshly shaved and pink. He wore a black tie against
the gray shirt with the commander's silver leaves on the collar
flaps. He had on the gold-filigreed cap and the blue jacket.
"Are we ready to get underway?"

"Engine room hasn't reported ready, sir," said Ewell.

"Tell 'em to bear a hand."

"Aye, aye, sir."

I looked at Buchan and thought that this would be the last
time he or anyone else would wear a tie until we were in port
again.

Buchan walked on long legs to the chest-high steel wind
guard around the wing and glanced up at the flag blowing,
twenty feet above him, from the foremast at the rear of the
bridge. The flag waved easily in the wind and pointed away
from the pier. That was good. It would help the *Dee* away
from, not push her into, the pier. Buchan, if he was pleased,
did not show it. He looked down, nearly forty feet below, to
the brown river water where it surrounded the thick black
posts that were the dolphins of the pier. The white swirl that
would tell of a current was not there. That was good, too.
Buchan moved two short steps away from the wind guard.

The talker said something to Ewell. Ewell walked heavily
to the captain.

"Engine-room reports ready, sir. All stations manned and
ready."

"Very well. All hands stand by to get underway. Tell the
engine room to answer all bells."

The talker parroted the words into the mouthpiece.

The *Dee* had no tugs to assist her. Buchan could have re-
quested them; he had not.

He leaned over the wind guard again to stare down at the
forecastle. Jake Warwick, big-bellied in the unfastened blue
jacket, stood between the black anchors chained to the deck
on either side of the bow. Ranged by the tripled spans of the
thick, brown Manila lines holding the ship to the pier, were
men in groups of four and five. They wore white hats, blue
bell-bottom trousers, and the blue jackets. In the middle of the
forecastle was a bareheaded telephone talker.

Receiving the message from the bridge, the forecastle talker called: "Stand by your lines."

The men moved closer to the cleats.

On the dock, ready to cast off the lines, were six seamen in dungarees. The cargo ship across the slip had sent them. One stood at each line where it reached the pier, three by the forecastle and three by the stern.

The captain looked at his men on the forecastle, at the others on the pier, at the short dips of the tripled brown line between the pier and the *Dee*, and turned to the talker waiting behind him.

"Single up."

"Single up," repeated the talker.

"Single up," brawled the man with the phones on the forecastle.

The men on the pier lifted the top loops of the six lines from each dolphin and let the loops fall, the loops dangling from the edge of the *Dee*, then getting shorter and finally vanishing through the round steel chocks on the ship's side as the men on the forecastle and the stern pulled the lines in hand over hand.

All the lines holding the *Dee* to the pier were now single strands. Buchan looked up at the flag again, then back at the stern.

"Cast off the after lines," he said.

"Cast off the after lines," said the talker.

I watched the three men on the pier raise the stern lines from the dolphins and toss them to the *Dee's* fantail.

The *Dee's* stern was free.

Now, pointing straight toward the river, the stern eased by inches away from the pier until the two made an angle of fifteen degrees. Then it stopped moving. The captain put both hands on the wind guard and leaned far over to look back. Then, his eyes still on the stern, he said, "Cast off Two and Three."

The forecastle talker yelled the order to the men on the pier. They cleared the second and third forward lines.

Now only one line held the *Dee* to the pier. It ran straight through a chock at the tip of her nose.

"Cast off One," commanded the captain.

"Cast off One," said the talker on the bridge.

"Cast off One," cried the talker on the forecastle.

The sailor by the line on the pier put both hands on the loop, lifted it from the round post, and with an underhanded, basketball throw motion, tossed it over the *Dee's* lifelines to the forecastle.

The *Dee* was underway.

"All engines back one-third," said the captain.

I felt that thrill that always hits when that last line comes in from the dock. It is the feeling of a complete break with the world, a quickly rejected but instantly returning sensation of defiance of the universe. As the umbilical cord of that last line holding her to the land is severed and the ship takes on her seaborne life, she becomes a world to herself. It is a world of rigid order, inflexible laws, and one all-powerful deity, The Captain, and it is a world spinning toward its own inescapable destiny, whatever that may be and wherever it is to be found.

The world for us, as the *Dee's* last line jerked aboard, her whistle sounded one long, dirge-like blast, and she backed arrow-straight into the stream, became a shell of steel as long as a football field and one tenth as wide as that, propelling itself towards something we did not know.

The *Dee* backed past the end of pier and made a wide quarter-circle into the river. Then Buchan stopped her engines and reversed them; she halted her rearward progress and moved ahead, along the river to the channel that led to the sea.

A ferry, oval-bodied and freshly painted in black and white, her passengers visible along her railings, crossed the *Dee's* path a half-mile ahead on her way from one side of the river to the other. Buchan stopped the engines and let the ship glide without power until the other vessel had moved clear. Then the engines took her ahead again.

The *Dee* steamed slowly downstream, changing course to one side and the other to avoid ships approaching or standing out of slips. The men on the forecastle were lined, at quarters, in two white-capped blue rows facing the right bank of the river. Jake Warwick was at the end of the forecastle, between the two anchors. The men stood easily, not at attention.

"You can smell your way out of this port."

Buchan, his eyes fixed on the river ahead, said it to nobody. He did not talk any more except to order course or speed changes, but stood, one hand on the wind guard, scarcely moving, as the *Dee* cut along the river and finally turned from it into the channel to the sea.

She left Cape Henry lighthouse a hundred yards on her starboard hand. The lighthouse was white with a red top where the light was. It stood on sand that was dull tan in the sunless gray light. The *Dee* made a turn and the shore shut off the bottom of the tower. You could only see the top, the white tapering over the brown sand until it flared into the red crown that held the light which mariners on a tall bridge could see for more than thirty miles in the night.

The *Dee* was in salt water now, not at sea but in a path running to it. She held her course for three miles and twenty minutes, then approached a large red and black buoy, with a skeletal body like a derrick and white letters on it. The *Dee* closed, the letters revealed themselves as "2CB," she passed the buoy fifty yards to her left, and then turned left to head almost due east.

She was at sea, but still not at sea; she had to course a buoy-marked swept channel for eighty miles eastward until all the charted roadways to port were behind her and the shore was below her horizon.

"All engines ahead one-third," ordered Buchan. "Tell the engine room to make five knots."

The *Dee* was making ten when he gave the command. You could hear the sound of the engines soften and feel the ship slow as the speed dropped. She rolled easily, going ahead at bare steerage way, in two-foot-high, gray waves.

An overcast covered the sky. The sun was behind it and never broke through. At intervals, a shapeless orange smudge came close to the surface of the overcast, but it always faded behind the layer of clouds and left the gray unbroken.

The captain moved away from the post he had held for more than an hour. He walked briskly down the port wing and looked back over the stern as though he were expecting something. Then he turned and walked back.

"How about some coffee?" He said it to Johnny. "Cream, no sugar."

"I'll send for some."

Peters, all in white, brought to the bridge moments later a silver tray with a silver pot, flanked by a silver cream pitcher and a silver sugar bowl, and four white cups with blue anchor markings on the sides.

He held the tray out to the captain. Buchan picked up the pot, poured coffee into a cup, set the pot back on the tray, and lifted the little cream pitcher to dash the white liquid that was not cream but condensed milk into the coffee. He jiggled the cup to mix the milk and the coffee. Peters supported the tray while Johnny and I poured our coffee. Then he took it to the executive officers inside the charthouse.

"Fresh for a change. Some strength to it, too." Buchan held the cup in his right hand. He turned to Johnny. "Secure the special sea detail and secure both anchors for sea. Set Condition Three." Condition Three was the regular steaming watch for the crew; one-third of the ship's guns were manned in Condition Three.

"Aye, aye, sir."

Johnny told the telephone talker. The talker echoed the
order into his mouthpiece.

The talker on the forecastle, sitting on the circular stump
of the capstan in the center of the deck, stood and shouted,
"Secure!"

Jake Warwick and six seamen began to work with the
anchors to change their rigging for sea. Both anchors had
been ready to let go in an instant while the *Dee* stood out of
the close waters of the harbor. On the bridge, a new helmsman
and telephone talker relieved the men at those posts. Two
new lookouts climbed the ladder from the port wing to the
flying bridge on top of the wheelhouse. On the forecastle, Jake
and his men stood back from the anchors. The forecastle
talker, standing close to Jake, said something into his phones.

The bridge talker said to the captain: "Both anchors
secured for sea, sir."

Jake and his men filed off the forecastle through a door
to the well deck behind it. Only the talker, taking off his
phones and coiling the rubber-covered line carefully around
them, remained. These he put into a metal box welded to the
bulkhead of the bridge structure at the back of the forecastle.
Then he, too, left.

Ewell was standing unobtrusively behind Buchan to receive
his orders. He was still officer of the deck; the first watch at
sea was his because he had had the last, unfinished watch in
port.

Buchan turned to look down the channel over the stern
again, then said, "Have the lookouts keep a sharp watch for
two destroyers standing out. The *Hilliard* and the *Donahue*.
We'll be operating with them." He looked at me. "Better stay
up here to handle the communications until we get squared
away."

The *Hilliard* and the *Donahue*. Now, whatever we were
going to do, we knew who was going to do it with us. We knew
the two ships. Every destroyer in the four-stacker Navy knew
all the others. I had swapped drinks with the gunnery officer
and the first lieutenant of the *Donahue*, a week before, in the
club at Norfolk. They had not even hinted of the operation.
Probably they had not known, either.

I looked over the stern at the gray water behind. I saw only
the black spindle of the last buoy three miles away, the
uneven black edge of the shoreline against the gray of the
sky, and, between the buoy and the coast, the wide black
body of a merchantman standing out to sea. She was taking
a chance alone. A year before, submarines had made the
waters off the end of the channel a graveyard for steamships.

Things were not like that now, but she was still taking a chance.

We passed the next buoy on our port hand. It was black and also shaped like a derrick, and had a black placard on the side with white letters that said "S1." It was the first of fifteen channel buoys.

"Log Sugar One abeam to port," Johnny called to the quartermaster of the watch, inside the wheelhouse.

I looked at my watch on the salt-faded khaki strap. Three-fifty-two—1532 hours. We had been underway almost two hours. I looked down the channel behind the *Dee*. Nothing new showed: only the coast, the merchantman, and the buoy. I walked to the flag bag. The flag bag stretched across the whole back of the bridge. Sitting on the forward edge were two signalmen.

"We going out with those two cans, huh, Mr. Taylor?" one asked. His name was Wilson.

"Yeah. Watch for them back there."

"Any other word on the setup?"

"No word."

I walked forward on the wing. The next buoy was about two miles ahead. There were five miles between buoys. This next one was Sugar Two. Sugar One was three miles behind. Buoy 2CB was five miles behind that. We closed Sugar Two slowly. At five knots, it would take twenty-four minutes to run two miles. I looked at Sugar Two with the glasses. A swirl of white showed in the gray water around the black base. The buoy grew larger very slowly.

"Here they are," called Wilson from the flag bag. He had the three-foot telescope we called the long glass to his right eye. "Two destroyers coming into the swept channel. About eight miles."

Through my binoculars I could see them full length, one behind the other. They were about to turn past Buoy 2CB to start down the channel. They were destroyers, all right. You could tell it from the sharp bow, the long forecastle, and the big hump that the bridge, deckhouses, and stacks, merging in the distance, made, the four points of the stacks rising out of the hump.

They turned left at the buoy, one behind the other, to come to the same course as the *Dee*. I put the binoculars on them. They came on tall and thin, like the cutting edge of a knife seen from ahead. White water suddenly spurted from the bow of the first. That meant they had put on speed. They had seen us. Coming up from behind, the bow wave higher with still more speed, they got bigger fast. In fifteen minutes, the first was only four miles away. That was signal-light distance.

The captain walked back to the flag bag to watch them. "Call the *Donahue* on the light," he ordered Wilson. "Tell her, 'Reporting for duty.' "

"Aye, aye, sir."

The port signal light was mounted on the wind guard where the guard met the flag bag. There was a foot stand under it. Wilson stepped to the stand, turned the switch of the light, and began to work the handle that controlled the shutter that spelled out words in dots and dashes. The shutter clicked in irregular rhythm. A flashing light answered on the leading destroyer.

"First one's the *Donahue*, cap'n," said Wilson, not turning his eyes from it.

The captain nodded.

Wilson clicked the shutter again. The light on the *Donahue* answered. He stepped down from the foot stand.

"Message sent and receipted for, sir. *Donahue* says to take number two position in column."

"Very well."

The *Donahue*, running up fast, pulled abreast of the *Dee* on her starboard side. She was making a good twenty-five knots. She was something to watch, rising and falling like a sea bird in the shallow waves, her knife bow slashing the water into high white froth, the flag on her mast blowing hard and straight back in the wind she created. In the blue and gray paint, she was a three-dimensional mirror of the *Dee*. The only difference was the white number on her bow. An officer on her bridge waved as she pulled even and drew ahead.

The other ship, the *Hilliard*, had cut speed and had dropped nearly a mile behind the first. As the *Donahue* left the *Dee* behind, Buchan increased speed and swung the ship into column between the other two.

"Hoist on the *Donahue*," Wilson said. Bright-colored signal flags danced on her halyards. He looked at them through the long glass. He called each flag by name to me and I looked for the meaning of the signal in the signal book, even though it was a familiar one.

"Standard distance one thousand yards. Standard speed fifteen knots. Make two-thirds speed," I reported to the captain. That meant the distance between the ships was fixed at one thousand yards and that their speed would be ten knots.

Wilson and the other signalman ran up the same flags on the *Dee*. The *Hilliard* did the same. The *Donahue* dropped her flags.

"Execute!" yelled Wilson. The other man yanked down on the halyard and the flags fell in a heap on the deck. The signal was now in effect.

Buchan appraised the distance between the *Dee* and the *Donahue*. From the *Dee's* bridge, the other ship's stern, the back of her fourth stack, her after deckhouse and the white water of her wake showed. He called to Ewell.

"Give the deck to the exec. And get all the officers in the wardroom."

It seemed that this time he was going to tell us what we wanted to know.

7

THE OFFICERS sat in the wardroom and waited for the captain. The door opened and he walked in, bareheaded and in grays, with his tie still on and in his right hand the brown briefcase. He slammed the door shut with a backward jerk of his arm, walked to the head of the table, and sat in the empty chair. He laid the briefcase on the green cover cloth.

"Here it is." He put his hand into the case and pulled out a sheaf of paper a quarter of an inch thick and laid it before him, his right thumb ruffling the edges with a card-shuffling rasp I could hear at the other end of the table.

"This is the operation plan. We're part of Task Unit Twenty-one, thirteen, nine. It's a carrier-destroyer group. Elements are one escort carrier and three destroyers." He named the carrier.

"They call this a hunter-killer group. All it does is look for submarines. That's all. Just look for submarines. The planes conduct searches in the day, but they can't operate at night. At night, the destroyers are the only effectives. Our primary mission is to protect the carrier. In this function we are considered expendables."

He said all of it in a flat, business voice that told you nothing more or less than the words said. Neither did his face.

"This is the second one of these killer operations that the Navy has attempted. On the first one, planes from this carrier achieved surprise to a high degree. Which is to say they caught the Enemy with his pants down, in the middle of the Atlantic where no planes had ever caught him before, and they knocked his balls off. The carrier claimed thirteen kills, nine probables, and four possibles on that first trip.

"This time it's different. The Enemy knows what's coming.

All officers will consider this a continuous combat operation and conduct their departments accordingly."

He looked around the table at the officers, his face in its professional mask and unchanging in expression.

"We'll be at sea a long time and we'll cover a lot of water. Our operations area runs from fifty degrees north, right off the tip of the United Kingdom, down south to Casablanca. We're responsible for the whole Atlantic Ocean between those latitudes. We'll be at sea for a month before we put into Casablanca for supplies and repairs, and probably another month after that, or close to it. It'll be January before we get back.

"This task unit is scout force for a big convoy that leaves Norfolk in December. It's supposed to be a hell of an important convoy to the invasion, whenever that is. We're supposed to do a good job of cleaning up for the convoy."

He lifted the paper sheaf one inch from the table.

"This is the operation plan. I want every officer to read and be familiar with it in the next six hours. That's all."

He stood up. The other officers stood, too, and left the wardroom to do the things they had to do.

8

SUNSET CAME after five o'clock, but there was no sun. Twilight was only a deeper shade of the gray afternoon. A thin fog had rolled into the channel from the ocean, and the mist was cold and clean to breathe. The fog and the twilight and the overcast colored the sea and sky around the ship into a dull gray broken only by whitecaps and the wake and wash of the three destroyers in column. Through the fog you could see for a good sea mile. From the bridge, I watched the stern of the *Donahue* ahead and the white wake trailing back from it, and I looked back to see the bow of the *Hilliard* cutting the gray water into white foam half a mile behind the *Dee*. In the light both ships looked black.

I had come to the bridge to read the operations plan. It was in the chartroom behind the wheelhouse. I left the spot on the starboard wing where I had been standing and walked six feet to the door of the chartroom. The door was closed. I turned the foot-long steel handle of the door catch, that was to the Navy a "dog," and opened the door. The room was dark. When inside the chartroom, I shut the door and turned the dog to lock it, the lamp went on. It was connected to the dog, so it went off when the door opened. That way, light never showed through the door at sea.

The light lashed my eyes. I squinted. A table jammed against the right bulkhead of the six-foot-wide room. On the other wall, hooked flat against it, was a bunk. It was for the captain, who seldom used it. Under the bunk was a long gray cabinet for the charts, sextants, and binoculars. Over the table was a gray shelf that held the navigation books and tables.

"Hello," I said.

At the table, Beirne, the chief quartermaster, sat on a high three-legged stool, bent over a yard-square white chart thumb-tacked into the black hard-rubber table top. The lamp, mounted on a short brass rod on the table, hit the chart from one foot above. The chart glared in the yellow light. Beside the chart on the table, weighted with an empty brass twenty-millimeter shell, was a piece of yellow paper. Beirne looked at the paper, then made measurements with the two-legged steel dividers on the latitude scale at the side of the chart.

I stepped closer and looked over his shoulder.

"Sub reports?"

He said nothing, but kept his eyes on the chart. I glanced at the yellow paper and recognized it. It was a copy of a message I had decoded two days before. It was a report of enemy submarine locations. He was marking them on the chart.

The chart was a scale map of the North Atlantic Ocean. At the top, thrusting in black outline into the uncolored white space that was the ocean, was the foot of Greenland ending in Cape Farewell, and, east of Farewell, Iceland. On the left side was the coast of North America. It started with Labrador and curved through Newfoundland, Nova Scotia, New York and Norfolk, then downward through Charleston and Miami to give way to the Bahamas, Cuba, and the islands of the Lesser Antilles. On the right, the east side was Great Britian and Eire, the shorelines of France, Portugal, and Spain, and the jutting hump of Africa. Gibraltar almost joined Spain to that continent, and on the circling corner of Morocco was Casablanca. At the bottom, the equator cutting through the land masses on either side and the open sea between them ended the chart. That was the North Atlantic.

"Sub reports."

Beirne answered, nearly half a minute after I had asked him the question, and took the dividers, set them for a distance on the latitude scale, marked off the distance from the 30-degree north latitude line cutting the chart below Norfolk, and carefully made a dot on the chart with the pencil fixed to one leg of the dividers. Then, shifting his grip, he made a small, neat X over the dot. It was on the edge of a cluster of X's. They were northeast of Norfolk, and, by the chart scale, about five hundred miles away. A straight line connected Norfolk and the X's. That was sure to be our first course.

Each X stood for one submarine.

"Fifteen there." Beirne put his finger on the clump. I counted: fifteen.

"First stop, I guess. When do we hit it?"

"Two days, at fifteen knots. If we hold that course."

On the charted ocean were other X groups. One was just north of the Azores Islands off the west coast of Portugal. Another was south of the Azores, and west, by almost a thousand miles, off Casablanca. Just south of Cape Farewell and midway between Eire and Labrador was a thick nest. There was another seven hundred miles east of St. John's, Newfoundland. Three small shoals of two and three X's each were scattered over the middle of the Atlantic.

I looked at the X's and wondered, for the hundredth time, by what sort of intelligence men sitting at desks before map-covered walls in London and Washington could say. "There are so many submarines operating here," and make a pinpoint in the ocean. But they did. They fitted together pieces of a puzzle: reports from search aircraft, intercepted enemy broadcasts, stories from survivors of sunken ships, intelligence from spies at Kiel or St. Nazaire and the other U-boat bases. Then, fragment by fragment, they made a shadowy picture. They were not infallibly right. But they were good. They were very, very good. Now the X's they made on the maps on the wall had become our signposts. We had to translate black penciled crosses on white paper into torpedoes, depth charges, and death.

"Got the operations plan?"

Not replying, he handed me a red folder from the shelf above the chart table. Standing at the table, I opened the folder and began reading. The formal Navy English on the first two pages told me what the captain and the chart had already made clear.

The task unit would hunt from one cluster on the chart to another. We would hunt the Enemy and destroy Him. That was all, and that was everything.

The search area started from a line joining Casablanca and Norfolk and ran northward almost to Cape Farewell at the top of Greenland. It was bounded on the west by Labrador, Newfoundland, and the northeastern coast of the United States. It stopped on the east with the United Kingdom and the coasts of Portugal and Africa. This was a sea more than three thousand miles long and one thousand miles wide, and it covered four million square miles of water. That was the battleground.

The ships had a clear division of labor. The planes from the carrier would hit the submarines on the surface—when the planes could find Them. The destroyers would attack the submarines when submerged— if the destroyers could find Them. The destroyers, also and primarily, would protect the carrier from the submarines—and there was no doubt at all that the submarines would find her.

There was a catch. Planes could not land on the seesawing box-top flight deck at night. Some day they would be able to, but now they could not. I wondered what would happen if a dozen submarines went after three obsolete destroyers and a pony-sized carrier when it was black dark. That was an interesting tactical problem. I put it out of my mind and read the plan. I finished it and put it back on the shelf.

"Learn it all?" Beirne asked, looking at the chart.

"All of it."

He looked up from the chart and put the dividers down.

"Listen to that sound gear," he said. "They've started it again. I'll be living with that damned pinging sixteen hours a day from now on."

"We'd be in a hell of a shape without it."

I had not been aware of the pinging. Now I suddenly heard it, clear and sharp, the way you sometimes hear, all at once, the beating of your own heart. It came from the sound shack that was separated only from the chart room by the partition.

Each ping was like the sound a rock makes dropped into a lake, silvery, searching, and finally vanishing but never dying. The pings were even-spaced and regular, second apart, like a dead-slow heartbeat.

The pings were sound waves. They searched for submarines. They were our eyes, and ears, and nose, under the sea.

They came from a steel dome on the bottom of the ship. The dome pitched the sound into the ocean. It amplified the noise of each wave and sent it to the listening device in the sound shack. If the wave hit something under water, an echo bounced off what it hit. Then the dome received and transmitted it to the sound shack. The echo was our only spoor. We chased the echo. It might be the Enemy. It might not. But the sound gear and its pings were all the *Dee* had to hunt Him with. The heartbeat of the pings was her reason for existence. When they stopped, she was nothing.

"Better get used to it," I said.

"Guess I'll have to."

I opened the door, stepped through it, closed it, turned the dog, and started for the wardroom. My next watch came after dinner. The pulsing of the pings followed me down the ladder to the deck below.

9

THE FOG and the overcast buried the stars and smeared the sea and sky together into a sphere of black that had the *Dee* at the bottom. On the bridge, I could see nothing except the white sides of the V she carved in the water, the wake of the ship ahead, the bow wave of the one behind, and, on my wrist, the green luminous figures and hands on the watch dial that said seven-thirty-nine. The wind, blowing cold and hard, carried the wet, fresh smell of the fog. The channel swells were stronger and they lifted the *Dee* higher and dropped her lower than two hours before. But her ride was still easy. The only sound on the bridge was the pinging: a ping, four seconds of silence, and the ping again.

I stretched my left hand forward to touch the flag bag and to feel, by it, my way around the back of the bridge to the port wing. My eyes, adapting slowly to the dark, made out Johnny's big back on the wing, just outside the door to the wheelhouse.

I touched his shoulder. "Hello. Ready to relieve you."

"Steaming as before." He moved deliberately from his spot at the corner of the wing to face me. His face was shapeless and white in the dark. "Making ten knots. We just passed Sugar Fourteen. The sea buoy coming up, old X-ray Sugar, and then your ass is at sea and the fun starts."

"How about the carrier?"

"We've got her on radar, eight miles back. She contacted us on radio half an hour ago."

This is something, I thought. Here we are starting a show without even a look at the star and director, we are taking orders from a boss that is only a yellow amoeba on a dark electronic screen and a voice talking out of a small round box on a steel bulkhead. Well, we would see the carrier tomorrow. We would, God knows, see all we wanted of her before this was over.

"Any orders on forming up?"

"Just what was in the plan. The cans set up the defense screen and the carrier steams right into position behind them. Then we all guide on her. Can you see yet?"

"Not so good. Give me another minute or two. Captain on the bridge?"

"In the wheelhouse." He gestured with his thumb at the open door two feet away.

I looked straight ahead. I still saw only the phosphorescent white wake of the *Donahue* bubbling on the black of the water half a mile away. Over the stern at the same distance, the white bow wave of the *Hilliard* rose clearly in the dark. That was all I saw of either.

"I see as much as I'll ever see," I said. "I relieve you."

He lifted his binoculars from his neck, where they hung by the leather cord, and put them around mine.

"Okay. You got it."

I heard his heavy footsteps on the steel deck as he walked toward the ladder on the other side of the bridge. I had said the magic, all-absolving, to him who heard them, words, "I relieve you." Now I had the deck. I had the responsibility and control, subject to the captain's orders, of the ship.

The job now was to keep the *Dee* in column behind the *Donahue* at the thousand-yard distance. The helmsman was steering the *Dee* straight for the white wake ahead.

"Looks like we got the sea buoy two miles ahead," said the man on watch at the radar screen inside the wheelhouse. The radar control equipment was inside the sound shack with the sound gear, but there was a repeater, for the benefit of the captain and officer of the deck, in the wheelhouse. This repeater scope gave a picture of all the objects in a circle around the ship, with whatever radius might be set. The ship was the center of the circle. The picture on the scope looked like one you would see from an airplane directly over the center of the circle. Except there were no photographic likenesses. There were only the yellow pips on the dark, distance-marked screen. It took time to learn to read the radar.

I looked ahead and to the left with my binoculars for the sea buoy, so called because it marked the end of the channel and the start of the open sea. The buoy had a small light on it. I did not see it. All I saw was the white wake streaking through the blackness ahead.

I lowered the glasses. The ship cut the water, rising and falling at the easy ten knot pace. I raised the glasses to look again for the buoy; then, not seeing it, let them fall to jerk on the strap that held them around my neck. Seconds later, I made another try.

In the darkness ahead, just to the left of the wake, was a yellow point of light. It might have been one mile away or it might have been thirty. But I knew it must be the buoy and I knew it was close. The light got bigger, slowly, as the *Dee* closed it. The faint tolling of a bell sounded, it, too, on the buoy, in a one-two beat that I could hear between the pings on the bridge. The bell was louder and the light brighter as the ship drew close to the buoy, came even with it, one hundred yards away, and moved past it.

The *Dee* was at sea.

I went into the wheelhouse to tell the captain. He was standing beside the wheel, looking, through a porthole, at the darkness ahead.

"X-Ray Sugar abeam to port, sir," I said.

"Very well." He did not move.

I returned to the wing. The notes of the bell grew fainter and then were gone. The yellow point of light, falling further and further behind, still pricked the dark. Finally the light also vanished and only the blackness was left.

I was suddenly aware that the captain was beside me. He had walked through the door from the wheelhouse to the wing, his footsteps so light I had not heard them.

"Swing her right and take station in the screen off the *Donahue's* quarter." He gave the order softly, as though not wanting to disturb the silence of the bridge that was broken only by the wind, the waves and the never-stopping ping.

"Aye, aye, sir."

I brought the *Dee* right to a new course to take her to station in the anti-submarine screen. The screen would be a three-cornered spearhead. The *Dee* was to be at the right corner, the *Donahue* at the apex, and the *Hilliard* on the left. Getting distances on the *Donahue* from radar, I took the *Dee* to her station and swung her back to base course. The spearhead was made and waiting for the carrier to come up behind it.

"How far back is the carrier?" The captain spoke through the door to the radar operator inside the wheelhouse.

"Four miles now, sir."

The destroyers were making ten knots and the carrier about seventeen. It would be more than half an hour before she came to position.

The *Dee* sliced through the darkness. The waves were higher and the wind freshening. It came across the wind guard to hit my face and strike faint moans from the signal halyards overhead.

"She's starting to blow," said the captain.

The pinging, never stopping and never breaking the even-spaced rhythm, carried over the bridge, like an unceasing and repeated melodic theme. The *Dee,* plowing ahead, began to pitch, not hard but in an ominous suggestion.

"It's going to blow up a rough night," the captain said again. "I'd make sure everything is lashed down."

"We're in for some weather, all right. The barometer's down two points in the last hour."

In the dark, I could see him nod. Then he asked radar again, "How far to the carrier?"

"Only two miles, sir. She's coming up fast."

Buchan turned to me. "She's only a thousand yards behind station now. Stand by for a speed change when she gets there. Keep station forty-five degrees on her bow at three thousand yards as soon as she gets there. She'll take the guide then."

Waiting, I listened to the pinging, the wind in the halyards, and the waves washing against the side of the ship as she cut through them. The wind was colder now, and the fog was heavier and closing in fast.

"Thirty-five hundred yards on the carrier," reported the man on radar.

The captain stepped back inside the wheelhouse. He stood by the radio telephone just inside the door. This was the voice radio for use between ships in formation, and did not reach beyond the horizon. It was the TBS. Buchan was anticipating a message from the carrier on it.

He did not wait long. From the speaker above the door came a crackling static that always preceded a transmission, and, after it, a deep voice.

"Hello team, hello team, this is Coach." These were the code words for the destroyers and the carrier. "Commence my operation plan. Commence my operation plan. Execute to follow. Speed red purple. Corpen white green brown. Stand by." A pause. "Execute."

The order swung the task unit from its due-east course to one north northeast, zero three-five on the compass, straight for the first cluster of submarines. It also set its speed at fifteen knots. The *Dee* had to go ahead faster to take her proper position as the formation turned.

"Let's go," said the captain.

"All engines ahead full," I commanded. "Left standard rudder. Come to zero one five."

"Zero one five," acknowledged the helmsman.

"All engines answer ahead full," called the man at the engine annunciators.

The *Dee* started with the new twenty-knot speed. She pitched heavily, and the wind, increasing with the ship's speed, was louder in the signal lines. The fog had pushed in so close I could not see beyond the bridge, and its outlines were dim and shadowy. The other ships were only oval pips on the radar screen. We saw nobody, neither our friends nor the Enemy, as we began whatever it was we were beginning.

"Take her to flank," said the captain. Flank speed was the highest speed the annunciators could demand from the engines. It was twenty-five knots.

"All engines ahead flank."

The annunciators rang up the speed.

The hum of the engines became a snarl, the *Dee* sprang into the oncoming seas, and, as the wind screamed in the halyards, icy white spray lashed her open decks, and the ping of the sound gear beat like an unseen heart over the bridge, she drove into the fog and blackness of the North Atlantic.

That was the way it started, off the Norfolk channel in November. That was the way it started, and none of us, in the wardroom or through the crew's quarters, on the bridge or in the engine rooms, at the guns or by the depth charges, knew what it was that we had started.

The task unit was alone on the sea, with nothing to protect, nothing to attack, nothing to flee from. All we had to do was hunt. We had to hunt over a terrain of water that covered almost four million square miles. We had to hunt an Enemy we could not see, but tracked with pinging sound waves that spread through the ocean fathoms under the jagged surface that barred us from what we hunted.

Whatever it was that we had started and wherever it might take us, we began it that night off the Norfolk channel.

Part Two

10

I STOOD by the sideboard in the wardroom and poured a cup of coffee from the glass bowl on the hot plate. The coffee was amber, and I could see the bottom of the cup through it. It was also tasteless. I drank another cup. The white hands and figures on the black dial of the clock above the door said seven-thirteen. I wanted to see the carrier before breakfast. I leaned over the closed bottom half of the pantry door and said to Peters, sitting, eyes closed, in a cane-bottomed chair against the opposite wall: "Put some coffee in this Goddamned stuff." Then I went to the bridge to look at the carrier.

On the bridge, I walked back of the charthouse to the port wing. Rocky was there, both hands holding binoculars to his eyes. He was officer of the deck.

I looked the way the binoculars pointed, diagonally back from the *Dee*.

"So that's her."

"That's her, that's our baby." He half chanted the answer, almost to the old tune, "Yes, Sir, That's My Baby," and let his glasses down easily, turning to me. "The white hope of the Yew-nited Stytes Nyvy. Look at her, boy, look at her. Get used to her. We're going to be her foot-servant and vassal from here on. Take a good look."

I did. She was on a line going back almost exactly forty-five degrees from the *Dee*, almost exactly three thousand yards away. The operation plan had set the bearing and the distance.

She and the three destroyers together made a diamond, the *Hilliard* on the left corner, the *Donahue* at the top, the *Dee* on the right, and the carrier at the bottom. Looking at the carrier from the forty-five degree angle, I saw her from a bad viewpoint, neither head-on nor in full profile.

"Let's see your glasses."

Rocky gave them to me. I put them on the carrier. Her hull was mottled into a piebald blue and white camouflage. Her shape was not easy to see from the angle.

"Right to zero-eight-zero." I moved the glasses to look at

57

Rocky. He had a white card in his right hand and was inspecting the watch on the back of his left wrist. The ship leaned as she turned right.

"Zigzagging?"

"Yeah." He looked back at the slip of paper. It had the courses of the zigzag and the times for each. Zigzagging was a tactic of evasion. It was supposed to make it hard for submarines to track or to torpedo you. In a zigzag, ships made frequent course changes at times ordered by the zigzag plan in use. The plan set the changes from base course and the time for each. All ships in a formation made the changes simultaneously. There were many plans, and they were in a green paper-backed book. Any plan in the book could be used. The plans were worked out by mathematics professors somewhere. Zigzagging was first used in the first world war. In this one, its value was doubtful. Still, we zigzagged.

"Steady on zero-eight-zero, sir," said the helmsman from the wheelhouse.

The other ships had turned simultaneously. They had not altered their true positions in the diamond, but on this leg of the plan, they had changed their relationship to each other. The turn had placed the *Donahue* even with and paralleling the *Dee* and the carrier directly behind us. Now I had a perfect head-on view of the carrier.

She had a straight flight deck that protruded over the sides of her hull. The hull tapered down almost to the point of a V where it met the water. The flight deck and the hull together looked like a Roman numeral five with the bottom chipped off. Rising from the extreme right of the flight deck was a tower. It gave the carrier a lopsided look; this one-sidedness was what struck you when you looked at her from ahead. The tower was her bridge. They called it the "island." It was built on the side to give the planes a straight runaway the length of the deck, which was, at best, not long.

"That flight deck is nobody's LaGuardia," I said.

"It looks too damned little to take planes. They'll earn that flight pay three times over just landing on that box top in the North Atlantic. I don't see how they can do it."

"They do it."

I wanted to see her in profile; I waited for the zigzag plan to bring the ships ninety degrees to the left, so she would be even with the *Dee*. It took two course changes to the left and twelve minutes to get her in that position.

I looked at her again with the glasses. This time she looked symmetrical. From the side, the tower almost bisected her length. The flight deck jutted over the ends of the hull as it had done over the sides. The side of the hull looked like a not-too-slender parallelogram.

"She looks squat."

"Why shouldn't she look squat?" said Rocky. "She is squat. She's just a merchant hull with a flight deck pasted on top. She's no fleet carrier. Fleet carriers are for the gentlemen's war. This out here ain't no gentlemen's war."

Through the glasses, the carrier did not look stubby. They called her a CVE. Regular carriers were simply CV. The E stood for escort.

There were, so far, not many CVE's. She was one of the first two built, and she was still new. This was only her second trip. On her first, she had made extravagant claims concerning the sinking of submarines. Maybe they were true, maybe they were not. But the Navy was counting on this one and the others like her, afloat and still building, to beat the submarines in the Atlantic. She was, as Rocky said, a white hope.

Now she was not pitching but seesawing. One end of her pudgy box-like bulk dipped as the other reared up.

I looked in the sky for planes. I saw none.

"Any aircraft up?"

"Four. They're all scattered."

I looked back at the carrier. "So that's her." I said it for the second time before breakfast.

"That's her. Why don't you go down and tell Arbry to get it up here and relieve me?"

I went down.

"Tickle the tit for me," Johnny said.

It was midafternoon of the same day, the first one out of Norfolk, and the wardroom clock said twelve minutes past three as Johnny and I sat alone at the table.

I reached down and pressed a button on the steel leg of the table. It made a buzz in the pantry, and brought a mess boy through the pantry door into the wardroom. His eyes were heavy-lidded from sleeping and he was buttoning his high-collared mess jacket that was bleachedly white against the deep brown of his skin.

"You ring, Mr. Ewell?" He blinked, still waking.

"What kind of sandwiches you got in there?"

"Same kind, Mr. Ewell. You want some cheese and jam?"

"Yeah, bring me some cheese and jam. And some fresh coffee."

Johnny slung his leg across the green-covered table. His skin above the roll of his black socks showed white against the green cloth. I looked at his leg.

"You want to buy champagne?"

"Hell, my foot's not on it."

There was a house rule that any officer who put his feet on the table bought champagne for the wardroom. It was just a rule. Nobody ever bought any.

Johnny grinned. He had charm. He was big and rough and he could be tough, but he was an authentic diplomat. He could insult a man and make him like it. Or a woman. Perhaps particularly a woman. It was a valuable trait and he used it for what it was worth.

I looked at him, sitting there grinning. He was a big man, big all over. He was at least two inches taller than six feet, and he weighed two twenty and maybe more. He had a big, smooth, and I suppose handsome, face, and thick well-combed hair above it. He had been a celebrated athlete at one of those small southern denominational schools in Georgia. He played fullback on the football team, right field in baseball, and in track putted the shot. I suspected he was the All-American Boy, the local pride, in his Georgia town, where his father had a law office into which he would go after the war. If, of course, he lasted the war. The Navy had pulled him out of his second year in law at the University of Virginia, given him four months' training, pinned gold ensign's bars on his collar, and sent him straight to the *Dee*. He joined her two weeks after I did, a year and a half before. Now he was sitting at the table in the wardroom, grinning, as the *Dee* rolled through the Atlantic swells on her hunt.

"Well," said he. "We're out of Norfolk, anyway."

"We're out of Norfolk, for sure."

"Maybe you're not so hot about being out of Norfolk. Maybe that tender little flier's wife was good duty."

"You have a low mind."

"You don't have to flatter me. I like to see the fly boys get burned. It was one of them that spoiled my happy romance."

"When did you have a happy romance that lasted longer than a night in the hay?"

"I did, sure I did. But it got fouled up. A fly boy fouled it up. Not that I'm complaining. He was just around and I wasn't. Plenty of times I've been around when the other guy wasn't."

"Over a period of years it evens up," I said. That was one of the wardroom epigrams.

"Yeah, over a period of years it evens up. Well, it was good duty while it lasted. I hope he enjoyed it as much as I did."

The gray curtain across the door swung monotonously with the roll of the ship. It was a fair roll today. I had the queasiness in my stomach that·comes with the first day back at sea. I looked through the porthole in the left wall. As the ship rolled, the hole was like the mouth of a gun moving up and down. At one end of the roll, with the hole pointing down, I saw only the gray sea below the horizon; then, the roll starting and the porthole rising, the horizon; and finally, at the other end of the roll, nothing but the gray clouded sky. Then the ship rolled back and I saw them in opposite order: the sky, the horizon, the sea.

"You're going to give that poor girl a guilt complex," Johnny said. "Aren't you ashamed? Don't you think you ought to be ashamed?"

"The pot insulting the kettle."

Jason brought out the sandwich. The cheese showed orange against the light brown crusts of the thick white bread. Jam oozed, purple, over the crusts.

Johnny picked it up in his big hands. He bit into it, deeply.

"Good." He said it with his mouth full. He chewed, swallowed, and took another bite. "So we're a scout force. You ever been a scout force before? What do we scout?"

"Oh, anything. Simply anything. Redheads, Scotch, ten-day shack-ups. You name it, we scout it."

"That I approve of."

"In our spare moments we look for a submarine or two."

"There are no submarines in the Atlantic Ocean. I personally have never seen one." He finished the sandwich quickly, stood up, and ran the back of his hand over his mouth. "It's so stuffy down here I think I'll put on some foul-weather gear and go up on the bridge. I think I might even stay there for a few hours. Say, about four." He had the next watch. Each watch lasted four hours.

"You know where you can find me." I had to relieve him.

"I always know that. Sleep well. I'll be seeing you. About four hours."

He walked through the passageway from the wardroom to his stateroom. I could hear him humming as he dressed.

11

I STAYED at the table, doing nothing. The motion of the ship, of which I had to become a part all over again, came up, revolving, through my belly, and moved my weight in the straight-backed chair, while I continued to look through the port at the gray sea and sky and the white curlers in between. Anson and Rockford came in, grunted greetings, and sat.

"Three-handed?" Anson asked, and Rockford said, "The hell with it."

So we sat, talking little, and I, at least, thinking much. About what we had left. Behind. Norfolk was not much, but it was without watches or general quarters or freezing winds or churning guts, or the gray monotony. While with the officers' club with double bourbons at the three-deep bar and fresh butter and milk and pink-centered steaks in the high-vaulted dining room, and, everywhere, the fur-coated, high-heeled women whom you could, if nothing else, admire. And this last time I had provided well for myself. Yes, I thought, I had indeed. Well, I could forget about that now. Somebody else was taking care of the providing. The providing would not keep. That was one thing you could never go back to. Those who live by die by. Or something.

A white hand came from the side of the gray curtain behind the table, pushed the curtain to one side, and Crandall made his entrance. That was what he did. He did not come in: he made his entrance.

His khaki shirt and trousers were transparently new and un-laundered, the creases of the manufacturers' first folding still showing, and the twin bars on each flap of his collar glistened like sterling plate. He correctly and quickly took off a cap with a bright gold strap above an unclouded black visor.

We all stared at him.

"Gentlemen." He looked around the table at us all, made the smile, and I remembered it and felt again the rush of instant dislike. Then he pulled a chair from the table and sat in it, very straight, folding his white hands on the green table covering.

He looked about him, the smile set on his face, waiting for a reciprocal greeting. None came.

Until I said: "Well, how do you like destroyer duty?"

He broadened the smile slightly, and produced from his left breast pocket a silver cigarette case, small enough to fit there but built to please. "Very much." The voice was polite, with the condescending courtesy of a new chairman of the board addressing his assembled vice presidents. "I'm sure the tour will be immensely profitable." Something snapped in the case and the lid sprang back to expose an even row of white tubular shapes. He proffered it, in turn, to each of us, and, after we refused, took a cigarette himself.

As sure as hell he will break out a silver lighter to match the case, I thought. He did, from the other breast pocket.

It made a quick bright flame the first time he tried it, and he put the flame to the cigarette, snapped off the flame, and restored the lighter to the pocket.

"You see," and now the smile was meant to be engaging, "they're planning to give some of us with experience in the bureau executive officers' billets on these buckets and they think we need a little actual destroyer duty first."

"Do they really?" Rockford murmured with great politeness. Which was, with him, an ominous sign.

"I'm sure they're quite right." Crandall nodded and leaned toward Rocky to show he really was sure they were quite right. "Nothing like learning your job, is there?" The smile. "Even if one can walk right into a job if he has to, it's always better if you get the feel of it first. That's what I used to say in my own organization." He waited for somebody to pick this up, but no one did. "Don't you agree?" He asked suddenly, of Rocky.

"Oh, I don't know." Rocky had committed himself completely to the soft, polite voice that was to be entirely mistrusted. "In the case of a really capable man—"

Crandall laughed deprecatingly. "I'm sure a couple of months on the *Dee* will do me a lot of good."

"I don't suppose it can hurt you, anyway." Rockford smiled, warmly and sympathetically, at Crandall. *He has him where he wants him now,* I thought.

"The funny thing"—and Crandall tried to make his own smile even more engaging—"the funny thing is they said they'll probably assign me to this very ship. As exec, I mean."

"That certainly will be splendid. In two months, you'll know all about the *Dee*." Rocky's expression became even more beatific.

Crandall laughed the modest laugh, and said nothing.

"You've been in larger ships before?" Rocky's warm, friendly voice dropped a note lower.

"Well, no." This time Crandall's laugh was not deprecatory but nervous. And I saw again what it was I had seen as he walked up the pier. Whatever it was. "As a matter of fact, I've never had sea duty before. Not officially, that is."

"Oh?"

"Of course, I made quite a few training cruises on the Severn River when I was in Washington. And I spent almost a week on the old *Wyoming* in Chesapeake Bay last year."

"You're all set, then." Rocky continued to smile sweetly and admiringly at him.

"What sort of duty did you have in Washington?" I asked. I was embarrassed, not so much by Rocky's playing him as by his total inability to see that he was being played.

"I was with the Bureau." He turned toward me, less polite

than moments ago. "The Bureau of Personnel. In the officer section."

"That must have been easy to take," said Anson.

Crandall did not like that. "I asked to go to sea as soon as I accepted my commission, of course. But the Bureau thought that my executive experience in civilian life would be of greater value in an administrative post, and I had no choice in the matter. But as soon as I put in my year on the beach, by God, I demanded sea duty!" On the last, he raised his voice, thrust his chin forward, and looked belligerently around the table, in a ludicrous parody of bluster. My embarrassment became really acute.

"They just can't keep a real sailor on the beach, can they?"

"I'd had quite enough of that shore duty. I wanted action." Crandall brought the cigarette to his lips, puffed on it, and blew out, hard, a stream of curling blue smoke. He turned his mouth down at the right corner and glared belligerently ahead of him.

Johnny, his face showing nothing, looked straight at me across the table.

I looked at Crandall; at his smooth white face still wearing the comi-dramatic toughness, at his white hand on the green felt that held, between two fingers, the blue-smoking cigarette. The hand seemed to move, yet stayed where it was, and then I saw that the movement was not of the hand at all, but of the thumb: Crandall was wagging it in a curious, circular gesture.

"There's nothing like sea duty," Anson's voice was, perhaps, not satisfactorily sympathetic. A delicate pink spread over Crandall's white cheeks.

Rockford saw his pleasure disintegrating, and moved to hold on to it. 'What sort of business were you in, before?"

Crandall's face went from the toughness to a kind of urbanity. "Textiles." He turned again to Rocky.

"Really?"

"Oh, yes." Now he was elaborately casual. "I ran a little factory"—and he smiled the minimizing, deprecatory smile—"in Peoria. Various cotton goods, mostly men's wear."

"Why, you must have been president." Rockford's voice admired the achievement.

"Oh, no. Only executive vice-president and general manager." He said it as he would have said "only the Navy Cross."

"Is that right?" Rocky's awe deepened. "Gee, with that kind of background, I'm afraid you won't find our little problems very interesting."

"I wouldn't say that at all." He was friendly, sure, condescending again. "The experience is useful, of course, in han-

dling men. Handling men is the big thing, wherever you are."
He paused, drew on the cigarette again, and worked on a profound and wise aspect. "It's the ability to handle men that makes an executive, I always say."

"I think you're absolutely right."

Crandall patted Rockford on the head with another smile. Once more the worldly executive, he said, "Incidentally, who's the first lieutenant? Graham tells me I'm to be assistant first lieutenant, temporarily."

"I'm the first lieutenant," Rocky said, very gently.

Crandall glanced, almost imperceptibly, at the single bar on Rockford's collar as he had done at mine the first day, and I could see his mind working. "Fine." He sounded just the right note of pleased enthusiasm. "When can we get together to talk over my . . . duties?" He smiled at Rockford as though the "duties" were a private joke between the two of them and added, "Boss."

"Tomorrow ought to be soon enough." Rockford smiled back. "No rush."

"Good enough." Crandall glanced at the clock above the door. "Then I suppose I'd better continue my indoctrination tour now. Find out what's what on the old *Dee*." He stood, picked up the cap, included us all in his farewell smile, and walked out of the door. The catch clicked as he closed it behind him.

The three at the table looked at each other, and for a moment, said nothing.

"I've seen it." Anson shook his head, slowly. "I've seen it, but I don't believe it."

"You haven't seen anything," I said. "Wait till the Bureau actually makes this character an exec."

Rockford laughed, to himself, rose, and walked, carrying his empty cup, to the hot plate. He lifted the glass bowl by the black plastic handle and poured the brown coffee into the white cup, then set the bowl back on the hot plate, and turned to us.

"But right now Mr. Vice-President general manager handler of men ain't exec," he said. "Right now he ain't nothing but assistant first lieutenant."

He smiled. And now his smile was neither admiring, nor warm, nor sympathetic.

12

I REACHED for the light switch on the bulkhead by the door,
snapped it, closed the door, and was alone in the room. The
room was like every other officer's stateroom on board, except
for the door. It had a door because it was not in officer's country but was on the other, after side of the wardroom. The room
had: double bunks, one under the other, against the bulkhead
away from the door; a desk, between the bunks and the opposite bulkhead, or wall, which were the same thing, the desk
filling all the space between the bunks and the bulkhead; a
basin at the foot of the bunks; by the basin, a tall steel clothes
locker. The room was eight feet wide, ten feet long, and deep
enough for a very tall man to stand as straight as he wanted.

I walked to the desk and picked off it an Office of Naval Intelligence pamphlet, on the pale blue cover of which the captain
had written in black ink, "All officers." I opened it. This one
was a description of U-boat operations in the Atlantic in Sep-
tember and October. I turned the pages, looking at the pictures.
They were photographs of submarines under air attack, all the
pictures shot by attacking aircraft. One showed two white
splashes erupting from each side of the black U-boat, and the
caption said, "A kill by TBF from patrolling escort carrier."
The second line under the picture named the carrier: it was our
own. The torpedo bomber, carrying depth charges instead of
torpedoes, had made the attack during the carrier's first patrol, which was also the first patrol made by any escort carrier
in the North Atlantic. On this patrol, she claimed to have sunk
thirteen submarines beyond all doubt, probably to have sunk
nine more, and possibly four besides those.

It was an incredible claim. I did not believe it. Still, if she
had sunk even half that many, the score was astounding.

That first trip she had had the advantage of surprise. The
Germans simply had not expected enemy aircraft in the middle of the Atlantic, and had made naked targets. That phase
was over. Now we would have to work for every shot.

I looked at the picture of the submarine again, at the wide
waist tapering almost to points at each end, at the abstract,
geometrical shape between the two white spouts, and thought:
They look almost the same from above as from the side, they
are the same from wherever you see them. Long, slender,
round-pointed. And black.

In the picture, something rose from the middle of the U-boat.

From above, not showing clearly, it looked like a circle. That would be the conning tower. In front of this circle, perfectly outlined for the camera, was the long, pencil shape of a gun: the four-inch. Behind the circle was a thinner, shorter pencil: a machine gun, the twenty-millimeter.

No men were on the decks, or at the guns, or in the conning tower. They had dropped inside the submarine prepared to dive. It seemed natural that the picture showed no men. You did not think of men in connection with them. Though of course men ran them, just as we ran the *Dee*.

I turned to the front of the booklet and started to read. The third paragraph said:

The U-boat type almost exclusively in use by the Enemy at present is the 750-tonner, a medium-sized, highly maneuverable submersible capable of nine or ten knots speed submerged and about twenty on the surface. It cannot maintain top submerged speeds for long periods but must recharge batteries frequently. Operating doctrine provides for recharging every 24 hours, where possible. Early aircraft successes were scored during daylight recharging while submersibles were surfaced. It must be assumed that hereafter they will recharge at night only.

The 750-ton craft has a complement of about fifty men and five officers, and is commanded usually by a korvettenkapitan (lieutenant-commander). It mounts one four-inch gun and one twenty-millimeter machine gun, although some may have been modified to carry four twenty-millimeters exclusively. Number of torpedoes is not known, but this is enough for the craft to make long patrols of an indefinite duration.

These submersibles generally operate in a loose organization that may number five to twenty craft. They normally make separate patrols within a very small area and remain in fairly constant contact. Very frequently they will operate as a tactical unit, with the senior submarine commander, of more rank and considerably more experience than the other captains in the group, in tactical command.

Most heavy concentrations are still in the sea lanes of the North Atlantic.

We knew that already, I thought. The book had little new, except the pictures. The pictures were very satisfactory.

I closed the pamphlet and dropped it on the desk. Then I turned out the light and crawled into the bottom bunk.

On the other side of the steel bulkhead, which was only six inches from my left ear and was itself five-eighths of an inch thick, I heard the sea striking, not hard but in an easy wash as the *Dee* rose and fell through it. On my back on the bed, I felt my weight shift slightly with the roll of the ship, but the roll did not move me. Footsteps clanged on the metal ladder from the main deck to the small platform deck just outside the door. We were at sea again.

How many days had we been at sea in the last year and a half, my year and a half on the *Dee?* I tried to figure. In eighteen months, and I took the round figures, there were 540 days. We were at sea, again roundly, three-quarters of this time. One-quarter of 540 was 135. Three times 135 was 405. That made, roundly, about 400 days at sea. If I had lived 400 days of my life at sea, how many deck watches had I stood? That was easy. Standing one watch out of three, you stood two watches a day. Two times 400 was 800; 800 sea watches. How many hours? Four hours in a watch. Four times 800—3200. Three thousand and two hundred hours on the bridge of the U.S.S. *Dee* had I spent. Not counting general quarters and special sea details. It was an impressive sum. Or was it? There would be at least as many more on the same bridge on the same ship. Or would there? I was optimistic.

Life was the watches, the general quarters, the sea details, and the necessary functions, biological and other, between. What had existed before these was a memory well chewed at the edges, which I did not now really believe. It was like a motion picture seen and remembered. It had stopped being real when I no longer wondered who she was sleeping with. Or cared. That had been almost a year ago. Until then, every time I lay on this bunk and put my right arm over my eyes, I wondered. I did not actually wonder who he, the he of the moment, was. What I wondered was how she looked, if she closed her eyes and opened her mouth, breathing quickly through it; what she said, did she murmur soft words of endearment or whisper four-letter eroticisms in the dark; what she did, whether she moved her body slowly and rhythmically, or twitched in a spasm of desire. Then, not all at once but a little at a time, I stopped wondering, and when I stopped entirely, everything that had been before the *Dee* became the motion picture I remembered. I did not think about the after. The now was all there was. The now was the *Dee*, the North Atlantic, the six weeks at sea and the two in port, New York if we were lucky and Norfolk if we were not, the watches, the work, and the general quarters. That was the now and that was all there was.

Was it better to be an officer? That was a matter of taste.

I liked it better. Why were officers officers? Because they were natural leaders, had great moral and intellectual superiority, or came from such nice families? No. It was because they had a little piece of paper somewhere with bachelor of something printed on it in fancy scrollwork. Where the paper came from did not matter. It could be Kalamazoo Teachers, Harvard University, or the U.S. Naval Academy. If it was not the last, you had to do other things for four months before they let you buy the blue uniform with one gold star and one gold stripe on the sleeve, but after that it was all the same.

My piece of paper came from the University of North Carolina, where I had been neither an athlete nor a scholar nor a man of distinction nor remembered for anything except a Delta Kappa Epsilon fraternity pin, much trouble with and one suspension by the dean of men, a box full of empty bottles in my room in the fraternity house, and a rattly yellow Chevrolet convertible with a well-worn back seat that my father had bought for me, second-hand, for $600 when I was a sophomore, the year his cotton crop was big and the prices high, and which I sold to a used-car dealer for $200 the week after I graduated. That week was two weeks before I went into the Navy.

In the Navy, by virtue of the piece of paper and the four months, I put on, in time, the uniform with the one stripe, and started to learn my job. Being an officer was like any other job. You had to learn it, and you often got bruised in the process. It always annoyed me to read, anywhere but particularly in books about the war written during the war, that leaders and officers were not made but born. That was a lie all around. The job was something you learned as you went along, and which, if you believed in it, you never stopped learning.

Until now, the job, the *Dee,* and the war had all blurred into a pastless and futureless present. But this, the hunt, was different. It was different in more ways than its military and operational aspects. Exactly how it was different I did not know. But I knew that it was. I was trying to decide what made it different when I went to sleep.

13

I HEARD the door opening and knew what it was, all before I was awake. I hated the knowledge now, instantly and automatically, still sleeping, as I had hated it the hundreds of times before, and would hate it, if I were lucky, the hundreds of times

to come. These were the only times I really hated the Navy:
when they came to call me for the next watch.

"Mr. Taylor."

The voice and the light flooding through the open door hit
me together and I was completely awake. I turned my head to
the left to look at the form framed in the doorway, outlined
black against the yellow light from outside. It was Flattery. He
was boatswain's mate of the watch.

"Time to relieve the watch, sir."

"Very well."

I started to sit up but nothing happened.

"A little cold, sir, but dry. No spray." Flattery knew his
business. He always talked until he was sure you were awake.

"It's all right, Flattery, I'm awake." He stood there, black
in the doorway, until my legs swung over the side of the bunk.
Then he stepped backward, the door shut after him with the
metal click, and I was in the near dark again.

I sat there, not moving, for what seemed a long time, on
the wooden rim of the bunk that was an inch higher than the
mattress. I knew I had to get up, dress, go to the bridge, and
stay there for four hours, but I still did not move. The green
figures on my wrist said three-thirty-five—1535 hours. I was
due on the bridge in ten minutes. Each four-hour watch was
relieved fifteen minutes before the hour it started. The hour
starting the watch was a multiple of four: four, eight, and
twelve o'clock, A.M. and P.M. Or 000, 0400, 0800, 1200,
1600, and 2000 hours, if you liked it that way. One watch on,
and two watches off, and in the two watches off you ran your
division, you did your work, you went to your battle station,
you ate, you evacuated, and, when you could, you slept. It
made a long day. Then I remembered: Johnny had been qualified as officer of the deck. This trip we would stand one watch
in four instead of one in three. It was a boon. When an officer
qualified for top watch, as a senior officer of the deck, there
was always cause for jubilation. It meant less watches for the
officers already standing them. This qualifying of an officer,
the entrusting of the safety and direction of the ship to his care
for four hours, took a long time. With Buchan, it took a particularly long time. He wanted to make sure before he turned
his ship over to anybody. He had qualified none of us as officers
of the deck until we had been on the *Dee,* standing junior
watches, for a year or more; then he let us handle things with
a minimum of supervision. Most other destroyer captains
qualified their officers for top watch in a half or a third that
time, then breathed down their necks forever after. It was

not that way with him. He did not put you there until he was sure of you. After that, he let you alone.

Now I had to get up there.

"Christ." I said it out loud in the dark. "Oh, Jesus Christ."

I slid off the edge of the bunk, the two-inch-wide strip of wood raking hard over my buttocks and then my feet solid on the rolling steel deck. I took three steps to the desk and turned the lamp on. The desk, gray-enameled, was against the after end of the room. It was a combination bureau and desk, the hinged top folding straight up and shutting. The lamp was over the open desk top. At the other end was a tall, green metal cabinet to hang uniforms in. Next to the cabinet was an aluminum sink, with a mirror over it and the brass steam pipes beside it. Against the wall that shut out the sea were the double-deck bunks. Mine was the bottom one. The one above it was a steel rectangle with springs, lashed by a chain at each end to the bulkhead. On the side facing the bunks was the door, and, alongside it on the wall, four hooks for winter clothing. On two hooks were masses of blue clothing, and on the two others were green oilskin coats with sheepskin linings and fur collars.

The room had space enough for one man to dress, if nobody else tried it at the same time.

I walked from the desk to the sink and turned on a shaded light over the mirror. Why didn't you turn that on first and save six steps, I thought. I looked at my face in the mirror. It was puffy, the eyes half closed and the hair tangled.

"Hopeless." I said it out loud again.

I turned on the cold water, cupped my hands and filled them, and sloshed the water on my face. Then I rubbed it hard with the thick white towel on the rack by the sink. I combed my hair. I looked in the mirror again. Now I looked awake.

I took the blue clothing from the nearest hook. It was made of a thick substance called jungle cloth and was supposed to be waterproof. There were two pieces; the jacket and a ballooning pair of pants with suspender-like straps at the top to hold them up and laces at the end of each leg to hold them down. In very cold weather, a pair of thick overshoes called "arctics" went over the pants legs, but I was not wearing them today. I pulled a black turtle-neck sweater over my head, smoothed it, and then started to put on the blue jungle-cloth pants over the gray trousers I was already wearing. To stand on one leg and slide the other inside the pants, I had to brace against the roll of the ship with one hand on the side of the bunk. I took the suspender straps of the pants, brought them over my shoulders to hook on the buttons on the other side, then picked up the blue jacket. I did not tie the laces on the bottom of the legs. I did not take the fur-collared coat, either; I wanted to save that until it was really cold. Carrying the jacket over my left arm and holding my officer's cap in the same hand, I walked out of my room to the small platform deck outside, and opened the door to the wardroom. My room was not with the others, back of the wardroom curtain. It was on the other side of the wardroom, beyond the door and six feet from it, and you passed it on your way from the wardroom to the bridge.

I went into the wardroom, closed the door behind me, dropped the cap and the jacket on the table, and poured a cup of coffee from the glass bowl.

The coffee was black. I took one swallow. It was old and quite undrinkable.

Jason was in the pantry.

"Goddamn it, Jason." He grinned, white-toothed, when I started. "This coffee tastes like fuel oil. Make some fresh. We want it fresh every watch. Every watch, you boys pour out the old and make some fresh. Fresh coffee, every watch. Got it?"

"Yessir!" He grinned again. "I tell the boys."

"I tell the boys." I mimicked him. "Well, I bet the boys have it the same way tomorrow and the next day and the day after."

"Oh, I tell 'em, Mr. Taylor. Don't you worry. We gonna have it fresh all the time for you."

"I bet. But get a cup from the galley and bring it to the bridge. I have to go up."

The wardroom clock said sixteen minutes of four when I walked out the door. I crossed the small square of deck outside, passed on my right the door to my room, went up the ladder to the well deck outside, turned left, took two steps to the ladder to the bridge, and climbed it.

On the bridge, I put on the jacket and zipped it closed. Johnny was standing behind the compass repeater on the port wing, big and shapeless in the floppy blue jungle cloth. He was watching the carrier and the two other destroyers with his binoculars and did not see me until I was right behind him.

"So. You made it."

"I always make it. What's the hot dope?"

He gave me the technical information. The *Dee's* station was the same, on the right of the carrier, to the side and ahead. However she might wander, we were to keep that position in the three-pronged screen ahead of her. As before, the *Hilliard* was on the left and the *Donahue* in the middle.

I looked out at them, all profiling clearly in the gray light, the four smokestacks that were their trademark of antiquity standing in rows above the sharp destroyer bulk.

"How's she behaving?" He knew I meant the carrier.

"Like cherry pie. I haven't had to change speed for half an hour. One-ninety-four turns is your magic number. It'll keep you right there." One-ninety-four turns were engine revolutions for seventeen knots.

"Check the bearing?" he asked.

I took a compass bearing on the carrier with the repeater. The repeater was mounted on a four-foot pedestal, and I had to bend to line up the two sights on the bearing circle with the carrier. The bearing showed the *Dee* was, nearly, on proper station.

"Okay."

"Here's the zigzag plan." He handed me the white card with courses and times printed on it neatly in ink. Scotch tape was pasted over the inked figures. "Next course change is at sixteen hundred even. You come right forty-five degrees and you're on base course for a while. You got it?"

"I got it. I relieve you, sir." Those were the words that counted. Now it was my watch and my responsibility. I threw a mock salute with my right hand and watched his big back in the blue jacket recede as he shuffled away. Then he turned the corner of the sound shack and was gone, on his way to the ladder to the other side of the bridge.

I turned back to the ships. Evening twilight had not quite come. There were heavy clouds in an overcast and no sun, and the sea and sky met in a montony of gray. The wind blew from the east, and a deep swell ran steadily with the wind.

The *Dee* pitched with the swell. The sea caught her slender bow and lifted it effortlessly toward the top of each wave, then dropped it almost caressingly into the trough behind. The pitch was easy. No water broke over the bow.

We had a couplet:

> "Pitch, pitch, goddamn your soul.
> The more you pitch, the less you roll."

And when she rolled, we said:

> "Roll, roll, you mean old bitch.
> The more you roll, the less you pitch."

Today both roll and pitch were painless enough. I turned the glasses to the other ships. The carrier, stubby as ever, was still seesawing. The *Donahue* and the *Hilliard* were pitching like the *Dee*. They were good to watch. There are few things better to watch than a destroyer running into a head sea.

Through the two-inch opening made by the unclosed door to the sound shack came the pinging of the sound gear as it threw the waves searching into the water. I moved to the door and opened it to see what was going on inside. The sound operators had a facility, on occasion, for turning their guiding handwheels in perfect rhythm while scrutinizing the comic-book adventures of Superman or Captain Midnight with true scholarly zeal. This one was engaged in no greater misdemeanor than looking incurably bored.

"Getting many disturbances, Daniels?"

"No, sir." He was eighteen or nineteen, maybe twenty. "No fish, no water effects, even. Nothing at all."

The pings not only found submarines; they also made echoes on large fish and small ones, in schools and alone, and they sometimes returned to the listening apparatus strange, inexplicable blurping sounds that were lumped together as water noises.

"Good enough. Keep a taut watch." It sounded completely spurious as I said it.

I looked above Daniels at the bulkhead. There, facing the door, were various paintings of naked women's bodies. One was further enhanced by pencil marks where some artist, like Daniels, had wished to complete the young woman.

Daniels looked at me and grinned. I shook my head at him.

"Like to have a little of that, huh?"

"It might do."

"Might do? Why that's fine. Man, could I use that fine thing down in the sack when I got off watch. Man, could I use that." Talking, he turned his head over his shoulder to look at me, while he kept his right hand on the six-inch wheel in front of him and turned the wheel in short, regular arm movements. The wheel aimed the sound waves underwater. Above it was a compass circle numbered to three hundred and sixty degrees. It was a compass repeater, like the other repeaters on the bridge, wired to the master gyro compass below decks. On the circle a green point of light moved, in five-degree steps. It showed the direction of the ping and the bearing of any target they hit.

"You better forget about that fine thing and worry about your pings."

He laughed. I pushed the door almost shut and moved back

to the wind guard to watch the carrier. The sound of the pings kept coming through the crack in the door.

I checked the bearing of the carrier. The *Dee* had moved ahead one degree. I cut speed to drop back.

It was fifty-eight minutes past four by the watch. The gray of the sky had deepened. It was almost time for sunset, but there was no sun. I walked up and down the wing. It looked like a quiet watch. The sea kept coming in the easy swells. The other ships held their places in formation tightly as we zigzagged. Using the watch and zigzag card, I gave the course changes to the helmsman as they came up.

After a month in port, I felt the responsibility of the deck. It was not small. As officer of the deck, you had the ship and the crew in your hands, and you could, by incompetence, wreck them. You might freeze three seconds and wait that long to change course. And that three seconds was quite long enough for a torpedo to hit instead of miss. So the three seconds would become, instead of another chance, the end of all chances for one hundred and fifty men. Whom you could, in the dazzling instant of crisis, save or destroy. And any of whom could, in another instant, save or destroy you and all the rest. It was a paradox of human endeavor that in our sea-speck universe, where divisions of rank and responsibility meant everything up to survival itself, they also meant less than nothing. A seventeen-year old seaman yet to have his first shave could annihilate us all as surely, as finally, as could the deity who was the captain.

The sky got darker; night closed. I felt good about the one watch in four. That would break the four-to-eight watch into two two-hour watches, though this one would be longer than two hours because of dinner. Right after dinner Rocky would relieve me. I would get a full seven hours in the sack, maybe, before they called me at three-thirty in the morning for my next watch. It was a good feeling to have one in four. Feeling good about it, I walked up and down the wing, always watching the carrier. It was three minutes after five. Sunset was at five-seventeen. Forty-five minutes after sunset we would quit zigzagging. That would be about six. At six-thirty Rocky would relieve me, I would go down and eat, go through some messages in the radio shack, and get to bed at eight-thirty. I would have seven hours there. If they did not wake me to decode messages. If we did not go to general quarters for an attack. I wondered what was for dinner. I had been crazy to twist this operation 'nto something mystic; it was good duty. This was a good watch.

"Sound contact at zero-six-zero. Range one three double-oh. Target appears to be submarine." Daniels yelled it from the sound shack.

I looked along the compass in the direction of zero-six-zero. Nothing showed on that bearing but the Atlantic ocean. If he had a real contact, it was a submarine, and if it was a submarine, They were starting early.

"Bearing clear," I called. "Verify contact."

We were in the reflexive routine of battle. It was a routine of machines. Machines did the work. Men simply turned the wheels, pulled levers, or said words. Only the machines really counted. The signalman called the captain through the voice tube to his cabin. The telephone talker received the orders from me and repeated them into his telephones. The telephone talker was a two-legged, wire-trailing machine. He said the words someone else told him into the round, black chunk of carbon brushing his lips and the words touched off a chain reaction over the *Dee*. He said no words of his own. Someone else gave him the words. He parroted them into his mouthpiece and they might start the *Dee's* guns blasting, plunge her depth charges into the water, shoot her torpedoes streaking from her sides, set the speed of her engines, and jerk her men through movements they hated, like strings on puppets. The words he said into the telephone were everything, but they were not his. He was an all-powerful, completely powerless robot.

The captain was on the bridge.

"Target at zero-seven-zero, eleven hundred yards, drawing right, no range rate yet." I gave him the information rapidly. I had swung the *Dee* from her course and headed her for the target.

He nodded. "I'll take her." He was bareheaded and had only a brown leather jacket over his gray shirt and trousers.

"Sound general quarters, cap'n?"

"Wait."

"Right cut-on, zero-seven-two." From the sound shack. "Target appears to be widening rapidly."

"Yeah," said the captain. "Another Goddamned fish."

"Target breaking up." Daniels was embarrassed. "Target appears to be a small school of fish."

"Get back to station in the formation." Buchan was pointedly annoyed.

"Set depth charges on safe," I told the talker, then said to the helmsman, "Left to zero-two-zero."

The carrier had passed the *Dee* and the task unit was nearly three miles ahead of us and to the left.

The captain said something expressive and left the bridge.

I walked to the sound-shack door.

"How about that submarine?"

He did not answer and I did not press him. I started moving the ship back to station.

14

THEY WERE at coffee at the table when Carter, Farnsworth, and I came into the wardroom from the bridge. They did not look up when we sat. They were laughing loudly.

"They've all got one," the captain said in the dying laughter, straight down the table to the Flattop at the other end. The Flattop had a high color. "It'll take you a long time to learn it and you're hell-set on doing it the hard way, but remember what I tell you. They all got one." That was one of his favorite aphorisms.

The laughter rippled again. I was sorry I had missed what went before. That closed the joke, whatever it was. The talk broke into splinters. Jason set a heaped plate before me. On it were green peas, two round browned potatoes, and hash with symmetrical meat cubes. I ate it, too fast, not talking. Jason took the plate and put a piece of meringued chocolate pie in its place. I looked at it and thought of the destroyer fat creeping over my legs and belly and behind. Then I ate it.

"Chow's still holding up, I see." I pushed the pie plate, now clean, away.

"Sure, there's plenty now," said the Flattop. "If we don't get some more from the carrier, though, you'll be eating sea biscuit in a couple of weeks."

"She'll take care of us."

"She better."

Rockford cut in. "We've got an old industrialist aboard now, captain," he said, in a voice like velvet. "Mr. Crandall here used to be general manager of a textile factory. In Peoria."

Crandall looked modestly at his plate.

"Is that right?" The captain was not interested. "Ought to be good background for his new job." Then, looking straight into Crandall's face: "You've got the after part of the ship now, you know. You'll be responsible for the upkeep back there."

Crandall returned the gaze steadily enough, but his face changed subtly. Exactly how I did not know. But I sensed again what had repelled me the first time, as he walked up the pier, and every other time that I glimpsed, but did not recognize, it.

"No coffee." Jason was at my elbow with a cup. I got up, left the table, and made for the head. It was on the other side of the curtain, at the end of the short passageway between the officers' staterooms. Two staterooms were on each side of the passageway. Two officers lived in each room. The head was beyond the last stateroom on the left side of the passageway. Across the passageway from it, behind a canvas curtain, was the shower. The twelve officers, not counting the captain, who had one of each in his cabin, shared one toilet bowl and one shower. At sea, the salt water in the head erupted with pulse-beat regularity and made a foot-high geyser inside the bowl. Six navy yards had failed to fix it. We called it, variously, the Fountain of Youth, Old Faithful, and the Douche Bowl. Tonight, it functioned according to its wont.

On the way back to the wardroom, I stopped at Arbry's. It was the first on the right going from the wardroom to the head. The gray curtain in his doorway was open. He was sitting, feet on his desk, reading. I stepped over the high steel door sill.

"What you got there?"

He held the back of the book so I could see the title. It was Conrad's *Tales of Hearsay*.

"Anybody ever tell you asking titles is a hell of a habit?"

"Many times. It never does any good." I sat on the wooden edge of the lower bunk, leaning forward to keep my head clear of the tubed steel side of the one above.

"These are all right." Arbry nodded at the book. "They're pretty good. He's been there."

"Oh, he's been there."

I glanced at the small row of books on the short, gray steel shelf on the bulkhead above his desk. For no good reason, some had always seemed a little out of place in a career officer's collection. Beside the inevitable trade tomes, Knight's *Seamanship*, Mixter's *Principles of Navigation*, and *Naval Regulations*, there was a Dante, a *War and Peace*, and a novel that was having a fling at the time.

Arbry was a departure from the norm. He was also a graduate of the U.S. Naval Academy, and this made his exotic development difficult to comprehend; Annapolis usually stamps its products into a uniform, extroverted, uncomplicated mold. He did not care much for women. It was not that he was homo- or even bi-sexual. He just did not care much. This some found hard to understand. Graham did not chase women, either, and spent his time on the beach getting decorously drunk, but he was married. Arbry was not, and his careless celibacy perplexed his friends. He did not shun women; he just did not have the sailor's eternally presumed, single-minded absorption in the institution of the Shack-Up.

He liked to read, well enough, but his real passions were jazz and gunnery. He was clearly happier firing his three-inch battery, that is, when he was firing it well, than he was any other time. As far as those guns were concerned, the *Dee* and the rest of the four-stackers were still fighting the war before, but Arbry had fashioned his obsolete weapons into an effective instrument. He spent days conceiving gunnery problems that he might have to face some day, and ways to beat them with what he had. So far, he had solved them only in practice. The *Dee* had never fired a gun nor a torpedo in combat in her twenty-odd years of existence. All she had ever used, in earnest, were the depth charges.

His jazz records made a two-foot stack in the corner by the desk. They had titles I had never heard. He said they were classics. He would play them on the wardroom phonograph, sit, listen intently, and indicate approbation only by the lift of an eyebrow or the clenching of a hand. He spoke seriously of New Orleans and Memphis and Chicago styles. At first I thought this critical approach a pose. Later I knew that with Arbry it was authentic.

He was the son of a banker, had had a protected boyhood in Connecticut, and had been to Amherst for a year before he went to the academy. Why he decided to become a naval officer I did not know. By the time I knew him, he was a good one. He was slight, with a pale, thin, almost handsome face that often looked in need of a shave, had straight, not thick, black hair making a point above it, and was, I guessed, twenty-four years old.

Now he closed the book and laid it on the desk top and swung the swivel chair to face me on the bunk.

"Anything break on your watch?"

"No," I said. "Daniels got a hot contact. Then it turned out to be a fish school."

"Daniels." He laughed. "The frustrated fire eater. He'd like to drop charges every watch. Got a hell of a good ear, though. Best ear on the ship."

"Maybe he'll be happy soon. We're due in the first concentration area tomorrow. If there are really fifteen of Them there, we might scare up one. Reckon?"

"We might. Might not, either. They aren't asleep this time. This is nobody's turkey shoot. They got hit hard when the carrier made her first trip, and now they'll be careful. And they'll be dangerous. This trip could get rough." He said it matter-of-factly.

"Maybe. We'll have to wait and see."

"We'll wait, all right. You can count on plenty of waiting on this duty. You can wait your balls off."

"You got any?"

He lifted the book and faked a throw at me. Then he was serious again.

"This thing shapes up funny to me. Before it's over we'll be wondering who's hunting who."

"You mean who's hunting whom. You trade-school bastards can't even speak the language." I stood up. "I'm going. I got a date with my sack. Have fun on the midwatch."

I left his room, walked through the wardroom to the half-deck on the other side, and opened the door to and walked inside my own.

I took off the gray shirt, threw it on the back of the chair by the desk, noticed that Farnsworth was already asleep in the upper bunk, and looked at my face in the mirror. I decided to shave. I filled the sink half full of cold water. Then I turned the handle to a short, quarter-inch-thick brass tube that ended under the water and was connected to the steam pipes of the radiator. The steam made a hissing sound when it hit the water. The water bubbled. I kept my finger in the water until it was hot. Then I turned the steam off. My room was the only one that had arrangements for hot water. An assistant engineer, who had had the room before the war, had fixed the tube. The other officers had to have water heated on the wardroom hot plate to shave. I lathered my face and pulled the razor over it, very slowly, because of the ship's roll. I finished, washed off the lather, brushed my teeth, took off the pants and shoes, turned off the light over the sink, and went to bed. I was still in the two-piece, long underwear. That way, you had it on when general quarters tumbled you out at night; you had that much of a start.

"Do we hit that first sub pack tonight?" Farnsworth said in the dark from the upper bunk. He had not been sleeping, then.

"It's not a pack. It's just an area where They are supposed to be. We don't hit it until tomorrow night."

"Oh." He felt better.

I lay in bed, under only a sheet because the room was warm from the steam in the pipes, and thought. I thought about what Arbry had said, about the things I had thought before that nobody had said. I had the feeling of things about to happen. It did not mean a thing. The last time I had it, the only things that happened were to Johnny. He caught the crabs from a British WREN in Gibraltar. Still, the feeling was there. I lay awake with it for awhile and then went to sleep.

15

THE NIGHT was fading into the dark gray of early dawn. The stars burned dimmer, and the formless black bugs that were the ships outlined slowly into space. Sunrise was more than an hour away. I felt tired. The first onset of day on the morning watch always brought with it an illusion, or perhaps a first awareness, of weariness.

My watch said five o'clock. On this, the third day of the hunt, I had been on the bridge for an hour and twelve minutes. I was cold, I was tired, and I had in my belly the before-breakfast nausea that comes at sea. I checked the bearing of the carrier with the bearing circle on the compass. It was all right.

I looked up to the top of the mast, at the cage of the radar antennae, that was a dark, revolving shadow, and called, through the voice tube inside the wheelhouse, to the radar operator also inside the sound shack.

"Range on the carrier."

"Two nine double-oh," came back through the tube.

That was twenty-nine hundred yards, so the range was all right, too. The assigned distance was three thousand yards and two hundred either way was all right. The carrier had behaved smoothly and predictably. So far it had been an easy watch. But dawn was almost here and it was a danger time. They liked dawn, and dusk.

I put the glasses to my eyes and began to search the sea from the ship to the low stars, starting straight back from the wake frothing white at the stern, moving the glasses ahead inch by inch, trying to see into the white-ribbed darkness rolling at us under the gray-breaking skies, always moving ahead, until I had swept the port side, passed the bow and moved beyond it to starboard, swinging backward now down that side until the steel walls of the wheelhouse shut off the search.

I let the glasses down and looked at the watch again. Five-ten.

"Time to call the cooks."

That was for Clay, the boatswain's mate of the watch, sitting on the signal-flag bag at the end of the port wing. He stood, reluctantly and painfully, and walked in heavy steps toward the ladder on the other side.

The TBS, the inter-ship radio, sputtered inside the wheelhouse. I moved closer to the door to the wheelhouse, where I could hear what came over the radio and at the same time keep the formation in sight.

"Hello, Team, hello, Team. How is the Team? This is Coach." The voice over the radio was deep, heavy and very much itself. It had a fine disregard for procedural amenities that only the boss could afford.

It belonged to the captain of the carrier, the commodore of the task unit. Talking into the radio telephone, he would be at this moment standing on his open bridge in that tower on the side of his flight deck, looking down now at the deck, his planes perhaps rolling off the elevators that lifted them from the hangar space below, through the suddenly yawning apertures in the floating, wood-splintered airstrip. The voice was deep. He might be a big man. He might be a little man with a big voice. I tried to picture him but could not. He remained just the voice, the omnipotent voice that ordered our destinies with no particular regard for them, no particular regard for his own, no regard at all for anything except what he was here to do: hunt Them and destroy Them.

Now the voice said: "Prepare to commence flight operations zero six hundred. Over."

The ships acknowledged by code name.

The *Hilliard:* "This is Fordham, Roger, out."

The *Donahue:* "This is Yale, Roger, out."

And I, pushing the talk button in the middle of the handle of the phone, said softly into the mouthpiece for the *Dee:* "This is Georgia, Roger, out."

The carrier was going to send up the dawn patrol at six o'clock. This I reported to the captain through the megaphone fitted into the sound tube that led to his cabin.

"Very well." He answered clearly, at once. He never seemed to be really asleep. You never had to call him twice, you never had to repeat. You told him something and he had it, all at once; as soon as you told him, he knew and was in charge of what was happening.

The wind blew hard from the north across the port bow at a forty-five degree angle. The carrier had to turn into it to launch her planes.

The sky was a flannel gray; the stars were going fast. The horizon was a blade-sharp line between sea and sky, and from the other side of the bridge I heard Graham, shooting the morning stars with his sextant, cry "Mark!" The smell of coffee boiling came up from the galley. I sent Clay, now sheltered from the wind inside the wheelhouse, to the galley to get some.

Suddenly the captain was standing beside me. I had not heard him come up the ladder. He had on blue jungle-cloth pants, his brown leather jacket, and on his feet an unfastened pair of the big overshoes. He had no hat, and the wind whipped his long red hair back from his face.

"Good morning, Captain," I said, not saluting. We did not salute much at sea. "Still waiting for the signals."

He nodded, not taking his eyes from the carrier.

"Watch her close." I spoke to Gerard, the signalman of the watch, and his two apprentices, called "strikers," now unlashing the canvas cover to the signal flag bag. "She'll be running up something any minute."

It was getting lighter fast. In the wheelhouse, a steel dipper clanged against a pot, and I knew Clay was back with the coffee. On the carrier's yardarm flags suddenly flew. Through my glasses they were tiny, unreadable daubs of color. Gerard had the long glass on them. He shouted to his strikers, and the same flags ran up on our halyards. They spelled out the course and speed for the aircraft launching.

"All right," said the captain. "Start hauling ass."

I started hauling. "All engines ahead full. Come left to zero-zero-five."

The carrier dropped her flags and turned into the wind. The *Hilliard* and the *Dee* had to shift with her and stay out front for submarine protection. The *Donahue* was dropping back astern to act as plane guard, and to pick up any plane crews who might take the big bath.

The *Dee* made knots ahead. She vibrated as she never did at lower speeds, and, charging straight into the seas, she pitched harder. The seas broke over the bow, and she shipped green water along the forecastle deck. The wind tore at my face, and spray from the bow wave flew back stinging and cold.

We came to station fast. The carrier had launched one plane while the *Dee* was getting there. Now another crouched near the forward edge of her flight deck. The glasses revealed life-jacketed figures of mechanics standing beside it. You could not see the propeller, but you knew it was turning; they would hold the plane there until she was up to full power and then they would let it go.

The plane hung there motionless, then leaped from the deck, almost straight up, as though catapulted, climbed steeply, circled the ships, and flew away, showing in profile as it passed the big belly and long cockpit of the TBF Avenger.

Another had rolled up to the brink of the deck. Behind it, waiting, were others. They were all TBF Avengers, torpedo bombers, loaded with depth charges.

"Count them," said Buchan. "Keep track of the number in the air."

Six more went up, each in the quick, rocketing, almost vertical jump, bodies black and their engines whining as they made the turn around the formation and fanned away in different lines, all radii of a circle that had the carrier for its center. And that was the dawn patrol.

The planes had to fly their patrol courses, looking for submarines on the surface. If they found one, they attacked with depth charges and cried, by radio, for help. Then more planes and two of the destroyers would rush to join what might be a kill.

The carrier hoisted more flags. The formation wheeled right to the old course, and the *Dee* this time had to slow and fall back to reach her station.

Far away the planes flitted in and out of vision, small and black against a shadeless gray sky. The east glinted orange and rose, and across the forecastle the sun came up.

16

"I WANT TO SEE Crandall," the captain said. He had eaten breakfast, put on winter clothes, and was on the bridge for business. His face, framed by the blue cloth helmet with the long ear flaps and pinked by the wind, had the ice-hard look that meant he was angry. "Get him up here."

"Aye, aye, sir." I was glad, inevitably, that someone else was the target today. And then suddenly I knew that I was glad that Crandall was in trouble, that I was glad he was going to be humiliated, and I felt a shame at the knowledge. But I was still glad.

I called the wardroom by telephone, got Crandall, and told him.

He was on the bridge a moment later, the fur-collared green coat over his khakis and the cap with the bright gold strap cocked—I was sure carefully—at a salty angle. The captain faced him as he walked from the ladder towards us.

"Yes, sir?" Crandall asked cheerfully.

The captain, for an instant, did not answer, but seared him with a look. Crandall blanched, the unnamable something showed again, and I felt again the strange mixture of pity and sympathy.

"Have you been on your afterdecks this morning?" Buchan scorned him with his eyes.

"Why—" he halted and swallowed. "Not yet, sir. I was just—"

"I'd suggest you have a look. Oil rags scattered all over the deck. A bucket of paint turned over and still kicking around. Some pigpen, and one hell of a good way to start a fire."

Crandall swallowed again.

"Goddamn it, Crandall, when you're in charge of something you're supposed to inspect it. Do you understand that?"

"Yes, sir." Crandall was standing stiffly at attention.

The captain turned sharply and walked inside the wheelhouse leaving Crandall suspended as in air, waiting. Crandall did not move, but stood as though stunned, rigidly erect. Then he slumped, turned and walked slowly, his eyes on the deck, to the ladder.

Buchan had been hard with him out of all proportion to the offense, I thought. But I also thought I knew why. He wanted to shock Crandall into awareness, to jar him loose from that factory in Peoria and the mahogany desk in Washington. He wanted, quite simply, to tell Crandall the score.

Now he had. And I had enjoyed the lesson, even though I felt sorry for him. I was ashamed, disturbed, and puzzled that I had. But I still had enjoyed it.

Crandall had other lessons ahead. What he told us, concerning himself, made it clear just how many. For Crandall was not, exactly, secretive. Before he had been aboard forty-eight hours, we knew:

His college (University of Illinois, class of 1932); his fraternity (Sigma Chi); his wife's first name (Dorothea); the number and gender of his children (two female, ages nine and seven, one male, age five); his car (Buick Eight, six-passenger, price in 1941, eighteen hundred and ninety-five dollars); his house (twelve-room, two-story, semi-colonial, price in 1939, sixteen thousand dollars); his clubs (Chamber of Commerce, Rotary, Iroquois Cotillion); how many men worked for him (second quarter, 1942, ninety-three); and what his mother thought about Roosevelt, stag parties, and the Japanese (she was against them).

Other things told more. So much more that I could see it: the day of Crandall. Crandall the executive.

It would start at nine. Though not precisely at nine. For he would arrive two, perhaps three, but never more than five, minutes earlier: to Set an Example for the Employees.

At two, three, or five minutes before nine, the brass knob of the door to the Big Office would turn metallically, the door would open briskly, not wide but perhaps two feet, and in would walk Crandall. He would shut the door with just the right amount of force: hard but not a slam. Then, looking neither to the right nor the left, he would walk straight down the aisle between the desks toward the office with the door with the frosted glass window that had black letters spelling, on one line, W. G. CRANDALL, and on another beneath it, GENERAL MANAGER.

Walking down the aisle, he would be pleasurably certain that he was an imposing figure, in the black Homburg, tilted at just the right angle for a young, but responsible, executive, in the fitted, double-breasted brown cheviot overcoat, in the polished brown shoes glittering under the lights, and in the yellow silk scarf, knotted at his throat to give just the splash of color so earnestly recommended by *Esquire* and the *Apparel Arts*.

In the corner of his mouth, angling upward, would be an imposing cigar. Which he would not be smoking but would know was imposing because it cost fifty cents.

He would stride down the aisle—seeing, in his mind, the word "stride" in printed letters.

The stenographers and clerks, who had come early because they were afraid for their jobs, would call out from desks on either side of the aisle: "Good *mor*ning, Mr. *Cran*dall."

And he, still striding, still not looking, and still holding the imposing cigar imposingly upward in his mouth, would answer with just the proper executive brusqueness: "Good morning."

Then he would open the door with decisive determination, close it behind him as he had closed the other, and, now inside, would take off the brown overcoat and hang it carefully on the one coat hanger on the coat rack. He would carefully unknot the yellow silk scarf and hang it, exactly in the middle, over a hook on the rack. He would place the black Homburg, very carefully, over the same hook.

Then he would snap the black switch on the wall, the two long incandescent rods would flicker indecisively and then burst into light, and Crandall would sit behind the glass-topped desk and put the flame of his silver-plated, monogrammed lighter to the cigar. He would take four, maybe five, puffs on it to ash it properly. Then he would lay it on the silver-plated tray on the desk.

When his secretary came in three minutes later, give or take fifteen seconds, she would see him sitting at the desk engrossed in the papers: a fine figure of an executive. A very fine figure of an executive, indeed, in the sharply pressed, double-breasted gray worsted suit, with the white linen handkerchief making four exactly even points in the breast pocket, and the precise red-on-black, Brooks Brothers necktie bisecting the V of the coat lapels.

"Good morning, Mr. Crandall," the secretary would say, cheerfully.

"Good morning," he would answer, very jovially this time, thus proving that he was, to his more loyal, trusted, and intimate subordinates, a good, a very good, fellow.

"Well," he would continue, shifting to his best let's-get-at-it voice: "Let's get at it." And he would gesture with his cigar, as though it were a baton.

Then he would frown and say, "Let's get at those reports."

"Yes, sir."

The secretary would sit in the chair beside him, balance her pad on her knee, and poise her pencil over it, waiting.

And so would begin the day of Crandall, the executive.

Or so it used to begin. Now it would start quite differently and end quite differently and would be very different in between. As this afternoon, when he sat at the wardroom table, without Brooks Brothers' tie or four-pointed white handkerchief, or properly ashed cigar, and Rocky asked with a voice that was not friendly. "Have you finished those hull reports?"

"Not yet. I only received them an hour ago." Crandall flushed.

"Then would you get at them. Please."

And later in the afternoon, after Crandall retired to his stateroom—quite possibly to work on the hull reports—the executive officer thrust his head through the curtain separating his room from the wardroom, and said: "Get Crandall for me." He added, "Please."

I walked through the doorway and down the corridor between the staterooms on the other side, stopped at the second on the left, and looked inside.

Crandall was sitting at his desk, writing on half-sized monogrammed paper with a silver-topped fountain pen. He looked up, and his right thumb, that had been pressed against the pen, began to revolve slowly.

"Exec wants you," I said. He nodded, and laid down the pen, while I saw, for the first time, the two pictures on his desk. On the left was a carefully, expensively posed portrait of a carefully, expensively groomed woman with blond hair. Wife. On the right was a militant, glaring woman with gray hair. Mother. The picture of Mother had been cut on the

left side, as though to fit the frame, and I saw at the edge something dark, like the start of a man's coat sleeve. Perhaps,
Father.

Crandall flushed slightly as he saw me stare, while his
thumb began to wriggle a shade faster. Annoyed at my own
lapse of taste and feeling the curious sympathy again, I with-
drew quickly from the door.

The next morning, I had business in the after crew's quarters, and, at number four stack on the afterdecks, fell in with
Crandall. He was going to make his morning inspection; the
captain had made an impression.

He went down the ladder to the compartment, me behind
him, and started forward along the center aisle between bunks.
Then he stopped, so abruptly that I bumped him.

I stepped back, but he had not moved; he was standing, very
still, straining without moving inside the sharp-creased khaki
trousers and the green oilskin coat, looking ahead, and I saw
what he had seen.

It was an enlarged photograph, the size of typing paper, held
to the bulkhead by short strips of scotch tape at each corner.

Then Crandall moved. He turned to me. "Do you see that?"
His nostrils quivered and his eyes were open wide. "That!"

"Oh, yes," I said. "Yes, I do."

The picture was of a girl. The girl lay on a bed. The girl
wore no clothes. The camera had been between her feet.

Crandall stepped forward. His arm jerked theatrically, and
I was looking at four pieces of tape dangling from a bare
bulkhead.

Crandall set his lips together, held the picture in both hands
at full arm's length, and I waited for the tearing sound. It
did not come.

"Look at that." He was, indeed, looking at it. "Just look at
that." And he moved his right thumb, which was partially
obscuring the most interesting aspect of the view, a little to
the side.

Accommodatingly, I looked. With the thumb out of the
way, the view was unobstructed.

"Isn't that—" He shook his head, not moving his eyes from
the picture.

"I wonder who took it," I said.

"It's disgraceful." He brought the picture closer, and the
thumb inched, involuntarily, toward the spot it had just left.
"Absolutely disgraceful."

I was still waiting for him to tear it up. He was waiting for
something, too, for he kept looking at the picture. While his

thumb slid, almost imperceptibly, back and forth over the glossy surface. "I never saw such a thing."

Then he extended his arms, as though pushing the picture away, and tore it carefully down the middle. He took the halves and tore them. And he started to tear the quarters, but they did not tear easily, so he wadded them instead and flung the wad into a wastebasket against the bulkhead. The wad popped loudly as it hit the loose paper in the basket.

"I certainly won't stand for that." His lips were still together tightly, and he was very pleased. "They can rest assured I won't tolerate that sort of thing." He was enormously pleased.

I did not say anything.

"They'll find out I won't stand for that," he said.

After lunch, Crandall had, officially, his first general quarters. Rockford, padded and swollen in the winter clothing, shambled into the wardroom to tell about it.

"You ought to have seen my boy today." He worked, with difficulty, out of the heavy green coat and dropped it on the transom, then unzipped the blue jacket and laid it on the coat. "Crandall in action." He shook his head in mock, exaggerated wonder. "It was worth the price of the tickets."

"What the hell did he do?"

"Wait till you hear." Rockford laughed again, and put one hand against one of the brass rods running between the deck and the overhead. The black turtle-neck sweater masked half his white throat and the straps of the winter outer-pants hooked over the sweater like suspenders. He looked at us, laughing, his brown hair pressed into strange shapes by the helmet he had removed minutes ago.

"He's in charge of the after repair party now, you know. Today was his first day, and I told him to take it easy back there, just look around and see what it was all about.

"And I told my chief, Harris, to take care of him and give him the word. You know Harris. Patient and long-suffering.

"He said, 'Yes, sir, we'll show him how it works.'

"Well—" Rocky was pouring himself coffee. "The alarm goes off and I go back to see that he gets started right and he isn't there.

" 'You seen Mr. Crandall?' I ask Harris.

" 'No, sir, he hasn't been back here yet,' Harris says.

" 'Now where for Christ's sake is he?' I say, and then Harris blinks and looks hard down the deck and then goes absolutely stone-faced.

" 'Here he comes now, sir,' he says, and I turn around and there's Crandall, clopping down the deck, and you know what?

He's got on his forty-five, so help me. He's got the forty-five strapped on his right side and a big long sea knife on the other. And there he comes, walking down the deck like Admiral King."

Rocky pursed his lips and swung his body, stiffly, in caricature.

"I go out to meet him and ask him, 'Why the small arms?'

"And he gives me the look"—Rockford pulled his chin almost into his neck and jerked his head from side to side—

" 'Regulations. Setting an example to the men.' " He parodied Crandall's voice. " 'Help maintain discipline, you know.'

" 'Oh,' I say.

"So we go back to the party. I hear a couple of snickers. They see the gun, all right. But Harris doesn't let on anything, just keeps that poker face.

" 'Lieutenant Crandall will be the officer in charge back here,' I tell him very formally.

" 'Yes, sir,' Harris says, and he starts to say something else, but Crandall butts in in that general manager's voice and says:

" 'Everything in good order, chief?'

" 'Yes, sir,' says Harris. Absolutely straight-faced.

"Crandall says 'Good' "—Rocky puffed his chest and grunted the word back in his throat.

" 'Yes, sir,' says Harris.

"Then somebody runs up to report the last watertight door is closed, so the chief tells the talker to tell the bridge Condition Able is set aft.

" 'What was our time?' I ask Harris, and he says, 'Two minutes and fifteen seconds.'

" 'Not bad,' I say. But here comes Crandall again.

" 'We'll have to beat that, chief.' " Rockford assumed the voice and posture again. "We'll have to cut some seconds off that.'

" 'Yes, sir,' says Harris. He doesn't show a thing, but you can imagine. Here's this guy who's never seen a real damage-control drill before telling him how to run it. The rest of them can hear what's going on, and I hear the snickers again.

" 'Suppose the chief shows you the damage-control closures and instructs you in the procedure,' I say, to both Crandall and Harris.

"Crandall blinks." Rocky blinked. "That word 'instruct' gets to him. He's just chewed the guy who's going to do the instructing.

"But he says, 'Very good,' and the chief says, 'Aye, aye, sir,' and I go to my forward repair.

"About twenty minutes later, I come back to see how it's going. I don't see Crandall. Harris is standing there, looking pissed off.

" 'Where's Mr. Crandall?' I ask him.

"Harris says, 'He wanted to make an inspection by himself, sir. He wanted to see if we'd done everything right.'

" 'Oh,' I say. 'Well, let's find him. I want to talk to him.'

" 'I think he went down into the after living compartment, sir,' Harris says.

"So I go down, looking for Crandall. I hear some kind of pounding on the deck, but I don't pay any attention to it. I go through the compartment, into the one on the other side, but I don't see Crandall. I keep hearing the pounding on the deck, and then I can tell it's something in the compartment.

"So I try to find it. And, by God, do you know what it is?" Rockford paused, for drama. "It's somebody knocking on the hatch to the depth-charge locker, from the inside. And the hatch is shut and locked."

The depth-charge locker was the space directly under the after crew's quarters. A hatch in the deck was the only opening to it.

"So I figure somebody's locked in, and I figure it's Crandall, and I run get the key and unlock it, and sure enough it is Crandall.

"There he is, standing on the ladder. In the dark. Without even a flashlight. He couldn't find the light bulb. And he's as white as this saucer. Not looking a damn bit like Admiral King."

Rockford sipped coffee from his cup. "To spare you the details, this is what happened. He was making this big inspection, not knowing what the hell he's inspecting, and he goes down in the locker to inspect it. Then somebody comes along, sees the hatch cover open, and closes it. Not knowing Crandall or anybody else is down there."

"Of course not," I said.

Rockford grinned. "Of course not. It was a very regrettable error. But understandable. Entirely understandable. That's what I told Crandall, but he didn't seem to appreciate it.

"He was only down there five or ten minutes. Couldn't have hurt him. You really ought to have seen him, though. It was something."

"I'll bet." I could see him, locked in the strange dark, pounding frantically at the locked, dark cover with his fists waiting for somebody to hear. It was not funny, and then it was. It was very funny.

Then I felt, all at once and stronger than ever, the sympathy and pity for Crandall that I could never completely dismiss. But I pushed it away, and permitted myself to think, only, that it was very funny.

At dinner, the captain, regarding Crandall with the smile that might have been amused, or taunting, or pitying, or omniscient, or all of those things together, but not, for certain, any one of them alone, said: "Hear you had a little mishap this afternoon."

Crandall, paling, grinned wanly. "Yes, sir."

"Good indoctrination." The captain laughed, softly and deep. "Good indoctrination." And if his laugh was not kind, neither was it unkind.

Crandall looked at the tablecloth, grinning, and the grin, fixed, immovable, and unaltering, was an open wound into which I did not want, was perhaps afraid, to look. Then, slowly, and by stages, his mouth turned down at the ends, and his look moved from the tablecloth to the soup on his plate.

His right thumb revolved in the curious, wagging circle. Then staring at the clear brown liquid sliding back and forth in the bowl, he picked up a spoon.

The captain called down the table:

"How are your cold feet, Flattop?"

17

TOWARD MIDNIGHT, the sea had kicked up. This was midnight of the third night of the hunt, six hours and twenty minutes, by the chart, before we steamed into the first submarine cluster, the one that had fifteen of Them.

Dressing in the room for the midwatch, the deck rolling high on one side and sliding downward on the other, then coming straight up at you and dropping fast away, was hard. It was harder with two trying together, both fighting the clothes and the heaving deck in the space between the bunks and the bulkhead and the desk and the sink. It was harder, as always, to dress for the midwatch than any other, when you had quirted yourself to wakefulness and out of bed just as sleep was taking full possession, leaving the covers with the bitter knowledge that you had ahead on the bridge the dark hours between midnight and four o'clock.

Farnsworth fell against me as I put on the heavy over-pants. "I'm sorry."

"That's all right."

Sharing a room with your JO was not so convenient, after all. I had thought it was going to be. I was dressed in the watch clothes before he had on his shirt and trousers.

"Better shake it, kid." I leaned against the door to get out of his way.

"Christ, what a hell of a way to live."

His legs stuck thin and white from the gray shirt he was buttoning in the dim yellow light from the lamp over the mirror. He was twenty-one years old, wore a college haircut, had spent three days at sea, and was about to be seasick.

"Oh, boy, sea duty. On the *Prairie State* they told us, 'Some of you aren't going to be lucky. You aren't going to get to go to sea right away. You'll have to wait on the beach a few months.' "

He staggered as a roll caught him and put his left hand on the side of the bunk.

"They all shook my hand when I got my duty. A destroyer. Boy, was I lucky. A real, honest-to-God destroyer, right out of the hat. No lousy time on the beach waiting, no crappy shore duty. Boy, didn't the instructors wish they could swap places with me. Didn't they wish they could get out of that God-damned New York. Didn't they wish they could go to sea. And on a destroyer, too. Boy."

Now he had on the gray shirt and trousers, both rumpled and yet to have their first washing. He reached for the jungle cloth garments. He was losing color fast. It would not be long.

He put one leg into the blue over-pants. He followed with the other, losing his balance again, and had to grab the chair to keep from falling. He worked his arms inside the shoulder straps and sat in the chair to put on his arctics, bending to pull them over his black shoes. Then it started to come up and he fought it and kept it down and got the overshoes on and then it started up again and this time he could not keep it down but dived for the wastebasket and was sick with his head inside it. I was truly sorry. Seasickness is not funny, not to those who have known it. A piece of shrapnel in your arm does less damage to your morale.

He was sick for two or three minutes. When he was through, I helped him up. He would feel better for a while.

"I'm sorry," he mumbled.

"It's all right."

"Christ, I feel lousy. Christ, what a hell of a way to live."

He washed his face in the lavatory. He started to put on the other clothes, the jungle-cloth jacket, over-pants, and weather helmet, a long-eared headpiece that looked like a flier's. We both picked up the sheepskin coats and went out the door.

"Aren't you going to get coffee?" He was turning toward the ladder, not the wardroom.

"What for? I couldn't keep it two minutes." He went up.

I remembered the wastebasket, went back into the room, picked it up, turning my head away, and set it outside the door. I walked into the wardroom. One light was on. Sandwiches were in a silver tray fitted into a hollow in the wooden sideboard. I took one and poured a cup of coffee. It was too old to drink. I drank it anyway and made a note to have another talk with the mess boys. Still eating the sandwich, I started for the bridge.

The pinging came to me as I was still on the ladder to the bridge from the well deck. I heard it over the thin partition in the chartroom, as I read the captain's night order book by the table light that had been masked in red tissue paper. Red light did not break your dark adaptation; it did not show more than a few feet away here.

I initiated the orders and went to the port wing, then performed the ritual and relieved Johnny. The task unit was not zigzagging. It had stopped after sunset. Carter, the other junior officer of the watch, had the conn. That is, he was giving orders to the engine and wheel and controlling the ship. I was still responsible, as senior officer of the deck, for what he did.

"How's Jerry?" he asked. Carter had been aboard almost six months. He was a salt.

"Not so good."

"Sick?"

"Once in the room, maybe again later. He on the other wing now?"

"Yeah, he's over there. Poor bastard. He'll get used to it, though."

"Some guys take a long time. He hasn't really eaten since we left Norfolk. I think I'll see how he's doing."

I walked behind the charthouse, the pings following, to the starboard wing. Jerry was there. He was sweeping the ocean with his glasses.

"Feel better?"

"I did, right after I heaved. It's coming back now."

"Why don't you eat something? Let me send down for a sandwich."

"I couldn't even get it down."

"Let me know if you change your mind." He wanted to be alone. I went back to the other wing.

Later, a familiar noise came from the starboard side. I walked over. Jerry was leaning over the side, holding to the wind guard as he bent over it. He was making agonizing sounds. I knew what they were. He finally stopped and straightened.

"Nothing comes up." He sounded miserable in the dark. "I try to heave and nothing comes up."

"You need ammunition. Don't argue. Just do what I tell you. Clay." He came out of the door to the wheelhouse. "Get some crackers from the galley, please." He started for them.

"Sea duty," said Jerry. "I'm sure glad I got sea duty."

"Want to go below?"

"Hell, no! I can stand my watches."

Talking might help, I thought. "We ought to hit Casablanca in three or four weeks. Be some good liberty there."

He did not answer.

"All these African ports are good liberty. Plenty of vino and plenty of women. You'll make out all right."

"Yeah?" He did not really care.

"Sure. The vino is bad but the women are good."

Clay was back with a box of soda crackers.

"Eat these. Even if you don't want them, eat them. They'll give you something to throw. You don't want to get the dry heaves again."

He took the box and sorrowfully munched a cracker.

"Eat another." He did. "Feel better now?"

"No."

"You will. Keep eating. Whatever you do, keep eating." I returned to the port wing.

I relieved Carter of the conn. We alternated at hourly intervals. This gave me some rest and Carter experience. Tonight there was nothing to do except change course and speed minutely to stay on station.

The watch was quiet. Nothing sounded except the pings of the sound gear, loud when you listened for them but unheard when you did not. That was one thing about the midwatch. There was little doing. Daniels reported a sound contact, but two seconds later said it was a school of porpoise.

At two-thirty, Carter took the conn again. I went to the other wing. I saw Jerry's back faintly in the dark. He did not see me. He was singing. Then he stopped his song and leaned over the wing guard. He did what he had to do, ate some crackers from the box, and started singing again. I stepped close to him.

"You sound pretty good. The crackers help, huh?"

"Some." He turned around.

"Still sick?"

"Sick as a dog."

"Why are you singing, then?"

"I don't care any more. The worst they can do is kill you.
That's all any of them can do, is kill you."

He was happy about what he had discovered. I left him
singing and walked back to the port wing.

The moon had not risen, and, across the sky, clouds floated
to mask the stars. Through the glasses the carrier was a blur
that smudged against the ink of the sky and sea. The destroyers, blotted into the black, did not even show in the glasses. On
the bridge were only spectral outlines and shadows.

We were almost in the waters marked on the chart by the
fifteen X's. If They were really there, if the chart was true, we
might, now, this watch, find one. Or two or three or four. Suppose more than one, suppose the three or four? What then?
What if They came in together from the compass points
around us? Coming in awash in the dark, slipping along the
broken black surface of the sea with nothing to fear from
our blind guns, could They get us with torpedoes before we
had a chance to depth charge? Maybe, maybe They could,
maybe They would try. If They did try, we would not see Them
with our eyes. We would see Them, on the surface, with the
round dark screen of the radar, the screen showing Them
against itself as shapeless yellow blobs, small blobs because,
above the water, They would be small. If They ran in submerged, hidden in fathoms of black sea water, we had only
the pinging to find Them.

"Radar." I said it through the voice tube to the radar operator, sitting back to back with Daniels, inside the sound shack.
"Watch close for small targets on the ten-mile scale. If you get
anything report immediately. Carter." I called through the
wheelhouse to bring him from the other wing.

He came through, a shadow with a voice. "Yeah?"

"Inspect the watch. Scare the lookouts. Tell 'em how close
we're supposed to be to the first pack. Tell 'em they better
keep a taut watch tonight." The shadow disappeared around
the corner of the sound shack.

The lookouts were members of the gun crews on the after
and galley deckhouses and on the flying bridge on top of the
wheel house. What they could see tonight, except a torpedo
wake, I did not know. Still, they had to try.

Something breathed heavily in my ear.

"It ain't worth it." The voice rasped like a saw in the dark.
I relaxed.

"What ain't worth it?" I said, in ritual.

"The foggin' you get ain't worth the foggin' you get," the voice said.

"No, Kaintuck, it ain't worth it."

"Nawsir, it sure ain't worth it."

This was all ritual.

The physical embodiment of the voice glided beside me, a black apparition that produced sounds of a heavy breath, working jaws, and the quick explosive "ptuh" of tobacco juice spat. This was Kaintuck. Kaintuck was the chief signalman and king of the enlisted men who stood watches on the bridge. What he was doing here now I did not know. He did not have the watch. For no reason, he had just appeared. Perhaps he had a feeling.

"What the hell are you doing here? Don't you have enough to worry about? You got to come up to this graveyard in the middle of the night to find something else?"

"Couldn't sleep so good."

Kaintuck came and went as he was moved. He lived on the bridge from reveille to taps; there, at any moment of day or night, you might find him at your elbow, his teeth stained yellow in the black of his beard, his gravel whisper telling the newest morsel of filth he had accumulated, his goat laughter exploding in final peroration.

Kaintuck was an institution of the old four-stacker Navy that had once dotted the world. Before the war, he had been a legend in the Asiatic Squadron. He had a name, but nobody used it and few knew it; some of his liberty mates could scarcely call it. Even the captain never addressed him as anything but Kaintuck. On the sleeve of his blue chief's dress uniform he wore four diagonal red stripes, each for a four-year enlistment. The stripes would have been gold, for good conduct, if he had not once disobeyed the orders of an egregious ensign and thus saved the ensign from himself, and if he had not remained in the company, five days after a leave was up, of a peroxide blonde who called him Pappy.

Now he stood beside me in the darkness.

"What the hell are you doing out here?" I asked him. "Why aren't you back in the mountains? You'll never make a crop here."

"Nawsir, I ain't going to make no crop here. Got to go back to make a crop. Never shoulda left. But there was a guy come around the place recruiting, with pictures of pretty girls in grass skirts waving at sailors. All the sailors had shoes on. I ast the guy, does everybody get shoes? Everybody gets shoes, he said, they give you shoes. I was fifteen and didn't have no shoes and couldn't go to school so I passed for seventeen and

signed the papers. I had to go to Knoxville barefoot, and
the recruiting officer give me an old pair to wear to boot camp.
When I got to Norfolk they give me shoes and clothes and all
the chow I could eat and I knew right then this was for me.
But I never shoulda left. I ain't making no crop."

The moon was suddenly uncovered. It was like a torch
lighted over the ship and the sea. It turned the carrier and the
destroyers into black hulks that you did not need glasses to
see, it made a cold yellow lane on the dark of the water, and
it struck and revealed the whole bridge. Beside me, Kaintuck's
beard was black and scraggly against the white of his face.

"They can see us now," he said.

"Wish we could see Them."

"We ain't never going to see Them. Not till we get one. Or
till one gets us. Don't never worry about seeing Them."

Somebody was on the other side of Kaintuck. I looked to
see who. It was the signalman of the watch. The crew called
him Fuzzy. You could see why: even in the moonlight his
face looked guileless and young.

Kaintuck ogled him. "Man. Man. Look at him. He come
to see his old sea daddy."

"Shut up." Fuzzy blustered. He was eighteen and the crew
had one word for him: tender.

"Yeah, he's come to see his old sea poppa." Kaintuck
smacked his lips and slapped Fuzzy on the buttocks, the slap
thudding deadly against the heavy overpants.

"Look out now," Fuzzy growled.

Kaintuck abruptly spun him around by the shoulders and
clapped both hands on his chest.

"Call me sea daddy!" he cackled. Fuzzy tried to twist free.

"Leggo me, you fogging queer." Fuzzy could not get loose.
He was panting.

"Call me sea daddy."

Fuzzy made a sound in his throat. Kaintuck released him.
Fuzzy stepped back in a boxing pose, left foot advanced, and
flicked his left fist under Kaintuck's nose. This was their ritual,
perfected by many repetitions. Kaintuck cackled again. Then
he said, "Go get your sea poppa some coffee. I relieve you."

Fuzzy went into the wheelhouse for the coffeepot.

"Man, you wait till I retire on twenty and get me that
farm," Kaintuck said to me. "You wait till I get that three-
room house with the well in the backyard and a built-in
head. Ain't going to have no outside privy in my house. Ain't
going to work, neither. Gonna go down in front of the store
and chew tobacco and tell sea stories. Won't nobody believe
'em though. Them people won't believe nothing you tell 'em.

Once I went home on leave and told my pappy about the flying fish, how they'd scoot around in the air and fall on the forecastle sometimes, and he swore up and down I was lying. Son, he says, this is yore pappy. What are you trying to give me? Never could tell him different. But just wait till I get that twenty in. From then on, look for me in them cane chairs in front of the store."

"You're a long way from that store now."

The watch ended without a sound contact.

18

ROCKFORD relieved me, I wrote the log, and started to go down. I was walking toward the head of the ladder, when I saw, dimly in the moonlight, four shadows together on the port side of the galley deckhouse, across the narrow space between it and the bridge.

"You son of a bitch." The words, harsh and without jocularity, came across the space, the rest of the speech drowning in the wind.

Something was happening. I went down the ladder, holding with each hand to the smooth steel rail along the side, crossed the well deck, and climbed the ladder to the deckhouse.

The forms still clustered together tightly. They bristled with a tautness I could sense in the dark. Three of them were circling, menacing, a fourth.

"Goddamn you, Malloy, do you know—" The voice broke off as I stopped at the circle.

"What's going on here?" Under the moon I could see the three white faces trained accusingly at the other.

Nobody answered. The three faces did not swerve.

"I said what's going on here?" I made it tough.

"Ask Malloy," said one of the surrounding faces.

Another face said: "Yeah, Malloy. Tell him. Tell him what it's all about."

"Goddamn it, I'm not playing games. What's all this?"

"I—" The croak came out of the fourth, trapped face. Nothing followed.

"Come on. What is it?"

"It—" The croak stopped again and the fourth face looked, in supplication and one by one, at the other three. They had no pity. "It wasn't nothing, sir."

"Goddamn it, Malloy, tell him."

"Tell him, you bastard."

Malloy saw there was no way out. I heard him swallow. "I guess—" The whisper was dry, thin, and tortured. "I guess I dozed off for a minute. Sir."

"You on watch?"

I heard the swallow again, and the racked whisper: "Yes, sir."

"You were asleep on watch then." My words were a sentence.

The white, afraid face nodded.

I started to say, "Do you know what Articles of the Navy say about that?" But I did not say it. I said instead, "Okay, Malloy." Which was all there was to say.

"Mr. Taylor." One of the faces in the circle of three swung toward me. "Don't put him on report. We can take care of this."

"No," I said.

"Let us handle it, Mr. Taylor. Please."

I started to say "No" again. But I looked at the three faces. "All right." I said. "Handle it." And I left the deckhouse.

If he had been overleave on the beach, I thought, they would have covered for him. If he had been in a scrape with the shore patrol, they would have lied for him. For any infraction of abstract discipline, they would have perjured, suborned, or jeopardized themselves, for him.

But this was something else.

I did not see Malloy for two days. When I did, he was very quiet and very grave, and I did not think he would sleep on watch for a while.

19

AT BREAKFAST, at the table suburbanly set with fresh white cloth, shining silver, and white china plates with blue anchor borders, the officers talked carefully around the cluster of fifteen submarines, of which, by the chart, the task unit was in the center.

The gray battle curtains in front of the wardroom door swayed with the roll of the ship. The row of a dozen books, loose between the ends of the unpainted tin shelf welded to the wall, tipped from one side to the other. In my coffee cup, the round brown surface of the coffee slid against the cup sides. My weight shifted on the leather-covered seat of the straight-backed chair. Rocky and I, the last two at the table, were still there, facing each other, when the others had gone.

"Eggs are still fresh, aren't they?" Rocky, not a polite man, said politely as he spread a sliver of yellow butter on a thick slice of brown toast.

"They're okay. I'm not much for breakfast, though. Too damned early to eat." Half of my eggs, the yellow smeared over the chips of white, were still on the plate. My stomach felt queasy, a little, with the morning sickness that comes at sea when you are dragged out of bed at seven, having gone there at four, lain awake with coffee and fatigue until five, and slept uneasily, dreaming, until the dark form in the white coat showed in the doorway, twanged "Seven o'clock," and slammed the door with a metal-on-metal crash to insure the shattering finality of your awakening.

I picked up the second and last piece of toast on my bread plate and made myself eat it. You did not want to get an empty stomach on a destroyer in the North Atlantic.

"How is it out this morning?" I asked through a mouthful of toast. Rocky had relieved me at the end of the midwatch, then had been relieved himself just before eight.

"Lousy. No sun, drizzle, hard wind, and a strong sea. Gray as a blanket all over. We took some sprays on the bridge my watch."

"Isn't this lousy weather? For the old days down in the Caribbean." The old days had been four months before.

"The good old days." He gave it a twist.

"Remember the time in San Juan we hid from the shore patrol under the tablecloth? With the girls slipping the drinks under it?"

"That cloth was a regular damned tent."

"No restricted places up here."

"No girls either."

"We might get a little activity today." I brought up the cluster, deliberately, for the first time. I was tired of avoiding it.

"We sure might. Supposed to be fifteen in the neighborhood, huh?" He knew how many there were supposed to be.

"That's what the chart says. But you know how those reports are. Hell, they might be five hundred miles from here, a thousand, even. You can't tell."

"They might be right here, too."

"Let's wait and see."

"Aren't you used to waiting by this time?" He got out of the chair, walked to the transom at the side of the room, picked up his cap with the salt-greened band on it, said "I've got to check 'em on the deck-painting," and went out.

My stomach was still not quite easy. I was not going to be sick, but I had the sea feeling where it counted. I finished my coffee and left the wardroom. In the radio shack, I checked the coded incoming messages on the message board. None had a high priority. Over the ship, I inspected the cleaning stations that my men in the communications division were responsible for. On the small square of the half-deck outside my door, which for no good reason was assigned to the division, were Daniels and Stenton, another sound operator.

Daniels was squatting, buttocks on heels, on the deck, his right hand sweeping dirt with a short-handled brush the men called a "foxtail," into a trash tray he held in his left. I stopped and he looked up.

"How's it going?"

"Dirty." He held up the tray to show me the dirt. "Everybody walks over this son-of-a-bitch deck. It stays dirty. You sweep it down, they track it up. Sweep it down four times a day and it's still dirty. What can you do?" His face took on a noble, long-suffering look and he began to enjoy himself.

"Fill out a sympathy chit and I'll sign it."

He looked at me reproachfully, then, brightening, said, "Maybe we'll get a little action today, huh, Mr. T? Right in the middle of 'em this way we sure ought to get some action."

"Don't be sure about being in the middle of anything."

"That's what the chart says." He liked the idea and nobody was going to take it away from him.

"The chart. They don't just sit still and wait for you, you know."

"Oh, They're around." He was having no argument. "Those boys that put out the sub reports put out good dope. They're sure as hell around. Maybe we'll get one this time."

"You're really eager. The Navy likes to see them eager like you." The last was a flick. He did not like official approbation. He was afraid it might stamp him as orthodox.

"Ah, the Navy." It had pricked him. "The Navy wants you to chip rust and sweep decks when you're right in the middle of a sub pack, it don't want you to fight. Just sweep and chip, chip and sweep, that's all the Navy gives a fog about. It don't care about nothing else, just so you sweep the decks and chip the rust."

"Don't fret. You'll get a chance at something else."

He was working the foxtail under the ladder to the well deck when I started up its rungs to the topside. There, I walked over the open decks. Men were crouched on the decks chipping away, with flat-ended, sharp-edged rods, the rust that salt sprays had made in the four days out of Norfolk. They were covering the patches of bare metal with yellow zinc paint: They were greasing gun breeches, washing swabs in soapy buckets of water, tightening lifelines, swinging the torpedo tubes over the side and back again. The work was going on.

In a sense, Daniels was right. Wherever we were, whatever we did, the work never stopped. It might be laid aside for general quarters, but it never stopped. Not in a submarine concentration nor in Long Island Sound, not in the heat of the equator nor the cold of the North Atlantic. One battle that never ended was with the sea. If you did not protect yourself from her, she would, like life, destroy you, one way or another. With rust, with salt, or, if you grew too defiant, with pure pounding fury. About the last, there was little to be done, but the first, the rust and the salt, you could beat if you never stopped working.

On the well deck, I stopped to look off to port at the other ships, black in the gray of the day. The wind, blowing in strong, whipped a spray from the side that hit my face, the impact a cold wet shock to the cheek-skin and then the taste of salt in my mouth. I rubbed my handkerchief over the wet place. It still felt cold and wet.

Then I stepped down the ladder, right hand carefully holding the side rail because the rungs were worn smooth and easy to slip on, to the half-deck, which Daniels and Stenton had left, and then went into the wardroom. Rocky was sitting at a table with his small notebook open before him, his cap, that he loved dearly because the weather had beaten it into such disrepair, on the green cloth beside the notebook. I walked around the end of the table to the gray tin routing box for mail. From my slot, which a typewritten strip of paper pasted across the bottom labeled, "Communications Officer," I took three pieces of printed mail. The captain had written in ink on each "All officers," and stamped on each was an inked box with lines for initials.

I sat down, across from Rocky, and skipped through them. They did not amount to anything. I tossed them over the table at him. He looked up.

"For you," I said.

"Christ, I don't have to read them, I can quote them. 'All who have not done so will do so immediately.' Give me the Goddamned things." He picked up the first and started to read. "Now. Now here is one. This is what they've got to worry about at DesLant. Did you read this? Listen." I had seen it but he read it aloud anyway. " 'All ships under this command will exercise all personnel at a regular period of calisthenics daily.' In the North Atlantic on this Goddamned bouncing vomit-bucket, we will exercise all personnel at a regular period of calisthenics daily. Get your jock strap ready. You will be exercised at a regular period of calisthenics daily. Jesus."

He initialed that one with the yellow pencil in his right hand and was picking up the next, when the gray curtain to the exec's room in the right corner of the wardroom swung to one side and Graham stepped out with the long, black-covered ship's navigation log in his hands. He looked at me.

"Taylor."

"Yes, sir?"

"You didn't write your four-to-eight log yesterday." He put the log, open to the day's entries with blank lines following the penciled "4-8," in front of me, frowned, opened his mouth to say something, then closed it, turned, and went back into his room, his back somehow managing to look military in the blousy gray shirt.

"Aren't you something?" Rocky made his face grave and reprimanding. "Didn't write your log. Stood a watch and didn't write your log for it. Suppose everybody didn't write their log?" He knew Graham could hear him and he got pleasure from flagellating the exec's sense of proprieties. "Where would the Navy be? Where would I be? Where would you be?"

"In the sack."

"In the sack. A fine place for an officer. You know the trouble with you? Trouble with you is you don't know what you're fighting for. None of our fine American boys know what they are fighting for. They are not properly indoctrinated. Their leaders have failed to indoctrinate them properly. Now you. Take you. What do you think you're fighting for?"

"Ten days leave. I'll settle for five. And if you throw forty-eight hours in my face I'll take it."

"You get a forty-eight? Not a chance, not a chance. No forty-eight for you. You missed a log. What would you do with a forty-eight anyway? What woman in the universe would spend a forty-eight with you? I'll take your forty-eight and use it constructively."

"Yes. You'll take my forty-eight. And I'll stay on board and stand your watches and shine your shoes and kiss your rosy red. Won't that be dovey?"

"Just dovey. I'll count on it."

"I wouldn't if I were you. You won't get off the ship. You realize you've been making heretical utterances?" I slipped into his way of talking. "We don't stand for heretical utterances around here. We don't pass out forty-eights to those who make heretical utterances. In the end you'll stay aboard for me."

He told me in what part of a pig he would stay aboard for me. I picked up his pencil and started to write on the blank lines near the top of the page. I wrote, after the 4-8: "Steaming as before. 0533 commenced zigzagging. 0618 executed sunrise." I skipped one line and signed, "Peter Taylor," then dropped one more and put "Lt. (jg) USNR."

I stood up, picked up the log, and took it to Graham in his room. I laid it on his desk. He nodded curtly. His displeasure was entirely sound. There was no excuse for not writing it on time. I went out, thinking automatically about Graham.

Graham was all-Navy. Everything he was had long ago been channeled into the grooves of the service. His existence was a straight line from one job, one ship, one promotion to the next, and it was a line walled inflexibly by the written and unwritten taboos of the Navy. He did not think about this, he had probably never consciously thought of it, but he knew and accepted it. He was, as nearly as a man can be, a type. The captain was a force, but Graham was a textbook officer. He could have stepped—almost—right from the pages of *Naval Leadership,* a thin book with a blue cover. He did not have and would not have what it was that Buchan could pull out of the air when he had to, but he was what his superiors called a "sound officer." He was little older than his own officers. He was from the class of 1939 at the Naval Academy and six months before, this job had been a good one for him, but now, with new destroyers coming out of the yards like automobiles, it was not such a good one. He would have a better soon. That was another thing he did not think about but accepted.

Though a disciplinarian, Graham had a sense of responsibility toward his men that was not always there in officers who pride themselves on their "drive" and "determination." All of the crew consequently respected and some even liked him.

He had married, as soon as regulations permitted, an equally conventional, equally uncomplicated, very pretty girl from his home town in Ohio, and was, so far as we knew, completely faithful to her.

Thinking of Graham on my way back to the wardroom table, I decided he was to be envied.

There were no sound contacts in the morning or early afternoon.

The routine of the watches gave me the first dog watch, that was supposed to extend from four to six in the afternoon but actually lasted until almost seven and well after dark.

On the bridge in the late afternoon gray, I watched the carrier and the other destroyers, spaced like points in a geometri-

cal design, wheel with the *Dee* in the ballet chorus movements
of the zigzag. I saw the planes, black slivers in the sky, move
in and out of vision, sometimes the purr of their motors filtering in faint with the distance, until, when the afternoon was
nearly gone, the four that were aloft converged in a circle
around the carrier and, one by one, dropped to the flight deck.
Toward twilight, the sky and the sea shaded into a deeper and
deeper gray, never changing but always darkening, until an
hour after the sunless sunset, both were almost black and the
other ships were the shapeless forms of the night. The wind
was hard and made the halyards cry. The pings, never slowing,
never speeding, thumped in their heart beat over the bridge.

I was alone on the port wing and then Kaintuck was beside
me like a materialized spirit.

"Don't look like we're going to raise anything." I saw him
clearly as he said it: the black beard, the ragged hair, the face
white in the darkness that was not yet absolute.

He turned his head, deliberately, toward the side and spat
tobacco juice into the driving wind.

"I think we would of raised one by now if They was here.
I don't think we going to find anything here."

"What the hell do you care what we find? Nobody can stir
you out of the sack for GQ because you're on the bridge all
the time anyway. What do you care if we raise one or not?"

He spat again. His breathing was loud, slow, and spaced.
"I'd kind of like to get one. Man gets tired of just hunting
Them without ever getting a look. Man gets tired just waiting."

"You haven't started to wait."

"Mr. Taylor, I done a lot of waiting in my time. I can wait
with any of 'em. I can wait as long as I have to wait."

That night, I did what I had not done since my first trip on
the *Dee*. I slept in my shirt and pants. The shirttail was outside the pants and up around my neck when the boatswain's
mate woke me at three-thirty for the morning watch.

20

ON THE WATCH, the sun curved out of the sea at six-nineteen,
exactly as Graham had forecast in the neat, stiff penciled figures on the slip of paper pasted on the bulkhead just inside
the door of the wheelhouse. Before, the ships had started, in
the last dawn darkness, the zigzag, and the planes, in the first

clear gray light, had jumped from the precipice of the flight deck and snarled away on the morning patrol.

This was the first sun in three days and I was glad to see it. It struck the sea and turned the gray to green, and, cutting across the *Dee's* bow from the east, glinted off the gray hulls of the destroyers on the other side of her to leave them bone-white in its glare.

The task unit was still in the charted submarine cluster. At three o'clock, having steamed beyond what the chart said was the cluster's perimeter, it had reversed course and was now cutting back through the same water it had searched, impotently, for twenty-four hours before.

The pings, always searching, struck off time like a loud, slow clock.

"Clay." He came out of the wheelhouse, red-eyed and heavy-footed in the shambling overshoes, to me where I stood alone by the compass repeater on the port wing. "How about some joe for the watch?"

"Yes, sir. I could sure use some myself."

"Me, too. You really start feeling it about this time, don't you?"

"Yeah, about here it really gets you. You feel like you been up a week. Well." He moved away. "That joe ought to wake us up. I better get after it."

He took two steps to the sound shack, turned the dog to the just-open door, opened it and stepped inside, then came out holding the long aluminum coffeepot by the handle across the open top, the steel ladle inside rattling around the circular edge, and he walked behind the wheelhouse toward the ladder on the other side.

My empty stomach rumbled. I caught a smell of the coffee in the galley. How it got to the bridge, in the face of the head-on wind, I did not know. But there it was. I felt saliva run into my mouth as I smelled it. I stood still, rolling from the ankles with the rise and fall of the ship, smelling.

I was tired of keeping station, of making the tiny changes in course and speed that kept the *Dee* on the same bearing at the same distance from the carrier. I called Carter from the other wing.

"Want to take it?" Not waiting for an answer, I handed him the card with the zigzag courses. "Your next change is at six-twenty-six."

He nodded, looked at the card, then at his wrist watch, then at the carrier, and, two minutes later, watching carefully the second hand on his watch, said through the open door to the helmsman inside the wheelhouse, "Come left to one-nine-zero."

The *Dee* started to turn, the turn easy and wide so you scarcely felt it as she came around, and on her left, the carrier and the *Hilliard* and the *Donahue* turned with her, cutting smooth quarter-circle tracks that you could see with the glasses in the rolling green sea behind them, then they all came out of it together and straightened on the new course they would hold until the next leg of the zigzag.

"That was a good one." Carter said it looking at the compass repeater that came almost to his chest to see that the helmsman had steadied. Then he bent to sight the carrier along the markers of the bearing circle fitted on top of the compass. "We came out of that one right on bearing."

"Good enough."

"What a day." He looked away from the carrier, at the sea and sky along the horizon. "Look at that sun. The exec ought to get a real sun sight today."

"He ought to get a good noon position if it stays out."

"Know how long we stay in this concentration?"

I shrugged and shook my head.

The wild shrieking static of the aircraft radio, a speaker tuned to the frequency over which the planes and carrier talked to each other, erupted from the wheelhouse. I stepped through the open door to hear what was coming, but could not understand, above the babble, the thin words that rasped out of the round metal box above the opposite door.

But the man on the carrier, The Man, did. The deep voice, that we knew now to the last note and inflection, spoke clearly in return.

"This is Coach. Roger. Out."

Then, on the other radio, the one for the ships alone, the voice called the *Dee*.

"Georgia, this is Coach. Over."

I pushed the "on" button in the tiny black box under the telephone that was our sending radio, lifted the French-style phone from the hook that held it, straight up and down, under the black box, pushed another button on the telephone shaft and said into the mouthpiece:

"Coach, this is Georgia. Over."

The voice spoke its next message in the silly, unrelated words that were code. I wrote down the words and took their meaning from the sheet taped beside the phone. Translated, the message said: "Submarine contact reported on bearing three-three-zero, fifteen miles distant. Investigate."

I called it to the captain through the little brass megaphone screwed into the sound tube that went to his cabin and ended here in another megaphone. I put my ear to the megaphone to get his answer.

"Start on over there." His voice, metallic and hollow through the tube, came back.

"Right standard rudder. Come right to three-three-zero."

I gave it to the helmsman.

"Three-three-zero."

He repeated the course, and hand over hand turned the spokes of the steam-driven wheel to the right to start the *Dee* turning, hard in the swing that took her around for more than a quarter of a circle, then turned them the other way to ease her out of it to her new course. She had settled on the course, north north-west, when the captain, fully dressed in the blue winter clothes and helmet, with the fur-collared green coat over his arm, walked through the door from the starboard wing.

"Steady on three-three-zero at seventeen knots, captain."

He nodded. "I'll take her. Sound general quarters."

I put my right hand to the red-painted, black-tipped handle for the general alarm, the handle resting against the metal stop on the left of the red box that held it, then pulled it hard to the other stop on the right, jamming it tight against the stop, and over the ship the claxon that was the general alarm jangled its "drrr-drrr-drrr" in bursts fast following each other that had the ugly shock of a summons to judgment.

Thunder broke over the ship, in three hundred feet jarring her decks. Voices repeated a single shout, "All hands general quarters!" until it became an animal cry in the disciplined frenzy of a warship's crew manning their battle stations. I walked to the port wing and looked back to see men make a blue stream spurting up the ladder to the galley deckhouse. On the deckhouse, the guns swung straight over the side and the men in the crews, single men again and no longer drops in the stream, rammed their arms into the gray pillows that were life jackets and yanked on their heads the round blue bowls that were helmets.

Beside me, the telephone talker, engulfed in a blue tub that surrounded his head and his earphones, fed me the reports from the stations.

"Main battery, manned and ready. Machine gun battery, manned and ready. Condition Able set forward. Depth charge manned and ready. Torpedo battery manned and ready. Condition Able set aft. Engine room manned and ready."

With the same precipitancy that it had burst into battle condition, the *Dee* fell into silence. I heard only the wind and the sea striking the ship. And the pings.

I went back into the wheelhouse. The captain's blue back was in front of a port hole to the right of the wheel. Left arm resting on the curved edge of the port, he looked straight ahead through the round, glass-paneled hole.

"All stations manned and ready, cap'n. Condition Able set forward and aft."

"Very well." He did not move nor turn his head to answer me. "All engines ahead full."

This took the *Dee* to twenty knots and she pitched harder with the new speed. It would take her to the point of the reported contact in three-quarters of an hour.

I went through the door to the port wing and stood there, just outside, where I could hear the radio and, if I had to, answer in a hurry. I looked back along the ship. On both sides of the galley deckhouse, a three-inch gun thrust over the steel wind guards and cut an arc through the air as the *Dee* rolled. A sight setter stood on the pedestal of each gun to set target range on the sight scales. In the saddle seats on each side of the guns sat pointers and trainers, heads bent to look into the sight telescopes and hands on the wheels that swung the guns up and down and from side to side. Three men made a line between the breech of the guns and the open ammunition boxes. The twenty-millimeter machine guns, just ahead of the bigger ones, stuck like black toothpicks from the chests of the gunners strapped to them.

Further back, angling from behind both sides of the deckhouse and close to the water, I saw the three finger tips of the torpedo tubes. What I could not see were the men in the repair parties, on the depth charges, in the engine room, and on the after deckhouse guns.

The pings struck off the seconds as the *Dee* cut ahead. On the left, the carrier and the two destroyers ahead of her, steaming from us at more than a right angle, slipped further and further away, became smaller and smaller miniatures of black on the green sea table, dipped over the horizon to show their superstructures, then only their masts, and finally disappear. Thirty minutes after she left them, the *Dee* was alone.

Ahead, maybe ten miles, maybe twelve, a black flyspeck showed low in the sky. Closer, it grew into a fly, making wide circles over the green water.

I put my head through the door. "Captain." He had not moved but was still standing, arm on the edge, in front of the port. "There's our plane ahead."

"So I see." He did not turn his head to say it.

The plane got bigger as the *Dee* closed it. Fifteen minutes after I had sighted it, the aircraft radio screeched again in the wheelhouse. I stepped inside. Over the caterwauling of the wind and the static the pilot said, this time so I could hear: "Georgia, this is twenty-six Mitchell. Thought I saw a periscope about here. Not sure. Dropped a stick of bombs anyway. No apparent results. You can find the spot by the green dye. I'm over it now. Out."

The captain brought the ship right five degrees to head for the plane. He turned from the porthole, and walked through the door to the port wing. I followed him.

"Have all stations watch for the green dye ahead."

"Aye, aye, sir." I relayed the order through the telephone talker.

The plane, its features sharp as we closed, made tight circles over the water to show us the dye. Almost under it, Buchan cut speed to fifteen knots, the standard attack rate, and the *Dee* eased her pitching.

The pings kept beating in their timepiece search.

Buchan was standing in front of me on the wing, against the wind guard, looking ahead. I raised my glasses and played them over a small belt ahead of the ship.

"There it is." I saw a discoloration in the water. "Dead ahead, about five hundred yards."

Buchan looked with his own glasses. "That's it, all right."

The *Dee* came alongside it. The dye made a pea-green splotch, running off at the edges into the darker green water around it. The plane had dropped the dye with the depth bombs.

"Break out the stop watch and the search plan," Buchan told me.

The ship moved ahead for a quarter of a mile, until, reading the stop watch and the open, yellow-backed pamphlet in front of me, I said to the captain, "Stand by for the turn. Mark."

"Left standard rudder." He brought the *Dee* ninety degrees to the left and held that course longer than the one before. This was one of the basic submarine search plans. It began at the point of last contact with the submarine. The ship started from that point and made an ever-widening orbit about it. But she did not circle. She coursed in straight lines, each a little longer than the last.

As the *Dee* plodded in her geometric groping, a creature of the stop watch and timetable, the plane overhead swept around her in wide curves, sometimes heading out and away, then returning with a head-on black rush and the sudden-booming motor roar, to start her circling again.

It was almost nine o'clock. In the east, the weak yellow sun was still low over the sea, and scudding gray clouds made shifting patterns in the pale blue sky. The sun had little warmth. Inside the heavy clothes, I was cold; I was tired, too, from nearly six hours on the bridge. Nobody had had breakfast. My stomach was empty and a little unwell.

"Captain, shall we send breakfast to the stations?"

"Very well." He said it as though he recognized, but begrudged, the necessity.

I sent a signalman to the galley to tell the cooks. Breakfast, less than fifteen minutes coming, was hard fried eggs between pieces of thick white bread. I picked one from the aluminum tray set on the flag bag. I broke it in two and bit into the first piece. The egg yellow broke and ran over the bread, that had already soaked up the cooking grease. It was good. I thought I had never been so hungry. I ate the sandwich, both pieces, in six bites, and took another. All this time I was looking at the stop watch to time the next turn.

We followed the search plan until after ten. Then Buchan said decisively, "There's nothing out here now. Let's get the hell back." He pushed the TBS radio button and picked up the telephone. "Hope we can contact the outfit." The task unit might be too far away for the short-range TBS.

"Coach from Georgia, Coach from Georgia. Over."

He waited almost half a minute, then repeated the message.

The box sputtered and the answer came back, thinly.

"Georgia, this is Coach. Over."

The captain said, "Results of search negative. Suggest we rejoin. Over."

The big voice came back:

"Rejoin at best course and speed. Our course at ten hundred, red brown purple." That was code for zero-one-zero. The task unit, then, had reversed course to permit us to return.

The voice opened up on the aircraft radio and told our plane to come home, and the plane, by this time certainly low on gas, wheeled and lined straight away.

Graham, who had been inside the sound shack, stepped out and went into the chartroom to figure, on a sheet of paper with small green squares, our course to rejoin the formation. He came to Buchan on the wing five minutes later.

"Cap'n, course is one-two-zero at seventeen knots."

The captain nodded and brought the ship to course. He turned to me. "Secure from general quarters, set the steaming watch."

"Secure from general quarters, set the watch." I gave it to the telephone talker in the tub helmet.

"Secure from general quarters, set the watch." The talker sent it into the mouthpiece.

"Secure!" yelled the sight setter on Gun Three on the galley deckhouse, and the one word, "Secure!" bounded over the ship like an echo, touching off a weak mimicry of the human explosion that had rocked the ship when general quarters sounded.

On the galley deckhouse guns, the men slung off their helmets and life jackets, jammed them into the racks, and ran down the ladders to the deck below, clanging the rungs with heavy feet. On the bridge, the helmsman and the telephone talker gave way to new ones. While I stood there waiting for my relief, the *Dee* dropped into the steaming, hunting routine as quickly as she had jumped out of it.

The men on the galley deckhouse gun watch squatted on the deck under the gun mounts, leaving only two lookouts on their feet. The feeble sun brought a laziness and odd detachment. I cursed Rockford for not having relieved me already; I wished he would hurry.

He came around the corner of the sound shack, buttoning the green coat over the blue trousers as he walked. The long ear flaps of the blue cloth helmet hung below his ears. Black mittens stuck out of the left pocket of the coat. His mouth turned down at the corners as he stopped beside me.

"Another fogging watch. Another fogging watch on this fogging bridge."

"You should bitch. You don't have three hours left. I've been here six."

"My heart bleeds for you, you know where. What's the dope?"

"Anchored as before." That was a bromide, never very funny. I gave him the information, he said, "I relieve you," and I was, all things being relative, a free man. I went into the charthouse to write my log. This morning I had enough to write. Reading from the scrawl in the quartermaster's notebook, the source material for all deck logs, I wrote the entry for the watch. Then I went below.

In the room, I kicked off my arctics and watched them curve in space to bam on the deck like small bombs. I took off the heavy coat, unzipped the blue jacket and twisted out of it, then unhooked and stepped out of the blue pants and left them curled on the deck where they dropped. I dropped face down on the bunk. I was tired in every cell. My thighs had the stiffness of standing for hours. I turned over on my back and spread my arms and legs apart, like a game beast stretched for skinning. I could not sleep, I had work to do—I told myself, knowing the real reason I would not let myself sleep was that

I did not want the exec to find me in the bunk—but I had a physical compulsion to suspend all sensation and movement from my body. I gave myself ten minutes and lay, not moving, except once to turn my wrist to look at the watch. At the end of the ten, I gave myself five more. Then I got up, washed my face, and went into the wardroom. I drank a cup of coffee, took three publications from the communications safe under the mail routing box, and began to correct them. The corrections were on strips of paper stuck between appropriate pages of the publication and were supposed to bring them up to date. You were always behind with corrections; as soon as you caught up, there were new ones to be made. I felt good, after the fifteen minutes, and made good time. I was almost through with the third publication when I had to leave the table so the mess boys could set it for lunch.

Washed and combed again, I sat with the other officers after the captain called through the voice tube from the bridge that he would not be down.

"Another wild-goose chase." Arbry, on my right, said it, taking his napkin, now showing stains of five days, from the silver ring inscribed "Gunnery Officer."

"What's one more or less? No liberty here."

"Liberty, but no boats." That was time-tested.

"It's a tough war." So was that.

"You're damned well informed it's a tough war."

Peters set a soup bowl in front of Arbry, then before me. A tiny cloud of steam rose from the brown-red liquid inside the white china sides. Vegetables swam just under the surface. I dipped the spoon into the soup, then lifted it, holding it in the air an instant to cool, and brought it to my mouth. The soup was beef and vegetable broth. It was the best the mess had ever had. I dipped the spoon again.

The jangle of the general alarm stopped the spoon in the air. I dropped it into the soup with a plunking splash that sprayed red droplets over the tablecloth. Chairs scraped on the deck. I ran for the door. Arbry's light body hit me on the way, bounced off, and jumped through the doorway ahead of me. I sprinted into my room to snatch the winter clothing to carry to the bridge. We might be at battle stations the rest of the day. And night. Or maybe for ten minutes. There was no telling.

Before I took the last step from the ladder to the bridge, the pings told me we had a sound contact. There was the ping, then after it, the echo, clean and solid but lower-pitched than the ping. The ping had hit something and the echo came back from what it had hit. The ping and the echo made a bouncing ball noise together.

Buchan was on the port wing conning the attack.

"Target moving right. Right cut-on, zero-seven-zero." Daniels' voice came loud through the voice tube from the sound shack.

"Right to zero-seven-zero," Buchan gave the helmsman. His voice was as detached as though he had ordered a course change in the zigzag plan.

Now he had to lead the target with the ship the way a hunter leads a duck with a gun. Late in the run, he would cut even more sharply ahead of the target, drop the charges, and hope they hit. The submarine, if it was a submarine, would try to turn away and not get hit by the charges. It was a stimulating cerebral exercise, particularly, I supposed, for the submarine commander.

The bridge was like a picture screen with background music suddenly cut off, and the only sound the dialogue of the actors: the ping and its echo bouncing back, the echo clearer and closer to the ping every bounce, the quick excited reports from Daniels, and Buchan's quiet commands to the wheel.

Then the *Dee* was peeling off in her last attack course and the captain said: "Fire on the recorder."

"Stand by to fire," Graham called from the sound shack.

"Stand by," said the captain to Wilson, the signalman, standing by the two levers and the push-button board that fired the depth charges. He crouched by the levers, big-boned and tense, his right hand tight on the green lever, the arm rigid behind it.

"Fire one." From Graham.

Wilson bent and pulled down hard on the green lever, that would drop one charge from the starboard stern rack, then straightened and brought it back in one smooth motion. On the bridge you could hear a faint splash as the charge rolled over the stern and hit the water.

"Fire two."

Now he pulled the red lever, for the port rack, and swung it back, paused as though counting two seconds to himself, and pushed two buttons in the panel above the levers. They were for the K-guns. The guns pommed loudly and the charges, cylindrical and black against the sky, arched up and out and tumbled into the sea with a heavy white splash, a hundred yards on either side of the ship.

Then a blast, muffled as though heard from far away, rocked the *Dee*. That was the first charge, hitting its depth and exploding, three hundred yards astern and one hundred and fifty feet under water.

"Fire three." Wilson pulled the green lever and pressed two

buttons, and the ship shook heavily, the steel of her body shuddering and rattling, as the second salvo, strong as the first multiplied by three, went off. A coffee cup fell from the flag bag to the deck and shattered itself in pieces.

"Fire four."

"Lost contact," Daniels cried.

"Fire five."

The ship bucked as each salvo went off. I clutched the wind guard to keep my feet.

"Right full rudder," ordered Buchan. The *Dee* heeled as she turned and straightened as she came about. Now the pings lanced out alone. The echo was gone. The job was to find it again.

The pings reached out for it. Buchan cruised the *Dee* back and forth over the area, the pings always pounding in their search. No echo came back. He went into the geometric search plan, the one that had found nothing earlier. No echo. For two hours, we followed the plan, always pinging. But no echo.

Then Buchan said, in a voice that did not quite mask disappointment, "Secure from general quarters."

Clattering down the ladder, I thought of the soup again. Washing my face for lunch for the second time, I thought of the soup. Sitting at the table, unfolding the not-quite-clean napkin, remembering the first, only taste, I thought of the soup.

Peters set a plate, already served with smelly cabbage and ham, in front of us.

"What about the soup?" But I knew as I asked it, with bitterness and defeat in my heart, what about the soup.

"Soup?" Peters blinked.

"Soup."

"Ain't no more soup. We threw it away when GQ went."

I did not say anything. I picked up the fork and poked it into the cabbage. Then I laid the fork on the plate and looked fixedly at the bare white center of the tablecloth.

"It's a tough war," said Arbry.

21

THE CLOCK over the wardroom door said nine-eighteen, and the gray light filtering through the uncovered ports told it was morning. I took four official letters from my slot in the tin routing box, dropped them on the table, and the general alarm and underwater blast, this very close and rattling the china on the board in the corner, went off together.

Half the depth-charge pattern had been fired when I reached the bridge. I was strapping on the helmet when the voice from the sound shack called, "Target breaking up. Target definitely a fish."

Buchan, standing by the open door to the shack, said through it, tonelessly, "Very well," and, to me, "You'd better help Crandall check for leaks." He did not need to explain further: why Crandall needed help.

"Aye, aye sir."

After every dropping of depth charges, it was necessary to look into all the ship's spaces that were separated from the sea by only the steel plate that was five-eighths of an inch thick. This was to see if the underwater explosions had ripped holes in the plate. They could.

I left the bridge and walked to after repair. Crandall was standing four or five feet away from the twelve men in the party that was now a loose, shifting circle in front of the after deckhouse, the blue steel helmet looking prankishly misplaced on his head, his lineless face ridiculed by its sheltering overhang.

Standing apart and erect, looking sternly straight ahead but not at all at his men, who were laughing, too loudly, he sparked the unvarying revulsion that I had not, yet, been able to define. And something else. I wanted to laugh, spit in his face, and pat him on the shoulder, all together.

"How did it go?" I tried to seem friendly.

"All right, all right." His unconcern was a little too heavily unconcern. "Those damn things do produce quite a sensation, don't they?" His grin was not as nonchalant as he had tried to make it. "Is it all right if I smoke?"

"Why not? We've secured."

He sighed, almost gratefully, and untied the top laces of the chin-high kapok life jacket to bring from his shirt pockets the silver case and then the silver lighter. I watched him bring the flame of the lighter to his mouth, and saw his hand was shaking. He drew, deeply and happily, on the cigarette.

"I thought I might help you check for leaks," I said.

"Thanks." He inhaled again. "But Rockford and the chief are already inspecting." Then quickly: "I'm standing by with the party in case they find any damage." He wanted, really wanted, to be useful, and I saw it and was surprised. I had not considered that before.

"Oh," I said.

So the charges got to him? Why not? The first time, they could get to anybody. The first time I had heard concentrated machine-gun fire at a training school, far from all menace except the New England winter, I had wanted to dig under a rock. Again I felt the odd kinship with Crandall.

"I'll kill a few minutes, if you don't mind," I said. "Any excuse to stay off the bridge."

"Certainly." He was all right now. I hoped he had not shown too visibly how the charges had hit him, and I hoped that the men had not seen.

A voice, from the circle behind us, said loudly and innocently, "This old bitch going to sink herself with these charges some day." And I knew they had been.

Another voice: "Man, and it's cold in that water." Also loud, also innocent. There was nothing to do.

"Yeah, just wham, wham, wham, and we're all in that water."

"How long you reckon a man can last down there?"

"They say twenty minutes."

"Twenty minutes your ass. You can't last ten."

"Just wham, wham, wham, and there we are."

I looked at Crandall and saw that he comprehended.

But he could not have done anything too shameful. Probably he had only looked scared. It was not important. Not important enough, even, to tell in the wardroom.

But I did.

That was the first concentration; a hunt for ghosts and a quick flicking brush in the dark that was over almost before it happened, that we could not be sure had happened.

The task unit left the area and steamed, through seas like gray hills that rolled and beat against the ships day after day, northward. The course was not north but a little to the east of it, to where the bunched X'es on the chart were. Each day was colder than the last, and the nights, too, were colder than the mornings. Each sunrise was a little later and each sunset a little earlier than the one before.

But these were no more than pencil marks in the navigator's notebook, for there was seldom a sun. Sometimes it would break weakly through the fuzzy mucous of the overcast and show for an instant, a washed-out yellow hall blurred at the rim, and then the heavy gray mass would swallow it again. Graham haunted the bridge and waited for it, then, fighting the pitch of the ship, he raised his sextant as it came out, shot it swiftly and angrily, cursed, and walked into the chart room to translate the sextant reading into a line of position on the white space of the chart.

Now the ships began to zigzag twenty-four hours a day.

They made sharp quick turns together, as though obeying the baton of an unseen director, tracing the undeviating patterns laid down by the thin green book. Every day, the pattern was a new one, and the ships cut back and forth, automatons of the green book, through the day and night.

Three times a day, the carrier turned into the wind to launch her planes, and they rocketed into the air, dwindled into single dots of black crawling across the gray sky, and finally vanished. Like well-trained hounds, they hastened home when she called, and she turned into the wind again to take them down. Every time she swung to a new course for her planes, the destroyers scurried quiveringly to new stations to guard her, then rushed just as frantically to the ones they had left when she came about to her old heading.

Through the day and night the Dee *threw her pings, trembling like the tones of a tuning fork, into the under-ocean, and the man crouched before the round dial kept turning the hand wheel and listening for the echo that would mean we had found what we hunted.*

That was how we hunted. We hunted from the first concentration to the second, from the second to the third, through and between them, and we found nothing. Then we turned back from the third to the second again, and we still found nothing. We began to hunt back and forth through the middle of the North Atlantic, moving in a slow shapeless orbit from one concentration to another. We still found nothing.

But we kept hunting. And waiting. You had to get used to waiting. In this war, you had learned, finally, that you would have to wait a very long time.

22

I SEARCHED THE SEA that stretched as far as eyesight from the ship to the circle the horizon made around her. Inside the circle was only the ship, a black splinter on the dark gray table of the sea under the lighter gray dome of the sky. The horizon cut the sea and sky apart; at the straight line of the horizon they contended and were not the same.

The *Dee,* having been detached from the task unit for this one of uncountable times to investigate a plane's reported, doubtful glimpse of something breaking water and disappearing, having run at full speed to the area and hunted over it without a contact, and having abandoned, after three hours, the search, was on her way to rendezvous with the other ships at a previously designated point of latitude and longitude that was six hundred miles southeast of Cape Farewell on the tip of Greenland.

"We ought to pick them up about dead ahead, Pete." The captain turned his face back, out of the wind, toward me.

"Aye, aye, sir."

He seemed about to say something else, but did not; instead he walked, in heavy, slow steps to meet the pitch and roll of the ship, into the wheelhouse to look at the radar scope.

I stood on the open wing and looked ahead with the glasses for the carrier and the other destroyers, which would be hull down over the horizon when sighted. And I looked, on the microscopic but never to be neglected chance that we might find something with eyes instead of pings, for what we hunted. In the month we had been hunting, we had never found, with certainty, what we hunted, and now, sometimes, I did not think we would ever find it. Still, we had to keep looking.

I stood there, looking, and watched the North Atlantic ocean attack. It pounded from ahead in deep slate-gray swells that rolled higher and higher to break at the top in white ridges and then plunged down and on to make way for the next. One swell swept in right behind the other. They never stopped and never broke formation.

From the bridge, I looked down and ahead to see them hit head-on and toss like a pencil this floating sliver of steel the Navy called a destroyer, each swell lifting the knife-pointed bow up to a peak of nothing, poising it there for an instant out of time, and plunging it like a guillotine blade into the trough behind. On top of the swells, you were on top of the world and could see it all clearly to the horizon; at the bottom after the ship dropped, you looked up and saw only the next sea, coming at you fast and straight like a long gray charging mountain with white snow at the crest. Every time the bow fell, it struck from the sea a quick, booming whoosh, as a man makes when something knocks his wind from him, and the impact exploded the water into a white geyser of spray that leaped at the ship and whipped across the bridge, forty feet above the water line.

I timed each sheet of spray to turn and take it on the back, I did not escape, there was no escaping, but the sprays hit the oilskin cover of my coat instead of the naked skin of my face. I held with the cold-deadened fingers of my left hand to the chest-high strip of steel that circled the bridge. The deck rolled hard in a side-to-side, up-and-down, four-way violence, and you had to roll with it, your feet wide apart and solid on the deck and your body swaying from the hinges of your ankles, to stand.

You could feel the ship shudder as the seas lifted her, and your stomach fell away from you as they let her fall. That rise and fall kept running through my belly as I stood, wide-legged and hunch-shouldered behind the wind guard, looking, between sprays, at the ocean with the short, double-barreled black binoculars that curved tightly into my right hand and hugged the nose bridge between my eyes.

"Son of a bitch." Wilson, the signalman, standing behind me, had just misjudged a spray and taken it in the face. He rubbed his face, pink and dripping water, with his left arm in the blue winter jacket, like a small boy wiping his nose with his sleeve.

"Remember to duck." I turned, saying it, and felt through the oilskin cover and sheepskin lining of the coat the lancing chill of the spray as it hit my back.

I was, for the thousandth time, grateful for and ashamed of the coat. The signalman did not have a coat. Only officers had the coat. Now the sprays had soaked its fur collar through, and the collar was cold and wet against the back of my neck and the line of my jaw. Feeling had left my face where it rubbed against the cold, wet collar. Feeling was almost gone, too, from my hands inside the wet, black wool mittens, and from my feet in the wool socks and the heavy, shin-high black overshoes. The cold had driven it from all those places. Water ran down the sleeves of the green coat and kept the black mittens steadily and completely wet. The shoes and the thick, blue, waterproof-but-not-quite-waterproof pants that tucked inside the shoes were protected from the sprays by the wind guard and were still dry.

From the bridge I looked back to the galley deckhouse, at the guns there and the men on the guns.

"Look at Lockridge," said Wilson, flattening himself backwards against the wall of the wheelhouse to avoid a spray. "He's getting it."

Lockridge, the gunner on the Number Two twenty-millimeter on the edge of the deckhouse and in the line of the spray, was strapped to the shoulder rests of the gun and could not duck. The sprays lashed over the side of the deckhouse to hit his face under the round helmet every time the ship plunged, and I could see his chin quiver below the helmet and knew his teeth were clicking. He pulled a white handkerchief from under his life jacket and wiped the water from his face, that had the hamburger red of a man who is very cold. How cold did a man have to get before his face turned blue, I wondered.

We still had not seen a blue face. Maybe we would, though, maybe if this lasted long enough.

"That poor son of a bitch," said Wilson from the wall.

"It's a tough war."

Lockridge was the only man at the guns the sprays pelted. On the other, the starboard, side, flying back before the wind, the sprays curved impotently out and away from the ship inches from the opposite machine gun. The bigger, three-inch guns were, on both sides, set behind and further back from the edges than the twenty-millimeters, and were safe from the spray. In the saddle seats beside the long, gray barrels, pointing like twin phalli from the ship, men crouched over round wheels with their hands on the handles, ready to swing the guns wherever they had to go. They looked like roundheaded, blue-legged hunchbacks in the gray life jackets that swaddled them from their helmets to their waists. The loaders were sitting on the deck, three in a line between each open gun breech and the short, steel ammunition lockers opened to expose the brass bases of the three-inch shell cases. They were in position to service the guns and were out of the wind, too. It was a small favor, but to be thankful for.

The captain was back on the port wing. He stood, his left hand on the wind guard, and stared, as though really not seeing them, at the white splotches on the waves. His body swayed, like a tall pendulum, with the *Dee's* roll. The sprays struck him, like Lockridge, as they whipped over the wind guard, but except for a quick roll of his head that pulled his face out of the way, he ignored them. His face was tired and older than it had been that last night in Norfolk when he walked over the gangway to his waiting rendezvous. If you had dropped suddenly out of the sky to the bridge, you would have known him at once as the captain. Even in the blue pants, the green coat, and the round helmet that swallowed all identity.

He turned to his talker, who, trailing the telephone line behind him, followed the captain around the bridge. He said, "Secure from general quarters."

The talker pressed the button to his strap-suspended mouthpiece and repeated the order, and, from the bridge, I could see the soundless moving of the lips of the talkers at the guns, their voices gone in the wind, as they heard it and passed it to their gun crews.

On the guns, the pointers and trainers slid from the seats, the loaders rose stiffly from the deck, Lockridge exhaustedly unfastened the canvas belt that bound him to the machine gun and the sprays, and they all slung off the rusted blue hel-

mets and writhed out of the life jackets that had swollen
them as with pregnancy; then they put each of these carefully and automatically in steel racks by the guns, and filed one
at a time down the steel ladder that led from the deckhouse
to the main deck below. The ship had gone out of Condition
One, her battle disposition. The crew was no longer at general quarters.

I unstrapped the canvas chin strap of my helmet and took it
off. My head felt light and freed from the weight. I bent to
stack the helmet on top of two others in the rack built against
the wind guard.

"There are the other ships, cap'n," Wilson said, crouched
to look with one eye through the long glass that he held on
the wind guard. "Bearing about three-four-five relative. Down
over the horizon."

I put the helmet in the rack and straightened. Wilson, now
upright and looking back at the captain, was pointing with
his right arm a little left of just ahead.

I looked with my binoculars the way he pointed. In the
circle of the glasses, I saw three masts, sticking like matches
above the horizon, one taller and thicker than the other two.
They were our friends.

"Head over and rejoin them," Buchan said to me. "Call me
when we're back where we belong."

"Aye, aye, sir."

The captain walked away. The thick soles of his overshoes
shuffled softly across the deck as he walked from the port
wing to the other side of the bridge, and the steel ladder
clanged dully as he stepped down its rungs to the main deck
and his cabin below.

Wilson was out of the wind against the wheelhouse again.

"Nothing. Nothing again," he said. "No submarine, no nothing."

"No nothing."

That was it. No nothing. In the month of the hunt, we had
lived so completely with futility that it was part of us. We had
never seen what we hunted. Nor even, with sureness, touched
Them. We had failed again. If what we chased had been one
in the first place. That we never knew, and did not know today. This of today was concluded and no longer important,
with no more significance than the failures that had been before
and those that would come after. It was another empty pursuit
in a long succession of empty pursuits, and the book was
closed on it. We would start looking again.

Standing on the wing, outside the half-open door of the
sound shack, I listened to all the *Dee* had to hunt with: the

pings, each four seconds after the one before, in the remorseless monotony of their pulsation through the thick darkness of the undersea.

"We ought to be back with the others in about half an hour. You figure that?" said Wilson.

"About that."

Then, over the throb of the pings, something hummed from far off, and about three miles ahead a plane punched out of the low, thick cloud cover to silhouette black, big-bellied and slim-tailed against the gray sky as it began to curve in a wide circle around the ship.

"You'd think they'd get tired up there." Wilson looked up at the plane. "Whistling ass around in circles just looking at water, all cramped up in that little cockpit four hours at a time. I'd sure get tired."

"They get tired."

"You know what, Mr. Taylor?"

"What?"

"I'm tired down here."

"It's a tough war."

I made a noise that was intended to be a laugh, and looked up at the plane and at the masts beyond the horizon. Here, I thought, it is: the planes in the sky, the ships on the surface of the sea, and the pings under it, a trident in three dimensions. That was our hunt and our war. In this war, you never saw the Enemy, hiding in the unseen dimension where only the pings could find him. But He saw you. You could be very sure He saw you. It was a strange war that seemed without beginning and without end. You felt it had been forever since that day we started it.

Rockford appeared and relieved me. I took off the binoculars, wrapped the leather thong carefully around the center strip, put them in the green, felt-padded steel box, also welded to the wind guard, closed the box top, and walked back of the wheelhouse to the ladder. All the way down the ladder, I heard the ping.

23

It was the afternoon of a day, which one I did not know, for in the weeks since Norfolk I had stopped counting, of the hunt. I sat with Johnny, Arbry, and Crandall at the wardroom table drinking coffee. I felt my center of gravity shift in the chair with the eternal up-and-down, side-to-side surging of the

ship, and held my feet flat and wide apart on the deck so a
roll harder than the rest, that I had not seen coming, would
not spill me out of my seat when it leaned the *Dee* almost to
the horizontal in that irrevocable slow-death sweep that
seemed never to have a stop.

The door opened. Rocky walked in. He slammed the door
behind him.

"Goddamnit." He dropped into a chair, jerked his green-
banded cap from his head, and slammed it on the table. "Goddamnit all."

Red streaks lined the whites of his eyes. There had been a
long general quarters right after his midwatch, and he had not
made it to bed until nearly dawn. Then he had had to get up
less than two hours later to start some work on the decks.

He glowered at all of us. "What lousy duty. What lousy
Goddamned crudding rutting fogging no-good duty."

"What's chewing you?" Arbry raised his eyebrows.

"I wish I could sit some place besides this stinking wardroom. I wish I could talk to somebody besides you simple-
minded cretins. The same place, the same crap, you same bastards, day after day, and I'm sick of all of it."

"It's a tough war," I said.

"I'm tired. I'm tired of sleeping half awake because general
quarters might go and I'm tired of some son of a bitch waking
me in the middle of the night to tell me it's time to relieve
the watch and I'm tired of eating dung for food. I'm tired of
this whole mess."

"No doubt about it, it's a tough war."

"Yeah, you sure got it tough." Arbry mocked him.

It left him as quickly as it had come. He laughed and
called us cretins and said what lousy duty again and that was
all of it.

"You know you love this duty."

"Oh, how I love this duty." He meant his voice to be heavy
with irony.

Rocky was an explosive mechanism. He was set on a hair
trigger and you never knew when something might pull it. He
attracted or repelled instantly, and there was seldom a middle
ground. Some of the officers disliked him and some of the men
hated him, but there were others who would do anything for
him. I was for him.

He grinned. When he grinned he would make you forget
anything. He could be cruel and he could hurt but when he
grinned you forgot all that. He knew this and used it. His
face was nearly ugly, but recklessness and a mock arrogance
had stamped it into an attractive pattern. Women liked it.

There was something inside him that would never be satisfied and that would always keep him on the move, and that, too, showed, and they liked that.

"This is wonderful duty, all right." He grinned again, picked up his cap and twirled it on his hand, glancing at the tarnished green band that he was proud of.

"Did you ever hear the Arabian proverb," asked Arbry, teasing, "that paradise lies in the shadow of the sword?"

"I saw that movie, too."

"I wonder how much longer that bloodhound on the carrier is going to keep us at sea." Arbry set the cup back into the saucer. "It's time to go in for awhile."

"Frankly, I don't think he knows himself." Crandall pursed his lips and made his face pontifical. He was handing down a judgment. "Frankly, I don't think he has any idea. Quite frankly, I don't think he has the ability of a five-thousand-a-year executive." The last was his favorite opprobrium.

"But you have, haven't you, Crandall?" Rocky was being cruel now. "You were a really high-powered executive, weren't you, Crandall?"

"I was accustomed to responsibilities," Crandall said stiffly.

"So we've understood." Rocky looked at him.

Crandall did not say anything. His face went, almost imperceptibly, whiter, and he reached for his coffee cup. I felt an unflattering pity for him.

Johnny changed the subject, and a few minutes later Candall excused himself.

"I wish he hadn't left," Rocky looked at the door as it closed behind him. "I wish he had stayed. Maybe we could have heard about the factory he used to run in Peoria. Maybe we could have heard how he handled men. I love to hear how he handled men."

"Why don't you try not to be such a bastard?" Johnny was amused. He pretended to disapprove; actually he liked to watch Rocky.

"I'm a congenital bastard and screw you. Oh, I don't suppose he's his fault. They should have sent him to a battleship where he could lose himself. They should never send a lieutenant without sea time to a destroyer."

"He won't be around much longer."

"Not after this trip, I bet," Johnny said. "If it's ever over."

"It hasn't even got started good."

"These chart concentrations have just been a crock of it." Rocky leaned forward in his chair. "We didn't even get water noises in the last area. When do we hit the next one?"

"Couple of days."

Rocky stood up, walked to the gray cabinet that held the silver, and pulled two decks of cards from the top drawer. He sat down and shuffled them. They whirred in his hands. I liked to watch him. He did it like a professional.

"How about a little bridge?" He looked around, chipper and cocky again. "It's after four. Not even the Great White Father could mind."

We played. It was warm and pleasant in the wardroom and I tried not to think of how it would be on the bridge.

We played on until the mechanical voice from the round, gray loudspeaker box above the door intoned, "Darken ship, smoking lamp is out on all weather decks," and Peters leaning stiffly over the transom against each bulkhead, pulled down the steel shutters which fitted over the glass ports, and fastened, then tightened the bolts that held them in place until no light could show through to whatever might be watching outside. We kept playing until he stepped from the pantry in the white jacket with a white tablecloth under his arm and hovered, reproachfully, near the table.

Then Arbry, raking in the last trick and scooping it up with the others stacked in line before him, said, "Bid four, made four. And I guess we better get out before we alienate the staff."

We stood. Rocky picked up the two decks, rapped the sides of each against the table, and walked to the cabinet to put them in the top drawer, the catch clicking as he pushed it shut.

I went into my room, washed my hands and face, and sat in the swivel chair at the desk to look at the pictures in the latest *Life* we had, which was a month old. I put my left leg on the pulled-out, rubber-covered desk top, and held my right hand on the other side of the top to keep a balance, then turned the pages with the other hand, and read, half interested, the printing between, until Jason opened the door, stuck his head into the room, said, "Dinnerservedsir," and pulled it back out again. I shoved the magazine back on the desk, slung my leg off it. got up, and went into the wardroom. Only Anson and the doctor were there, sitting on the starboard transom and talking.

"Do you always get what you want?" the doctor was asking, derisively, as I sat on the other side of Anson. Neither looked at me.

"Yes." Anson was serious. "I've always had exactly what I wanted. I must confess it's spoiled me completely."

Looking at him, at the smooth, mature, unworried face, smelling only faintly of a decorous shave lotion, above the fresh khaki shirt with a single silver JG's bar on each collar flap, I had no trouble, no trouble at all, in believing him. I had seen few things balk him. Only, in fact, women, a situation which, when occurring, caused him more annoyance than frustration.

Anson had a face that you were always sure you had seen somewhere before but could never tie to a place and time. His unobtrusive good looks would have been equally well set against the backdrop of the Yale Club, a Long Island North Shore houseparty, or the oil-streaked bulkheads of a destroyer's engine room, and, in all of those places, he was equally secure. By having given himself completely and long ago to orthodoxy, he seemed older than twenty-six, and had a quality that placed him instantly on an equal footing with the oldest and most conservative member of whatever gathering he was in. As a result, he was group leader without portfolio and heir apparent to the executive officer, a position from which Arbry, who was senior and regular Navy, had excluded himself by his pronounced individuality. In any discussion of ship's politics, somebody always said, "Annie will get this command before the war is over," and, although he was only a JG, that was something else I had no trouble believing.

He turned from the doctor to me.

"I see we hit the next concentration tonight. You might have some fun on the midwatch."

"You can forget about that. I know all about those concentrations now. They got a staff officer in Washington that makes them up. He just sits back in his chair and looks at his nice big map on the wall and says, 'How can we keep those bastards chasing their tail a little longer?' and he comes up with the sub reports. Then he makes the X's on the map and sits back on his derriere and laughs his head off. That's where we get our concentrations."

"You might get fooled, bucko. You might get well fooled."

"Not tonight, I won't."

"Why not tonight?"

"I just won't, that's all."

"You will some night."

"Some night ain't tonight. I promise, I won't break you out tonight, not even for one small general quarters."

"See that you don't."

The other officers came in, one by one, and after them, the captain. We stood, he sat, and the rest of us took our places. The captain seemed in good spirits; at sea, he was unfailingly, perhaps calculatedly, good humored at meal times, whatever the operation.

He started it.

"Still with us, Flattop? I thought you might have committed suicide by this time, you've been away from it so long."

"I've given that up, cap'n. I'm going into a monastery when we get back."

"You mean a nunnery," Arbry said.

The captain laughed hard. "He'd last one week in a nunnery."

"Bet you on that," Flattop said.

"He'd have a thousand kids in a year in a nunnery."

"No," said the doctor. "In one year in a nunnery the Flattop would account for exactly three hundred and sixty-five offspring. Counting conceptions. No more, no less."

The conversation was in the old reliable channels. They had told us as midshipmen that women and politics were never discussed at mess. I tried to imagine a meal without them. After dinner, which was beef stew, tasting too heavily of flour, and rice, and dessert, which was two canned pear halves, I went to the room and finished *Life*. Jerry climbed into the top bunk while I was reading.

"Turn off the light when you finish," he said pointedly.

"Go to hell."

When I turned it off and, in my long underwear, pulled the sheet up, my watch showed five minutes of eight.

Three and a half hours later, the opening of the door, the flashlight in the face, and the softly implacable, "Time to relieve the watch," awoke me. I lay there, loathing the Navy, the sea, and the *Dee* for five minutes, kicked the hump Jerry made in the mattress, and got up.

"Get out of there." I turned on the light.

"Oh, Christ, what a hell of a way to live." Then he got up.

On the bridge, after coffee, I felt better; once up, even the midwatch was bearable. In the chartroom, with the red-covered flashlight, I read the captain's night order book, initialed the page, and walked to the port wing. I stopped in the dark behind the bulking outline of Johnny's back.

"What's the dope?"

He turned around. "As in the book. Hurry up and see these damned things. I want to hit my sack."

Since a half-moon hung under the clouds, it did not take my eyes long to adapt to the dark. He was still grumbling when he went below.

I took the conn myself. The carrier was docile, and I kept station with small course and speed changes, ordering the zig-zag turns as I watched the car and my watch with the red-lensed flashlight. It looked like a good four hours.

Only Clay, the boatswain's mate of the watch, was on the port wing with me. He moved up and stood behind me in the dark.

"How'd you like to be in New York tonight, Mr. Taylor?" he said without preliminary.

"How do you think I'd like it?"

"Wouldn't you like to be walking down Fifty-Second Street with some quiff on your arm, all lined up, though? You ain't married, are you, Mr. Taylor?"

"Not me. A long way from it. You married?"

"No, sir. Be a hell of a thing to be married with this war on, wouldn't it?"

"Why?"

"I been shacked with too many women that had husbands gone. When I get married I want to keep my eye on the gear."

"You probably got something."

"Yeah, I want it to be where I can keep my eye on it."

"You'll never go wrong that way. How's about inspecting the ship?"

"Aye, aye, sir."

Clay was a real sailor. You could talk to him. He knew when you stopped being an officer and were a man. He also knew when you started being an officer again.

"I'll get some joe while I'm down," he said, and went into the pilot house for the coffeepot. I could hear the ladle rattling in the pot as he walked down the ladder on the other side.

I was alone on the port wing with time to think, about the war, about the operation, about what was coming. Up to now, the *Dee's* war had been a very satisfactory war. It was a small, clean corner, related only by death and logistics to the sweating, stinking, excrement-smeared mess that was the rest of it. For us in our corner, the war was a way of life. You went out and you came back to the cream of everything or you did not come back at all, and neither way did you lose too much. It was the best way to live I had ever known or ever would know, and in moments of rare clarity I was aware of it. If it was the war, it was all right with me.

But this time I felt we would have to pay our dues to the club. I only wondered when the showdown would come. Because it would come sometime. It had to come. We had covered a real part of the world looking for it and it could not be postponed forever. It might be delayed but it could not be written off. There had to be a pay-off. So far there had been only a groping and brushing in the dark. But the pay-off would come. I only wondered when.

Nothing came that night. I had been right at dinner. We did not even pick up a water noise, although on the chart we were jammed neatly in a cluster of X's.

We kept steaming—and hunting. It was like no other hunt-
ing could ever be. Hunting without a spoor, hunting a quarry
you did not and would not see, hunting game that was as clev-
er, and as dangerous, as the hunters. They say the hunting of
man is the ultimate hunting, but we were hunting man. We did
not think of the submarines as man. They were an abstraction.
We thought and spoke of Them only as They, or Them, or One.

They were the Enemy, stripped of all humanity and cast into
long black shapes that were a physical symbol of death, carry-
ing within them only death, as they cut silently through the
silent, cold darkness of the under-ocean.

To find and destroy this Enemy was what we had to do.

And we hunted without a lure and without a bait.

No, not without bait. There was a bait.

We were the bait.

You would wake in the night and know that you were your
own bait and wonder when They would take it. You did not
know. You could only wait.

We waited.

24

THAT DECEMBER we hunted through many gales, and each was
like the one before and the one after. The gales brought high
seas that twisted and tossed the *Dee* and pounded unendingly
against the thin steel plates of her hull, hard hail pellets that
the howling wind blasted at you like shot from the gray sky,
freezing sprays that you could not always miss streaking
straight for the bridge, and the sorrowing whine of the wind in
the signal halyards that you knew, someday, would be all
of the gale you would remember.

In the gales, you did not want to go on the bridge, but once
there, you did not mind. You looked out at the gray world that
was the same everywhere: the white curlers on the mountainous
gray swells, the gray clouds a solid cover on the gray sky,
the other ships, almost black in the light, rearing and plunging
with the sea, and you flowed into the rhythm of the heaving
deck, the wind and sometimes the hail stung your face as you
dodged the flying sprays, and for a little while you became part
of it all.

But before the watch was over, you did not care about
being a part of it, but only wanted to escape from the wind
and the sprays and rub life into your face and your feet and
scald your guts alive with something wet and hot. Then you

were convinced that the storms were not dramatic but were only painful.

This day, we were hunting in a gale, more than fifteen hundred miles east of Labrador and six hundred south of Iceland. It was too rough to sit in the wardroom and work, so I lay on my back on my bunk in the room, watching the light over the desk throw shadows from the chair and the lavatory against the wall and looking at the blue winter clothes on the hooks opposite the bunk swing from side to side with the roll of the ship. My watch said three-twenty-five. I would have to get up, put on the clothes, and go to the bridge. I gave myself five more minutes in bed.

Then I decided not to use the five minutes, but swung my legs from the bunk and stood up, washed my face, worked into the clothes, and, carrying the big coat, went into the wardroom for coffee. I was hot inside the black turtle-neck sweater and the blue jacket over it. That would not last long, though, not on the open bridge. The coffee was weak, with the aged taste.

The doctor was on his back on the transom three feet from the hot plate. He twisted his head and looked at me with one open eye.

"Got the watch?"

"Yeah."

"Have fun then."

He turned his head back and put his right arm over his eyes. He said nothing else, and I walked out of the door.

On the well deck, on my way to the bridge, I tripped and nearly fell over two legs in the blue cloth that appeared suddenly between the hatch from below and the ladder to the bridge. They belonged to an apprentice seaman named Kerrigan, whose back was propped against the bulkhead, with his head thrown back, his hands across his stomach, his mouth making clear and articulate moans. This was his first cruise. As I listened to the sounds, I wondered if he had ever shaved. I did not hold the moans against him, for I knew they gave him a kind of relief. While I watched, he rose to his knees, crawled on them to the two-foot steel strip at the side, leaned over it, and vomited.

He finished and wiped his mouth with his sleeve, then looked at me, his face thin and white in the blue cloth headpiece, and tried to grin. He felt better now, and would for awhile.

"You eating anything?" I tried not to show sympathy.

"No, sir, I can't eat nothing. Everything I swallow comes right back up."

"Christ, you can't stop eating. Get some soda crackers. You can hold them."

"No, sir, I just can't eat nothing."

"You've got to have something to throw. Those dry heaves will kill you. Get some crackers. Tell Whitey I said to give you a box of crackers. Right now. That's an order."

He twisted, hip-first and his left hand pushing from the deck, to his feet, and lurched toward the passageway to the galley. A roll threw him against Number One stack, rising from the center of the well deck between the bridge and the galley deckhouse. I watched his back, weaving like a drunk's, vanish into the passageway at the right of the deckhouse. Then I climbed the ladder to the bridge.

Johnny stood close to the side of the wheelhouse on the port wing, looking at the sea roll at the *Dee*. He did not look away when I greeted him, but kept staring at the bow as it sliced under the surface to take water over the forecastle deck, the water turning from gray to white-rivered green as it swirled over, then rushing fast down the deck as the ship reared to spill over the sides and back into the sea. The sea and the wind came from about ten degrees on the starboard bow, and the sprays curved clear and away from the port wing.

"Dig, you bitch, dig," Johnny dared, watching. "This God-damned sea. Look what it does to us. Look at it throw twelve hundred tons of steel around like a bar of soap. You go up, you go down, you go down, you go up. Just like a bar of soap. This sea is powerful stuff. You can't beat it. You ever think about that? You can't beat it."

Power was something he respected, and he respected the power of the sea. I did not think he feared it because I did not think he feared anything except in a temporary, biological, wholesome kind of prudence, but the sea he admired and respected.

"You want to stay up and think about it for another four hours? I'll be glad to oblige. I'll just go below and leave you up here and you can think about it some more. I won't mind. I'll go right back down."

"Yes, you will. Come here and get the dope."

He gave it to me, I said, "I relieve you," and he went below.

I gave Jerry the conn, and he gave the helmsman the courses in the zigzag plan and kept the *Dee* on station with the carrier.

The ship rolled hard to starboard. Something banged on the well deck. I ran to the ladder and looked down. A cleaning-gear locker, a steel box four feet high and three feet across that had been welded on four thin legs to the deck, was lying on its side against the two-foot safety strip at the edge of the deck.

"That roll tore it right out of the deck," Carter said, behind me. He repeated, with relish, "Right out of the deck."

"Get Jake Warwick on it."

The ship rolled steeply to port, and the locker slid, in a flesh-crawling rasp against the steel of the deck, to a stop against Number One stack.

"Hurry."

Carter was starting down the ladder when Jake burst out of the hatch to the well deck from the living quarters below, a coiled piece of brown one-inch line in his right hand and two seamen behind him. The ship rolled, moderately this time, to starboard, and the locker slid away from the stack a few inches, and then, as the roll back followed, moved against the stack again. Jake, stepping behind his pot belly with unbeliev-able speed, whipped the line three times around the locker, grabbed the ends of the line, slung them around a piece of steel tubing circling the stack, and, jerking the line tight, tied the ends together. The locker did not move as the ship canted to starboard again.

Jake stepped back from the stack and looked critically at the locker and the line as the ship made two full rolls, then turned and climbed, swinging the belly before him, the ladder to me, standing at the head of it on the starboard wing.

"All secured now, sir." He breathed heavily.

"That was fast."

"I heard the son of a bitch go." He grinned.

"It sure went." That was all there was to say. He had known what happened before he saw it, and had done what he had to do before I could send for him.

"Those babies really make a noise when they go. I'd know that damned scraunch anywhere." He was breathing easier. "We'll weld her back when we get a smooth day. Couldn't do it now."

"Not by a damned sight. Think it'll hold the way you got it, Jake?"

"Yes, sir. It'll hold with that line we got on now."

"Fine." I looked at him, standing there in the khaki pants and the chief's cap and the blue jacket tight across his belly, and wondered who said, "No man is perfect." He did not know Jake Warwick. Because Jake was perfect. He was, completely and finally, everything that a chief boatswain's mate could be or could ever hope to be, and he was nothing else.

With most men in service there is at least a hint of what they were or what they might become in the world they call "the outside." With Jake there was none. You could not separate him from the Navy, because the Navy was what he was. He might have stepped full-blown, with his chief's hat set squarely on his head and his pot belly thrusting out in heavy dignity,

from a big wave that broke across some unsuspecting forecastle. He had been a boatswain's mate in the old destroyer
fleet before the *Dee's* keel was laid and before I was born. Another year, and he would have thirty years in, and would, as
soon as the war was over, retire on three-quarters pay.

In the first war, Jake had been welterweight champion of the
Asiatic squadron, and it still showed in the way he handled
himself, in the way he sped over decks and under lines, through
hatches and up ladders, always swinging the belly before him
with a dancer's grace. The belly was the only place he had become fat.

Now, standing on the bridge, he said to me, "It's a rough
day. I hope nothing else don't carry away. These farmers I
got for sailors now." That was the worst thing he knew how to
say, and, saying it, he shook his head.

"Oh, they'll come around." Jake would bring them around.
He had brought God knows how many men, and officers,
around before. He had taught all of us in the wardroom much
of whatever we knew; he had a tolerant affection for ensigns,
and made them aware, without ever transgressing the barrier
of military courtesy, of just how far they had to go before a
chief boatswain's mate could afford to take them seriously. He
took unsparing pains with their education, and upheld with
the men their new and sometimes uncomfortable authority.

"I guess they will. They'll have to. I'll get 'em there somehow." He sighed and shook his head again. "Those farmers."
Then, briskly, "Will that be all, sir?"

I nodded, and he clattered down the ladder to the well deck,
where a small knot of men had gathered to look at the locker.
His voice came up loud and strong to the bridge.

"I'd like to borrow a knife. Is there a sailor in the house?"

I laughed, and returned to the other side where I could see
the carrier and the other destroyers, bobbing up and down in
the sea, plodding onward, hunting. The sound of the pings
came clear and even through the open door of the shack.

*We were weary with hunting. Every day was cut from the
same gray bolt of monotony as the last. We searched, and
searched, and searched, and we found nothing. Sometimes the
pings found contacts and we chased them, but in the end the
contacts simply vanished or turned out to be fish. In the end
there was nothing. It was that way for both the ships and the
planes. We never really touched Them. It was a pursuit of
wraiths, and you began to doubt, in a little closet that you kept
locked even from yourself, that They existed. They were an*

allegory, a fable, They were a composite Evil One in a witch doctor's fantasy, and you would never really see Them.

The days ground you with dull and unvarying cruelty. The watches on the bridge struck as inexorably as the bells of a clock. Half your life you spent on the bridge; no night passed but that the hard hand on your shoulder and the malevolent light in your face jerked you from sleep made troubled and uneasy by the tossing of that steel shell that encased you and with whose destiny yours was so irrevocably welded. And the clanging call of the general alarm rasped you to battle stations, night and day, from sleep and from meals, always with the same emptyhandedness of failure in the end.

In all of this there were the cold and the weariness and the frustration and the seasickness. Those who had the last, for many days and without surcease, wished sincerely and with reason that they were dead. One of these one day slashed his wrist with a double-edged razor blade as he sat in the crew's head, with the sea water that splashed on the fantail and ran through the door to the head swirling around his feet. But he was not quite sincere enough, for the bleeding was stopped and he was in two days on watch and retching over the side as before, until one day he stopped being sick and was never sick again.

Through every day and night the pings kept searching. And every day not irretrievably sacrificed to the weather, the planes went up.

25

THIS DAY appeared to be one of those sacrificed. We had been running south of Greenland in the fringes of a gale for three days, and on each of them the planes had gone up, but today the gale had overtaken and struck us with full sixty-knot force. The wind screamed overhead, and dove over the wind guard of the port wing to bite and tear at my face and whip tears from my eyes. I tried to turn and shelter myself behind the fur collar of the coat, but the wind still found me.

Below, the wind ruffled the sea into long lines of white marking the crest of the swells, and the swells, which had been slow to follow the wind, were now deep and angry, worse, even, since daylight, four hours before. They ran before the wind with regular, booming violence, making rolling gray hills and valleys as they swept on.

I looked toward the ships to the left of the *Dee*: the carrier behind, the *Hilliard* screening on the opposite side, and the *Donahue* ahead.

The carrier rode the seas like a seesaw, the stern angling downward and the bow pointing halfway to the sky, then the stern rising and the bow falling until they had completely reversed positions. The destroyers took the swells like steeplechasers. The *Donahue* reared from the water as though to leap over the gray mountain that moved upon her, showing her naked, normally invisible, red underbody, almost to the keel at her ultimate bottom, the keel itself almost breaking above the sea. The next instant she dropped into the trough behind the swell to expose only the tops of her four stacks. Far to the left, on the other side of the formation, the *Hilliard* showed only when the swells lifted her to their peaks.

It was a bad day for planes. To me, it looked like an impossible day for planes.

"It's too rough even for that bastard." Carter, standing near me on the wing and speaking of the carrier's captain, was obviously thinking what I was thinking.

"It's too rough to land the planes. He could get them up, easy, but he'd never get them down."

"I'll bet that kills him, too."

"He's out here for business."

"Balls. He's out here for some more medals and headlines."

"That's not it. He wants to get Them. He has to get Them."

"He doesn't have to go up. All he has to do is stand on that fancy bridge and watch somebody else go up. And stick his mouth into that radio phone and give orders. He doesn't have to go up. And he doesn't have to ride destroyers, either."

"He's got enough to worry about."

"Maybe." Carter grunted. He put his glasses to his eyes and studied the carrier. "I'll be Goddamned."

"What?"

"They're moving the planes up." His voice was awed and unbelieving.

I lifted my glasses. He was right. Four planes, wings still folded, now ranged one behind the other from the forward edge of the flight deck.

"So it's not too rough after all."

"It's slaughter." Carter let his glasses down. "I don't see how he can send the planes up in this. What can he make?"

I did not know, either, but I said, "Maybe he figures They'll think the same way. Maybe he figures he can catch Them out today."

He was, beyond all doubt, going to send his planes up. The TBS was rumbling with the anticipatory noises that went before a broadcast, and then the big voice spoke the orders for the flight operations out of the steel box on the wall. I reported to the captain through the voice tube.

"Go to station at eight knots," his voice came back through the tube.

The *Dee,* on the right bow of the carrier, had to ease back slightly to take proper station on the carrier as she came ten degrees to the right to head into the wind. The *Hilliard,* on the other side, came sharply right and charged for the stern of the carrier, where, five hundred yards behind it, she would take the plane guard position. The *Donahue* was almost where she belonged.

The carrier did not wait for either ship to get there, but came about quickly to starboard and started kicking the planes into the north wind. The aircraft, looking small and forlorn from the *Dee's* bridge, breasted into the wind and climbed steeply over the formation, circled the ships once, as though for bravado, and fanned out on the patrol course. Only four were in the air, all TBF's, carrying depth bombs in their torpedo racks.

The carrier turned back to base course before the *Hilliard* ever reached her guard station to the rear, and, as she swung left, the destroyers went back to their former stations, the *Dee* moving ahead the five hundred yards she had to gain by increasing speed to twelve knots, two more than that of the carrier now.

From the aircraft radio came the strange, muted howl of the wind, all but engulfing the faint rasps that were the pilot's voices asking for courses, the jumble of wind, static, and words tumbling out in a shrieking cacophony.

The planes wheeled in their line of flight to circle and stay in sight, pinpointed in black against the gray cushion of the sky. They did not want to get too far from home.

From the bridge, I stood there and watched them, swaying with the jolting rhythm of the ship and one hand bracing on the wind guard, while the cold poured through the fortresses of clothing that had been thrown up to keep it out, through the sheepskin coat and the jungle-cloth jacket and trousers and the Red Cross-knitted turtle-neck sweater and the long, two-piece underwear that fitted like a fighter's tights under all the rest. The cold poured through these and went through you and there was nothing you could do about it.

I danced a heavy-footed clog, the big overshoes pum-pum-pumming against the deck, and swung my arms, feeling the weight of all the clothes against them, to work up heat. So did Carter. I wriggled my toes, hard, inside the shoes that were inside the overshoes, and tried to stir the blood in my feet. All of it helped. I decided all the men on the bridge needed something to burn their bellies.

"Tell the wardroom to send up some chocolate," I said to Carter. He went into the wheelhouse and called for it through the voice tube.

Ten minutes later, Peters, wearing only the white jacket and holding to his stomach with his left arm the tray with the silver pot and china cups, started up the ladder. From the space behind the wheelhouse, I watched him. He took only one step at a time, bringing both feet to the same rung before he advanced one of them to the next, holding tight to the rail at the side with his right hand. He stepped from the ladder to the bridge and started toward me. He set the tray on the flag bag, picked up a cup, and started to pour the chocolate. Inside the white jacket, both his arms shook and the cup rattled in the saucer.

"For Christ sake, Petey, put it down and go below. You want to freeze?"

"No, sir!" His chattering teeth were white against the brown of his face. He set the pot back on the tray and fled from the bridge.

I poured a cup for myself and a cup for Carter, who was now conning the ship, and took it to him. He gulped the chocolate inside. Some of it sloshed out and spilled on the deck as the ship dived. I held to the wind guard to drink.

"Hot and sweet." He lowered his cup, still holding the handle between thumb and forefinger. The chocolate had left a brown smear on his upper lip. "That's the way I like my chocolate and my women. Hot and sweet."

I looked at him: a shapeless, bear-wide mass in the winter clothes and a round, young, unrememberable face under the long-eared blue helmet. If there was ever an average, I thought, Carter was it. If all the reserve ensigns in the United States Navy were melted down and poured into one mold, the product would look amazingly like Melvin Carter, Ensign, USNR. High school in Cleveland, Ohio, sloppy clothes, fumbling initial attempts at drinking and love-making. Four years at Ohio State, more fashionably sloppy clothes, more adolescence, and only slightly less clumsy attempts at drinking and love-making. Straight from the university into the Navy, through indoctrination and midshipmen's school at Northwestern, to assignment on the *Dee*. There what he considered an upper-level, graduate seminar in drinking and love-making until he reached the limits of limited talents in both fields. He liked to say he was "sort of" engaged to a "girl back home."

That was Carter, who not only spoke in clichés but thought in them. He was Young America, in capitals, without identity and without individuality.

Now he licked the chocolate from his lips and said again, "I like 'em both the same way, hot and sweet, women and chocolate."

"You'll get along with chocolate for a while, friend." I poured a second cup and drank it. It was wonderfully hot. "Pass the pot around."

Carter took it into the wheelhouse. It was taboo for the men to drink from wardroom cups, but we were not concerned with protocol this December.

The chocolate felt warm and liquid in my stomach. Feeling good from the chocolate, I watched the specks that were the planes as they flitted, low and ever searching, against the pattern of the sky.

They never disappeared, but stayed in sight, on the rim of visibility, circling. And looking. And maybe wondering if they would make it home. It was a bad day to be up. The fliers undoubtedly thought it was a bad day to be down, in this sea on an old destroyer. It was. It was a bad day to be anywhere.

Then the big voice on the radio called them back. He was cutting the patrol short, landing them early because they might need all the extra time they could get. The planes converged from four directions and fell into a disciplined column astern of the carrier.

"They earn that flight pay here," Carter looked at them, now tight together in a small circle.

"I hope they get to spend it."

The planes kept circling off the carrier, then a light flashed from her bridge, and the first started in. It turned toward the carrier and began its approach, low and straight, like a black arrow in slow motion aimed at the pitching stern, the end of the seesaw, swinging up and down, making a dipping barrier that the plane had to clear to drop to the sanctuary of the flight deck.

It was going to be hard. The seesaw was sharply up and down. The plane had to pass the stern on its down swing to land.

The aircraft approached the stern, slowed, and eased toward the deck. But the stern rose sharply to meet it, the figure with yellow paddles poised at the end of the deck, who was the flight officer, waved the paddles frantically, and the plane climbed steeply up with sudden speed and engine roar to fly away and fall back into the circle.

The second, coming in right behind the first, was not even

close. The stern rose as the plane was over it, and the pilot did not need the yellow paddles to wave him away. He had already started climbing.

"Jesus," said Carter.

"Yes," I said.

The third came in higher than the others, timed the seesaw perfectly, passed the stern just as the stern started down, quickly cut speed and dropped hard to the deck. It bounced along the deck, still running ahead; then its belly hook caught the arresting gear and it lurched to a quick halt. That was one down. Through the glasses you could see the plane crews hauling it away to clear the decks for the next.

The fourth missed badly. Then all three that were left missed again, twice. Each time it was the same. The carrier's stern swung up like a gun they could not pass, and they had to snarl away and try again.

"This could take some time," said Carter.

In thirty minutes, two, finally timing the swing of the stern, got down.

"One more." Carter held the binoculars on it, already climbing away from another failure, alone in the sky. As completely alone, I thought, as I had ever seen a thing, as alone as a thing could ever be. It circled and started its approach. There was an unsureness about it. You could feel it. Two miles away and knowing nothing of flying, you could still feel it.

The run was bad. The stern nearly smashed the plane coming in and it just got away.

"The poor son of a bitch," said Carter. "This is probably his first carrier duty."

"Some duty."

My hands were sweating inside the wool mittens. All the men on the bridge were on the port wing, watching, silent. On the deckhouse, the gun crews were on their feet at the side, intent and not talking, watching.

The plane did it all again and missed. It kept trying and used up another half-hour. Every time it was the same: the low approach, the stern rising implacably at the wrong instant, and the frantic getaway.

"He must be running low on gas," said Carter.

The carrier captain must have thought so, too. His voice, strong and deep, sounded on the aircraft frequency radio. You could hear him over it clearly; it was only the voices of the pilots, coming from aloft where the wind was a scream, that were hard to understand.

"Thirty-three McGuire," said the voice. All the planes were called by number plus the pilot's name. "This is Coach. Over."

In answer there was the crying of the wind and a jumble of words.

"This is Coach." The voice was trying to be reassuring. "Come in higher next time. Come in as slow as you can. Gun it up to pass the stern just as it starts down. Take it easy. You can do it. Good luck. Out."

The wind and the static-drowned words acknowledged.

The plane started this approach from far back, fatalistic beyond all doubt. It came in slow and straight at the carrier, came close, then gained speed for an instant and passed the stern as the stern started down, not perfect but good enough. Then it pancaked to the deck, missed the first arresting gear, and slid crazily along until the second caught and tripped it to a jerky stop.

It was down.

"Goddamnit." Carter breathed hard. "Goddamnit."

The sound operator called from the shack, "Did he make it?" and the telephone talker yelled back, "Yes."

The men in the gun crew on the deckhouse were laughing now and moving away from the side.

"Maybe he'll spend that flight pay after all," said Carter.

"Maybe." I did not have time to think about it, because the carrier had come to base course and the *Dee* had to move ahead to station.

I heard, all at once, the steady beating of the pings from the sound shack, and realized that, while the planes were getting down, I had not heard them. But the pings had not stopped; it was I that had stopped listening, and now I listened to nothing else. The pings kept beating. The pings never stopped.

The indistinguishable days wove with each other a bare gray fabric of cold, fatigue, and failure, with the pings running an unbreaking, maddening thread through it. Never faltering, never slowing, never stopping, the pings never let you forget the hunt. Nor what it was that you hunted.

They were the cord that held the spheres of the hunt together. They were the single, shadowy link between reality, the surface of the sea, and the unknown, the dark fluid world under it. Even the planes in the third dimension of the air were bound to the pings by the identity of their common quarry.

The pings were the "Dee's" life-beat, and both her arms and armour; with the pings, she hunted interminably through the bleak wasteland of the North Atlantic. But neither she nor the other hunters, even with the pings, could bring Them to bay.

26

THE TASK UNIT, beaten without a battle in the northernmost clusters, turned southward again, and hunted in a slow-advancing path through the eastern half of the North Atlantic. We followed a southwest course that led consecutively to a concentration north of the Azores, to the Azores themselves, and then to Casablanca, the watering place. But there was no urgency to reach any of these, and the ships cut away from the course to hunt points where, by the radio broadcasts from Washington, single submarines had been reported. We did not find any.

As we ran south, the killing edge of the cold dulled, and, while I wore no fewer clothes on the bridge, they now kept me warm where before they had kept me alive. Close to the Azores, we slipped out of the gales, and the wind and seas eased. Two days, even, we had a sun, and on one of these, it shone all day.

We steamed into the charted concentration above the Azores, hunted, fruitlessly, back and forth through the area delineated by the black X'es for one day and one night, and turned toward the Azores to fuel.

"What's the name of it again? The town."

I asked it of John Ewell as, at ten minutes of four in the afternoon of the fueling day, I relieved him of the watch on the port wing of the bridge.

The *Dee* was steaming alone toward the fueling port, whatever the name was, on one of the islands, the other two destroyers having gone into it earlier in the day, one at a time, taken their oil, and returned to screen the carrier, which had no necessity to take fuel or anything else and was standing off the islands, waiting. The *Dee* was last to be sent in, and had not left the formation until almost three o'clock, when the *Hilliard*, coming up fast behind her with new-filled tanks, blinked on the yellow signal lamp, "I relieve you." Now, as the *Dee* moved ahead alone, only the masts of the other ships, patrolling back and forth, showed over the stern in the gray afternoon light.

Ewell answered my question. "Horta. H-O-R-T-A."

"Never heard of it."

"Me, either. But that's where we're going."

"Okay. I relieve you." I saluted and he left the bridge. Ahead, the low black mass of our island rose out of the gray sea, while, far off and to each side of it, smaller dark humps, other fragments of the Azores, outlined on the horizon. The island ahead grew larger as the afternoon faded. Twilight came and was almost gone when the *Dee* passed on her left the sea buoy that marked the start of the channel to Horta, the buoy only an unwinking yellow light and tolling bell in the beginning night as she went by it into the channel. In the channel, the lights of other buoys, blinking red and green in the deepening darkness, led her straight into the harbor that opened suddenly in a three-quarter circle rimmed by the dark shore and the yellow lights of the town above it.

"So this is Horta." The captain, standing almost in the doorway from the wing to the wheelhouse, was part amused, part scornful, part something else.

"Ever been here before, Cap'n?"

"No." He was looking at the piers on the opposite side of the harbor, nearly a mile away, lighted by ships moored there.

"Wonder what kind of a town it is."

"Like any other town." He glanced at. me and laughed shortly. "You can find anything you want if you look hard enough." Then he looked back to the piers on the far shore. "See that tanker there? The one lighted up like a Christmas tree? That's where we're going. Have 'em rig portside to."

At first, the tanker was only a smear of light across the dark water. Then, as we came closer, heading at a thirty-degree angle toward the light, she came into sight, and I could, a little at a time, make out her features. Two hundred yards away, now sharp in the light that flooded her and glinted yellow off the black of the water, I saw her clearly, her stern pointing with the pier toward the open harbor and her bow toward the lights on the shore. She was like no other tanker I had ever seen. Her bow flared up and out like an ice breaker's, her stern was high, and there was a heaviness of construction about her that told of service in the North, the North of the Norwegian Sea and the Arctic Ocean.

The captain, leaning over the wind guard to watch the side of the tanker and calling his wheel and engine orders through the open door, eased the *Dee* tight against the other ship. English sailors on her decks made the mooring lines fast.

Buchan, about to leave the bridge, stopped and looked at the tanker. "You know about her? She's a prize ship the British got from the Germans. Used to be the Bismarck's private tanker. She fueled the Bismarck right before the British sunk her. That was the last time anybody fueled the Bismarck."

"I'll be damned." I wondered how he knew the story but did not ask. "How did the Limeys get her?"

"That part I forgot." He looked at her again, appraisingly, walked behind the wheelhouse to the ladder, and stepped down it.

I followed him. On the well deck, a dozen men were standing, leaning over the side rail to stare at the lights that were lancing the darkness with a thousand yellow points.

"Looks like good liberty over there," somebody said.

"Any liberty is good liberty."

"Well you ain't going to get any liberty."

They stopped talking, and I could feel them thinking. Here it is, the lights were urging. Here is liquor, here are women, here is warmth and good cheer, and a respite from hunting. Come and get it.

Well, they could not come and get it, and neither could I, because as soon as the tanks were full, the *Dee* was going back to sea, back to the task unit waiting impatiently in the gloom off the island for her to return and get about business. Nobody was going to get anything.

They knew that. They knew it, and it made the lights they would not meet more beckoning, the liquor they would not drink hotter and stronger, and the women they would not sleep with more voluptuous and more passionate. Their guard was down. They did what they had to do and never cried out when there was no alternative, when there was nothing about them but the sky and the hunting. But when the choice appeared, when the sweets that were not part of their hard diet dangled, just out of reach, before them, they grew sick with hunger. And so they lined the rail and looked at lights on a shore they would not touch.

The last one, attempting comedy, repeated, "There ain't gonna be no liberty."

I left them, and went below to the wardroom and sat with the other officers to wait for dinner. Buchan entered, in the black turtle-neck sweater with the blue winter pants hooked over it. We stood, and sat at the table after him. The mess boys served the soup, a beef consommé. It was good to drink it again without keeping one hand on the bowl to balance it against the roll of the ship. The absence of motion had an enervating effect. The resolution and tension that made our standard protective mechanism ebbed away and left behind a kind of slackness. The captain was quiet, and did not want to talk. There were only the most desultory attempts at conversation.

After dinner, Farnsworth and I went back to the well deck. Two engineers were tending a fuel hose from the tanker, the hose lashed into place with its nozzle inside the manifold that opened to the forward tanks. The other men who had been there before were gone. But the lights on the beach were still there. We stood at the side, not talking, looking at the lights.

Rockford, coming out of the deckhouse passageway, jolted us out of it.

"Do you see this?" he brandished a half-full bottle of rum. "Those bastards."

"Where did you find it?"

"Aft. A dozen guys were drinking in the torpedo shack. They killed one quart before I caught them. This is the second bottle."

"Where did they get it?"

"From the British, I guess. Where else?"

"What are you going to do?"

"Don't talk like a fool. I'm not going to do anything."

"It's hard to blame them."

"Who said I blamed them? I just don't like 'em pulling that stuff on my watch." He drew his arm back and threw the bottle like a baseball, out from the ship into the darkness. I heard it plop in the water. He smiled. "I wish I was over there myself."

"Everything's over there."

"It doesn't help us."

"We'll be in Casablanca soon."

Hawley, the oil king, his face streaked with oil that showed grotesquely in the half-light on the deck, came out of the passageway to Rockford.

"All through, Mr. Rockford. Took seventy thousand gallons."

"Good. Log it and we'll get out of here."

Rockford went into the captain's cabin to report. A moment later, the loudspeaker commanded, "Set the special sea details." I went to the bridge. When the hoses had been returned to the tanker and all the stations reported ready to get underway, I told Buchan.

He acknowledged with a short nod, then, looking back at the stern, said, "Cast off the after lines."

The talker passed his order and the three mooring hawsers holding the stern to the tanker came in, and, after the stern swung out, Buchan took in the forward lines. Then he backed the *Dee* into the water of the harbor, turned her around, and started her down the channel, running between the flashing red and green lights that marked the way to the open sea. She passed, for the second time in three hours, the fixed white light that was the sea buoy.

"All ahead full," Buchan ordered.

The *Dee* moved faster, her engines throbbed, and she rose and fell swiftly as she ran into the sea. Behind her the lights that were the pleasure and the softness of land paled, slipped behind the horizon, and became a glow on the edge of darkness as she drove faster and faster into the murk of the North Atlantic.

27

THE LIGHT on the compass repeater above the wheel showed red from the wheelhouse. Behind the wheel, the helmsman stood black and shapeless. The telephone talker huddled on top of the small-arms locker inside the door, drinking coffee from the steel dipper that flashed silver as it caught the moon through the open door to the port wing.

"Eight days." The helmsman's voice was sepulchral in the silence. "Eight days to Casablanca."

"Eight days." The talker's echo had the same tomb-like hollowness.

Then, for a moment, neither said anything, and I, eavesdropping without rationalization outside the door, heard only the pinging, each ping tremulous and sad, complete to itself and yet part of an unending sequence, like the perpetually forming drops of water that fall in slow torture from the down-thrusting stone daggers of a cave roof into the dark, bottomless pool of water below.

Then the helmsman said, "We never been to Casablanca before."

"It won't be no different from Algiers." The voices kept the hollowness.

"None of these African towns are any different. All of 'em are just alike."

"I hope the vino's better than that Algiers stuff."

"That vino's the same everywhere, it's bad stuff. I seen kids flat on their faces from it. Right out in the streets. Puke all over their clothes. Couldn't move. The Shore Patrol had to carry 'em back to the ship just like they was corpses. That vino is bad stuff."

"It's bad stuff, all right, but what else you got to drink?"

"You got to drink it, but you got to watch it."

"You got to watch it."

"What I want is to get two or three bottles and a French woman and take 'em all to bed for two days. You ever sleep with a French woman?"

"I laid one in Algiers one time."

"Ain't they hot though? I never saw women get hot like these French women. They just don't care what. Those bitches are hot as firecrackers."

"You ever try an Arab?"

"An Arab? Christ no. I couldn't stand to smell an Arab. I never seen one that looked like they took a bath. I don't want no Arab."

"Boy, you ain't had anything if you ain't had an Arab."

"And I don't want anything if I have to have an Arab. None of them Arabs take baths."

"I knew one that did."

"Where?"

"I was shacked with her, all one night."

"How'd you work that?"

"It was in Algiers. I slipped past the MP's into the Casbah, see? They had a guard all around the place to keep the guys out, but I slipped in. Then I found this babe. You know how all the whores live in those holes in the wall? Well, she was standing up right outside one, not much of nothing on, just something upstairs and something down and that was all. She looked good and smelled good and she didn't have to ask me but once. I went inside. She had a nice place, rugs on the deck, big soft thick rugs. No beds. We got down on the rugs. She had on this Arab perfume that like to drove me crazy. Oh, she was really something. And she was awful clean, I kept thinking how clean she was. Next day I was bragging to the guys about it. The day after that I came down with the clap. Doc said it must be a record. Forty-eight hours of exposure."

"You get cured?"

"Yeah, I got cured, all right. The doc cured me right off with penicillin."

"It hurt you?"

"No, the way they treat it it ain't bad. It ain't no worse than a cold. I'm all set now."

"All ready to go again?"

"All ready."

I moved away from the door to the wind guard, where Carter, the red flashlight in one hand and zigzag card in the other, was conning. There, I was back in the terrain of the wind, and it hit me strong and fresh, though not so cold as seven hundred miles to the north.

"How is it?"

"Okay." His face profiled in white as it pointed toward the other ships. "No strain."

I raised my glasses and looked through them at the others, bulks without shape that were blacker by a shade than the blackness around them. I let the glasses drop to the end of the neck-strap, walked to the other side of the bridge, spoke to Jerry, there alone, and went into the wheelhouse to look at the radar.

The helmsman, talking as I came through the starboard door and went to the radar set four feet from the wheel to bend over the round, open-ended cylinder that circled the screen, said: " . . . read this crap about do we know what we're fighting for?"

"Yeah, I read some of it. What's all that anyway? Who wants to know?"

"The guys that write it. They want to know do you know what you're fighting for."

"What the fog is it to them do we know what we're fighting for? They don't have to do it. What do they worry for?"

"They like to worry. They want you to be educated."

"Christ, it ain't enough to be out here. Now you got to know why."

"If those cruds are so hot on us knowing, why don't they come out here? Why don't they come out and give us the word?"

I came up from the screen and said, "They don't need to come out. They know already. They know all about it. They want you to know."

"Oh, those foggers. Those mother-loving foggers. We'll put their ass on a tin can in the North Atlantic and give them the word, huh, Mr. Taylor? Then maybe they won't worry so much."

"Christ, Mr. Taylor." The talker had not moved but still sat on the small-arms locker, a hump with a white face in the dark. "On the outside they don't know how it is with a sailor. They don't want him to act like a sailor, they want him to act like a boy scout."

"They want you to listen to all that crap." The helmsman kept his eyes on the tiny rectangle of red light above his head that showed the compass heading of the ship. "You can't worry about all that. You start to think too much and you go to pieces. I've seen what happened to guys on the Iceland run that thought too much. You got to put it all out of your head, all but the liberty and the women and the liquor."

"And then they start all this about do we know what we are fighting for. All these jokers sitting on their ass in New York worrying about do we know what we are fighting for." The talker had worked himself up. "Jesus, what do we care? We go out, don't we? We stand our watches and our battle stations, don't we? What do they care?"

"I couldn't tell you," I said.

"You get cold and you get wet and you get tired and you keep going out and maybe you get it and maybe you don't, and if you don't get it this time maybe you will the next, and you come in for a little while and they want to know do vou know what you're fighting for. What's it to them? We go out. That's all they ought to worry about. We go out."

Then the sound operator called, through the voice tube, "We got something," and I moved fast to the wing to start the attack.

But the "something" turned out to be only a water noise, a sound without identity, filtering through the under-ocean from a source that was, also, unknown.

The hunt wore on, until it obliterated everything else. It seemed without beginning and without end, a search that encompassed all of time and all of existence.

You hunted ceaselessly through seas as barren and as cruel as life, you sought an Enemy as shadowy and as untouchable as Nemesis, and you looked for him with pings from a man-made device that were as thin, as short-reaching, and as unseeing as conscience. You did not see how you could win, how you could find and destroy what you hunted.

After a time, you did not care about winning. You only wanted, for a little while, to rest.

Part Three

28

THE SEA WALL came out of the sea like a stone fence rising from a New England landscape, the wall long and gray and its mortar chinks lined clearly, while the waves, green in the morning sun, rolled gently against it and fell back in a jagged streak of white that shifted, disintegrated, and formed again as the waves returned. The ships, in single file with the carrier ahead and the three destroyers trailing like dogs at heel, eased through the break in the wall that was its entrance into the outer harbor of Casablanca.

The *Dee* was third in column, second among the destroyers, and followed the *Donahue,* a thousand yards ahead, through the water, now brown inside the sea wall, of the outer harbor. The outer harbor, bounded on each side by the curves of the dark African coast and in front by the wall, was large, and we had miles to run to reach the inner harbor and the military installation inside it.

The ships today wore the stiff, scrubbed formality of men of war of the United States Navy calling at a foreign port. Ahead, on the low-riding stern of the *Donahue,* men stood in two blue, white-topped rows, as they did just below the bridge on the forecastle of the *Dee,* and astern, on the forecastle of the *Hilliard.* On the bridge, I wore blues, the white-covered cap, and the belted black raincoat. So did the executive officer and the captain, who, for the occasion, had on the cap with the gold-filigreed visor.

"Graham." Buchan, behind the compass repeater on the port wing, called it sharply.

"Yes, sir?" The exec, his face wrinkled, stepped from the door of the wheelhouse.

"Where the hell is Rick's?"

Graham grinned. Rick's was the Casablanca night club in the picture with Bogart and Bergman.

"The chart doesn't show it, Cap'n."

"You've got to find Rick's. In the picture it looked like a real operating base."

Buchan laughed. He was in good humor. Going into port,

151

he was always in good humor. He turned to me and said: "You ready to operate?"

"You never saw anybody so ready."

He laughed again, then looked ahead at the carrier and the *Donahue*. The column, led by the carrier, was winding sluggishly between the ships at anchor which sprinkled the outer harbor, though not too heavily, since most of the traffic now went inside the Mediterranean to Algiers or Oran.

Five hundred yards to port, we passed one of these with no flag at her mast. I put my glasses on her. Then I saw what she was: a hulk, a broken ship out of commission, with the turrets which had once housed her big guns now empty and impotent, and red dust streaking the huge black hull.

"Looks like a battleship." I said it aloud, to no one.

White letters showed on her twisted bow, and, with the glasses, I read them.

"Captain," I was, for no sound reason, excited. "That's the *Jean Bart*." I pointed with my left hand at all that was left of the battleship that had been, before the Americans shelled it into a wreck in the North African invasion, the symbol and pride of French naval power.

He nodded, had, apparently, seen and recognized her before I. "Pretty well shot up, huh? They tell me she plays hell with Franco-American relations here. Every time the French decide they're ready to kiss us and make up, they take another look at the *Jean Bart* and get worked up all over again." He laughed the short, scornful laugh. "The hell with them. The bastards ought to be grateful we came in."

A mile ahead, the carrier crept forward in her slow, lopsided massiveness. A black boat with a red canopy that covered it completely was trailing and gaining upon her; where the boat came from, I had not seen. It skimmed on, bounding along the flat brown surface and lacing it with a thin white wake, drew even with the carrier, turned toward her and pulled in to her port side, sheltered by the overhang of the flight deck. The boat hung there for almost half a minute, then veered out, and, turning in a wide half-circle, made for the *Donahue*, the red canopy and narrow black body under it expanding as the craft closed the distance.

On the carrier's foremast fluttered the red and white flag that means the same the world over: I have a pilot on board. The boat, then was a pilot boat; presumably it carried pilots for all three destroyers, too.

The yellow signal light flashed from the dark, slender solidity of the bridge structure on the right side of the carrier's flight *deck*. Kaintuck leaped to the foot stand behind the *Dee's* signal light at the corner of the wing, and the flag bag, and staring intently at the orange flashes breaking from the tower, clicked his own shutter in acknowledgment.

At the end of the message, he clicked it twice to sign off, stepped down from the stand, and called to Buchan, six feet away: "All ships, proceed independently."

"Wait independently," snorted the captain. "She's taken care of, and the hell with us."

The carrier lumbered on, past the jutting brown arm of land, crested with yellow wooden houses, that marked the beginning of the inner harbor. Then the white wake boiling from under her stern vanished, she moved perceptibly slower, and seemed to stop, about a mile from the tall, white stone buildings lining the shore that was Casablanca. Jerking to her mast went the round black ball signifying she had let go an anchor.

·"She's dropped her hook, Cap'n." I was watching the anchor ball go up.

"All engines stop," said Buchan. "We'll lay to and wait for our boy."

The *Donahue*, ahead, had already stopped, and, with no engines to keep her on course, was swinging slowly in the light wind to her left to parallel the beach. The red-topped boat came alongside her, and I saw, without glasses, a figure in black climb from the boat to the ladder on her side and up the ladder to her deck. Then the boat, already pointing toward the *Dee*, started for her.

It came in from ahead, and halted with a snarl of backing engines by the port side of the forecastle deck, rising and falling from the small swell it had itself created, and then, waved on by Jake Warwick, coasted with one quick engine grunt ten yards back to the steel ladder clamped over the side from the well deck.

I was on the well deck as the pilot's head, under a dirty white, black-billed yachting cap, popped over the side, to be followed, in six-inch sections as he climbed the ladder, by the rest of him: a short, wizened body in a double-breasted blue serge suit with a well-spread sheen and a red turtle-neck sweater under the coat. His face had a healthy tan that contrasted with his otherwise sickly appearance, but was negated by a wispy, colorless mustache that straggled up and down the sides of his mouth and gave him a half-comic, half-pitiful aspect.

We shook hands. As officer of the deck, I had to greet him as he came aboard.

"*Bon jour*," I said.

"Good morning," he squeaked.

That was the exchange of salutations, and, it over, I motioned to the ladder to the bridge. I climbed it behind him, getting a straight-up view of his shiny serge posterior.

He shook hands with the captain, saying again in his squeaky, nasal voice, "Good morning." That seemed to exhaust his English. I wondered how he was going to give orders to the helm and to the engines. But he had learned somewhere rudder and engine orders in the language, and, after he got the *Dee* underway again, squeaked them out with surprising authority, although he used the merchant-marine commands of "dead slow," "slow," and "fast." These I had to translate into speed by thirds.

The *Dee* coursed close to shore, trailing by half a mile the *Donahue,* and passed on her right the white and yellow buildings that made a ragged, broken line of stone against the sky, merchant vessels tied to the piers projecting from the beach, white laundry dancing from lines on their sterns and light brown smoke curling from their stacks, and the automobiles speeding down the broad concrete drive less than a hundred yards from the water's edge.

The Frenchman conned the *Dee,* following the *Donahue* as the *Hilliard* followed her, on the course paralleling the curve of the beach for nearly three miles, then, still in the smooth, widening wake the *Donahue* cut, turned nearly a quarter of a circle away, from south to east. We were now heading toward the base of the narrow promontory thrusting out of the shore that erected a natural barrier for the inner harbor.

Sticking like a long gray arm into the brown water, coming at right angles from the strip of land, was a pier. The pilot grasped the captain's shoulder and pointed with his right forefinger at the pier.

"La."

The captain, understanding, nodded.

Half a dozen men stood on the pier. Closer, I saw they were Lascars, barefooted, with cylindrical red fezzes on their heads, their bodies brown and bare to the waist. They were all immobile, waiting, and watching, uncuriously.

"I guess they'll take our lines," said Buchan.

The *Donahue* was approaching the pier. The pilot stopped the *Dee's* engines, and she lay off, until the other ship could complete her landing and tie up to the pier. The *Donahue* angled in sharply toward it, then, closer, eased away until she was almost parallel. She stopped. The thin white heaving lines flew all at once from the ship to the pier, and the Lascars,

suddenly alive, scurried up and down the planking to pick up
the lines and pull to them the heavy brown hawsers attached
to the other ends. All six of the hawsers jerked, guided by the
thinner lines, to the pier, and were made fast to the posts
rising out of it. To complete the landing the *Donahue* swung
her stern against the pier, and on her decks sailors pulled the
slack out of the dipping hawsers. Then, making a loop from
the remaining length of each big line, they passed it by hand
to the Lascars, and the Lascars dropped the loops over the
posts.

"She's doubled her lines, Cap'n," I said.

He nodded.

A blue and white flag ran to her port yardarm and waved
in the wind.

"She's hoisted Able, Cap'n. Ready to receive us now."

"I'll take her from here," the captain said, pleasantly, to
the pilot, who looked uncomprehending. Then Buchan added,
"I relieve you," and the pilot bowed stiffly. His ego was, perhaps, injured by the dismissal, but Buchan did not want a
foreign, unvouched pilot with little English bringing his ship
alongside anything.

"Starboard engine ahead one-third," Buchan called.

He curved the *Dee* alongside the *Donahue* as the *Donahue*
had done with the pier, then her lines shot over to the other
ship and she was made fast there. Only a rope-covered, ball-
shaped cane fender amidships separated the two destroyers.

"Here we are." Buchan walked away from the wind guard
on the starboard wing now, after the lines were doubled.
"And I hope to Christ we stay here until we get underway
again."

"How long do we have?"

"Two days," he said shortly, and walked back of the wheelhouse to say goodbye to the pilot, who had gone to the other
wing to disassociate himself completely from the landing.

Two days. And one would be lost to me because I had the
day's duty, for twenty-four hours, starting from noon. The
prospect did not make me happy. Still, two days in port were
two days in port.

I clattered down the ladder from the bridge to the well deck,
then turned forward and went through the open door to the
forecastle and looked down the length of the pier to the land.

The foot of the pier ran straight into a narrow, dirt, twin-
pathed road that curved, yellow in the sun, to a thoroughfare
set back a thousand yards from the water, extending the five-
mile length and cutting through the center of the peninsula.

This looked like a river of mud, and the plodding brown

Army trucks that lined it, like so many great turtles crawling through the muck, slow, blind, and resigned, concerned only with maintaining a tenuous physical contact with the one ahead and the one behind. Even at the distance, I saw the mud spew under the turning wheels, the fresh mud dripping like dung from the sides of the truck carriages, and old, dried mud caked in heavy lumps on the hoods. I heard the mass sound of their motors, a mingled, abrasive monotone in which all separateness was swallowed by the whole.

Showing over the trucks, on the other side of the mud highway, were tops of yellow wooden buildings, the ones I had seen as we passed into the inner harbor, shelters, undoubtedly, for Army and Navy offices.

On the near side of the big road, slightly to the left of the foot of the pier and just beyond range of the wheel-sprayed mud, squatted three figures, passive, unmoving, enduring, in robes that had ceased being white an eternity ago: Arabs.

"Let's go see if we can still stand up on honest-to-God land," said Johnny, now beside me in the nose of the forecastle. "Bet I can't."

We walked across the gangway, now being lashed into place by two seamen on the forecastle just under the bridge, to the *Donahue,* then passed across her forecastle and gangway to the pier.

"Man, feel that." Johnny stopped and pushed against the wooden planks without lifting his feet, like a diver testing a springboard. "Feel how stiff it is."

The wooden planks were solid and unmoving under my feet. I walked carefully ahead, like a half-drunk trying to achieve the semblance of sobriety. We went down the pier. I felt the exhilaration of quick, unfettered movement, the pure physical exuberance of a sailor, long at sea, who sets foot to land. We walked off the pier to the dirt road. It, strangely, was not mud, not soft even, but firm and well packed, yielding only enough to show footprints. It had the nostalgic smell of fresh dirt.

"Peace, it's wonderful." Johnny stamped his right foot against one of the two wheel tracks. "It don't roll. It don't pitch. It just lays there and looks at you."

I heard laughter from the pier, and turned back to look.

I touched Johnny's arm. "Look at that."

On the pier at the foot of the *Donahue's* gangway, a small brown and white dog, of untold bars sinister and obviously the *Donahue's* property, was running back and forth, lifting his feet high in the air and slapping them comically to the planks. Four sailors, his honor guard, stood watching, and laughing. The dog was puzzled; the pier did not move, did not rise up or fall away, did not roll to one side or the other. He dashed in one direction and then the other, in the same flopping, rolling gait, trying with offended gravity to solve the problem that someone had invented to tease him.

"Looks like Jojo can't get rid of his sea legs," I said.

"The hell with Jojo. Where's Humphrey Bogart?"

"Where do you think? He's over at Rick's."

"Let's get over to Rick's. In the picture there was all kinds of stuff hanging around Rick's."

"I'll have to wait till tomorrow to check Rick's. I got the deck this afternoon."

"Poor man."

"You're fogging well informed, poor man."

"My heart bleeds for you, you know where."

We walked back down the pier and crossed the *Donahue* to the *Dee*. On board, you could feel the excitement. It ran through the ship like an electric current; sparks crackled in the air. The crew had scoured the *Dee* into spotlessness before entering port, and today was strictly *fiesta*. Work was over. All over the forecastle, men made small blue groups along the lifelines, looking at the promontory and road ahead, and pointing at the white city across the water as though it were the City of God. Voices rose and fell, single phrases sounding clear over the composite noise. All had to do with the same subject.

Little Ski, in one of the groups, caught my eye and grinned: a wicked, omniscient, conspiratorial, you-and-me grin.

He sidled away from the group, moved close to me, and said softly: "We going after it today, Mr. T.?"

I clucked my tongue. Then I smiled back.

"Yeah." His face was satanically good humored as he half whispered it. "Yeah, I see we're going after it."

"I'm not going after anything today. I got the duty today."

"We'll go after it tomorrow."

"How you talk, Ski. How you talk."

But on my way to the wardroom, I thought: You might be right, Ski. You might just be right.

29

GRAHAM called me into his stateroom. Sitting behind the gray desk in his white shirt and neatly knotted black tie, the blue coat hanging on the back of the chair, the pile of typed papers

stacked precisely in a pile before him, the automatic frown
fixed on his face, he looked up at me as I swung the gray
curtain over the door to one side and stepped in.

"How about finding somebody to do the laundry?"

"Me?" The job belonged, by rights, to the mess treasurer,
Flattop.

"Chase has to line up stores. I wish you'd handle this."

"Okay." I knew it was an order.

I left the ship, walked down the pier and down the narrow
road that led to the mud highway. I picked a hole in the two
opposite-moving lines of trucks and ran across, feeling the
mud suck at my shoes as I lifted my feet. Across, I looked at
the mud smeared on my blue pant legs in the crossing, turned
left, and walked, beyond the line of fire of the mud, beside
the road, over rough, grass-covered ground, the soles of my
shoes twisting on the uneven surface, until, half a mile further,
I reached the first of the dirty yellow buildings.

Beside an unpainted sentry box in front of it stood a soldier
with a rifle, wearing the shapeless olive drab and leggings.
Sweat made paths in the dirt on his face. He had the sloppy
look of garrison troops who have been too long in a place.
He did not salute or come to attention.

"Got a telephone?" I asked.

"In there." He jerked his thumb toward the door of the
building. "Third door to the right."

I went into the building, walked through a corridor and
over a wooden floor, and turned into the third, doorless doorway. Inside, facing it from the opposite wall, was a green steel
desk with a soldier behind it. He was bareheaded and brown-
haired, wore a sergeant's stripes, though which grade I did
not know, on his sleeve, and was reading a red-and-green-
backed comic book. On the desk, in a brown leather field case,
was the telephone.

He looked up, explained, after I asked, how to use the telephone, and went back to the comic book.

I studied a mimeographed directory between broad card-
board covers, tied with a long white string to the desk. I
picked four numbers that might give me action. At each of
the first three, I spoke to the officer in charge; all of them told
me, with absolute certainty, that it was impossible, impossible
for me or Eisenhower, to have laundry returned in less than a
week. At the fourth number, I spoke to a sergeant in the
Army quartermasters' laundry.

"Sure." The voice came back through the earpiece. "I can
do it for you in twenty-four hours. Bring it around."

That surprised me. "We get underway day after tomorrow,

sergeant. If there's any chance you can't make it, I'd rather you didn't try."

"Lieutenant." The voice was crisp. "When I tell you I'll do it in twenty-four hours, I mean I'll do it in twenty four hours. Bring it around. And get it here by noon."

"Thank you. I will."

I hung up and looked at my watch: ten-thirteen. About two hours to find transportation, pick up the laundry from the ship, and carry it wherever it had to go.

I went back to the highway. Maybe I could, by bribery, commandeer a truck for the laundry. I edged closer to the road, to pick out one and stop it. I watched four go by, carrying two-by-fours in the back that clattered as the trucks bounced ponderously in the mudholes, and saw an empty one behind the last of these. I took one step closer and waved my arm to stop it. It jolted past without slowing and threw mud over my pants. I stepped back and cursed the driver. I stood ten feet from the road to flag the next. It stopped, all at once, without first slowing. I jumped to the running board, opened the door and sat on the dirty black seat in the cab, swinging my legs to the side to miss a rusty iron spring sticking through the leather seat cover, as, with a rumbling motor belch, the truck started off in the direction of the pier and the destroyer nest.

The driver was in civilian clothes, a tan sport shirt over muddy gray pants. He grinned at me, showing white teeth in a round, black-stubbled face topped by a wild spread of black curly hair.

"Bon jour," he said, and looked back to the road, slowing so as not to hit the truck ahead.

"Bon jour."

"Que voulez-vous? What you want?"

I struggled with college French. *"Je desire . . . d'aller au . . .* laundree." The last word was my own invention.

He glanced at me, contracted his eyebrows, and looked back to the road.

"Laundree." I made motions with my hands to represent washing.

"Ah." He brightened, happily. Now he understood. "Jigjig. You want jigjig." He nodded his head approving in enthusiasm, smiling.

"No, no." I shook my head. He looked sad. I pointed to my shirt, and made, with greater care, the motions of washing, wringing, and hanging to dry.

It worked. *"Blanchisserie."* He nodded again, with noticeably diminished enthusiasm. "You want *blanchisserie.*"

"Oui." I nodded.

"The cigarettes."

"What? *Qu'est-ce c'est?"*

"You give me cigarettes. How many?"

"One pack. *Un."* I held up one finger.

He grinned, shook his head, held up four. We compromised on three.

I motioned him from the highway to the dirt road to the pier. Pointing straight at us as we turned were the three destroyers, side by side like triplets in embryo, looking narrow-waisted and fragile, with only the sharp edge of their bows and the single slim gun above giving them a touch of arrogance and feminine menace.

He stopped the truck, at the foot of the pier.

"Wait 1 jumped out, went down the pier, over the *Donahue* to the *Dee,* and, ten minutes later, led three steward's mates from the ship to the truck, carrying on their backs as many sheet-covered laundry bundles. Inside the bundles were the pieces which the ship's little washing machines could not do: the wardroom linen and the officers' shirts and trousers.

The boys slung it in the rear of the truck. I got inside.

"Okay?" the driver turned to me.

"Okay."

He grinned again, and, with a groaning of gears, backed the truck into the highway, stopped, started forward and followed the road. As the road turned from the promontory to the mainland, it changed to gravel and hugged the shore closely. We drove over it for what seemed several miles, then turned through many streets and were on a boulevard where palm trees grew. We drove on, then stopped in front of a long, white frame building flying an American flag from a mast on the roof. A black and white sign posted just off the street said, "U. S. Army, Quartermaster's Corps."

"Bianchisserie." The Frenchman grinning, pointed at the building.

It was the laundry.

30

ON THE SHIP after lunch, the captain sent for me.

I knocked on the bulkhead beside his door.

"Come in

He was standing before a mirror, in a T-shirt, shaving.

Lather dripped from his face into the bare aluminum lavatory.

"You got the deck?" His eyes were still on the mirror as he pulled the gold safety razor over his cheeks, then flicked the soap from the blade into the basin with a snap of his wrist.

"Yes, sir." I had it, all right. On the first of two days in port, I had it. The luck would have been heartbreaking except for one thing: half the officers had to stay aboard, anyway. Consequently, I lost nothing.

"I want to have a birthday party for Arnhem tonight." Arnhem was the *Donahue's* captain. "Can the boys get a cake ready?"

"Yes, sir." I hoped they could. "Any particular kind?"

"Oh, any kind." He seemed cheerful. I was surprised that he was passing up an expedition into town for a party for his friend. It was a sacrifice. Particularly for him. He raised his chin, and, stroking upward from the throat, scraped the razor carefully over the taut skin under it. The blade made a rasping sound passing over the stubble. "Some of his officers'll be over with him. Our JO's may have to sit at a second mess." He ran water from the faucet over the razor and laid it on the lavatory. "I'll be leaving the ship at two o'clock for a conference on the carrier. Have my boat ready."

After dinner, the plates cleared from the white cloth that was fresh for the occasion, Morales, the chief steward, brought the cake in himself, and placed it ceremoniously in front of Arnhem, on the captain's right. The cake was lemon-yellow, with six three-inch orange candles burning in the center, and orange lettering spelling "Happy Birthday." Stew retreated to the pantry door and hovered just inside the wardroom, rubbing his hands together and grinning nervously. Arnhem made properly appreciative noises, and Buchan gave Stew the thumb and forefinger gesture of approval. Stew blushed, laughed his nervous Filipino giggle, and fled into the pantry.

"That's a beautiful thing," said Arnhem.

"Come on," said Buchan. "Blow out the candles."

Arnhem, an unobtrusive man with thin brown hair going back in a widow's peak and gold-rimmed spectacles on his nose, puffed his lean cheeks with air and blew out the candles with one gust. Buchan cut the cake and passed the slices down the table. Arnhem smiled as he tasted his. He was obviously pleased with his party. He and Buchan had been classmates at the Naval Academy, junior officers together on the Arizona, and, after that, in the same destroyer division operating out of San Diego.

The party was going well, when, after coffee, I excused myself and went topside to see that the movie was ready.

It was. The white screen was stretched on the back of Number Four stack, and benches and chairs, facing the screen, ranged back from the stack toward the after deckhouse. Behind them all, fifty feet back, the nose of the black projector pointed like a machine gun at the screen. Men were already beginning to fill the benches. The chairs in front, for the officers, were empty.

I walked to the gangway. Jerry stood there, with the officer of the deck's pistol and belt strapped around the middle of the brass-buttoned coat and the coat pouching like a sack from under the belt. He was, in port as at sea, my junior officer, and we took turns keeping the gangway.

"They all set up for the movie?"

"All ready," he said.

"I'll relieve you after the movie." He knew I was ordering him to stay at the gangway during the picture and consequently to miss it, and his face was glum as he nodded. I was amused by and sorry for him. That was the way things were done in the Navy, it was the way they had been done to me, and I was not going to change the pattern. Rank, even half a stripe of it, had its privileges.

I returned to the wardroom to tell the officers, still at the table, that the picture was ready. They all rose and started out of the room, except Buchan and his friend. They sat at the end of the table, talking in low voices and laughing at something remembered, and Buchan, glancing at me briefly, said, "We won't be up." They were still chuckling when I left the room.

I dropped into one of the three empty chairs in front of the screen just as the movie started. It was old, from the late thirties, and the heroine was Joan Crawford, tightly gowned and moving through situations almost grotesquely vulnerable to the Anglo-Saxon exhortations shouted from the audience that made the real entertainment at the *Dee's* movies. At the end of every reel, the picture went off the screen, while the operator fitted the next strip of film into the projector. In the hiatus after the fourth reel, I heard, over the chattering and calling from the benches, the sound of a single voice, climbing higher and falling and then rising again, coming from the quarter-deck. What it said was lost. I left the chair and went to the gangway.

There, standing on the deck, his arms dangling paralytically around the necks of two friends, who held him up, was Walsh, the first-class torpedoman. His hat was gone, and the scraggly blond hair that ringed the bald spot in the middle of his head was tousled and standing almost straight up. His eyes were glassy, red bruises splotched his face, and his breath, smelling of stale wine and vomit, hit me six feet away. He was singing, thick-voiced, and staring ahead, not seeing me, nor his friends, nor anyone else.

"Everybody loves the Navy," he croaked. "Everybody loves the Navy, of the Ewe-Ess-Aye." The song went high on the last note and broke off, but his voice, drunk and angry and wounded, blared on, "Bullshit. Nobody loves the Navy, nobody loves the Goddamn Navy. Lemme tell you, it's all a lie. Nobody loves the Navy." His body jerked queerly, in the unrelated movements of a puppet, as he tried to break away from his friends, but they held him. "I won't go back on this old bitch. She kills you, she breaks your heart. They'll never get me back."

"Take it easy, Walt."

He made a singsong of it: "I won't go back on the bitch, I won't go back on the bitch. Son of a bitch, I'll never get rich, but I won't go back on the bitch."

Then, as he smiled a pleased, vacant little smile, and hummed, without words, the same tune to himself, his knees unhinged, his head fell forward against his chest, and he hung, a dead weight, between the two friends that supported him.

"Take him to bed," I said.

They carried him off. Well, he had forgotten for a while, anyway. His troubles were over now for almost ten hours. It was something.

I looked past the *Donahue* to the pier. Six sailors were walking down it, one staggering and waving both arms, toward the three ships.

"They're starting back," I said to Jerry. Liberty did not expire until ten o'clock for the crew and it was now not quite eight, but they were starting to return. I would have to be on hand when they came aboard; if there was any trouble, it was my responsibility. "I may as well take it now. You can see the rest of the movie if you want to."

"Okay."

He unsnapped the pistol belt and handed it to me. I felt a little guilty at not having anticipated this development and let him see the picture from the start. But only a little. It was good indoctrination for him, I told myself. I fastened the belt, feeling the heavy, one-sided drag of the pistol on my right hip, and he went through the passageway toward the movie.

Two and three at a time, the men in the liberty section,

numbering half the crew, dribbled aboard, in various stages of drunkenness. None were as far gone as Walsh. As each came over the gangway, the sailor on the gangway watch took his identification card and put a pencil check by his name on the list typed on the sheet of white paper. At ten o'clock, I asked him: "How many still over?"

He looked at the list and counted the unchecked names with the rubber tip of his pencil. "Five." He named them.

"Oh, hell. The Shore Patrol'll probably haul them aboard about daylight."

But at ten minutes after, three of them crossed the gangway, on their feet and only moderately drunk.

"Want to log them late?" asked the gangway watch.

"No. Who does that leave now?"

"Just Daniels and Little Ski."

"Christ. Always those two."

My watch hands circled off the minutes. At ten-thirty, they were not back. Not at ten-forty. Not at ten-forty-five. At ten-fifty, I walked back to the galley. Inside, Whitey was mixing white pie dough in big brown wooden bowls.

"How about a horse-cock sandwich, Whitey?" Horse cock was the trade name for bologna meat. He made it, and holding it in both hands to bite into, I went forward to the quarter-deck.

I stepped through the door of the forecastle as Daniels and Little Ski walked off the gangway.

"Where the hell have you been?"

Little Ski grinned, winked at me, and did not answer.

"You're an hour late."

"Man," said Little Ski, still grinning. "Man, did we have ourselves something, Mr. T. Man, did we have it."

"You'll have it, all right. Wait till you hit that extra duty."

"You woulda gone nuts over it, Mr. T.," Daniels said.

"You're gonna love it here, Mr. T." Ski kept grinning, as though the grin were a special, coded communication from himself to me. "You're just gonna love it."

"Get the hell below." Ski looked over his shoulder, still grinning, as he, following Daniels, went through the doorway.

"Want me to log 'em late?" The gangway watch asked again.

"No." He and I looked at each other and we grinned.

Only four officers left now. He looked up from his note-book. Officers' liberty was officially over at one, but if any of them spent the night on the beach, it was all right, so long as they made it back by eight-o'clock quarters. "Arbry, Rock-ford, Carter, and Chase."

I was right on both counts. Rocky, Arbry, and Carter, wine-fully garrulous, stamped over the gangway fifteen minutes later. Without the Flattop.

"Goddamn it, Mr. Officer of the Deck." Rocky looked up and down imperiously. "Where are my sideboys? When I board this hunk of junk I expect to be received with full military honors. Is that clear?"

"Yes, sir. I'm sorry, sir." I bowed servilely.

"See that it doesn't happen again."

"Aye, aye, sir." I dropped it. "Where's the Flattop?"

"He won't be home till breakfast. He's connected."

"Ah."

"Yeah, the old Flattop connected. He won't be in tonight."

I followed them through the door to the well deck and down the ladder to the wardroom. Buchan and Arnhem were still sitting at the table when we came in.

"The pack returns." Buchan looked up at Rocky and laughed. "What's the matter, couldn't you get situated?"

"No suitable opportunities. You should have come along and got us lined up."

The captain, chuckling softly, still looking derisively at Rockford, was pleased. "Where's the Flattop?"

"Shacked."

The captain laughed out loud. "You can count on the Flattop. How was it, nice goods?"

"A matter of taste. Strictly commercial merchandise."

The captain and Arnhem looked at each other and laughed again.

"At this point you fellows shouldn't be too discriminating." Arnhem put a cigarette into his mouth, the hollows showing in his lean cheeks as he pulled on it to light it.

"When the ration board says no steak, you have to take hamburger." Rockford was a shade drunk. Whenever he was very loud, you knew he was a little drunk. When he got thoroughly drunk, he grew very quiet. Tonight he was only a little drunk, and he was loud. He liked the sound of what he had said, and said it again. "When you can't get steak, you have to take hamburger."

"Looks like you're observing meatless Tuesday." Buchan looked at him with that sardonic, half-amused, half-baiting expression compounded of a twist of the mouth and a narrowing of one eye.

"True. Most regrettably true. Steps must be taken."

"You won't take 'em here. Looks like you missed the boat in Casablanca."

When we went to bed, the two captains were still at the table.

31

THE NEXT AFTERNOON, after losing ourselves three times, we found the Naval Officers' Club, somewhere in European Casablanca.

There, the four of us, Johnny, Anson, Jerry, and I, sat at a wooden table on a balcony that looked over the street. In the middle of the street was a strip of planted green grass, and, rising from it, thick, gray-trunked palm trees that threw black shadows slanting across the white pavement on the other side. Along both sides of the green strip, singly and minutes apart, dainty, filth-covered horses carrying white-robed, filth-covered riders passed, as unhurrying as if they had eternity before them, their hoofs calack-calack-calacking on the concrete as they went by the balcony and down the street.

The balcony was in the shade of the building, and it was pleasantly warm in the blue uniform, like Carolina in early fall. From the shade of the balcony, we looked at the street glinting white in the sun, drank American whiskey with soda from tall glasses that sweated coldly on the sides, and ate American salted peanuts from an open blue can on the brown table top. The shadows the palm trees cast in the street grew longer and climbed up the yellow walls of the buildings on the other side, and the cool of the dusk came in behind the afternoon, still carrying the heavy, faintly rank smell, compounded of a thousand elements, that is the private musk of North African cities. A high-voiced French waiter in a wrinkled tuxedo stopped at the table and told us the last bottle of American bourbon for the day had been opened; after it was gone, there would be only African wine. We ordered a double round; he brought it.

"Time to start operating." Johnny jiggled the ice in his glass, the second drink of the double round. "Let's get going."

"Where?"

"Flattop says the place is right across the street. It's strictly a bar, but they call it some kind of officers' club. Plenty of talent there, he says, nice talent."

"Let's go, then."

We paid, left the table, walked downstairs and out of the club, and crossed the side street to a door declared by a red and white placard to be the Bar of the Officers of the Allied Nations.

Inside, there was a long bar close to the back wall. Above

the bar were pennants inscribed with names of French schools. On the left wall were American university pennants, and on the wall opposite, those of the British. Behind the bar was a tall girl in a green silk dress, with a wide red mouth and long black hair. She was pouring drinks from a champagne bottle into four stemmed glasses on the bar, for four Army fliers standing there in the light tan shirts they called "pinks" and the crushed brown caps set on the back of their heads. The bottle went dry before the last glass was full. She turned it upside down, shook it to work out the last two drops, and set it back on the bar. She made a sad face, threw up her hands, and said something. They laughed at it together, loudly; obviously, they had been drinking, like us, for some time. I looked back at the girl, posturing behind the bar, and admired the virtuosity of her gestures and exclamations; she was doing whatever she wanted with the fliers.

"There they are." Johnny motioned with his head. "The old Flattop sure had the dope."

"Flattop always has the dope."

In front of and to the far side of the bar were about a dozen black-topped tables, chromium chairs covered with brown leather at each, and, against the wall facing the bar, a long, brown leather-covered sofa. On the sofa sat three girls, and, at the two tables next to it, six more. They were all under thirty, more or less pretty, chic, and lightly rouged. I looked at their legs: their stockings were sheer silk and the shoes expensive-looking and high-heeled. In Africa, the whores were always the best-dressed women. Or the best-dressed women were always whores. It was a debatable point.

"They look bored," said Anson.

They did. Perhaps it was because it was now five o'clock and business was still desultory. It seemed the fliers only wanted to drink. The women were all looking brightly at us; one caught my eye and smiled. I smiled back but did not go over. Instead, we all went to the bar, and stood together a foot from the fliers. They noticed us with a quick look, and then ignored us. We ordered champagne with five glasses. One was for the brunette barmaid. She smiled, showing one gold tooth in the back of her mouth, and turned to get the bottle from the shelves back of the bar.

"Is it true what they say about women with big mouths?" Johnny looked at her backside, the green silk stretched tight over it, as she reached for the bottle on the top shelf.

"Shut up."

She came back with the bottle, uncorked it with a pop, and giggled as the unchilled wine bubbled over the neck of the bottle and spilled on the bar. She filled four glasses, and just covered the bottom of the fifth, hers, with the clear liquid.

"Comment on t'appele?" Johnny's French was as clumsy as mine.

"I am Suzy. And you speak French." She flashed the gold tooth again. "I am so glad to see an American boy who speaks French. Who knows words beside *coucher* and jigjig."

"Are there French words besides *coucher* and jigjig?" I said.

She threw back her head and laughed loudly, to show her admiration of the wit of the marvelous American naval officers.

"You work at it too hard," Johnny said.

"What?" She wrinkled her forehead; she had not understood.

"Shut up," I said to him. Then to her, "He says you keep very busy."

She pouted in mock self-pity and nodded her head. "Oh, yes, I work very, very hard. All day and half the night."

The last was a cue for somebody to ask what time do you get off, honey. Instead, Johnny said, "Let's have another bottle."

She brought it, poured into the five glasses as before, and said, "You must like our champagne."

"No."

"No?"

"No. You know what your champagne tastes like?"

"Shut up," I said.

"Let me tell you what it tastes like."

She leaned forward, smiling.

"Shut up," I said, again.

"It doesn't taste like anything. That's what it tastes like." He was drunker than I thought.

"Well, blow me." Johnny was looking past the three fliers with the pushed-back, floppy brown caps, hunched over and with their elbows on the bar, past the girls, waiting and watching and talking rapidly with mouths and hands, in the chromium chairs at the black-topped tables, past the dissolving clouds of smoke and the pennant-lined walls, to the only door. "Who have we with us."

I looked. It was Crandall.

Inside the door, now closed behind him, he stood, poised, commanding, aloof: Estimating the Situation. Above it all, but willing to use it, his secret smile said. Then he saw us, and his poise, command, and aloofness sagged, while his smile became more strained than secret. He waved his gray-gloved hand, uncertainly, awaiting invitation. I gave it with my own free, nondrinking hand. He started toward us.

"Oh, goody," Johnny said into his drink.

Crandall approached with an imitation of what he had shown before he saw us.

"Ah." The tops of his teeth greeted us. "Off to an early start! Commendable, highly commendable!"

"Isn't it?" Johnny said, and to the bar girl, "Another glass for our compatriot."

She set it on the bar and Johnny poured the yellow-white liquid into it, stopping to let it fizz in the glass, adding another spurt, and handing it to Crandall.

"I thank you!" Smiling, inclining his chin, he raised the glass, making the slight gesture of drinking a toast, then tonguing his wet lips as he put it back on the bar. "How are operations?"

"As you see. At the moment, suspended."

"In preparation, I should say. In the logistic stage."

"In some kind of stage, for true."

"You younger hands need an old head to show you how." He laughed. The hell-on-wheels operator. He lifted the stemmed wine glass again, drank all that was in it without stopping, and thunk-ed it on the varnished wooden bar: a swagger. "Yes, you need the old experience to point the way, gentlemen, the old tested experience." He believed it; he was, here and now, completely sure. He was bracing for a try at the girls at the tables. What does he want to prove, I thought, doesn't he know they're whores?

"Another bottle, my dear." He smiled, confidently, at the black-haired Suzy, who smiled back with automatic joy. Then, to us, with careful carelessness: "This one's mine, gentlemen."

"The hell it is," I said. "We split it. It's a whole bottle."

"I insist. Goddamn it, I insist. After all, rank still has some privileges." He was absolutely determined that he should buy the bottle and that we should drink it. This would establish something for him. He was going to buy the bottle.

"If you insist," said Johnny. "And you do insist?" He grinned at Crandall, and nudged my foot with his.

"Oh, I do," said Crandall. "I do insist."

Behind the bar a cork popped, and the bottle, foam spilling over its neck and trickling in drops down the sides, was on the bar. Crandall reached behind him and brought back a billfold of dark, smooth undirtied alligator, and took from it three one-hundred-franc notes. He tossed them on the bar in a gesture of magnificence, and said to the girl, "The change is for you." This was the first time I had ever seen him happy. He looked devilishly at the girl, now picking up the big, folded bills. "Anyone ever tell you you're a very pretty girl, mamselle?" He mispronounced the last word.

"Why, m'sieu!" She pursed her lips in burlesqued shock, and then laughed loudly, winked at him, and moved down the bar.

"You see? It takes an old hand." Crandall had great satisfaction. "Nothing like the old experience, gentlemen. You may be an old married man, but if you've got that old experience—" He poured the champagne from the bottle into all the glasses as we held them out, and, last, into his own.

"Yes," He was happy and satisfied. "A man may be married but he's not dead. If he's got it, he's got it."

He elevated the glass again, and, his blue-veined adam's apple pulsing against the stiff white collar as he swallowed, tossed off the wine at one shot. "Ah!" He smacked his lips in a cliché of appreciation. "That's fine, fine stuff. I'd like to smuggle a case of that stuff home, by God. For my cellar."

Johnny looked at Crandall disbelievingly, and made a face at his own glass. Crandall did not notice. He was busy being happy that we were drinking liquor paid for with his money. He poured again into his glass on the bar, watching proudly the thin pale stream splash on the curving glass surfaces and the bubbles swirl upward in the rising yellow pool. This one he drank slowly, sipping from the rim and surveying, masterfully, the girls at the tables at the wall.

"Yes, we'll have to start the old wheels turning, have to get to work. And for an objective—" his eyes stopped—"what would you say to our friend right there?" He motioned with his head at the black-haired girl in a red dress alone at a table, smoking a cigarette and staring, impassively, at nothing.

"Entirely adequate," I said. "Chic, in fact."

The dress, silk, fitted tightly enough to show that, though slender, she had everything she had any business having, while her face was pretty and would have been more than that with more flesh to round it, to fill the hollows under her high and delicately rouged cheekbones.

"Quite chic." He was impressed with the word. "Extremely chic. Let's hear what she has to say." And turning, laughing to show it was really a joke: "There will be no charge for this lesson, young men. Look, and learn."

He took a step toward the girl and Johnny caught his arm. "Take the bottle."

"Oh, no. That's for you fellows."

"Take it. You'll need it."

Crandall took it, and advanced, smiling, on the girl, while she gave him in return, as he closed, the inviting but controlled smile of the expensive whore.

"Watch him now," said Johnny, watching. "Watch him seduce this lily of purity."

He reached the table and said something and she looked straight into his face and answered. We could not hear either. It was like watching a pantomime, or a movie with the sound track gone dead. She said something else, still smiling, still looking directly at him, and gestured with her eyes to the empty chair beside her. He bowed, sat, and placed the bottle and glass on the table. She had a glass, was, in fact, revolving the stem between her fingers, but it was empty. He ceremoniously filled it from the bottle, then his own, and they toasted each other and drank. She began to speak, and to make fluent accompaniment with her hands, shoulders, and eyebrows, while he looked at her with a fixed smile and narrowed eyes which, I deduced, were to show wickedness.

I did not understand what he was trying to do, and then I did. He knew what she was, all right. But he had to make a production, he had to convince himself that what he was doing was achievement. It was as necessary to him as buying the bottle had been.

"Observe the look," said Johnny. "It invites, it lures, it compels. Like Charles Boyer. Only, of course, greatly superior to that of Boyer."

"Immeasurably superior."

The conversation rolled. She naturally knew English. Both talked animatedly, while Crandall maintained the look, breaking it twice to refill the glasses. After twenty minutes, he seemed no nearer to consummation.

"When is he going to close it?" said Johnny. "The babe is getting tired."

"He wants to give us plenty of time to study the lesson."

The three aviators on our right, between us and Crandall, were also watching. They had been for some time.

"Christ." It was the one in the middle, a captain with twin silver bars on his tan shirt. The army's bars were bigger and brighter than ours. "Is that jerk still jerking it with that whore?" He was not talking to us, but to his own companions.

"He's been over there for half an hour," said one first lieutenant.

"He's a slow roll," said the other first lieutenant. "He likes it slow. He wants to take his time."

"The hell with him," said the captain with the bright twin

bars. He was a little drunk. "The hell with him and his jerk routine. I'm taking over."

He walked, deliberately and arrogantly, to their table, his shoulders sloping under the shirt, his hat back on his head, and a half-empty glass in his right hand.

He stopped at the table, and Crandall and the girl, seeing him for the first time only as his trouser leg almost brushed the table top, looked up at him. From the bar we could see his brown back, to the right of that the girl and the red dress, and then Crandall in the blue uniform with the gold sleeve stripes. Both of them looking straight up at him: the girl showing nothing at all and Crandall, his smile gone and his mouth open and slack, looking shocked.

The flier must have been talking. The girl had the attitude of listening, of listening carefully. Crandall was still in shock. The flier's left hand slapped his hip pocket, where his wallet made a square bulge. The girl shrugged and raised her eyebrows, to indicate indifference, or acquiescence, or maybe nothing at all. She crushed her cigarette in the ash tray and turned and smiled, politely and mechanically, at Crandall. I saw her lips form words, and perceived, with delayed reaction, they were *"Pardonnez-moi."* She rose, and Crandall, his mouth ajar and his face completely numb, stared at her. Then he remembered to rise, as a gentleman should, came up from his chair a few inches, and dropped back. He watched, frozenly, the red dress and the brown shirt move away and disappear up the stairway in the corner of the room.

His eyes came back to the bottle, bought with the money he had been unable to use to buy something else, and he picked up the bottle, nervelessly, and tipped it toward his glass. Nothing came out. He lifted it and held it upside down, the mouth pointing straight at the glass. Two drops fell, protestingly, into the glass. That was all. The bottle was empty.

He sat it upright on the table and, biting his underlip, gazed at the open neck of the empty bottle. Which was, after all, too small.

"Poor bastard," I said, and meant it.

Crandall did not look our way, or rejoin us. In a few minutes, he was gone.

We forgot him and started another bottle. I took my last glass and went to the sofa to sit beside a blond, heavy girl with a blue woolen dress fitted tightly over breasts that tilted up like eight-inch guns.

"Bon soir," I said.

"Good evening." She looked up at me, speculatively, her

eyes blue in the round face that was, in the heavy way, pretty.
"You speak French?"

"Yes."

"I do not like American boys who speak French."

"Isn't that too Goddamned bad, now?"

She smiled, dutifully. All of these women were like those
in the toothpaste ads: She is Lovely, Until She smiles.

She leaned close, so that the eight-inch gun oreasts bored
into my shoulder. I felt them squash at the contact.

"You like Casablanca?"

"All right. Want a drink?"

"Thank you, baby." I gave her my glass, still half full. She
took it without moving, the firm, heavy warmth of them passing through the blue dress and my uniform to my skin. "You
with me?"

"I'm with you now."

"I mean you want to go to bed with me? Nous *couchons?*"

"You mean *coucher.*"

She laughed. "Same thing, baby. You want?"

"Later."

She shrugged and leaned back. My shoulder was sweating
where they had rammed it. She did not even look at me now.
I had been written off as a poor risk. She appraised the company at the bar. A dozen others were there now, all fliers except for two infantry lieutenants. The evening crowd was
starting to come in. She would be occupied soon.

I knew I ought to take while it was there, but it was too early;
I did not want to see the ast reel of the picture first. And I did
not want a whore. Not, that is, unless there was nothing else.
Now I was happy just to sit, completely apart from everything,
feeling almost without a body, w tching all that happened with
a liquified and O mpian detachment.

One of the girls was talking to Johnny at the bar. One of his
hands held a glass and the other lay high on the girl's hip. She
was smiling and he kept nodding attentively. I knew by the
solemn cast of his face that he was drunk. A thin redhead,
childlike without make-up, had taken Jerry over, at one of the
tables. Anson was drinking seriously with the first group of
fliers. Minus, of course, the captain. My lost love in the blue
dress rose from the divan and propelled the eight-inchers to
one of the infantry lieutenants at the bar. The perfume of the
women mixed with the smell of the wine at the bar and the blue
clouds of cigarette smoke. Jerry and the child redhead got up
from the table, walked to the other end of the bar, and turned
through a doorway which showed a stairway. I leaned back,
unmoving, against the leather cushions, in a vacuum, without

time or urgency, as though there had always been this, with nothing before and nothing after. The North Atlantic did not exist.

I sat there for what seemed a long time. Then Johnny came over from the bar.

"Let's get out of here. I don't like the setup." He sounded sober, and I was surprised. It always surprised me the way he could, even staggering drunk, take hold of the strings, pull them tight, and become in seconds almost sober.

"I don't like these *poules.*"

"The hell with the poules. Too easy, just shooting big fish in a small barrel. We don't want the poules."

"Why don't we look around for a while, anyway?"

"Yeah, we ought to look around. What we want is for love. Not for money. *Pour l'amour.* All for you, babee, all for you and lawve."

I laughed. "Let's go, all for lawve."

Anson was happy with his new friends, and, from the bar, waved us on without him. The girl in blue was staring, with meaning, at the lieutenant, who looked ready to buy. We walked through the door into the street.

It was night, and there were not many lights. The African night wind blew in clean over the smell of the town. We walked two blocks along the almost dark street, then came to a bar with light showing through an open door and went inside.

It was like a million bars, in Chicago, New Orleans, or on Fifty-Fourth Street: one bartender in white behind it and twenty stools in front. Only two were occupied, by a fat, black-haired French woman in a brown silk dress with a brown handbag beside her on the bar, and a short, thin, baldheaded husband on the stool next to her. They glanced at us, curiously, and briefly, and resumed their talking to each other. The bartender looked at us questioningly.

"Whiskey?" I asked.

He smiled, sorrowfully, and shook his head.

"Two champagnes, then."

We drank them and went out.

At the next bar, we sat next to a Frenchman who declaimed effusively, in English, "I will buy drinks for the American liberators. You will do me the pleasure of drinking with me."

He bought champagne, which seemed all there was anywhere, and we drank. Further down the bar, another Frenchman, the only other customer, sat alone. He turned his back, to exclude himself deliberately from participation in the approval of ourselves, the Americans. He raised the glass to his mouth, drained it, and walked stiffly out of the door. We bought the other, friendly Frenchman a drink, and left.

Three men in civilian clothes sat alone in the next bar. We looked in, turned, and walked out.

We walked slowly through the streets, stopping at every bar. There were no women in any of them.

"Well." Defeat was in Johnny's voice. "It looks like they were all over at the Allied Club, all the women loose in Casablanca."

"They're sure somewhere. Maybe they discovered what a fortune they were giving away."

"Yep, not for love tonight. *Pour* money. Let's go back and settle pour money."

We had a hard time finding the way back. When we saw the sign over the door again, it was 9:30, half an hour before curfew. We went inside.

The bar and room were full. Of officers. The air was thick with smoke, and there was the steady babble of many voices. They were two-deep at the bar. Anson, sitting at a table with the fliers, waved.

"Where are the girls?" Johnny looked over the room.

"Do you see any?"

"No."

"Neither do I."

"What do you think?"

"I think they've all been tucked in for the night. I think we've missed it."

We had. We had passed up what we could get to try for what we wanted, and we had wound up with neither.

Casablanca was a failure. For us as well as Crandall. We went back to the ship at the ten o'clock curfew.

The task unit left Casablanca the next morning, in full daylight.

Part Four

Casablanca was behind. It was behind, and there was nothing ahead but the sea, and, somewhere, the Enemy.

The reports said hunting outside the Bay of Biscay, more than a thousand miles off the coast of France, was good, and, from Casablanca, we steamed steadily northwest. Every day was colder, and every day the warmth of Africa faded further into the past. The third day out, we put on the heavy coats again. But we still were not back in the cold that slashed and bludgeoned and paralyzed, and the three days were good. Every morning there was a sun, and the seas were easy.

The hunt had not yet assumed its old shape of eternal futility, of searching and never finding. We were once more unbeaten, we were still fresh from land.

32

I LAY in the bunk, fighting, too hard, after the tension and coffee of the midwatch, for sleep. I looked at the watch on my wrist, the green hands and figures showing, in the dark, thirty-four minutes past four, making it thirty-two minutes that I had lain, between the sheets that now smelled faintly musty and in need of washing, awake. Lying there, I listened to the heavy, regular breathing, almost but not quite a snore, that came from Jerry's bunk above, and consequently hated him for sleeping. I listened to it, my eyes not even closed, my body, in spite of what I directed, tense and unsoftening, and then, somewhere, I crossed the line into sleep, because I was dreaming.

In the dream I was officer of the deck, and was heading the *Dee* straight for a line of rocks that stood black and jagged out of the gray sea, pounding and breaking in an unworldly white over the black rocks, and I could not move to spin the wheel or give the order to change course, but stood, frozen, as the *Dee* ran faster and faster, until she rose out of the water and was skimming like a gull low over the sea, for the black and white destruction ahead. The rocks reared high before me, the *Dee* almost on them, and then I was awake.

176

My body was rigid and the pounding of my heart sounded like a slow drum in the dark. I sat up, laughed, not out loud, and dropped back to the mattress, touching the hard wooden ledge around the bunk and smelling the stale smell of the sheets, deliberately and slowly, to obtain the reassurance of their physical tangibility. I breathed deeply and relaxed muscle by muscle, luxuriating in the immutable glimmer of red light coming under the door from the battle lamp on the half deck outside. I lay there, now glad to be awake, knowing fully that nothing that might happen in reality could equal in terror the things of a dream.

Then I heard the door open. The red light from outside grew brighter, then dimmed, and the door closed with a soft click.

Someone was in the room. He tiptoed to my bed and touched me lightly on the shoulder.

"Mr. Taylor." I recognized the voice; it belonged to Baxter, a radioman.

"Yes?" In the dark I felt his surprise at finding me awake.

"Sir, we just got an urgent message for the task unit on the Fox schedule." The Fox schedule was for messages direct from Washington. "I knew you'd want to break this one."

"All right." So sleep for this night was over. Resigned, I swung both legs over the side of the bunk and slid to the floor. I found my slippers under the desk and worked my feet into the fleece lining of them in the dark, so not to wake Jerry. The sweater and pants were where I had left them, on the chair, and I put them on and went into the wardroom.

Baxter was standing by the table, with the white paper in his hand. I took the paper, unlocked the gray cabinet that held the coding machine, set up the machine, and punched out the decoded message. I read it, pasted the strips from the machine on a sheet of paper, locked the machine, and went to the captain's cabin.

I knocked once.

"Come in." He had the priceless, for a naval officer, gift of waking all at once. He switched on his bed lamp as I walked in, and sat up in bed, clear-eyed, blinking only twice from the light.

"This just came in." I handed him the message.

His face expressionless, he read it, grunted, and handed it back.

"That ought to be something," he said, conversationally, and half turned toward the wall, to reach up and press one of a row of buttons above the bunk. It would sound a buzzer on the bridge, and bring the officer of the deck to the voice tube.

"Officer of the deck, sir." Rocky's voice, clear and sounding as though two feet away, came out of the brass megaphone suspended from the overhead in the center of the room.

"Expect a course change to starboard this watch." Buchan raised his voice so the open megaphone, on the end of the voice tube, would catch it.

"Aye, aye, sir." The other voice came back.

He nodded at me in dismissal. I left his cabin and went to the radio shack, four steps away. At the long table on the other side of the four-foot-wide room, Baxter was sitting, a typewriter before him and black earphones over his head. He looked at me as I came in.

"Type this up for distribution." Before I handed it to him, I read it again. It was addressed to the task unit commander, and said:

TWENTY ENEMY SUBMARINES REPORTED DEPARTING BREST X COURSE INTERCEPTING YOURS AND THAT OF UK CONVOY X TAKE ACTION YOU CONSIDER APPROPRIATE X

It added some latitude-longitude positions, and was signed "Cominch," commander-in-chief, United States Fleet.

I went down the ladder to the wardroom. I opened the pantry door and looked inside. On a cane chair, balanced on two legs with its back propped against the wall, sat the mess boy of the watch. His head, resting on the back of the chair, was tilted so far back that his closed eyes pointed almost at the ceiling. Slow snores passed through his open mouth, and his hands, clasped together over his stomach, made a black contrast with the white of his jacket.

"James."

His head jerked up and his eyes opened, blinking uncomprehendingly, his face a startled blank.

"Reveille, James, reveille."

Cognizance came back into his face, and he grinned, sleepily.

"How's about a bacon and cheese sandwich?"

"Yes, sir, Mr. Taylor." He yawned, and leaned forward, the two legs of the chair that had been in the air thumping the deck, and, still half asleep, he stood, stretched, and reached with extended fingers for the overhead. "You sure like those sandwiches, Mr. Taylor."

Moving like a sleepwalker, in the pantry he found the bacon, bread, and cheese, and brought them into the wardroom. He put an aluminum skillet on the hot plate and dropped two pieces of bacon in it, the bacon sputtering and popping in its own grease and its frying smell tantalizing me as I waited.

James made the sandwich, put it on a blue-anchored saucer,

and set it before me. I bit into it. It was good, the bacon crisp and the cheese softly sticky. Maybe, I thought, it would get me to sleep.

I finished the first half and picked up the second, and Rocky's voice came out of the megaphone over the table.

"Cap'n, sir."

"Yes?" Buchan's voice, clear and awake, answered. His cabin, the bridge and the wardroom were all on the same sound tube circuit, and anything said at either station could be heard at the other two.

"Change course to zero-one-five."

The captain answered, as though he had been waiting for it, as though he had known exactly what it would be, "Very well."

The ship heeled a little as she came right. It was not a big change, only twenty degrees. It would take the task unit into the submarines only a little faster.

33

In the morning, I lay unmoving on my back on the mattress after the figure in white intoned, "Seven o'clock, sir," and slammed the door, and knew the sea had intensified. My body pressed hard against the mattress as the ship rose, and then went suddenly weightless, as, leaving me suspended for an unmeasurable molecule of a second at the top of her pitch, she started down again. The new course was only one point east of north; we would be back in high seas soon, I thought.

I sat in the bunk with my legs over the side, tried to push myself up, and finally did it. For an instant, as I turned on the deck light, I thought I was going to vomit, but the feeling passed. I had slept one hour since midnight, and was as debilitated as you can be only on a destroyer in the morning: mouth brackish, limbs dead, eyes burning, and bowels churned into buttermilk.

At breakfast, Anson, freshly shaved and clear-eyed, looked at me across the table and said, "You look happy."

"Ecstatically." I did not want to talk, but lifted the cup and drank the coffee, which, this time when I needed it strong enough to walk on and bitter as wormwood, was pallid and tasteless.

"So pleasant, too."

I made an obscene, upward gesture with my middle finger, and then said to all of them at the table, which did not number the captain and the exec: "Did you get the word?"

Then I told them.

Over the ship, too, I learned as I made my morning inspections, the word was around. The men knew. They always knew. There was no way, ultimately, to keep what was happening to them from them. They knew where they were going, and why, and what was waiting, which were all the same.

On the bridge, while I was checking the publications kept in the wheelhouse, Kaintuck sidled to me, and, his voice whispering conspiratorially out of the black beard that came halfway down his chest, said, "Looks like we really going to play some grab-ass with Them this time."

"You reckon?"

"Man, it looks like they sure-God mean business this time. It looks like they really got their backs up, don't it?"

"Where do you get all that?"

He cocked his head and tried to look mysterious. "Don't you worry about me. I hear things, I get the word."

"You don't want to believe everything you hear."

"Oh, I get the dope, all right." He said it profoundly, and then, in a transformation of mood that I could not follow, sighed, "The foggin' you get ain't worth the foggin' you get." With that, he walked away.

Later, when I came out of the radio shack to the well deck, Jake Warwick happened, with elaborate casualness, to find himself walking beside me.

"I hear we got some news." He looked at the deck in front of him, not at me.

"Yeah, Jake. We got some news." I knew he could repeat the message word for word, knew, too, that as soon as Baxter had been out of bed for an hour, a quarter of the crew could do the same. It did not matter.

"What do you think?"

"What do you think?" I countered.

"I don't like to say what I think."

"I think something is going to break. Soon." I did not try to fool Jake.

He nodded, soberly, and then shrugged his shoulders. He caught sight of nearly a dozen seamen, broken into groups of two and three, standing on the well deck, beyond reach of the sprays and the wind, which was blowing in strong from the north once more. They were idle, and talking, not loudly.

Jake took two steps toward them, and bellowed: "Come on, you farmers, you ain't at the general store. Turn to. Get on those decks."

Chastened, they picked up their rust scrapers and paintbrushes, squatted on the deck, and returned to the unending slavery of guarding the *Dee's* steel plates from the sea and the weather. Jake drove them hard the rest of the day; they did not have time to think.

But they had time later. In the dying afternoon, on the four-to-six watch, I looked back from the bridge to the men of the gun crew on the galley deckhouse. Always before, three of them had squatted on the deck behind the shielding gun mount and out of the wind, while the other two stood, one on each side of the deckhouse, as lookouts. But now, all five were on their feet. The three on the port side were close together in conversation, not laughing, and, as they talked, kept watching the sea and the horizon. I was sure what they were talking about.

After dark, relieved of the deck by Rocky and on my way to the wardroom, I saw on the well deck three forms, in the blue clothing that almost merged with the night, standing before Number One stack. I knew Almerico, the engineer, by his voice, hearing him say two words, ". . . this time," before I went through the open hatch and down the ladder.

The belly-tightening feeling of something about to happen had the whole ship. And I knew that from here on, it would get stronger.

The others were at coffee when I sat at the wardroom table, and Peters put a bowl of red bean soup before me. Nobody was talking, when the Captain, half smiling, called down to Chase, "Flattop, how're your feet these nights?"

"Cold, Captain, cold. They stay cold all night long. It's murder."

Everybody laughed.

"You should have listened to me." Buchan mashed out the stub of his cigarette in the ash tray that was the brass base of a three-inch shell. "I told you to bring your talent along. If you'd listened, you wouldn't be in this mess."

"I couldn't get the talent to come."

"You're some glamour boy. Can't even talk your tomatoes into a little boat trip. You know what I think? I think you're slipping."

"You're right there. I think I better retire."

We laughed. Then Buchan, rising abruptly, left the table, and it went silent again.

The new course was taking the task unit to the North, to the waters between the northern tip of Britain and Iceland. There we would wait. The convoy for which we were an outpost was on its way now to the United Kingdom, and They wanted it.

They wanted the convoy because it was very necessary to some-thing very big: the invasion. Whenever and wherever the inva-sion would come. They wanted it badly, and the place for Them to get it was where we, and They, were going. There They would have to make a move, there we might, at last, find Them. We steamed north.

The carrier and the three destroyers cut through slate seas that were higher by the day. Every day, too, the cold was heav-ier and sharper than the day before, and soon we were in the gales of the North Atlantic again, in the winds that screamed and chilled and slashed. Then we were there, in the storm-lath-ered ocean badland between the Kingdom and Iceland. They were coming there, too, because They wanted the convoy. We had kept the rendezvous. Now we waited for Them.

We did not wait statically. We ran back and forth on the chords of a great circle, always hunting. And waiting.

34

THE DAY to fuel came, freezing, windless, and still, one of those rare rifts of calm that suddenly appear and suddenly vanish in the violence of the North Atlantic. The sea was smooth gray jelly, uncut by waves or whitecaps, thick enough to spoon.

"Good day fur it," said the captain in a mock countryman's voice. That was his favorite aphorism, which he applied, cathol-ically, to virtually all occasions, though chiefly to their suit-ablity for sexual intercourse. "Make enough speed to stay out of trouble today."

I looked at him standing on the port wing of the bridge, one hand on the wind guard that came almost to his chest, gazing at the carrier a sea mile away and not quite behind us. He was wrapped in the heavy blue jungle cloth with the fur-collared green coat over it, his face long and red-tinted under the blue cloth headpiece. He looked well rested; there had been no general quarters the night before.

"This is no place to be a sitting duck," I said.

He was right to be happy about the day. It was luck. Now there was no risk of heavy seas smashing the *Dee* into the sharp bulk of the carrier while she was alongside to take the oil. And in this sea the ships could make speed while fueling. They would not be slow targets in submarine waters.

The fueling figured to be right out of the textbook, which was good, because it had to be done today. Weather had pushed it off two days before, and the destroyers were low on oil. They were sprinters; they could not go the distance alone. They had to have almost constant transfusions of the heavy, black, turnip-smelling fluid that was their lifeblood to survive.

Buchan turned away from the wind guard to me. "We're last on the card. The *Donahue* first, the *Hilliard*, then us."

The *Donahue* was coming up behind the carrier now. She drew even, hung there, and spat her lines, thin as threads at the distance, to the lopsided mass of the big ship. Then, from the carrier, a black shoelace that was the oil hose, looking from our bridge to be suspended in the air, passed slowly to the dwarfed shape of the destroyer beside her. The two ships clung motionless together, the black shoestring and the slender threads dipping between, in a black and gray lithograph.

"She's riding easy." The captain was watching, too. "No smashups today."

Through the glasses I could see them moving, not in a real pitch but in an easy rise and fall, gentle and well curbed, that seemed no more than a cradle rock. They held together like that, as unchanging as figures in a painting, for more than an hour. Then one end of the shoestring fell from the *Donahue* into the water and the carrier sucked it up, the threads suddenly vanished, and the *Donahue*, no longer part of a picture, was cutting sharply away from the carrier, her bow wave rising white and high out of the gray velvet as she drove ahead toward the *Hilliard*, a mile away on the left side of the screen.

The *Hilliard* circled back, repeated the ritual, and, at eight minutes past eleven, it was our turn.

"Sound general quarters," said Buchan. He was taking no chances that he did not have to take.

The *Dee* wheeled to the right in a wide sweep that swung her behind and coming up on the carrier. We came closer, and the stern of the carrier, V-shaped under the overhanging roof of the flight deck, focused into clear lines. The number "11" was suddenly visible, dirty white on the rust-smeared blue hull. Men emerged in outline on the twenty-millimeter-gun platforms under the deck. As the stern got larger, their faces took shape, and, closer still, showed a half-pitying, half-derisive curiosity. The *Dee* nosed past the stern and crept up alongside the big ship, gliding ahead in the smoothness of her wake. I looked almost straight up to the flight deck. From it, four helmeted flying officers looked down with that same look of superior curiosity, observing, as through a microscope, how the other half lived.

"Get the lines over," commanded Buchan. The telephone talker repeated the order.

On the forecastle of the *Dee*, a seaman raised to his shoulder a gun that looked like a rifle, it cracked, and a line ending in a metal arrow fired from the gun shot uncoiling into the air, arced through the space between the ships, and dropped to a platform on the carrier under the flight deck. Her men hauled it in. On the end of the heaving line was a heavy Manila hawser. It followed the light line to the carrier, was made fast there, and with it, dipping between the two ships, the carrier was half towing the *Dee*. Then she, in turn, threw to the *Dee* a heaving line which guided a hawser to us. On the end of this one was the yellow brass tip of the black, fist-thick hose through which the fuel oil would pass from the carrier's tanks into the *Dee's*.

On the *Dee's* forecastle, twenty men strained at the line to pull the heavy hose aboard. The hose started from the carrier, wagged slowly through the air like a headless snake, then fell into the water between the ships and writhed, still like a serpent, in the white froth there, to climb out, finally, and up to the *Dee*. The men pulled the brass end under the lifeline and linked it to the *Dee's* own hose, stretched, ready, on the deck.

Two minutes later, the telephone talker reported to Buchan, "Ready to take oil."

Then the oil started pouring through the hose into the *Dee's* near-empty tanks.

The *Dee* rode smoothly alongside the carrier, the two rising and falling alternately in a slow, off-beat rhythm. The hose, now not a live struggling thing but a nerveless black corpse, hung deadly between them. Buchan, watching on the port wing the movements of both ships, the water between them, and, on the compass repeater before him, the *Dee's* heading, called one- and two-degree course changes to the helmsman inside the wheel house.

I looked back along the length of the *Dee*, at the slender three-inch guns swinging slowly through the air and pointing at the horizon, at the dozen men standing, in easy attitudes, along the port side of the galley deckhouse staring at the carrier, and at the white water bubbling from under her stern to violate the gray smoothness of the sea behind her.

Ahead, the *Donahue* and *Hilliard* zigzagged back and forth in their protective patrol. And from the sound shack came the ceaseless pinging. Time passed.

"The engineers say ten minutes more," the talker said to the captain.

Buchan nodded, and, half relaxing, put one arm on the wind guard, still watching the *Dee's* bow, so close to the carrier.

"Wish they were all like this," he said, as much to himself as to me.

The bow was glued in steady position alongside the bigger

ship. It had, indeed, I thought, been a textbook exercise. The soft, lulling gait of the ships, the unbroken placidity of the gray sea, and the windless cold of the air created, somehow, an almost dreamlike tranquillity, as though time had been suspended, as though we were out of time and had been caught and congealed in the middle of an unfinished movement.

Then the helmsman yelled from inside the wheelhouse: "Rudder is jammed at right fifteen!"

As he cried, the bow was breaking from position and swinging slowly but inexorably to the right. The thick Manila hawser between the ships snapped tight and the heavy black hose straightened ominously from its dip.

"Stand clear!" Jake Warwick shouted on the forecastle.

Jake snatched the emergency hand axe from the paralyzed sailor holding it as the knot of men around him erupted into single, fleeing pieces. Alone by the line, taut as a banjo string and crackling from the increasing tension, he raised the axe high over his head with both hands and smashed it down on the oil hose, where the hose came over the side. The hose parted on the second blow. He raised the axe again and slashed at the twanging line that held the *Dee* and the carrier together. The line parted with a pistol crack. The long end jerked into the sea and the short one whipped across Jake's left knee and knocked him to the deck. He lay there, doubled at the waist, both hands holding the knee and his face contorted.

This had all happened by the time you could count to fifteen. Now the *Dee* was free and circling out of control to starboard, like a horse with the bit in his teeth. Looking over the side at the stern, I saw a long piece of wire, which had held the hose to its guide line and which now trailed in the water, slip under the *Dee's* propeller guard and disappear. Sucked under, I thought. The *Dee* swung clear of the carrier and kept on in her circle. It was something that the rudder had jammed to the right; if it had stuck on the left side, we would have crashed into the carrier.

"Get somebody up there and take care of Warwick." As the captain was speaking, six seamen converged on Jake. They lifted him from the deck and carried him through the door to the well deck. The doctor would take care of him there.

Buchan tried to straighten the *Dee* from her circle by using the engines.

"Port stop. Port back one-third."

The hull began to shake. The shaking became more violent, and there was a heavy rattling on the bridge. Then both the shaking and the rattling stopped.

"What the hell is that?"

"I think we wound a long piece of wire around the port propeller, Cap'n," I said. "That wire on the oil hose got sucked under when we cut loose. I saw it slip under the prop guard."

He said nothing, but shook his head, took two steps toward the flag bag, then wheeled and took two more forward.

The talker was getting something on the phones. He said to the captain, "Engine room says the port screw won't turn over. They say something's fouled it."

"Goddamn it," said Buchan. He looked over the wind guard to the carrier, her stern toward us and getting smaller fast. "That's all we need. That's really all we need."

The *Dee* was still turning slowly to the right. Buchan looked at the shimmering circle of her wake, at the receding stern of the carrier again, and then wrote on a paper pad and handed it to the signalman, Kaintuck.

"Send this to her."

He was reporting what had happened. The *Dee's* rudder was jammed, one engine was useless, and she was out of control in dangerous waters.

Kaintuck flashed the signal light, and the carrier blinked her answer. He brought it, written on the pad, to Buchan.

"Effect emergency repairs and rejoin." The captain read it aloud. "Will provide air cover."

He handed the message back to Kaintuck, not looking at him, his eyes already back on the carrier. She was moving away fast. The *Hilliard* and the *Donahue* were still weaving from side to side in front of her; she was sending neither back to protect us. The other ships were now more than a mile away, and lengthening the distance. We were alone.

Buchan, staring at their diminishing shapes, decided what he had to decide. He turned his back on them and said: "All engines stop." Then, to me, "Bring the talker and some seamen to the fantail. We'll look it over from back there."

The telephone talker, his line coiled in his right hand, and I followed the captain down the ladder and through passageways to the fantail, the rear end of the ship.

From the fantail, I looked over the lifelines and saw, dimly through water half transparent near the surface, the clover-shaped brown propeller, its three blades thrusting, motionless, from the narrow bottom of the ship almost fifteen feet below.

The seamen came back to the fantail, and it began to fill with men, among them Johnny. They all stood in the center of the deck, silent and waiting for something to happen. The *Dee* was now dead in the water, swaying gently in the glacial sea. A perfect target for anything.

The telephone talker plugged his line into a socket on the

deckhouse bulkhead, and said into the phone, "Fantail, testing." Then he stopped, and I heard, in his earpiece, the sputter
of the answering voice from the bridge, until he swung quickly
to the captain. "Bridge reports the rudder is clear now, sir. It
answers the wheel, port and starboard."

"Fine." Buchan made a noise that might have been a laugh.
"That'll do us a lot of good while we're sitting out here." His
voice changed swiftly. "Tell the engine room to stand by for
quick changes on the port engine. I'm going to try to work the
wire loose from the prop." He could have steamed on the
starboard engine alone, but this would have ruined the turning circle for a depth-charge attack and would have left the
Dee almost useless. She needed both engines.

He ordered the engine ahead, stopped it, and reversed it.
Through the water, I saw the prop, turning slowly, as in pro-
test. The forced turning shook the fantail, hard. Buchan, hop-
ing by the quick starts and stops, to free the blade of the wire
that had entangled it, tried the procedure many times. It did not
work.

"Let's try the grapnels." Buchan's voice was impassive, but
his face showed he knew the grapnels would not work, either.
Carmer, the first-class boatswain's mate, functioning now for
Jake, obeyed. He lowered over the side of the ship a grapnel,
a three-pronged hook, on the end of a piece of line. Maneuver-
ing the grapnel by the line he held, he tried to work its hooks
into the wire that fouled the propeller and that he could not
see. He could not do it.

"Can't do any good with this, sir."

The captain acknowledged with a half-nod, then stood, saying nothing, waiting. He might have been thinking of the target the *Dee* made. I was.

Johnny stepped out of the ring of men around Buchan, and
said, casually, "Suppose I go down and take a look."

Buchan looked at him. He did not answer for several seconds. Then he said, "Okay. Go put on two suits of long underwear. And hurry it up." Johnny left. Then the captain told
Carmer, "Break out the shallow-water diving outfit." And to
the telephone talker, "Tell the engine room to secure that
screw. And I mean secure it. Tell them to plug it so it can't
turn over. And tell the engineering officer to report it plugged
personally."

We waited. As we stood there, the air cover appeared. Two
planes, knifing out of the clouds, began to circle the ship. One,
angling low over the mast with a quick-deepening motor snarl,
wiggled his wings. I was glad to see them.

Carmer came back with the shallow-water diving apparatus. It consisted of only a black rubber mask with three straps on the side, a round aluminum valve at the nose, and eye goggles above the valve, plus a sixty-foot air hose with an oxygen pump on the end of it. Carmer set the pump and hose on the deck, and held the mask in his hands.

Buchan looked at the mask. "Is it working?"

"Yes, sir."

The captain nodded. Then Johnny stepped around the corner of the after deckhouse to the fantail. His legs, white in the skin-tight underwear, protruded from under the green coat and ended at his feet in the black arctics.

"All ready?" Buchan appraised him.

"Yes, sir."

"Put it on, then."

Johnny took off the coat and handed it to a seaman. The sleeves of his underwear jersey ran into black mittens on his hands. In the underwear and mittens, he looked like a nineteenth-century prizefighter. Carmer knotted a line around his chest and handed him a pair of wire cutters that looked like oversized, clumsy scissors. Then he slipped the black mask over Johnny's head, and I thought, for an instant, of a hangman dropping the hood on his man. Johnny adjusted the nose valve with his mittened fingers. The mask gave him, too, the look of a gargoyle.

The circle of men around the captain and Johnny opened to leave a clear space above the propeller. The fantail was quiet.

"Mr. Anson says the propeller is secured, sir," said the talker. Now there was no chance of the screw turning while Johnny was working on it.

"Okay, Johnny." The captain faced him. "Shove off."

Johnny walked to the side. He bent and slipped between the two lifelines, now like a fighter going into the ring. He put his hands on the lower lifeline and let himself down to arm's length. Then the men playing the line around his chest took his weight on that and lowered him into the water. His feet in the black arctics went in, and after them, his legs. He involuntarily drew his legs up as the water first hit, and then the water rose around him, only his head in the mask showing and then it, too, under. Only white bubbles showed on the surface.

The water was almost clear. You could see through it as with opaque glasses. Johnny, head down, forced his way toward the propeller with long strokes of his arms. The propeller was nearly fifteen feet down. H reached it and wrapped one arm around the shaft that held it to the ship. His feet trailed up toward the surface until he was almost vertical. His long black hair swirled, above the mask, back from his head. Through the water in the white underwear he looked like a corpse. With his free right hand he was doing things with the wire cutters. His feet fluttered as he tried to kick them down. The cutters kept working, for more than a minute. Then he let go of the shaft and jerked on the line, his white body already starting to rise. On the fantail, the men tending his line hauled away.

The white substanceless form neared the surface, broke it, and the black mask came out of the water. They strained on the line to bring Johnny up. He was heavy, better than two twenty. They pulled him to the lifelines. Then he put his hands on the bottom line and finished the job himself.

The captain waited as they took the mask off. Johnny's face came out of the mask red, with his lips palely blue. His teeth clicked hard together. He could not talk. Then he started.

"Lots of little turns. On end of shaft." The teeth stopped him, then he started again. "Cut lots of 'em. Lots more left. Go down again, few minutes."

"No, you won't." Buchan looked at him sharply. "You're secured. Take him in there and warm him up." He pointed to the open door of the crew's head, in the after deckhouse, ten feet away. Carmer led Johnny in and closed the door.

Buchan looked around the circle, expectant but not asking.

"I'll get on my gear," I said.

He looked at me. "All right, Pete. But hustle it."

I ran to my room. In two minutes I was back, dressed as Johnny had been, in the long underwear with the coat over it.

"Ready?" said Buchan.

"Ready."

"Okay. You've to cut that line off the shaft. Make it good. We're in trouble every minute we're out here."

Carmer pulled the mask over the top of my head. The straps cut tightly into my neck and scalp. I could not breathe. The mask imprisoned me. I wanted to fight it and throw it off. I turned the air valve with my fingers. Air came in. I breathed again. But hard. There was not enough air.

Carmer put the cutters in my hand. I stepped through the lifelines to the rim of the deck outside, and, my hands on the bottom line, stooped, turned, and slid over the side. Then I was hanging on the line. I let go, and they were lowering me into the water. My feet went under. The water struck like shock. I turned to ice by inches as I went down. Water crept around me, went over my head, and I was completely under. The cold hit like a hammer at my chest. I swam down. The cold was paralyzing. I had to fight to move. I was suddenly

aware that I had no mittens on my hands. Nobody had noticed.
I made it to the screw. My feet started to billow toward the
surface as Johnny's had done. I kicked them down. I wrapped
both arms around one blade of the screw and the shaft. That
left both hands free. I was now between two of the three
blades, the edge of one pushing against my chest. It would be
fine if they started turning the screw. My face brushed the iron
surface of the blade. It was rough. My skin stung.

Through the goggles I could see the wire clearly. It was
wrapped, many times, tight around the shaft. I tried to work
the cutters into position under the wire. The wire was wound
so tight it was hard to do. Finally I started to cut. There was no
leverage for the cutters and it came slow. My fingers went
numb. I could hardly move them. The cutters were working.
Now they were biting through the turns of the wire.

A sudden and special coldness settled below my waist. I
looked down. Both the long, thick underwear pants and the
jockey shorts under them had slipped from my waist. For a gap
of several inches I was naked. The numbness was settling in in
that area. I yanked the underwear up and kept cutting. There
were still many turns. I did not know how much longer I could
stay down. Feeling had nearly left the fingers. I had ten of
them, I did not care about them, but I had only one of something else. The last I wanted to take no chance with. The
underwear kept coming down and I had to pull it up. The wire
still made many turns around the shaft. I cut at them and the
numbness got stronger below the waist. I had enough. I reached
behind me, tugged the line three times, and let go of the
shaft. The line pulled me up through the water. They hauled
me aboard. I was shaking like a skeleton. Somebody slung a
blanket around me. I tried to talk.

"Still some wire. Around it." I stopped to control the clicking of my teeth. My body shook inside the blanket. "Go down
again. Go down again when. When I get warm."

"That's all for you." That was the doctor. "You're through
going down. You won't stand any more watches today, either."
He held up a bottle of whiskey, and I, taking it, shivering,
noticed the label said "Seven Crown."

"Take a stiff one." I did. The whiskey felt like spreading
fire in my belly. They took me into the head. Flattop was inside, dressed in the underwear, ready to go down. The doctor
kept me in the blankets in the head for ten minutes, then he
led me, still in the blankets, below to Johnny's room. I took off
my clothes and the doctor rubbed me hard with two towels.
Then he put me to bed in the bottom bunk. Johnny was in
the upper one.

The doctor set another bottle on the desk, where I could reach it.

"Drink it all if you want," he said, and went out.

We started drinking. The whiskey hit hard, and fast. Then we heard the sound of the engines and knew that somebody, somehow had finished clearing the screw. I was quite drunk, scarcely feeling the pitch of the *Dee* as she went ahead at what I knew must be twenty-five knots, when I went to sleep.

Day followed day like sections of a cable that someone was winding tighter and tighter on a great, slow-turning spool. Our war was closing in. The battlefield had shrunk. The Enemy was still invisible and the terrain was still the never-changing, never-the-same sea, but the ship had the feeling of forces converging. It was not a thing that you could see or touch or describe, but it hung over the ship like cold, heavy fog, and it grew colder and heavier with each day.

The men, tightened, too. On watch, they had an intenseness that had not been there before; off watch, they clung together in small groups to shun the loneliness of even a moment. In the wardroom, meals passed in near silence; Buchan was no longer there to spark them. Now he never left the bridge. He had his food sent there and slept in the emergency cabin behind the wheelhouse.

We kept hunting. We had contacts, and almost every day the klaxon jerked the "Dee's" crew to battle stations. But these were only brushes in a great dark. The tremulous echo that was our only spoor either vanished abruptly or faded mockingly into nothingness.

We hunted. But we really waited for Them to make the move. It was up to Them. They would decide when.

35

CRANDALL was now almost completely an outcast: insulted by the officers and abused by the men, in the thousand ways they had of inflicting abuse without actually violating the sharp line of the law.

This contempt had crystallized that day—weeks or years ago—that someone had shut him in the darkness of the depth-charge locker. This had been the seal. From then on, he had been, in a sense officially, something to despise. But the despising had changed. In the beginning it was bawdy and teasing, rough but not really cruel, superficially good-natured. But, as the hunt wore on, the despising dropped its camouflaging rim of good nature, and the cruelty showed: thin but visible.

Now, as we steamed for what we were sure was the rendez-vous of decision, the cruelty and the contempt had intensified into an angry, vicious thing that had depth and solidity and shape I could not have conceived, those short eternal weeks before the hunt.

Crandall's defeat in Casablanca had been a seal, too. Of a different kind. This one he could see himself. And it must, consequently, have burned him like an unhealed brand.

Now every officer and man — except the captain, who stayed apart from it — competed to see who could drop the greatest defecations upon Crandall. Within the rules. On the side of the line. For the line was as clear and straight as though painted in black on the weather decks. The men observed it rigorously, because they were enlisted personnel dealing with a commissioned officer in the United States Navy. And the officers also observed it, because they were officers dealing with a commissioned officer in the United States Navy. But they all crowded the line to hit and hurt him.

Each time that I hit him, I felt, afterward, the same contempt, hatred even, for myself that I did for Crandall, and swore I would stop. But I never did.

Then one day the line was crossed. I was not there to see it. Nor was any other officer. But it was reported, as such things will be, with remarkable exactness, and was, by dinner of the day it took place, unrestricted property in the wardroom.

This was what happened:

Crandall found it necessary, shortly after four o'clock in the afternoon, to speak with Dorgan, the coxswain in charge of the cleaning detail on the after weather decks. Rockford had called Crandall's attention, pointedly, to two cans of paint and four paintbrushes left adrift on the open deck at the close of the working day, and suggested, with equal definiteness, that Crandall call it to the attention of the petty officer in charge.

Since it was after four, Dorgan would be, almost inevitably, in the after crew's quarters below. So Crandall went there to find him.

Crandall stepped, blinking, from the last step of the ladder to the red-painted, rusting deck and stood, not moving, for a moment, in the light of a solitary electric bulb that burned directly over him. Before him ranged four rows of three-tiered bunks, separated by aisles. Almost half the bunks carried prostrate forms in varying shades of light and dark, of dress and undress. The light threw long gargoyle shadows off the bunks that danced in creeping rhythm across the walls and the deck as the light swung back and forth with the movement of the ship.

One man in a stained blue dungaree shirt sat at the end of a table under the light, smoking a cob pipe and reading a magazine with a gun-drawing, bright-colored cowboy on the cover. He looked up at Crandall. It was Hawley, the oil king.

"Have you seen Dorgan?" Crandall asked it in the tone he had used with the men from the start, which was part peremptory and part something else.

Hawley did not answer, but raised his head and called at the bodies in the bunks: "Dorgan. Hey, Dorgan."

If Dorgan was there, he did not answer. Heads came up from pillows and looked toward Crandall.

"Dorgan. Oh Dorgan!" The chief made it louder. "Mr Crandall wants you."

No answer.

"Hey, Dorgan. Mr. Crandall wants to see you."

Then, from the shadows, an anonymous voice cracked like an inquisitor's whip, screaming and full of hate, becoming in its unpossessedness and for its instant of flight, the fused single outcry of the entire crew: "Ah, Cranberry, blow it out your ass!"

It was the pressing of a firing key. A barrage rolled up and out from the bunks, swelling and swelling, louder and louder, the five words chorused by two dozen men pounding at and shattering Crandall standing there a target.

"Blow it out your ass! Blow it out your ass! Blow it out your ass!"

The chorus thundered over the compartment, and then died, as suddenly and as without warning as it had exploded.

In the mass guilt, there was no culprit to punish.

Crandall stood frozen, his face sick and unbelieving and terrified as the light swung back and forth above him. In shock again. He did not move. He just stood there. As though the world had come to an end and was going to roll over on top of him. Or maybe as though it had already rolled on top of him.

Then, Crandall, the muscles of his white face working and his eyes rigidly, incredulously staring, turned and started up the ladder. At first, slowly and with dignity.

Before he reached the top, he was running.

At dinner in the wardroom while we, knowing, sat silent at the soup, Rockford said blandly to Crandall: "By the way, did you find Dorgan this afternoon?"

Before Crandall answered, the captain looked at Rockford. And now it was Rockford who lost color and studied his plate. Crandall shook his head, wordlessly, and the captain instantly said down the table to the Flattop: "Where are those blondes you promised to send up? You're a fine damn talent scout!"

So the captain knows, I thought. He knows and he is protecting Crandall. At the start, he drove Crandall without mercy, and now he is protecting him. Why?

And, why were we crucifying Crandall?

I wanted to know the answers. To both questions. Which were maybe the same question. If I knew the answer, I was sure, somehow, I would know a great deal more. A great deal more than just the answer to this question.

36

NIGHT WAS NOT really for sleeping, I thought, pulling up the stale sheet and the rough white blanket that stung my chin, which were, in the steam-heated room, all I needed. Though you did sleep. Night was when it would or would not happen. Each night you pulled up the covers thinking, with something far away and deeply buried, that this night might be the one, that They might make the move this night. For you knew that when They did, it would be at night.

"I'll see you at eleven-thirty," Jerry said from the upper bunk. "What a hell of a way to live." He turned out the light on the bulkhead by his pillow, and, except for the red light coming under the door, the room was dark.

Automatically, I looked at the watch, and, automatically, noted that the time was eight-thirty-two; three hours to sleep until the midwatch.

But I did not sleep, not for a while. I was thinking about the hunt. I knew now what made it different. It had taken me this long to learn, and I had not learned all at once but only a little at a time. Or so it seemed. Perhaps I had known it all at the start, and admitted it only a little at a time. Whatever, I knew now. I knew that the hunt was more than an operation. On another level, not the one you saw and spoke and heard, but the one you felt, it was a hunt for Evil. It was a pursuit to which we had been joined by no act of volition on our part but into which we had been thrust by the forces that controlled us. These forces were, on the first level, the office of naval operations, but on the other one, the one you felt, they were something else. We did not know why we were hunting Evil, or, at the beginning, that we were hunting it, but now something had pushed us into the hunt and we had to finish it.

This search for the unseen Evil, an Evil that was as much a part of his life as the submarines were of our hunt, was what every man had to do, and he was pushed into this by whoever does the pushing. For him, as for us on the hunt, there was no end until he hunted out the Enemy and destroyed it, or until, unseen, it destroyed him.

I thought about this parable. Then I laughed, at it, and at myself. What shit, Taylor. What utter, North Carolina bullshit. If you walked across the street for a drink, you would try to underwrite it metaphysically. You have been out here too long. What you need, like Ski, is a three-day shack-up with a bottle and a blonde. Blonde, brunette, or greenhead. Any pigmentation. Concentrate on that and cut out the metaphysical you know what. Stop trying to translate a shoestring North Atlantic operation with a bush-league carrier and three four-stack destroyers too old for anything else into an allegory for all humanity. You will be back soon. In the room with the girl of any pigmentation and with no particular face there will be an electric clock on the wall, circling your minutes away. On the table by the bed, next to the telephone, will be a bottle, half empty. Through the window, because you will be high above the street, the morning wind will blow in fresh, though not strong, for the window will be open only two inches. You and the faceless girl of whatever pigmentation will awake, without clothes and smelling muskily of loving, and you will pick up the telephone and order breakfast, and it will come in on a rolling table covered with a fresh white cloth, the coffee hot and fresh in a silver pot, the scrambled eggs and bacon and toast all hot and steaming under the silver containers, and you and the girl will eat the breakfast and start again.

That is what there will be for you, and please, please stop the metaphysics. What you have to do out here is very simple and what you want to do back there is very simple, so keep it in a simple, straight line.

You better get some liberty soon, I thought. You've been at sea too long. Then I went to sleep.

A yellow light burst through the darkness, and, from a great distance, a voice called. I traveled the distance in a timeless, heart-dropping rush and heard the voice again, now distinct and at my ear: "Time to relieve the watch, sir."

I opened my eyes and saw, above the yellow circle of the flashlight a foot from my face, a tall form that was more a shadow than a shape.

Now I was no longer asleep but awake, almost, and had to get out of a warm bed and put on infinite layers of clothing and had to climb a ladder to an open bridge and had to take, for four hours, the wind and the cold and the dark.

"You awake, sir?"

The voice prodded and cajoled me the rest of the way.

"Okay, Flaherty. I'm awake."

"Cold out. A little spray."

That was to clinch it.

"Okay, okay."

He stood on tiptoe, put the flashlight into Jerry's eyes, and called him, softly. Jerry awoke. He moaned, "What a hell of a way to live." Then Flaherty went out.

I lay still, being unhappy. Jerry's behind made a bulge in the mattress above me. I kicked it.

"Stop it. Christ, what a hell of a way to live."

I slid out of the bunk. The steel deck was cold to the bottom of my feet. Though the room was warm with the steam heat, the deck stayed cold. The ship was rolling hard. I had to put one hand on the side of the bunk for balance as I put on my pants over the long underwear, which, in bed, I had kept on. I sloshed water from the lavatory on my face, and then I was completely awake.

"Get your ass out of there," I said.

Jerry groaned, and got it out.

He let himself down slowly from the top bunk and stood, oddly frail, on the deck in the white underwear.

He stumbled toward the lavatory. "There's nothing like sea duty." Then he washed his face.

I put on the jungle-cloth outer clothes, picked up the big coat and the blue hat with the long earpieces, and went into the wardroom. He followed.

There were sandwiches in the silver platter in the brown wooden board that held it fast, and coffee in one of the glass bowls on the hot plate. Jerry picked up two cups from the grooves in the wooden board, put them in saucers, and, balancing one carefully in each hand, held them out. I poured coffee into them, took one, and a sandwich from the platter. The coffee was old. I bit into the sandwich. The bread was stale and bologna was inside.

The engines stopped.

It was like a heartbeat ceasing. The always-there noises of the ship that blurred together and were lost on the rim of consciousness were suddenly gone. Left in their place was a silence that screamed.

"Jesus Christ," said Jerry. Against the overwhelming fact

of the ship's sudden helplessness, he could only bring these two words, and he said them again. "Jesus Christ."

The cables of the engine telegraph, which ran through the wardroom, made noises against the ceiling.

"Here goes general quarters." I put the cup down and stood up.

The *Dee* was still capsuled in the vacuum silence. Her hard tossing had stopped. I opened the door, stepped through it, and the ship came alive again, with a quick, deep hum of engines and the loud exhalation of the ventilation blowers through which she breathed. The cables rasped again, and I felt her start ahead.

We went through the hatch to the well deck, then climbed the ladder to the bridge. Johnny was on the port wing. I knew, by the way he stood, leaning over the wind guard with his glasses at his eyes and pointed out at the darkness, that he was tense and excited. He did not look at me as I stopped at his side.

"What happened?"

"Everything." He took the glasses down and turned to me. "The engines just lost suction and we broke down. We dropped back a mile and a half from where we ought to be. The carrier's over there broad on our beam now." He pointed at a ninety-degree angle. The *Donahue's* screening in front. The *Hilliard* is way to hell and gone off somewhere. She got a sub contact and went after it. The rest of us changed course and got out of there."

"The *Hilliard's* all by herself?"

"All by herself. The carrier wants plenty of company."

"She needs it." She did. At night, unable to get the planes in the air, she was only a target. "Are the engines all right now?"

"Maybe, maybe not. They're turning over, anyway. The engineers are still working on them." He gave me the rest of the information. I looked at the carrier and the *Donahue* with the binoculars, and he said, "Are you going to relieve me or leave me up here all night?"

"I relieve you." I touched the cloth helmet with my right hand.

"Good night. Try not to get me up with general quarters."

"I'll let you get to sleep first."

"You probably will, you son of a bitch. Good night." He left.

There was no moon, and the carrier and the *Donahue* barely showed in the circle of the binoculars. Through the open door to the wheelhouse, I could see only the red point of light above the wheel.

"Pete." The captain's voice came from inside. I went in and saw him, his legs white in the dark, bending over the radar-scope. He had his heavy coat on over the long underwear. "We're still a mile behind station. Keep speed at twenty knots until we get there. I'll be back when I get some clothes on."

"Aye, aye, sir."

He stepped out of the door into the dark. I looked at the yellow pips on the radar scope. They made a geometric picture of the ship's position. The *Dee* was still behind the others, but moved ahead as I watched. The captain came back fully dressed. He stood before the scope, and I moved to the side to let him see.

"Gunfire on the port beam!" Jerry cried it out half inside the door.

The captain and I ran to the wing. Tracers curved red against the black of the sky, far to the left. It was very far. They floated with deceptive slowness in a roman-candle arc. There was no sound. The distance was too great for it to carry.

"Twenty-millimeters." Buchan had his glasses on them.

"Must be the *Hilliard*."

"It's the *Hilliard*, all right."

The tracers stopped, as suddenly as they had started, and where we looked, there was only darkness.

"Think she had one surfaced?"

"I don't think so." Buchan was still looking where the tracers had streaked the sky. "Somebody just thought they saw something. See how quick it stopped."

Now he let go of his glasses and they dropped to the end of the leather thong around his neck. He went back inside. Whatever had happened was, temporarily, the *Hilliard's* affair.

"Captain." The radar operator called him in a low voice. "We got something here."

I looked through the door and saw Buchan examining the radar screen again. "Four contacts," he said. "On our side of the formation, too."

That meant the carrier would send the *Dee* in to investigate them. Buchan picked up the radio telephone and reported them, by distance and bearing, to the carrier.

He put the phone back on the hook, and the *Dee's* engines stopped again in the sudden, life-ending cessation.

"What's the matter?" He called it through the voice tube to the engine room, and, though he was visibly angry, his voice was even.

"Lost suction again, sir." The answer came back through the tube.

"How long before you can get the screws turning?"

"Can't tell, sir. We're working on it."

Buchan did not answer. I sensed his bitterness; his ship was out of action in enemy waters, and he could not do a job that belonged to him.

"Somebody else will have to take those contacts," he said. As he stood there, the radio made its electric noises and the big voice called the *Dee*.

It said, "Georgia, investigate strangers, investigate strangers."

Buchan said into the phone: "Coach from Georgia. We cannot investigate strangers. We are blocked out. We are blocked out." That was code for broken down. He said it crisply and without apology.

There was silence. Then, the voice again:

"Yale investigate strangers. Georgia rejoin Coach when ready."

That was it. The *Donahue* was taking our assignment.

"Sound general quarters," Buchan commanded.

"Aye, aye, sir."

The *Dee* had been running ahead under momentum, but now had nearly lost all her headway. If she had to wait for it dead in the water, the crew had to be at their battle stations.

I pulled the handle of the general alarm. It pressed against its stop, and the Klaxon screamed. The ship awoke like a man seared with a hot poker. Running feet shook the decks and hatch covers clanged. Men shouted, "All hands general quarters." In the dark, I could see their white figures, still in underwear, as they climbed the ladder to the galley deckhouse. All stations reported ready. The ship was silent again.

The engines were still dead, the *Dee* no longer going ahead but wallowing in a trough, rolling unresisting with the sea. We waited. We could do nothing else.

Buchan stood, far back, on the port wing, by himself. The three-inch guns, further back on the ship, trained low over the water. From the bridge, the men on them were formless, dark shapes that took substance only when they moved. The ping of the sound gear stabbed the silence of the bridge. Nobody talked.

Then the engines started in the quick, explosive cough, as before, and the *Dee* trembled again in that tiny shudder that for her was life. She was underway. The captain snapped commands. The ship came out of the trough and drove ahead, dropping and rising with the swells as she ran faster and faster, the wind cutting over the shields like a bolo.

"This feels good." Johnny had moved away from his torpedo director and was standing by me. "This feels awful good. Those Goddamned engines better keep working. We've been a sitting duck three times this week. Our luck can't stand it again."

"I hope to heaven we don't have to try it again."

The *Dee* ate the sea at twenty-five knots. She overhauled the carrier fast, passed her to the left, and swung over to take station ahead.

"Secure from general quarters." Buchan wanted to give the crew all the rest they could get, while they could get it. They might need it.

I still had the watch and waited on the bridge, counting the minutes. An hour after general quarters, Rockford appeared to relieve me. It was ten minutes to four and the moon had risen. He seemed tired, and taut, and still sleepy.

"You can't win," he said. "You just can't win."

I went from the bridge to the wardroom. Crandall was sitting in a chair at the end of the table, staring fixedly ahead. I glanced at him without curiosity, then looked sharply back. He was raising a cup of coffee, and his hands were shaking. Coffee sloshed out and spattered on the deck. Neither of us said anything. I walked out.

Jerry was already in bed when I came into the room. I took off the winter gear, and, still in the sweater and trousers, lay down on top of the blanket. I looked at the red light from the battle lamp outside filtering under the door and went to sleep.

37

THE GENERAL ALARM riveted through layers of sleep to shock me into instant, unequivocal consciousness, and I was completely awake as I snatched the winter clothing from the chair and ran for the bridge that I had left, it seemed, only minutes before.

The alarm was still hammering as I dashed through the door from the starboard wing to the wheelhouse, the clothing over my left arm, to find and relieve Rockford. I saw over the wheel the luminous green figures of the clock showing six minutes past five. Rockford had taken the deck from me a little more than an hour before; now I had to take it back from him.

He was not in the wheelhouse. I hurried through it and out of the other door to the port wing.

"Here I am." I heard his voice, then saw him in the forward corner of the wing, where the wind guard met the wall of the wheelhouse, his face sharp and white in the dark over the bulk of the big coat.

"All right. Give it to me. What's the story?"

"We left the carrier." He was trying to control his excitement. "We got part of a message from the *Donahue* on TBS. Only part of it. 'Need assistance.' That was all we got. The carrier turned us loose and sent us to help her. Wherever she is. We don't know where. We've got to find her. Graham is trying to figure her estimated position and give us some kind of a course. The captain is coming and the navigator is on the bridge."

"I relieve you." I wished, for another, unnumberable time, that the planes could go up in the dark. He took off his binoculars, slipped the strap over my neck, and went below to his damage control parties.

"Graham." Buchan's voice, inside the wheelhouse, called through the voice tube to the charthouse on the other side of the thin steel plate. "How about that course?"

"Coming up." Graham's answer came back through the tube, and he added, seconds later, "One-three-eight, captain."

The course was a calculated guess, no more. There were too many unknowns. But it was all we had.

"One-three-eight," Buchan acknowledged, to Graham, and ordered the helmsman, "come right to one-three-eight. All engines ahead full."

The *Dee* sprang ahead faster, and you could feel the greater speed as you feel a horse, under you, break into a run. The sea, like the north wind, came in from her port quarter and rolled her hard, but she was taking no head-on beating and could hold twenty knots as long as she had to. Buchan zigzagged her sharply on either side of the course. That way she could cover a wider belt of sea. And she was a harder target for torpedoes.

We ran ahead for more than an hour. The black of the now moonless night shaded into the dark gray of morning twilight. Graham, a black sextant in his right hand, and Beirne, the quartermaster, behind him with a stop watch, walked from one wing to the other, looking for stars and waiting for the horizon.

The gray began to blanch, and the horizon emerged, but it

was fuzzy and shrouded instead of sharp and straight. The overcast blotted out the stars, and smeared the moon into a lineless, lightless slab of yellow. There were no morning sights. We would keep running on dead reckoning. Graham scowled and took the sextant back into the chart house.

It was solid daylight. The smell of coffee drifted urgently from the galley to the bridge. Mess cooks carried it in big pots to the battle stations. One came to the bridge. I waited for the men inside the wheelhouse to pass it to the wing, and tried to move my toes inside the shoes and the arctics. My feet were without feeling.

Graham came out of the charthouse and said, "Captain, I figure we're somewhere in the area now."

Buchan, his face a deep pink over the brown fur collar of the coat, nodded. "Let's circle around, then." He walked to the wheelhouse door, and said through it to the radar operator, "Got anything yet?"

"No, sir. We've lost the carrier now. No contacts at all."

"Very well." The captain moved back to the wind guard, and began to course the *Dee* in a big circle, about five miles in diameter, and cut the speed to fifteen knots. She held the pattern, leaning a little to the left as she made the easy turns. Looking, now with the glasses and now without them, I saw nothing but the gray sea, combed by the white ridges of the waves, and the gray tent of the sky bounding it at the horizon.

The captain walked back and forth in his four-foot space in the corner of the wing, trying, I thought, to keep warm, looking, always, at the sea.

"What time is it?" This to me.

"Ten to seven."

"Be sure to get breakfast to all the stations."

"Aye, aye, sir."

Knox, the radar operator, came to the doorway. "Cap'n, we got four contacts. On the starboard bow at eleven miles."

Buchan went into the wheelhouse to look at the radar scope inside, then, almost at once, came back.

"They look like the contacts we had before. The ones the *Donahue* went after. We'll go in for a look."

He swung the *Dee* to the right to head toward them, then started to zigzag her again.

"All guns stand by." He gave the order to his telephone talker, and I knew we would not have breakfast for a while.

The men at the guns, who had huddled together behind the mounts after the first flurry of general quarters, now manned them again. The pointers and trainers climbed back into the seats, and the leaders made a line between the ammunition boxes and the gun breeches.

The *Dee* was closing the distance between herself and the yellow blips on the radar that were reflections of tangible objects on the face of the sea. The objects themselves were now only eight miles away. In the dull gray light, I still could not see them. Graham plotted their course and reported it to Buchan. They were moving almost due south, in front of the north wind, at eight knots.

"Object on the port bow at five hundred yards," the lookout cried from the flying bridge above. Buchan and I put our glasses on the spot. I saw nothing. Then it appeared on top of a swell, slid under, and thrust out again, small, shapeless and black. It was going to pass close aboard.

"Could be a mine," I said.

"It's no mine." Buchan kept his glasses up. He, I thought, knew what it was. So did I. So may have everybody else who saw it. But nobody was saying.

It was still a formless chunk of black wallowing in the waves. It could have been anything.

The *Dee* passed it at less than a hundred yards. Then you could see. You could see the legs in blue jungle cloth protruding from the black life jacket. You could not see the face because it was down in the water. We did not stop. Buchan kept the *Dee* moving toward the radar contacts. Ten minutes later, two empty life jackets floated by. Radar showed the *Dee* seven miles from the contacts.

Buchan pointed ahead. "Look up there."

Something came into my glasses on the crest of a sea, tiny and dark and looking far away, too far to be another corpse, too low in the sea for radar to pick up. It dipped in and out of visibility with the sea, a single black comma on a white-flecked gray sheet of ocean.

The *Dee* made straight for it. It grew larger, until I could see it even in the sea trough, and it took outline. It was a life raft and men rode it. How many, I could not yet tell. They had seen the *Dee* coming and were sitting very still, not trying to get attention. They knew they had it. At a thousand yards, I saw the men clearly. There were six. They were in United States Navy winter clothing.

Buchan cut speed and maneuvered to come alongside the raft, heading in the same direction as it was drifting. He eased the ship into heaving-line distance from the raft and stopped the engines. He picked up the electric megaphone.

"On the raft. Stand by to take a heaving line."

One of the men raised his hands high to show understanding. On the black, float-rimmed oval they crouched on their knees and waited.

"Get it over," Buchan yelled to the forecastle.

On the forecastle, Carmer swung the lead-ended coil of line back like a discus and flung it at the raft. The line shot uncoiling over it and one man snatched the white thread as it dropped.

"Haul away," shouted Buchan.

The men on the raft jerked the heaving line toward them. On the other end was a heavy, five-inch mooring hawser. It snaked its way to the raft as the men pulled. There was nothing they could make the line fast to on the raft. All six of the men held it with both hands. One lifted one hand, waved, and put the hand back to the line. They were ready.

"Pull her in," Buchan ordered.

The seamen on the forecastle, one behind the other, gripped the line and, holding tight, walked back with it. The raft bounced toward the *Dee*, pitching hard. A steel ladder was already over the side of the forecastle for the men. On the raft, they clung tightly to the line as the raft worked toward the ladder.

I could see their faces now, but set, or maybe frozen, in numb immobility, they showed nothing, no surprise, no relief, no jubilation, no weariness even, but only desperate concentration on the steel ladder on the side of the soft-pitching ship.

One squatted low as the others held to the line, grasping the raft float with his left hand and stretching his right for the ladder. The raft reared on top of a wave and he jumped for the ladder. He caught it with his right hand, slipped, and flung his left hand to the same rung. Then he climbed to the deck. One by one, the others did it the same way. The last man had to hold the raft to the ship, with the line, by himself, and it was hard. He let go the line and leaped all at once. Both hands closed convulsively on the steel rods at the side of the ladder and he pulled his feet to the bottom rung, held himself there motionless for an instant, and then started up.

The raft, again adrift in the sea, slid away from the ship, tossing in the swells, and was gone.

"All engines ahead standard." Buchan deliberately started the engines at that speed instead of working to it by one-thirds.

Then he leaned over the wind guard toward the last man off the raft, standing on the forecastle directly under him, and, in a controlled voice that still did not quite sheathe what he wanted it to sheathe, called: "What ship?"

The man looked up, his face, that had been whipped by the wind and sea into raw meat, staring blankly at the bridge. Water dripped from the soggy blue clothing and the life jacket over it to the deck, and, inside them, his body shook in spasms. You could see him grasp all the strings of himself and pull them tight for one moment.

He looked up, and his voice, though weak, was unshaking as he answered: *"Donahue."*

The doctor, followed by three pharmacist's mates with white blankets over their arms, popped from the door to the forecastle and rushed through the circle of seamen that surrounded the men off the raft. They threw the blankets over the survivors, and started to lead them through the door and off the forecastle.

Buchan said again to the last man, as, supported by two of the *Dee's* sailors, he neared the door: "Can you talk?"

The man, wordless, nodded.

They brought him up the ladder to the captain. Only his raw face showed out of the hooded white blanket. The blanket shook with his shivering.

Buchan faced him, observing the face and the shaking blanket, but saying nothing, waiting, encouragingly, for the man to begin.

"We got it." The cold spasms halted him. Then he started again. "Early this morning. I think three times. Not sure but I think three."

He stopped. He was thinking each sentence out in advance.

"The ship was at general quarters. I was on the bridge. We were going in to investigate those four contacts. You know those four contacts?"

Buchan nodded.

"The last I remember radar said the contacts were two miles away. It was dark as hell. We couldn't see anything." The shaking stopped him again. Inside the blanket he worked his arms and shoulders to pull it tighter around him. He breathed hard, and then, in control of himself again, spoke. "Then something hit aft. It shook us hard but it didn't do no damage on the bridge. Then the deck came right up and hit me. We must have taken a fish right under the bridge. I was laying down trying to get up when another one hit. Somewhere aft. I don't know where. I finally got up. The bridge was all smashed. Some of the guys were already gone. The rest of us tried to cut the rafts loose. We got some in the water. I don't know how many. We jumped in the water after them. Six of us got this one."

Buchan asked his first question. "Did she go down?"

"She was going. We lost her in the dark."

The captain, his eyes intent on the other's face, started to speak, then stopped. When he asked the question, it was as though he knew the answer.

"Did your captain get off?"

The man was silent, as if, through all the things that the hours on the raft had done to him, he knew how important the question was to Buchan. Then he said, "No, sir," stopped again, and went on.

"One of the guys said they saw a mess boy standing on the deck crying. Lost his life jacket and couldn't swim. The guy said the skipper took his jacket off and gave it to the mess boy."

Buchan nodded again. "You better go below now. You're all right now." The two seamen led him away, his back big and without shape in the white blanket as it moved toward the ladder.

The captain stood looking over the wind guard at nothing. You could not tell what he was thinking from his face.

Then he turned abruptly.

"Radar. Range on the contacts." He had decided the contacts were more important than a continued search for survivors, which was, after all, the *Hilliard's* job.

"Four miles, captain." Knox's reply came back from the wheelhouse.

"We should have sighted something a long time ago," Buchan growled. He raised his glasses and looked ahead. "A long time ago." He might have been thinking what I was thinking now: that the contacts, whatever they were, must be very low in the water. Like submarines barely above periscope depth.

He kept jerking the *Dee* from side to side in a constant, irregular weave. He did not know what he was taking his ship into and he wanted to be ready, as ready as he could be, for anything. By always changing course, he made the *Dee* a hard torpedo target.

Two and a half miles away by radar, the contacts were still invisible.

"I'll be Goddamned." Something like awe was in the captain's voice. He moved his binoculars three inches from his eyes, then put them back. I looked. I still did not see anything. I wondered what it was that he saw. But I said nothing.

He laughed shortly. "They look like—like balloons. Son of a bitch."

Then I saw them. I had not seen them at all and suddenly I saw them very plainly, almost dead ahead of the ship. There were four of them, large, silvery sausages, almost the color of the sky, waving low over the water.

"Just like barrage balloons, by God." The captain had the glasses on them again. "Last I saw those was in London in 1941. By God."

The *Dee* zigzagged closer, and the sausages, now on one side of her bow and now on the other as she changed course, grew larger. Through the glasses I saw tiny shroud lines, like wire threads, stretched downward under them. The lines held the sausages to something under the water.

"They're no mines. They're moving too fast to be mines." The captain had already made his decision. "Let's pick them up." He walked back to the wheelhouse to the ladder going down from the bridge, and called from it to the well deck below, "Chief."

"Yes, sir?" Jake Warrick swung himself by the crutches under each arm to the foot of the ladder, his injured leg, stiff and white in plaster cast, swinging with the motion of his body. The leg had kept him from duty for two days; after that, he had forced the doctor to return him, helpless without the crutches, to the decks.

"We want to pick these things up." Buchan leaned over the top of the ladder. "Don't damage them. Get your grapnels in the lines and bring them aboard. But don't hurt them."

"Aye, aye, sir."

"We'll take them on the port side. I won't stop. You'll have to work fast."

Buchan brought the *Dee* past the sausages, then turned her ahead of them and at right angles to the wind, so that the wind was blowing them down straight on her. Carmer poised, a grapnel in his right hand, on the edge of the forecastle, against the lifelines.

"Be funny if they was mines," Kaintuck whispered to me. "Wouldn't it?"

The first was almost on the ship. Carmer tossed his grapnel at the shrouds under it. The three-pointed hook caught in the thin lines. He pulled on the grapnel line. The sausage eased toward the ship. Carmer snatched at the shrouds and jerked the sausage aboard. It was a balloon, all right. It bobbed up and down over the forecastle as he held the shrouds. Something was on the other end of them. Carmer and three seamen pulled on them, hand over hand. The something came out of the water and hung dead at the end of the line. They pulled it aboard.

They held it up for the captain to see. It was a cigar-shaped tube of white canvas, open at one end. Jake, standing on his crutches in the point of the bow, swung on them toward the bridge and yelled: "Drogue."

A drogue is a sea anchor for small boats. By filling with water, the canvas tube resists the forward movement of a drifting boat and slows or stops it. Here the drogue had served as a buoy for the balloons. It had held them close to the water as they drifted before the wind.

"One's enough," The captain said through cupped hands. "Bring it to the bridge."

Carmer climbed the ladder with the balloon, it dancing, long and shiny and silver on the shrouds, as he went up the steps.

He stopped in front of Buchan, and held the lines as the captain pulled the balloon down to examine it.

"Filled with helium," Buchan said. He rubbed his thumb against the balloon. "Feel that Goddamned surface."

I did. The surface was metallic, like super-thin aluminum or tin, though it was pliable enough.

"Got a knife?"

The signalman gave him one, and Buchan carefully scraped the balloon with the knife edge. The substance fell off the balloon skin in flakes like paint. A small patch of silk showed where he had scraped.

"Some kind of metal alloy." He rubbed the flakes between his fingers and then flicked them to the deck. "Specially souped up to give one hell of a radar contact. No wonder we got four contacts. They really set this one up."

He stopped and thumbed the balloon with his forefinger.

"Yeah, they set it up all right. These things drift with the wind. They give beautiful radar contacts, and they plot with a course and speed. You think the balloons are the subs, and the real subs submerge right around the balloons. You come in to investigate the balloons, and they pot you, one, two, three. Just like that, just like shooting fish in a barrel. Oh, they set it up."

He let the balloon go and it jumped to the end of the shrouds. Carmer pulled it back to him.

"Very sweet." The captain was now completely professional. "A very sweet little mousetrap. And the *Donahue* walked right into it." He was silent for a moment. Maybe he was thinking that if her engines had not broken down, the *Dee*, not the *Donahue*, would have walked into it. Maybe he was thinking that the torpedoes that had ended the *Donahue* had belonged to the *Dee*. Then he turned to Carmer. "Deflate this thing and take it to my cabin."

Carmer explored the bottom of the balloon for its valve.

"The hell with that. Put a knife to it."

Carmer took his deck knife from the scabbard on his belt and jabbed the point, like a pin, into the balloon. The gas rushed out in a long, dying whoosh. Then he folded the limp, silver-covered silk and left the bridge. And the machine guns liquidated the other balloons.

I heard familiar, heavy breathing at my ear, and turned to look at Kaintuck. He whispered softly out of the corner of his mouth, "Let's go thank the engineers."

The *Dee* turned left through a quarter of a circle and headed back to find the carrier.

Now the hunted had turned on the hunters. Or had They? Who were the hunters and who the hunted? Now I was no longer sure. Perhaps They had been the hunters all the time. Perhaps They had picked the time and the place for the kill and pulled us into it.

For it was They, not we, who had baited a trap and sprung it. It was They who had made the kill, and only an accident had made the victim the "Donahue" instead of the "Dee."

Then I knew there was no need to wonder who was the hunter and who the hunted. I knew with a chilling certainty, that if we were hunting Them, They, too, were hunting us.

38

THE *Dee* STEAMED EAST. She had to meet the carrier at the rendezvous point of latitude and longtitude, which, for such contingencies as hers, was always designated a day in advance. Now, in the middle of the morning, alone on the sea, she had almost a hundred miles to run; it would be afternoon before she rejoined.

"Radar." It was the captain, on the port wing, speaking through the wheelhouse door to Knox on the radarscope. "Watch for the carrier on the long-range scale. Let me know as soon as you get a surface contact."

"Aye, aye, sir."

Graham, coming around the corner of the wheelhouse, stopped close to the captain and me.

"Found out where we are?" Buchan grinned wryly, with one side of his mouth, at him.

Graham, half smiling himself, shook his head. "Still on dead reckoning, Cap'n. We can't be more than twenty-five

miles off our estimated position, though. We'll pick up the
carrier on radar, all right. If she makes the rendezvous herself."

Buchan, the one-sided, humorless grin still on his face,
shrugged his shoulders. "Well. We sure as hell better." He
laughed without mirth, and turned his back, standing against
the wind guard, staring ahead at the gray sea and sky, as the
Dee steamed on.

He held the crew at general quarters, but let them stand
easy at their battle stations. On the guns, only the lookouts,
single, forlorn, black figures, upright and unguarded in the
raking north wind, were on their feet; the rest of the crew,
huddled together for warmth under a canvas gun cover, lay
on the deck in the shelter of the mounts. The captain stood
apart on the port wing, the wind whipping his cheeks into a
deep red, and said nothing, except for a sporadic curt command, for hours, leaving his corner only to walk inside the
wheelhouse, look at the radar screen, and move noiselessly
back to the open wing.

Tension siphoned off, a drop at a time. On the bridge, the
men looked drained and tired. My feet were dead, my face,
frozen. I could not rub it with my hands because the mittens
over them were wet from the sprays. I was too cold, too tired,
too empty, to be adequately sorry about the *Donahue*. I decided I would be sorrier later.

At three minutes to twelve, I said to Buchan, formally, "Reporting twelve o'clock, sir. The chronometers have been wound
and compared," and he answered, equally formally but not
bothering to look at me, "Very well." That was a ritual of
the sea, to be gravely observed under all circumstances, and
it would take more than an enemy or a war to obviate it.

I heard the clatter of ladles in pots on the ladder, and two
mess cooks appeared. One had an aluminum tray piled with
sandwiches, the other, a tall jug of soup and almost a dozen
white china mugs cradled in one arm. The sandwiches were
cold to my touch, and the bread and bologna that made them
were cold in my belly, but the red beef soup, making a thick,
white spiral of steam above the china mug, was as hot as I
could stand. It burned my insides and scalded me into something approaching vitality. I remembered, drinking the soup,
that we had had no breakfast.

Then the mug was empty, the sandwiches eaten, and the
afternoon crawled along. At two o'clock, radar had no trace
of the carrier. Graham, his scowl deeper, even, than its cus-
tom, stalked back and forth from the port wing to the charthouse. But if Buchan, still standing, almost motionless, in his

corner and searching the jagged ocean ahead, was worried, he did not show it.

At two-thirty, the screen still showed nothing. Then, at four minutes to three, Knox said, "Two contacts at zero-seven-zero, fourteen miles."

"Yeah." Satisfaction was in the captain's voice. "That's her. Let's head over there." He walked, neither stiff nor clumsy under all the winter clothing, into the wheelhouse, and brought the *Dee* twenty degrees to the left. Then he began to zigzag her again.

Almost immediately, two black matchsticks, one taller and thicker than the other, masts of a large and of a smaller ship, bristled over the horizon. Then the top of an aircraft carrier's tower rose under the taller, thicker stick, and, after that, the tips of the four smokestacks emerged under the thinner one.

"There they are." I pointed, for Buchan. "Looks like the *Hilliard* got back before we did." He inclined his chin slightly and said nothing.

Fifteen minutes after their masts had broken the horizon, they were in full view, coming straight at us, zigzagging together, the thin-bellied destroyer and the one-sided carrier behind her pointing straight at the *Dee* and churning white bow waves as they came on, then showing almost broadside as they swung on another leg of the zigzag.

The captain walked the length of the wing to the flag bag behind it, picked up the signal pad, wrote on it, and handed it to Kaintuck. "Send this."

Kaintuck stepped to the foot stand above the deck, and whirred the shutter of his lamp. Yellow flashes from the carrier's tower answered.

Kaintuck brought the reply, written on the pad, to the captain, silently. Buchan read it and handed it back without a word.

Then he said to the helmsman, "Right standard rudder." The *Dee* was almost back in formation, and he maneuvered her into position on the right side of the screen. Now there was only one destroyer to the left. It seemed that half a dozen ships were missing.

I walked toward the flag bag, where Kaintuck stood. "Let's see it." His face, for once, impenetrable behind the black beard, he gave me the pad. I read:

BT HILLIARD PICKED UP FORTY FIVE MEN THREE OFFICERS OFF DONAHUE X YOUR SIX MEN BRINGS TOTAL NUMBER OF SURVIVORS TO FIFTY ONE MEN THREE OFFICERS X ONE HUNDRED MEN NINE OFFICERS MISSING X ARNHEM NOT AMONG SURVIVORS BT

"Taylor." That was the captain. I handed the pad back to

Kaintuck and walked, four steps, to Buchan. "Secure from general quarters. Set the watch."

I gave the order to the telephone talker, and he passed it over the battle circuits. I watched the men on the galley deckhouse guns. This time, they made no pistol-shot rush to abandon their stations; instead, they dragged slowly to their feet and took off their helmets and life jackets in a kind of frozen apathy, not hurrying and seeming not to care, looking too tired and too cold either to hurry or to care, as they clumped, deadly, down the ladder to the deck below. They had been at general quarters for ten hours.

So had I. And all of them on the bridge, as officer of the deck. Now, by the schedule of the watch, I would have to take the deck again at four o'clock, for the first dog watch. That was thirty minutes away. I had thirty minutes to rest before I came back for another two and a half hours.

Because, by the schedule, the twelve-to-four watch was his, Johnny relieved me to finish what was left of it.

"Have a long rest." He took the binoculars from me. "I'll see you in half an hour."

"In half an hour. Some days you just can't win."

"My heart bleeds. You know where."

I was too tired to come back at him. I went below. There was not enough time to sleep, so I walked into the wardroom, poured a cup of coffee and sat in a chair. I stretched my legs, stiff and nerveless, in front of me, and drank the coffee. It was hot and strong, though old, and now I did not even mind the last. I leaned my head against the back of the chair and closed my eyes. I heard the door open and close and I opened them. Buchan stood by the table, in the blue clothing, his hair tousled, carrying the big coat.

He was all business. "Get all the top watch officers in here. Tell Ewell to leave his junior officer on the bridge and come down."

Rocky was in his room, the last on the other side of the gray curtain, lying in his clothes on the bottom bunk with his arm over his eyes, already asleep. The light burned over the desk. He started when I touched him.

"In the wardroom. Captain wants all watch officers."

He sat up, put his fists in his eyes, and shook his head. He was on his feet, bending over the basin to wash his face, when I left.

I called Johnny by the telephone from the wardroom to the bridge. He came into the wardroom in his heavy clothes, the coat over his arm. He slung it on the table and dropped into a chair. He was the last. Rockford, Arbry, and I were waiting.

Buchan, sitting at the end of the table, said without preface: "They don't know that we found those balloons. They'll probably try the trick again. You can spot the balloons easy if radar gets them. They'll plot on the same course as the wind. If the course runs dead with the wind, you'll know what you have. Notify me of all contacts, and start plotting right away. That's all."

We got up. Johnny paused at the hot plate to pour himself coffee. He was uncharacteristically serious. He drained the cup, scooped his coat from the table, and walked out the door.

I followed. I climbed to the main deck and went to the radio shack to check messages. Nothing important was on the board. Two radiomen sat silent before typewriters, head phones on their ears. I went out.

I climbed the ladder to the galley deckhouse. Why, I did not know, but I did. I stopped and looked at the gun crew. Three, wrapped in dirty white blankets, sat on the deck, their backs against the ammunition boxes. The other two were standing the lookout watch, and vigilantly; the glasses did not move from their eyes.

I walked over to Villarubia, the gunner's mate, on the starboard side. He lowered the glasses and grinned at me, then snuffled through his nose. The nose ran with the cold to smear the black stubble on his red face.

"Cold?"

"Cold as a whore's heart." He pawed his nose with a black-mittened hand. "Not as cold as down there, though." He pointed over the steel safety strip circling the deckhouse, at the sea below, falling away from the ship in a breaking line of white.

I looked at him. He might be starting a crack-up. He grinned again, and I relaxed. He was all right. Without the coat, I was shaking. I went to the wardroom for more coffee, then took the coat from my room and went back to the bridge.

The sky had its unchanging gray glaze when I took the deck. Twilight came quickly, and sunset was at four-fifty-three, though without a sun. By five-thirty, darkness had dropped again. If the night brought more cold, I could not tell it. My feet were already dead, and my face chopped and numb. Looking into the blackness with the binoculars, I had to get used to one black shape ahead of the carrier instead of two.

"Pete." I looked around. Rockford was behind me. It was not quite six, more than half an hour before I expected him.

"What the hell are you doing here?"

"I thought you might have a bellyfull of it for one day." He was still buttoning his coat. "I grabbed a sandwich and came up. You can still make dinner."

"Christ, you shouldn't have done that." I had never seen anybody do it before. I was embarrassed and did not know what to say. "Thanks a lot, but you shouldn't have done it. Go on back down and eat."

"Oh, shut your ass and give me the dope. Don't I have enough to worry about without your yapping? Give me the fogging dope."

I gave in without another murmur. In my room, I sat down, took off the artics, then the shoes, and rubbed my feet through the stockings until I could feel in them again. I washed my face in cold water, rubbed it hard with a towel, and went into the wardroom. The others were already sitting, and the mess boys passing the soup. Chicken, I thought, tasting it, rich grains and butter flecks showing in the yellow, thick liquid. None of the officers talked as they spooned the soup.

I looked around the table at them and thought: We have all changed. One by one, I could tell how each had changed. The change had been evolving all the time, and this of today, of the *Donahue*, had made it nearly complete. Something, a kind of virginity, had gone out of all of us. In its place was a new knowledge, the knowledge of defeat and failure. We had not quit, none of us had quit, but we knew now what we had never known before, what it was to be beaten without fighting, to be beaten by an Enemy you could not see. And this knowledge showed. It showed in all of us. In Johnny, Rockford, Arbry, and Anson. In the Flattop, Graham, Crandall, Jerry, Carter. In the doctor. In me.

No, it did not show in all of us. It did not show in the captain. If he had changed, he kept it to himself. He was still the captain.

Now, his hair neatly combed and his fresh-shaved face white and pink above a black wool shirt, he looked at the silver platter that James brought in from the pantry. My eyes followed his. The platter was piled with white and dark meat.

"Turkey?" For the first time I could remember, he showed surprise. "What's the occasion?"

Then his mouth twisted and he leaned back in his chair. "I'll be Goddamned. Today is Christmas."

He looked down the table. His eyes stopped, at the other end, on Flattop, and he said: "What did Santa Claus bring you, Flattop?"

We had met now what we had steamed fifteen thousand miles hunting. We had found it. They, the hunted who had become the hunters, had picked the time and place, They had made the move, and They would finish what They had started. For we knew it was not finished, but only begun, and we knew that there would be a finish.

It did not come the night after the "Donahue," or the next, or the next after that. But it was coming. We knew it was coming, and we waited. We knew, too, that the waiting was nearly over.

39

THE NIGHT was a black wall, unpierced by moon or stars, that rose, impenetrable and unending, wherever I looked. I stood on the port wing and tried to cut it with my eyes.

"You won't see either one of them. You might as well relieve me now." Johnny was beside me, waiting. "You can look for an hour and you still won't see them."

"Couple of minutes more. Let me try it with your glasses."

I raised the binoculars from his chest to my eyes, not lifting the strap that held them around his neck but stooping slightly to reach them as they came to the end of the strap. Through them, trying to pull the *Hilliard* and the carrier out of the black solidity, I still saw nothing. I let the glasses down, waited for three breaths, and tried again. This time I caught the two ships, inky, shapeless amoebae a half-shade darker than the wall, that vanished into it when I lowered the binoculars.

"Okay. I see them now." I lifted the strap from his neck and put the glasses around my own. "Any radar contacts?"

"No contacts, no nothing."

"I relieve you. Go hit your sack."

"Such is my intention. Good night."

"Good night."

Then he was gone and I stood alone in the corner of the wing, in the darkness and the silence. The bridge had the waiting, expectant stillness of an empty room; the cadenced mourn of the wind and the sobbing heartbeat of the pinging were not sounds but part of the silence, that did not emerge from it unless you deliberately listened to them.

Three-fifty-three, the green watch hands said in the dark. Starting the routine of the watch, I gave the conn, symbolized by the red flashlight and zigzag card, to Carter, and sent Jerry to inspect the ship.

The Enemy

I walked behind the wheelhouse to the starboard wing, then through the door from it to the wheelhouse. Above the radarscope, looking down at it, was Knox's face, faintly outlined by the red light from the radar. He moved away, to let me see the screen, as I stopped beside him. I looked down at the screen. It was a black circle with the red rings on it. Each ring was an equal distance from the other. They marked the range by miles. The *Dee* was the center of the circle. Close to and to the left of the center were two yellow, oval-shaped pips, an eighth of an inch long and half as thick. They were the carrier and the *Hilliard*. Any other pips that appeared were not friends.

"No contacts, huh?" I said.

"Nothing showing."

"Watch it close on the twenty-mile scale. Watch it for small contacts." I was thinking of the balloons.

"I'll watch it close."

I went back to the port wing. Time inched on. By four-thirty, the watch seemed two hours old. The cold had set in, in my feet and face and body. I walked to the other side and back to warm up, then I sent Clay to the galley for coffee.

"How's she doing?" I said it, for conversation, to Carter, standing by the wind guard with the red flashlight in one hand and the zigzag card in the other.

"Fine. No strain."

"Good. Looks like an easy watch."

Knox said from the door, "Can you come in a minute, Mr. Taylor?"

I went in.

"Take a look. On the twelve-mile line."

I looked down at the dark screen with the red rings. In the upper left corner, almost touching the middle ring, was a yellow pip, half the size of the ones made by the carrier and the *Hilliard*.

"Jerry." He came to the door from the starboard wing. "We got a contact. Go in the charthouse and plot it." Then, through the voice-tube megaphone, "Captain. Surface contact bearing two-nine-five, twelve miles."

His voice, hollow in the tube, came back, "Very well."

I started the stop watch to run the plot on the contact, and watched the yellow pip on the screen. Exactly every minute, I gave Jerry, through the tube to the charthouse, the range and bearing of the contact. With four of the minute positions, he could determine the course and speed.

I gave him the range and bearing for the third minute, and Buchan walked in through the starboard door. He was fully dressed, in winter clothing and the coat. He had probably been sleeping in his shirt and trousers. He walked straight to the radarscope, and, as Knox and I stepped to the side, looked at it without saying a word.

"Breaking up." He kept looking. "Two there now. What does the plot say?"

"We haven't finished." The second hand of the stop watch was close to the sixty-second mark again, and I said to the charthouse, looking at the two small yellow splinters of the pip, "Stand by. Mark. Range, eleven miles. Bearing, two-seven-one."

"Wind still from the northeast?" Buchan said.

"Almost dead from the northeast, Cap'n. From three-three-five or three-four-zero."

I saw him nod in the red light coming up from the screen. "Reciprocal would be," he stopped to figure, "about one-six-zero, then."

"Yes, sir." I knew what he was thinking, that if the course of the contacts was the same as that of the wind, we had found the balloons again. The wind, blowing almost from the northeast, had a course of one-six-zero, or a few degrees on either side of it. If the contacts were moving in the same direction, they were moving with the wind. And if they were moving with the wind, we knew what they were.

"How about the course and speed?" I said to the charthouse.

"Right away." Jerry was excited. I wondered if I had made a mistake in giving him the job. Maybe I would have to turn the deck over to Buchan and plot the contact myself. Neither Buchan nor I talked but stood, waiting.

Jerry's voice came out of the tube: "Target speed, eight knots. Target course, one-five-seven."

That was it. The course was with the wind. We had what we were looking for. The balloons. I put my hand on the general alarm handle and looked at Buchan, not needing to ask, and he said. "Go ahead."

I pulled the handle from one side of the electric box that held it to the other, and the clanging exploded the *Dee* into general quarters. The crew manned their battle stations.

Buchan was calling the carrier on the TBS, reporting the contacts. I heard the last of what he said into the telephone: "Request permission to investigate. Over."

The crackling, then the voice answered, "Permission granted. Out."

Then the voice ordered a ninety-degree turn to the left for the carrier and the *Hilliard*.

Now the *Dee* was by herself with the contacts. And what

was with them. The contacts were, and now we were sure of this, the balloons, balloons like those that had pulled the *Donahue* into the trap. But the balloons were only the bait. Waiting, ready to spring the trap, was the Enemy. Now, more clearly than ever before, the identities of the hunter and the hunted had merged. Each was the hunter and each the hunted. What lay somewhere between the *Dee* and the contacts, what we had hunted for fifteen thousand sea miles, was now hunting us.

We started in. But not clumsily. Not straight into it.

Buchan spun the *Dee* in a tight circle and headed away from the path of the contacts. What he meant to do was plain. He was coming in from behind. That would not fool Them. There was no more fooling. But it would break up the trap. It would even the odds. It would also let Them know that we knew.

The *Dee* had to run a big half-circle to do what he wanted her to do. It would take time. But she could still run it faster than They could cut back and take a set position on the other side of the balloons.

Buchan jumped the speed to twenty, then to twenty-five knots. The sea drove in from the side and rolled the ship in a hard, pendulum dip that dropped one side almost into the waves and shot it steeply into the air, while the *Dee* flew ahead in her up-and-down gull swoop and the wind lashed sheets of spray at the bridge and darkness was a black barrier inches ahead.

"Range on contacts, twelve miles." Knox had been ordered to make reports on the contacts every minute. The range was opening as the *Dee* drew away. It would close when she came in on the contacts from the other side.

Sea miles were rushing under the *Dee's* stern. Buchan kept changing the course to hold the half-circle pattern. In an hour, she had almost completed it. The contacts were abeam, ten miles away.

"Left full rudder." The captain turned her toward the contacts. Somewhere between the *Dee* and the contacts was what we were looking for. We went in to find Them.

He cut speed to seventeen knots, because the pings were no good at faster speeds. The *Dee* ceased her world-ending violence and slipped into her easier weave. With the slower speed, she was an easier target. Buchan began to swing her in a jerky zigzag stripped of any pattern. He never held a heading longer than thirty seconds. The ship heeled hard with the turns. I had to hold to the wind guard with one hand to stand.

"Set depth charges for shallow," Buchan snapped. That was

forbidden. They were supposed to be set only after an attack had started. The Navy ordered it that way when the men on the *Reuben James* were killed by her own, pre-set charges when she went down. But Buchan did not care about doctrine now.

The pinging sliced through the silence. In what we had to do, it was all we had: our eyes, our ears, our everything.

In the darkness, I did not see faces on the bridge. I did not hear words. I only guessed at what was happening to men. Men were blurred into the corporate identity of the ship. That sense of corporate identity was a great propellant. It was like a horse. It would take you places you did not want to go yourself. I held on to it, and I was sure the others, that I did not see, held on to it, too.

I looked over the stern, at the green-white phosphorescence of the *Dee's* snaky wake.

"Sound contact bearing at zero-seven-zero, range eleven double-oh." Daniels' yell came out of the sound shack.

"Come right to zero-seven-zero. All engines ahead standard." The captain was starting the run.

The ping was bouncing off what it had found. The echo came back softer and lower. The echo was the spoor. We could not lose the echo.

Buchan was running straight in on the target, taking no more evasive action. He had committed the *Dee*, completely and singly to the attack, leaving her open to torpedoes. In her climactic act of destruction, she was, like a matador going over the bull's horns with a sword, vulnerable to the same destruction.

"Range, seven double-oh." Distance was closing. The pings still bounced truly off the target, and the echo came back.

"Range six double-oh. Target bears zero-nine-zero."

"Right full rudder." The captain was peeling off to lead his target in the final attack course. The ping and the echo were close together.

"Stand by to fire," Graham said from the sound shack. This was no decision that he made. It came from the machines that governed the pings. The machines made all the decisions.

"Stand by," repeated the telephone talker on the port wing.

"Fire one." Through the sound-shack tube to the wing.

The bridge was noiseless except for the pings and the now-ricocheting echo. On the wing, Kaintuck's body dipped from the waist as he swung the release lever that sent a depth charge spinning from the rack on the stern into the sea. That was the first charge in the diamond-shaped pattern of underwater explosions that the *Dee* would lay. I wondered if the

pattern would hit, if the crashing wave of the charges would
smash into a steel shell a hundred feet underwater and break
it to pieces. I realized suddenly my hands were clenched
tight, and I opened them and moved the fingers.

"Fire two."

Kaintuck's body dipped twice as he pulled down the levers
for both the port and starboard stern racks. Then he pressed
two buttons on the K-gun firing panel. The K-guns pommed
together, loud, and on each side of the ship, though you
could not see either, a depth charge was end-over-ending in
the blackness and down into the water, hitting with a splash
that you could hear.

After the splash, so quickly after it that the splash might
have been the trigger that touched off the other, I heard something else, an underwater blast, sounding muffled and far
away. It shook the *Dee* like a terrier a rat, and the *Dee* could
not resist but only plow ahead. The blast was the first charge
exploding as it reached its depth, one hundred feet down. The
second group would explode underwater, almost together, at
about the same time that the third was fired from the ship.

"Fire three."

Once more the ritual of the firing, the bursts of the K-guns,
and then the muffled wrenching explosion of the second group
of charges, the blast louder and the shaking harder this time,
because four charges, instead of one, were going off almost
together.

"Fire four."

The blast. Then the shaking.

"Fire five." The last drop in the pattern, a single charge
rolled from the racks, the point of the diamond. No K-guns,
but silence. Then, in sequence, the blast from the last two
groups.

That was all of the depth-charge pattern. The job now
was to get the contact again. The pings had lost it, as they always lost it, when the ship was close enough to the target to
drop the charges. That close, the target slipped under the
sound waves that were the pings, and they could not find it.

"Right full rudder." Buchan brought the ship about through
a quarter of a circle and headed out to open the distance between her and the target, so the pings could hit it again. He
took the *Dee* almost a thousand yards from the last depth-
charge drop, then swung her back toward the same spot.

The pings beat alone now with no echo, as unhurried, even-
spaced, and relentless as always. Sounding under the pings
now were strange gurglings and rumblings: underwater disturbances created by the charges and the *Dee's* wake. They

would make it harder than ever to regain contact. Coming in, I heard only these noises, the pings, and the ooo-ooo-ooo of the wind, and felt a cold tightness in my belly and a fluttering in my thighs.

"Contact bearing zero-six-zero!" Through the noises, Daniels had found it. "Range one two double-oh."

"Stand by depth charges," said Buchan. "Come right to zero-six-zero."

The *Dee* was in another run. Through the sound-shack tube now, each ping sounded clearly, and, a full second after it, the muted, watery imitation that was its echo, the echo and the ping drawing closer and closer together as the *Dee* charged in.

The lookout screamed from the flying bridge: "Torpedo on the starboard bow!'

I saw it coming. From the port wing, looking ahead and across the bow, I saw the wake, a long white arrow streaking across the blackness at the *Dee*.

Watching it come, I hoped, without fear, that it would hit some other part of the ship, not the bridge, that whoever it got, it would not get me. I knew and was ashamed to know that I would rather it got ten people or fifty people aft than me on the bridge, but I was, watching it come, completely without fear, only selfish. I was surprised, watching it come, that I had had more fear in a high-school dressing room before playing basketball. Maybe there was not enough time for fear. These things I did not think, or even sense, in sequence, but they hit me all at once in a timeless instant, even before Buchan yelled, "Right full rudder."

The *Dee* hesitated for what seemed forever, as the arrow came at her. Then she swung toward it, making a target only as wide as her thin waist, and the white arrow, coming and coming at her through the black passed down her starboard side a hundred yards away.

"Look for a contact dead ahead." The captain had abandoned the first target and was charging at what had just fired the torpedo, back along the white phosphorescence that the torpedo had left.

"Contact!" Daniels had it. The echo was as clear as a horn.

The submarine must have been shallow when it fired. It was not far away.

Buchan went into his final attack course.

"Fire one."

"Fire two."

The charges were dropping, with the pom of the K-guns, the

explosions muffled by tons of sea water, and the tooth-shaking shudders that ripped the ship.

"Fire three."

"Torpedo on the port quarter!"

The captain wheeled. The wake boiled at the *Dee* almost from behind. It was going to be wide. He did not change course, but held the heading to finish the pattern. The echo stayed clear and strong until it vanished. The run looked good.

"Fire five." That was the last charge in the pattern.

"Torpedo astern!"

"Right full rudder." Buchan glanced at the wake and gave the order almost together. He was turning away; he turned away from the torpedoes when they came from behind and toward them when from ahead. That way, he left the smallest possible target.

This one was going to be close. The white line of the wake bubbled under the stern, so close, it seemed, that you could have thrown a rock into it from the fantail.

Buchan brought the *Dee* hard right again. He pointed her toward the origin of the last wake. He changed speeds and jerked the ship from side to side as he took her in, an evasive action to keep Them from figuring her movements.

The sound gear was alive with the underwater churnings now. Then, cutting through them all, the pings had their target again. The echo sounded, one time and sharp, over the bridge before Daniels cried, "Contact!"

He held the contact as the *Dee* closed, the echo and the ping closer and closer together until they were like beats of a punching bag. The *Dee* dropped her charges, circled out, and started back.

The pings searched through the wakes and water noises, blurred together now in a rumbling whisper. The *Dee* cut back and forth for a quarter of an hour without an echo. The underwater whisper was dying. Then the pings hit something, and we attacked again, to leave the sea flashing with the white phosphorescence of the *Dee's* wake and the explosions.

"No more depth charges topside," the talker said to Buchan. "They're breaking them out of the magazine."

"Very well." Buchan knew he did not have to tell them to hurry.

He whipped the *Dee* over the piece of sea she had already crisscrossed so many times. It was alive with wakes, her own and those of the torpedoes. You could hear the gurgling noises of the wakes on the sound gear, between the pings.

"K-guns loaded," the talker said.

"Tell the ammunition parties to keep breaking out the charges. We'll need all we can get."

"Contact at one-one-zero!"

The *Dee* went into another attack and began to drop the pattern.

"Fire one."

"Fire two."

The K-guns boomed, the pings, now echoless, pounded alone, and too late to dodge, a thin white wake spurted at the bow through the blackness, and the *Dee* smashed something hard and unyielding that flung her backwards staggering and lurching like a drunk. All at one time, I plunged against the wind guard, grabbed it with both hands, and saw, through a spouting white geyser of water, the bow leap up like a gun shot animal and fall back again.

That was all. It was over. The *Dee* had taken a torpedo somewhere and was still going ahead, the pinging as miraculously undisturbed as though she were still inviolate. She was still afloat.

The blast had flung Buchan against the wind guard, too, and now he pushed himself away from it and stood on his feet. "It got the bow." His voice was hard. "Tell forward repair to investigate the damage, report, and make emergency repairs."

The talker said into the mouthpiece the order that would send a dozen men deep into the ship, far under the water line. If she went down, they could never get out.

"Tell them to hurry."

"Contact!" Daniels yelled from the sound shack. The repair party was below decks and there was no way to tell how long the *Dee* could stay afloat. The captain started an attack.

The charges shook the ship. We were still waiting for the repair party to report when the last charges in the pattern went off.

The telephone talker said, "Forward repair reports no damage on this side of frame fourteen. They're shoring the watertight door in the chief's quarters."

"That means we lost just the tip of the bow." Buchan's relief showed. "Tell them to shore that bulkhead with everything they've got."

Below, they would be shoring already, bracing the thin steel wall that stood alone between the *Dee* and the sea with all the two-by-fours that they had.

"Tell the engine room to trim us down by the stern." That would lift the bow, or what was left of it, a little higher out of the water, and take a fraction of the sea's assault off the too-thin plate.

"Let's get out of here." The captain had made his decision: the *Dee* could do no more. "Tell all stations to report casualties."

The talker repeated the reports as they came in to him.

"Gun Two, no casualties."

"Forward engine room, no casualties."

"Forward repair, no casualties."

Gun One, on the forecastle, close to where the torpedo had hit, should have been the first gun to report. It came in last.

"Gun One reports one man missing, sir."

"Who?"

"The second loader. Kosciusko." That was Little Ski.

"All stations check on Kosciusko. See if he's anywhere aboard."

The talker got another report. "After repair says Mr. Crandall is missing, too."

"What the Christ could have happened to him? Look for him, too."

Buchan was heading the *Dee* back toward the carrier and the *Hilliard,* zigzagging and making seventeen knots, as much speed as he dared with the cutting edge of the bow gone.

"Radar." He walked to the door. "Any surface contacts?"

"Just those two little ones that we had all the time," Knox said. Those were the balloons, the bait in the trap. "Nothing else."

"They aren't chasing us on the surface, then." Buchan was, without question, pleased by this, but his voice did not show it. He turned to the talker. "How about Kosciusko and Crandall? Anybody found them?"

"No, sir. They're still looking." The talker stopped to listen to something coming over the phones. "Forward repair reporting, sir. They say the torpedo took a chunk out of the bottom corner of the bow. It got all the forward peak tanks." We were carrying salt water for ballast in the peak tanks before it hit. "Mr. Rockford says that looks like all the damage."

"Very well," said Buchan.

"It didn't break our back then." I was talking about the keel. Buchan snorted. "If it broke our back, you'd know it."

The *Dee* moved on. There was an ominous, slow heaviness in her roll and pitch now, and the deck slanted forward a little,

The captain, who might have sensed what I was thinking, said, "We've got nothing to worry about as long as that bulkhead holds. These ships have been shot up a lot worse than we are and still made it all right. If the bulkhead stands up, we've got no real worries."

He walked into the wheelhouse, came back, and said to the talker, "Anything of Kosciusko and Crandall?"

"Anybody find Kosciusko and Mr. Crandall?" The talker waited after he said it, then said, into the phones, "Bridge, aye," and to the captain, "They can't find Kosciusko, sir. They're pretty sure he went over the side when the torpedo hit."

"I guess he did." Buchan's voice was flat. He said nothing for a moment, then, "How about Crandall?"

"After repair says he was right with them just before the fish got us. After that, nobody saw him."

"Tell them to keep looking." Buchan went back into the wheelhouse to look at the radar.

So Ski would never go after it again. Now he did not have to worry about nice girls or any other kind. Close out the service jacket on James Aloysius Kosciusko. Age, 23, Rate, seaman, first class. Next eligible for promotion, February 1. Length of time on present ship or station, eleven months and some days. Place of residence, Brooklyn Heights, N.Y. Person to be notified in case of death, injury, or capture, wife, Marie Kosciusko. Other relatives, none.

The pings, never slowing and never missing, kept beating as the *Dee* steamed west in the darkness.

And Crandall was still lost.

"Crandall couldn't have gone overboard aft, where he was." Buchan was back on the wing. "What the hell could have happened to him?" He was close to me now. "Go find him," he said. "Find him, if you can."

"Aye, aye, sir." I went down the ladder.

Then, half crouching, rolling with the ship, walking, feet wide apart and arms swinging, across the well deck, while the wind, now blowing from behind, flicked both cheeks with ice, I knew. All at once.

The knowledge had been buried there a long time. Now it had worked up and out, through the layers of whatever it was that had buried it, and I knew. Now I wanted very much to find Crandall.

Because now I knew who Crandall was.

40

I KNEW who Crandall was. I knew why I felt the uneasiness as I saw him the first time, stepping with that graceful hesitance across the gangway to the deck of the *Dee*. And I knew why I had come to hate him.

Not because of the outside thing, which was simple enough to see, and which was, also simply, that Crandall was a phony. He had not been able, in his own success argot, to deliver the goods. He had come to a place where bossing secretaries, writing reports, making sales talks, wearing Brooks Brothers rep stripes, were not enough. He had had the show, but nothing behind it, and where he had come, he needed more than the words and the gestures and the smile.

But that was not why we hated him. It was why, or partly why, we had laughed at him. Not why we hated.

Why we hated was something else. Which I now knew clearly and had known, not clearly, for a long time. Though fighting and refusing to recognize the knowledge. Now I knew why I hated and why the others hated.

We hated Crandall because each of us saw, in Crandall, himself.

The worst part. The part that he kept in chains and in his deepest hold. The part that he had to keep deeply and forever locked to remain a man.

And Crandall was that part in the flesh. Out of the hold. Unchained. Walking the deck, breathing the air, staring each of us in the face. We could not escape him so we had made it impossible for him to escape us. We felt bound to destroy him before he destroyed us.

What was this that he was? Not the pure Evil, the death Evil, like the phantom black shapes we had hunted through four million square miles of sea.

But as much the Enemy as the other. Harder to fight, because not only impossible to see but impossible to separate from yourself. Because it was yourself.

He was weakness, fear, whatever it was that would, if you let it out, capture and leave you not a man but something else. And in however deep a hold you chained it, you knew it was always there. You were always afraid that it might get out. If it did get out it would conquer you and become you and there would be no difference between the two.

That was Crandall. He had been conquered, and had become what it was that had conquered him.

Which was, as I have said, part of every man. A part to be hated, a part to be feared, a part to be beaten.

So we had hated, and feared, and beaten him.

Now that I knew why we hated, it was no longer necessary to hate, or to fear. Because, whatever he had been to us, he was, still, a human being. Not a really bad one.

That was why the captain, toward the end, had shielded him. He had seen what Crandall, underneath the success boy, was, and why we were committed to his destruction. Seeing, he had tried to save Crandall the man from what we were bound to do to Crandall the other. But the fury had been too much. Even the captain, against it, had been as a smoke wisp in the North Atlantic wind.

So now I knew. Now I would try to find Crandall.

41

ALL OF THIS I thought in the dozen steps across the well deck. Through the black burrow of the galley passageway, in the open, wailing darkness of the open deck between the torpedo tubes and Number Four stack, I still thought of it, but more than the rest I thought of where to find Crandall. Working hand over hand along the safety line stretched between the stand and the after deckhouse, the line wet and thick and hairy to my palms and sea water swirling over and sucking at my arctics on the deck, I pulled myself to the deckhouse and the after repair party: the party first a huddled dark mass and then separate black forms touching each other against the deckhouse, waiting.

"Who saw Mr. Crandall last?" I asked it, blindly, of the huddle.

One of the forms detached itself. "He was right here and then he was gone." It was Dorgan. His voice was subdued. Awed even. "He was here, right next to me, and then the charges went off, and the next time I looked for him he was gone."

"He couldn't have been wounded. Where could he have gone?"

They were all silent; repentant, I thought, and wondered if they knew. Then Dorgan spoke in the same voice, "I guess he went over."

I agreed, silently, but said, "We'll look for him anyway. Get a couple of men and we'll start."

They all stirred, moved forward in a heavy rustling of clothing and shuffling of feet, to volunteer, perhaps to declare atonement for what they had done to Crandall by searching for him now.

It is a little late for all of us, I thought, and swiftly after that, we are not to be blamed.

Dorgan picked his two. We, four now, followed our fingers

along the cold slick side of the deckhouse to the door opening
into it. Then we went through the door and down the ladder
to the after living compartment.

The yellow bulbs, swinging unendingly, cast the dark moving
shadows, and we walked among them, through the corridors
between the rows of bunks, looking in each bunk and under
the rows, for Crandall, knowing he would not be there. He was
not.

"Let's try the steering engine room," I said.

It was behind the crew's quarters and was the last compartment at the stern of the ship. I opened the half-size steel door
set two feet above the deck. In the dark inside, the engine
clanked, as in agony, as it moved the rudder under the keel
at the command of the wheel far away on the bridge.

The coming yellow beam of my flashlight made a solid yellow circle that danced over the black surfaces. No Crandall.

"Let's go topside."

We closed the door, tightened its steel dogs, and went back
through the compartment, up the ladder, and outside. I was
sweating from the stuffy heat of the compartment. But on the
weather decks the wind whistled across the ship like an ice-
breath, freezing, petrifying, but pouring into my lungs to
create a sensation of freedom and release that was not free
from a fear of the nameless dark. Desperately aware of mor-
tality and perishability, I was hollowly, shamelessly grateful
that someone else was lost in the dark. Not I.

On the sides of the ship reared the great black swells combed
with the green-white streaks that seemed to fly all about and
over the *Dee*, diving at her as she rose and sliding harmless
under her as she defeated the forces that could have broken
her by riding unresisting with them.

This flickering darkness enveloped us. Somewhere in it was
Crandall, and it was completely necessary to find him. If he
was to be found. If he had ever been lying on this stretch of
deck, that we now crossed only with the taut, cold, slippery-
wet rope line, he was not to be found.

Jets from the seas ripped over the sides and across the deck.
We passed Number Four stack and the end of the line. Now
the torpedo tubes made a buffer for the sea. The torpedomen
were standing easy at the tubes, ready but not manning them.

"Seen Mr. Crandall?"

"No, sir." It was Walsh's voice. "We haven't seen him at
all."

The four of us moved on into the galley passageway. I did
not know how he could have ended there. But I did not know
how he could have vanished with such finality, either. I did

not, in fact, have any idea where he could be. Except the one idea.

In the passageway, I turned the beam of light into the recesses and crannies under the projections thrusting from the bulkheads. I saw a pile of potatoes, their eyes staring, immobile and bug-like under the light, and a discarded life jacket and a rusty helmet. But no Crandall.

On the well deck, outside again, we had to look without the light. The forward repair party was standing by the ladder to the bridge.

"Jake?"

"Yes, sir?" The thick-middle shadow came a step closer.

"You seen Mr. Crandall?"

"No, sir. Not all night."

"Any idea where he might be?"

"Yes, sir."

I paused and heard, under the wind, his heavy breathing. "You're probably right. Where else?"

"Nowhere else."

Still we had to push the search to its absolute limits and then beyond. Finding Crandall had become as necessary as crushing him had been before.

"You check the forward crew's quarters," I told Dorgan. "I'll try the wardroom."

We went down, and I left them at the wardroom door. Inside the wardroom was only the doctor, sitting at the table, in khaki shirt and trousers and nothing else. Two black bags with medicines, gauze, and surgical instruments were open on the table beside him. The wardroom was the battle hospital.

The doctor glanced at me as I closed the door, and then I saw that he had an open copy of the *Saturday Evening Post* on the table in front of him. Is he really reading it, I wondered.

"We secured yet?" His voice was flat.

"Not quite. We're looking for Crandall. You seen him?"

"No. Something hit him?"

"I don't know. He just disappeared."

"What the hell could have happened to him?" He was surprised, concerned, and yet relishing a little, the excitement.

"You tell me."

"Want me to help look?"

"We're through now, as soon as I look in the rooms."

I walked through the open doorway to the officers' staterooms, and down the little corridor between them, stopping and looking into each of the four rooms as I went by. Then I went back to the wardroom.

The doctor looked at me. I shook my head.

"I guess that's where he is, all right." The doctor, having, through circumstances, participated less in the war against Crandall than the rest of us, felt a less compelling concern in finding him. "Let me know if you need me."

And he returned to the magazine, which he had or had not been reading, as I left.

I had to tell the captain we had not found Crandall.

He was not on either wing of the bridge. I stepped through the door from the port wing and looked in the cramped darkness of the wheelhouse. Someone, big in an officer's coat, was bending over the radarscope, and, close, I saw it was Buchan.

He was looking into the scope, and the dead red light striking up from the screen glinted off his face.

"Yes?" He had not looked at me, he did not look away from the screen now, but he knew I was there.

"We didn't find him."

He kept looking into the screen, not at me, his face, that I could just see, sharp-cut and fixed as though frozen in the cold red glow. He said nothing, still staring at the magic circle that could tell what there was to be told about the surface world outside, and I waited.

Then he said, his voice saying nothing except the words it made while I watched his lips move in the pale redness: "Did you try the depth-charge locker?"

And, dropping down the ladder, fast, its rails cold and hard against both my hands, I, too, was sure. Really sure.

42

IN THE RED DECK of the after crew's quarters, the hatch to the depth-charge locker was a big square of blackness, nothing showing inside or under it. The ladder to the locker had been pulled out to speed the moving of the charges. A piece of line, with knots a foot apart for hand-holds, ran from a deck stanchion, over the hatch rim, and vanished into the black void.

I stood, alone in the compartment, at the edge of the hatch, trying to see into it, and then turned as I heard the ladder to the compartment, behind me, rattle with footsteps. The ammunition party, all twelve of it, was following me.

I hooked the square battle light on my belt, stooped, took the line in both hands, and eased myself through the opening until I was completely inside, my body hanging on straight arms. I looked up and saw, through the square and in the yellow light, staring white faces pop from nothingness into a ring around the hatch. Then I started to work down on the knots.

It was like lowering into the sea, the other time, I thought, but now no cold sea water rose over me: only darkness.

I let go the line when I thought I was inches from the deck. I was further. I dropped nearly two feet and hit stiff-legged, the hard shock running hurting up through my ankles and the steel plates clanging loud and hollow and then echoing in the darkness.

I groped overhead for the light bulb, found it, and turned the switch. It did not work. The blasts from the charges probably had jarred loose a connection. I pulled the light from my belt, where the long hook had held it, and snapped it on.

Its yellow fingers moved along the stacked rows of gray cylinders that looked so like garbage cans. As I went ahead through the center corridor, each step a slow and completed movement, I saw only the thick gray bodies and the shadows they made and the darkness thickening off from the light beam. The charges had, all of them together, enough TNT in their thin steel shells to blow a destroyer division to hell. I shivered, feeling suddenly cold and bloodless and brushed by death. And by what it was that was outside in the dark.

I wanted out of there.

Someone shouted, from the square of light that now seemed far away: "Do you see anything?"

"No."

My voice bounced off the death-packed gray bodies and flew back at my ears in a dozen hollow ghosts.

"Look in the far corner." The call through the yellow square came down clear and unshattered. "The corner on the left."

I moved toward the back bulkhead, that was almost on me now. One step and then the next.

A tiny strip of space ran between the bulkhead and the last row of charges. I turned into it.

The yellow circle hit a new bulkhead now, that had been on the left, and moved up and down it. But I saw only the bulkhead. And in the tapering darkness on each side of the thin shaft of light, the charges and their shadows, the shadows now not round or thick but long and slender and black, like the shape of the death against which their death was committed.

The two bulkheads met in a corner, and nothing was there.

I came closer, and swung the light straight at the charges. Nothing. Then something. Black and just big enough to see. Rising over the top of the corner charge, two feet away from each wall.

What?

I moved ahead, fixing the light on it, and the darkness and the death in the chamber converged on my back.

I was almost even with the last charge. I stopped. I could not see.

I did not move.

Then I took one fast step ahead and wheeled and rammed the light at what it was and I saw.

Crandall.

He was sitting on the deck, two depth charges cupping his back, and the top of his hair, that I had seen rising infinitesimally above them.

His knees were drawn to his chest. His face was slack and shapeless, and his eyes looked black, wide and unblinking into the light. In his mouth he had his right thumb. The useful, right thumb. The thumb he had jabbed at the office girls.

"Crandall." I reached my hand forward to touch him, then dropped it. "Crandall."

He stared raptly into the light.

"Crandall."

His lips tightened on the thumb, and I heard noises of a baby sucking.

Then I turned away and started for the hatch. Not one step at a time.

And then I pulled myself up the rope, upward and upward, faster and faster, toward the square of yellow that swelled bigger and bigger, closer and closer, until my head burst through it and I had returned to whatever it was I had returned to. Which was, it seemed, the after living compartment.

The ring of faces moved back as I pulled out of the hatch and to the deck, and they all asked the question, silently, as I stood there panting.

"Go down and get him," I said.

They handled him very tenderly as they lifted him from the locker and carried him through the compartment. It was surprising how tender we had all become, now.

43

AT SEVEN O'CLOCK, we picked up the carrier and the *Hilliard* on radar. By eight, we had rejoined them, and the task unit returned, in the full force of one escort carrier and two, or more precisely, one and three-quarters, four-stack destroyers, to the area of the attack. The carrier put a double patrol, eight planes, in the air. They never looked so beautiful before.

It was almost ten when the task unit reached the waters, which, by Graham's dead reckoning, were those where the *Dee*, nearly five hours before, had dropped her depth charges and taken the torpedo. Radar got no contacts. From the port wing, I saw only the white-frosted gray of the sea, and the clouded, low-ceilinged gray sky over it.

The ships began a search plan to cover a ten-mile square, looking, as were the planes, not only for contacts, but for signs of damage that the *Dee* might have inflicted.

Half an hour after the search had started, the flying-bridge lookout called down, "Water discoloration at three-five-zero, over one thousand yards."

That was just to the left of dead ahead. With my glasses, I saw it, less than half a mile away: a smoothness in the water, darker, it seemed, than the sea around it, though only a little.

"Captain." I pointed to it. "Think that's a wind slick?"

"Let's go see." He changed course to the left and the *Dee* headed for it. Through the glasses, I watched the dark spot get larger, until the *Dee* was brushing it with her port side as she crept by it at five knots.

Buchan, Graham, and I leaned over the wind guard to look down at it. It was faintly brown, less than fifty yards wide, and trailed off at the edges.

"That's no wind slick," said Buchan. "That's oil. We hit one and it leaked oil. And the slick's still here, after five hours." He straightened. "Looks like we did some good, anyway. Maybe we sank her, maybe we just shook her up. No way of knowing."

The *Dee* had passed the slick now, and, over the stern, I watched it get smaller and smaller and disappear.

We had steamed fifteen thousand miles in the hunt. We had hunted through four million square miles of ocean. We had been at sea for almost two months. And that tiny, ragged, brown patch of smooth water, now lost in the tossing white-caps, was all we had to show for it.

That was all. Or nearly all. The "Dèe" went into Reykjavik for emergency repairs and rejoined the task unit, which hunted until the big convoy, the one it had been protecting, the one that was essential to an invasion, somewhere, later in the year, reached the United Kingdom. The convoy arrived, and we, never having seen it, started home.

Nor had we ever seen the Enemy. We had steamed twenty thousand miles hunting Them, we had bloodied Them and They us, and we had never seen Them. There semed no real victory

*and no real defeat. If either had won anything, we had, because
the convoy had made it.*

*But you felt there was no clear winning. And it seemed
natural and inevitable that there was no clear winning just as it
seemed, somehow, natural and inevitable that we had never
seen Them.*

*Because you never really saw your own Enemy, and you
never clearly beat Him. You hunted Him, and you fought Him,
and if you were lucky enough and tough enough, you survived.
If you were unlucky, like Little Ski, you got blown overboard,
or if you were soft, like Crandall, you tried to dive back into
the womb. If you were neither of those things but were instead very lucky, you went back to New York and you Shacked
Up. Wherever your New York was. And whatever your Shack-
Up might be. Wherever and whatever, it was only for a time.
In the end, you always had to go out again.*

44

THE SEA BUOY beginning the Norfolk channel was twenty miles
away. The ships were steaming for it, not zigzagging now but
going straight ahead, in the inverted V, the *Hilliard* and the
Dee abreast and a mile and a half apart, the carrier the same
distance from each on the point of the V behind them. The
Hilliard cut smoothly into the four-foot waves, gray under the
unchanging gray sky, her rise and fall just enough to see from
the *Dee's* port wing, while the carrier breasted imperviously
through them.

The wheelhouse blocked the north wind from the wing, and
it was not cold there. The wind blew a light spray from the
other side across the forecastle, the forecastle now lower in the
water by a foot than before the torpedo, but the spray did not
hit the bridge.

The TBS speaker crackled. This was what we were waiting
for. The three signalmen of the watch, the telephone talker,
the two junior officers and I crowded near the door, two feet
from Buchan, standing by the TBS telephone inside the wheelhouse. He picked up the phone and waited for the message.
Out of the round gray box on the bulkhead came the voice,
bigger, deeper, it seemed, than ever before.

"Hello, Georgia, hello, Georgia. This is Coach. Over."

Buchan pressed the button on the phone shaft and said,
softly, into the mouthpiece. "Coach, this is Georgia. Over."

"Georgia from Coach. Still think you can make it to the big town?"

"Af-firmative." I saw Buchan's lips, close to the telephone, smile as he said it.

"Georgia from Coach." The voice became consciously formal. "You are hereby detached from Task Unit Twenty-One Point Thirteen Point Nine. Proceed independently in accordance with previous orders."

"Will do." Buchan's smile twisted. "Next time we hope we have less trouble with the engineering."

"We hope so, too," rumbled the voice. "And have one for us at the Stork Club. Goodbye and good luck. Out."

"Will do. Goodbye and good luck to you. Out." Buchan put the phone back on its hook, pushed the "off" button on the black box under it, and the red button of light on the box went out.

For the *Dee*, the hunt had ended.

"Right standard rudder," Buchan said to the helmsman. "Come to zero-two-zero."

The *Dee* leaned to the right as she went into the turn, then eased back as she came out of it and settled on the new course, the one that would take her to New York. Though the sea was now rolling at her from almost straight ahead, it was easy, and the pressure bulkhead, that took all its force, was by this time triply re-inforced. We should have no trouble.

I watched, from the wing, the *Hilliard* angle to position ahead of the carrier. The two made a straight line, going away, their line and that of the *Dee*, diverging by more than ninety degrees, taking them further and further from her. I watched them, black figures always receding, until the top of the carrier's tower and the tips of the four stacks were all that showed against the gray of the sea. Then Johnny relieved me, and, with a last look at the tower and the stacks, standing alone above the horizon, I went below.

The wardroom clock showed four minutes to four as I poured coffee and sat down. There was a bridge game at the other end of the table. I looked, idly, and saw Rockford, Arbry, and Flattop, and then I looked again. In one of the seats, holding his cards fanned in front of him, was Graham. And, as he raked in a trick, he smiled.

Arbry looked up from his hand at me. "Did we get rid of 'em?"

"Once and for all. I hope."

"Thee and me."

The door opened and Buchan walked in. He dropped the blue cloth helmet on the green table cover, unbuttoned the thick green coat, took it off, and laid it beside the helmet. Then he pulled a chair from the table and literally fell back into it. He stretched his legs straight ahead of him and let his arms dangle from his shoulders. The game stopped. We all looked at him.

"I am goddamned glad that's over." He grinned, wiped his fingers across his brow, and flicked imaginary sweat to the deck. All the control, all of what it was that had held him, and the *Dee*, together through what they had had to do, seemed, in that one instant, to have drained completely out of him, and he was sitting here grinning, only a very tired, very relieved, man. He said it again, "I am goddamned glad we're through with that."

"You can say that again, Cap'n," said the Flattop.

The captain laughed, loudly, and looked at the Flattop. He sat up straight in his chair. "You know what I bet?"

"What's that?" I said.

He laughed again, still looking at the Flattop, and leaned forward. "Bet anybody five even money that Flattop is the first guy to shack up."

45

I DRANK COFFEE from the steel ladle, the metal burning hot where it touched my underlip and the coffee hot all the way down. Warm with the coffee, I moved from the wheelhouse door to the wind guard on the wing, into the wind that blew in cold and fresh from ahead. I looked out from the ship. The dark of the night was breaking, and the stars were sharp and yellow in the dissolving gray of early morning.

"Any sign of her?" Buchan's voice was at my ear.

"No sign."

"We ought to be picking her up soon." He moved away to the forward corner of the wing, and stood there, his left arm on the wind guard, as though carved, looking ahead.

The *Dee* dipped gently in waves that would not have harmed a rowboat, their whitecaps breaking small and far apart in the near light. I listened to them wash softly against the sides of the ship and fall back as she went through them.

Ahead somewhere was Ambrose Lightship, the start of the channel that ended in New York.

From the decks below, I heard the heavy streams from the salt-water hoses spattering over steel plates as the seamen washed down the weather decks. Reveille had been early; the crew was already making preparations for entering port. The sky was fading. The stars slipped behind it, and, over the stern, pink showed.

Buchan walked back to me. "See anything?"

"Not yet."

The *Dee* steamed on. The sun rimmed, orange, over the line between the sea and the sky.

Then I saw the masts, thin black toothpicks, one taller than the other, rise straight out of the sea ahead.

"There she is, Cap'n." I pointed.

He said nothing but looked with his binoculars. Then he muttered, half to himself, "That's Ambrose, all right."

A little at a time, her body climbed over the horizon, and she expanded as we came closer, like a picture telescoped with infinite slowness, until, one by one, her details showed clearly: the line of her bow, the squares of her deckhouses, the solid red paint on her hull. Very close, you could see, against the red sides, the big white letters, AMBROSE, and the black anchor chain dipping from the hawse pipe to the water.

The *Dee* passed her to port, three hundred yards away. A sailor stood by himself on the forecastle, a dark and lonely figure profiling against the lighting sky. He waved his right arm as we passed. I waved back.

Buchan turned from the lightship to me. "Get one anchor ready to let go." His voice was crisp; he was the captain taking his ship into port.

I sent Clay to tell Jake Warwick. In moments, a dozen seamen, bulky and awkward in the blue winter clothing, filtered through the door to the forecastle, and edged toward the twisted, upbent point of the bow.

Behind them was Jake, swinging on his crutches, his belly pushing tight against the blue jacket, his leg stiff and straight in the thick white cast. A sudden, sharp gust of wind whipped a sheet of spray across the forecastle to lash his face. Looking down, I saw the drops of water roll down the red, wrinkled skin and his upraised hand brush them away. Then I looked up from his face to the ancient chief's cap above it, to the tarnished green anchor and, under the anchor, the three corroded brass letters that stood for United States Navy. He jerked his head and leaned forward on his crutches.

"Come on, you farmers," he bellowed. "Get that hook ready to let go!"